KILLERS

THE BAX MYSTERIES BOOK 1

PATRICK HODGES

For
Trina, Cheyanne, Crescent
and everyone else who inspires me

CHAPTER ONE

He heard me. There's no way he didn't hear me. I am so
dead.

I duck down behind the van. I can't even look, so I
listen. For anything. The sound of a doorknob turning, floorboards creaking, anything to remind me just how big a mistake I
made by coming to this awful place. I picture the man plowing
through his doorway, with any of a variety of deadly weapons in
his hands, ready to pick off the idiot with delusions of grandeur
who thought he could tackle the boogeyman all by himself.

Yeah, like I said, a mistake. Not the first one I've ever made,
but it just might be my last.

How did I get here, anyway?

Jeez. A girl's life is at stake, not to mention mine, and I choose
now to get introspective?

Maybe I should start at the beginning. Like, the day I discovered I had superpowers.

Don't get excited. Despite what you've read in comic books,
it's really not all it's cracked up to be. I mean, if I'd been lucky
enough to find a glowing meteorite in the woods and it gave me
invisibility or super-strength or the ability to shoot lasers out my
butthole, that would've been cool.

Me? No, my big moment came in the alleyway behind the coffee shop where I work. I touched a piece of what I thought was trash, got a massive migraine, blacked out, and woke up with my face half-in, half-out of a puddle that smelled faintly—okay, not so faintly—of motor oil. Images flashed through my mind like a movie being played on extreme fast-forward, too fast for my pain-addled brain to make any sense of. Memories of a little girl's kidnapping, confinement, and murder. It wasn't until later that I even learned her name.

Sarah Blankenship. Ten years old. A fifth-grader at Desert View Middle School. A girl who loved her teachers, hot fudge sundaes, and her pit bull puppy Lucy.

A girl who would never see her family, her friends, or Lucy ever again.

But...wait. That's not the beginning either, is it? Man, I suck at this.

I peek around the van again, my palms slick with sweat and my heart thundering in my chest. Still no sign of movement.

There was a time, not so long ago, when I was a loser, the poster child for not giving a crap. I was destined for prison. Or an early grave. And if I'd stayed that way, with my head lodged firmly in my ass, that's how my story would end.

Well, the early grave may still happen. But by God, if this is it for me, it's going to be for a good reason.

Scrape.

He's right behind me, isn't he.

Shit.

CHAPTER TWO
ONE MONTH EARLIER

M y stained, tattered duffle bag rests on the bed beside me as I scan the walls of my bedroom. I do my best to keep my face blank and to not stare at the head of the man kneeling at my feet, removing the device that's been chafing my skin for the past eight months. It's a tough task since the dude's comb-over is the most hideous I've ever seen. If the few remaining hairs on his head had ever been able to cross the vast distance to all the other ones, they couldn't now.

He's taking his sweet time. If it were my job to go from screw-up to screw-up, releasing them from electronic prison, I'd probably want to stretch the minutes out too. He didn't bother introducing himself as he entered my bedroom...for the record, *without* knocking. Good thing I was already dressed.

With an electronic *boop*, the ankle monitor shuts itself off. Mr. Comboverski tosses the device into an open satchel, stands, shoots me a "have a nice life" glance, and departs.

I resume staring at the walls of my room, the one I've shared with a kid named Kyle Hagan since my arrival at the Asterly Halfway House. My half of the room is a stark contrast with his. While his walls are plastered with posters of WWE stars like Jinder

3

Mahal and Kevin Owens, I opted for a more conservative approach. Which is to say, completely empty.

I lock eyes with Kyle as he shuffles back into the room, depositing himself on his bed. Kid's fifteen, short, with thick, nerdy-looking glasses and scruffy black hair. I sense a pang of sadness in his expression, and I well up a little inside. Eye contact is not his thing, so I take it seriously when it happens between us. We've not had many conversations since becoming roomies, but those we've had have been pleasant enough. My life might be crap, but it's Minas Tirith—complete with blaring trumpets and gleaming ivory spires—compared to his. Whatever happens from here on out, I hope he finds an outlet for what must be a crap-ton of rage, one that doesn't involve an ankle bracelet.

"Happy birthday," he says with a thing that's as close to a smile as his face is capable of making.

"Thanks, man." I take a moment to wonder if I'll ever see him again. Probably not.

I think I'll actually miss him. God knows there were much worse roommates I could've had. Never once did he mouth off to me, or curse me out, or get in my face about my snoring. Because, yeah, I have a snore that could set off seismographs, or so I've been told.

"Any idea where you're going?" he asks.

I give a noncommittal shrug. "Sheila told me she had a full morning planned. I'm just waiting for her to get here."

He jerks his head at the room's only window. "You mean your social worker? She just pulled up. Unless you know someone else who drives a green Spark."

Curious, I rise to my feet and move over to the window. There, parked on the curb right behind Carl's weather-beaten Buick, is a snug little two-door the same color as ripe jalapenos. In front of the car stands its owner, pretty much the only person on the planet who gives a shit about me.

She's wearing her usual silk, floral print blouse, a light brown skirt, and white sneakers. From this distance, she can't possibly see me through the filthy screen covering the pane, but I'm sure the smile she shoots up at my window is indeed meant for me.

"Your ride's here," says a gruff voice from behind me.

I turn to see the now former master of my universe filling the threshold to my now former bedroom. A smile plays over the face of Carl Benz, the administrative gorilla who runs Asterly House, which is a rarity on par with a Cubs' World Series victory. In lieu of Netflix, unsupervised Internet access, and dirty magazines, needling Carl over his career choice has been my one major source of entertainment for the last eight months. My favorite dig is reminding him that he shares a name with a brand of car he'll never *ever* be able to afford, usually by referencing his nonexistent girlfriend, who I've named—

"Is it Mercedes? She's treating me to a spa day. Because, you know, eighteen." I flash him an evil grin. Kyle chuckles under his breath, earning a stern frown from Carl.

Carl meets my eyes again, and he bares his coffee-stained teeth at me. "Dream on, asshole. It may be your birthday, but I'm the one getting the present...namely, your eternal absence." His beer gut vibrates as he suppresses a chortle. "It fills my heart with joy to know that the next time you strike out with the law, you'll be sent somewhere more appropriate." He eyes me up and down, his smile morphing into a self-satisfied leer. "Somewhere, there's an itchy orange jumpsuit just waiting for you to come along and fill it. The day you put it on, I hope you think of me."

I notch an eyebrow. "Stop it, Carl, I'm getting misty-eyed."

His resolve cracks. "Grab your shit and get outta here. I gotta get this space cleaned up and ready for the next loser."

An audible sigh from Kyle fills the room. I see him sitting there, hands on knees and contemplating the threadbare throw rug someone paid five bucks for at Goodwill. It occurs to me that the kid's next roommate may not be as compatible. Knowing Carl, he'll stick Kyle with some bulked-up Neanderthal who likes to torture small, furry animals.

With a deep exhale, I grab my duffle bag and sling the arm-strap over my shoulder. Time to blow this shithole. But first...

I amble over to Kyle, hand extended. "Take care, man. Don't let this place get to you. Don't let *anyone* get to you."

He looks up, a mixture of resignation and dread on his face. He limply takes my hand in his, letting me shake it for him. "See ya, Bax."

I don't bother saying goodbye to any of the other residents on my way to the front door. A couple of boys in the TV room shoot me a "smell ya later" look, but that's about as cordial as it gets in this place. I let the screen door slam behind me and don't even look back as I descend the steps for the last time.

"So, where we headed first?" My eyes are glued to the side-view mirror as Sheila hangs a left at the intersection. Asterly House disappears from sight. I heave a sigh of relief.

"Sadly, your first day as an adult is going to involve a lot of adult stuff. I'll do my best to get you through that quickly, as you have a lot of things to celebrate." A sly smile curls the corners of her mouth. "Did you have anything specific in mind in that regard?"

I use my thumb to wipe away the thin layer of dust covering the car's tiny digital clock. "Let's see...it's just past ten a.m. We have nine hours before I can get that lap dance I know you're dying to surprise me with. After that, I'm partying till I puke. We'd better stop by a CVS so I can pick up a pack of Trojans." I give her a playful wink. "You know, just in case I get—"

Sheila slams on the brakes, causing me to pitch forward and bonk my head on the dashboard. I yelp in pain. "Seatbelt, smartass," she says without a trace of apology.

I straighten up, slapping my hand over my aching forehead. "You did that on purpose."

Her eyebrows raise, disappearing into her grayish-brown bangs. "Who, me?"

Our eyes meet for a few moments, and I let out a guffaw. She faces forward and proceeds through the now green light.

"I guess we'll have to find a cheap motel for me to stay at until I figure the rest of it out," I muse, brushing a lock of unkempt brown hair out of my eyes. "Hopefully, one next to a barber shop."

She shoots me a reassuring smile. "If today goes as planned, a motel won't be necessary."

"'As planned?'"

"You *do* remember when the court appointed me your guardian *ad litem*, right?"

I stare blankly. "Of...course I do."

Sheila lets out a huff. "Boiled down, it means that I act as your representative—in financial matters, for example—until you're able to look after yourself."

"You mean the money Dad left me...that's *real*?"

"It is."

"Like, for *real*, real?"

"Yup."

I haven't been paying attention to where we're going, so it's only when we enter the parking lot of a bank that I become aware of my surroundings. The bald eagle logo grimaces down at me from the sign above the entrance as she pulls the Spark into an empty space.

She meets my gaze. "Before you go off half-cocked, promise me you'll give me the day to convince you that you can do much better than a cheap motel."

I barely hear her over the *cha-ching!* noises inside my head, but I somehow manage an "I promise" as she kills the engine.

"Good." With a smirk, she adds, "Lunch will be on you."

"It will?" I mock-gasp.

"Bax, in an hour you're gonna have more money at your

disposal than I make in a year. After everything I have set up for you today, a nice lunch is the least you can do."

I brighten. "Holy shit, there really is a lap dance?"

"Course there is." She grins evilly. "Though I warn you, I'm a little out of practice."

All the blood in my body goes straight to my face.

She rolls her eyes. "Oh, for God's...let's go already." She steps out, slamming the door shut.

Through the windshield, I shoot her a hairy eyeball. "What, you think I'm gonna have an appetite now after picturing that?"

After swallowing my mild disgust and exiting the Spark, I make a show of brushing dust particles from my plain white tee and jeans and find myself regretting my decision to not wear my jacket. Early October in Phoenix is usually quite temperate, but today there's an uncomfortable chill in the air. It seems to have gotten colder since I left Asterly.

We head inside the bank, where a white-haired guy in a blazer and tie sits me down on the other side of his desk and shows me a mountain of paperwork. Oh, joy.

My brain checks out as I fast-forward through ninety long minutes of signing my name to a gazillion documents, which is even more tedious than it sounds.

Even so, I leave the bank with an actual smile on my face, now the proud owner of my very own checking and savings accounts. I am officially fifty thousand dollars richer, with similar deposits to be made on my birthday for each of the next nine years. In my head, I'm already mulling over dozens of ways to spend the cash, each more outlandish than the last.

The sound of Sheila slamming the car door brings me crashing back to reality. Fifty grand is a lot of money. It's more money than most eighteen-year-olds have, but it's not going to buy me a Lambo, a luxury yacht, or even a house that doesn't have a "Condemned" sign attached to it.

In the passenger seat, I slip the generic ATM card and five twenty-dollar bills into my worn faux-leather wallet and eye Sheila as we head for the next stop on her itinerary. I decide to preserve the mystery and let it happen. I'm probably still on a high from having actual cash money in my pocket again.

Five minutes after we leave the bank, Sheila turns the car onto Grand Avenue, heading northwest. "There, that wasn't too painful, was it?" she asks.

"Not at all," I reply. "I kept waiting for Mom to come charging through the door, screaming her head off that I didn't deserve a penny." I snort. "Wonder if she even knows today's my birthday."

"Probably slipped her mind between trips to the liquor store."

"Yeah."

"I don't suppose you've spoken to her lately."

I feel my stomach clench, and for once it's not from hunger. Why'd I have to go and bring up Mom? "Nope. Haven't talked to her in over a year. Wouldn't even know how to reach her if I wanted to. Last I heard, she was shacked up with some guy in Prescott Valley."

"Dwayne. They're still together, as far as I know. But enough about her. Let's talk about you."

Here we go. I brace myself for the impending lecture.

"This isn't going to be a lecture, don't worry," she says drolly.

I swear this woman is telepathic.

"I won't sugarcoat it, Bax, you've had a tough last few years—"

"It's been a shit sandwich."

"But thanks to what your father left you, you have something most boys in your position don't have—a real chance to turn your life around."

"Whatev."

"Bax..."

She leans forward, and my eyes return to her concerned face. She means well, and deep down, I appreciate that more than I show it. Over the last two years, I've given her every excuse to write me off as a loser, to cut me loose the same day the system

9

did, but she's stuck by me through thick and thicker. Sheila Dunbar truly puts the "social" in social worker.

I decide to change the subject. "Don't you have other kids to bring back from the Dark Side?"

She flinches a little. "Course I do."

"Do you chauffeur all of them around on their birthday?"

I glance at Sheila in time to see a tiny smile disappear from her face. "Only the special ones," she says.

I realize she's dressing it up, so I let her. Most delinquents—or at least the ones I've been forced to cohabitate with—carry an unhealthy amount of rage. It could be against their parents, their ex-girlfriends, or just the almighty system in general. Many of them see Sheila as the face of that system and use her to vent their spleen on. When they finally cross that legal line from childhood to adulthood, I imagine many of them give her whatever equivalent of "eff you" strikes their fancy and never look back. Which is totally unfair. Sheila's maybe the one person in their lives who truly cares. She doesn't coddle them, but she doesn't patronize them either. It's one of the things I admire about her...I sure as shit couldn't do what she does.

"What makes me so special?" I hide my grin by facing the window.

"You're a good kid, Bax," she says in that voice that almost makes me believe it, "and you're a lot smarter than you give your-self credit for. I think you can truly make something of your life if you set your mind to it."

"Uh, thanks." I tug at a loose thread on my T-shirt.

Sheila lets the subject drop, fiddling with her cell phone as we slow down to drive through a construction zone. I don't own a phone, so I pass the time by wondering just what the hell I am going to do next.

What does a kid my age with above-average intelligence, no goals beyond the next party, and no direction in life do after inher-iting a truckload of money? Well, "go nuts" is probably the short answer to that question. I could blow it all in no time on fancy clothes and bling, not to mention a gas-guzzling luxury car that I'd have to sell once the money ran out.

Or I could do what so-called "responsible" people are supposed to do—get an apartment, a job, and a nice TV with a gaming system so I don't die of boredom. Yeah, I'll go with that for now.

Sheila looks up at me, and again I feel her telepathic fingers crawling through my mind. It'd be impressive if it weren't so scary.

I never set out to be a delinquent. Somewhere along the line, though, that's what I became.

Is that what I still am? Can I ever be anything else?

Chapter Three

I start to wonder where the hell we're going when we turn off 59ᵗʰ Avenue and into a residential area. Decent-sized houses line the streets on both sides, peppered with the occasional park, school, or apartment complex. The cars that I see parked on the homes' wide driveways are mostly family sedans, and not a beater among them. The houses themselves don't have much personality or variation, as they were likely all built from the same manual judging by the adobe-shingle roofs that top every one of them, but they look livable.

This is my new neighborhood? Sweet. I'm so gonna need that haircut. And a new wardrobe. And I'm definitely favoring that gaming system. There's also this thing called Roku that I want to check out, though I still say it sounds like a Pokemon character.

A concrete slab with a huge plaque bearing the words "Arbor Vista Townhomes" catches my eye as Sheila makes a right turn into what looks to be a large, sprawling complex of buildings. My eyes widen in anticipation as I step from the car. My gaze sweeps over the length and breadth of the place. There's a community pool, a set of playground equipment that looks brand spanking new, and dozens of trees with a few greenish-yellow leaves clinging to them for dear life.

I turn to Sheila, eyes wide in disbelief. "Are you freaking kidding me?"

Sheila drops her keys into her purse and skirts the car to face me. "What do you think?"

"It's a complete dump."

"Glad you like it." She grasps my arm and nudges me toward the rental office. Still shell-shocked by Sheila's resourcefulness, I let her guide me through the door.

The Arbor Vista Townhomes property manager is a short, squashy-looking man with a walrus mustache that comes well past his upper lip. He runs a skeptical "this is the guy?" eye over me, and for a second I'm reminded of Carl's trademark leer. No, not creepy at all.

After a two-minute conversation between him and Sheila, he grabs a set of keys from a desk drawer and beckons us to follow him.

During the hundred-yard walk to what I assume is a vacant unit, Walrus Guy—his real name is Ted, but that's gonna take a while to stick—recites a long list of things that I'm *not* allowed to do should I decide to take up residence. This includes loud parties, inviting "shady" people over, giving out the number to the security gates, yada yada. Jeez, it's like he thinks I'm going to invite a motorcycle gang over for a beer-and-gunfire party the moment he goes home for the night. If I didn't resemble the delinquent he obviously sees me as—and that I am, to be fair—I'd probably be offended. But if the price is right, this is a place I definitely want to live, so I'll happily screw on a smile and treat Ted as the King of Arborvistania.

He gives Sheila and me a five-minute tour of the townhome, a one-bedroom, one-bathroom affair which is already moderately furnished with a bed, a couch, a kitchen table and chairs, and a working fridge. Utilities are free, and the rent is just under eight hundred bucks a month, a number which would have been out of the question three hours ago. I add a dresser, two end tables, and a microwave oven to the mental list of things I need to buy, which is now as long as my arm.

Ted gets a text that sends him scurrying to another unit two seconds after he locks the door, leaving Sheila and me to check out the grounds. There aren't many people about, which I guess is not surprising for an early afternoon on a Friday. Arbor Vista has that lived-in feel without being rundown, warm and homey while still retaining an upper-middle-class sense of security. Not for the first time, I find myself impressed by Sheila's choice. Did I say impressed? I'm thunderstruck. Compared to Asterly House, Arbor Vista is frickin' Wayne Manor.

As if reading my mind—get out of my head, lady!—Sheila asks, "I may be wrong, but you look impressed. It's so rare that I see that look on one of my kids."

I nod, the snark having abandoned me for the moment. "How'd you find this place?"

She shrugs. "I have my resources. By the way, do you like children?"

Aaaaaand the snark returns. "Depends on the sauce."

Sheila slugs my arm so hard I wince.

I assume by "children" she means, like, preteens and under. "I mean...yeah. I...guess?"

"Good," Sheila says. "You notice those schools we passed on the way in?"

"Yeah, what about them?"

"A lot of those kids live here." She checks her watch, then points to the expanse of grass stretching between several buildings. "In a few hours, there'll be kids flying up and down this lawn, ready to start their weekend."

I frown. "No one my age?"

"Not that I saw, but there are ninety units, so maybe." She strolls back toward the rental office, and I fall into step beside her. "I have a few other places we could look at, but this is my favorite. I'd definitely want to live here." Wink, wink, nudge, nudge, say no more.

"It's nice, but..." I scratch the back of my neck. "I don't think Ted likes me much. Dude was giving me the stink-eye the second I walked in."

"Pfft," she scoffs. "I know his type. He's harmless. Pay the rent on time, follow his rules, and he'll mellow out."

"Hrm."

She flashes her most motherly smile. "So...you'll take it?"

Oh, that smile. Warm as sunshine, powerful as the Death Star tractor beam.

"I'll take it."

"Whew," she says. "Thank God, because I was totally lying about having other places to show you. Now about that lunch... I'm feeling like barbecue today." She disappears back into the office.

I laugh, and there's no stopping my grin.

I've heard about that strange, floaty sensation people get when experiencing extreme joy. Sweet Jeebus, I think this is it.

Hello, new life. Great to finally meet you.

Suck it, Carl.

Walrus Guy—sorry, *Ted*—looks surprised when he runs my debit card through his swiper thingy, and my first month's rent payment goes through. This, after yet another hour of listening to him repeat every rule in the Arbor Vista manual and signing papers. I swear, I've signed my name more times today than every day in my entire life. Combined.

It doesn't stop me from smiling when he hands me my townhouse and mailbox keys, and the code to the walk-in and drive-in gates. Sheila's grin is even larger, which doubles the warm fuzzies.

Several hours later, we're back in the Spark, its backseat and trunk full of stuff I've spent the last few hours purchasing—clothes, shoes, a microwave, an alarm clock, three bags of groceries, and some basic toiletries. Our last stop before the barbecue restaurant was a close-out furniture store, where I picked out a pair of end tables that looked both durable and cheap.

I face forward, my stomach reminding me in no uncertain terms that indulging in the restaurant's bottomless baked beans was not a good idea. I'm gonna be reenacting the campfire scene from *Blazing Saddles* later, I just know it. I give a weak groan, hoping Sheila will take that as a cue to bring me home and let me slip into a food coma until the end tables arrive. But no, there's apparently one more stop we need to make.

We're only about a half-mile from home when Sheila unexpectedly turns into another parking lot, right across the street from Glenview Community College. I scan the signage above the cluster of storefronts that make up one of many, many strip-malls in this part of town. From right to left, I see a taqueria, an income tax place, a ninety-nine-cent store, a barber shop, a Middle Eastern restaurant/bakery, a dry cleaners, a cell phone outlet, and a hip-looking coffee shop. The parking lot is packed, but the greatest cluster of vehicles fill the spots closest to the coffee shop, Hill O' Beans. Sheila expertly squeezes the Spark in between two SUVs, and in we go.

From the clock on the wall, it's going on four-thirty and every one of the twelve tables in the place is filled. Mostly with teenage girls. And I'm not talking high-schoolers, I mean girls my age. I instinctively run my fingers through my unruly mane in a haphazard attempt to make myself more presentable. I hope the coffee here is good. Judging from the mixture of pleasant aromas wafting past my nostrils and the lack of available seats, it is. Too bad I've already had my fill o' beans today. Heh. I kill me.

I nudge Sheila's shoulder. "I'm stuffed, Sheila. I'm not even thirsty. What gives?"

She steps in line behind four other customers. "We're not here for a meal."

"Then what?"

She hits me with the motherly look again. "You have your

freedom, Bax, and that's great. It's also not enough. Today repre-
sents a huge turning point for you. But the question is, in what
direction will you turn? Will you go back to being an immature
hooligan, or will you make an effort to be a productive member of
society?"

I stare blankly at her. That ton-of-bricks feeling people get in
moments of clarity? I just got it. I've known for months that this
day would come, and I have no...plan...whatsoever.

For most of my childhood, Mom seemed to think my one
ambition should have been to be as awesomely great at everything
as my brother AJ. One only had to look at his trophy shelf, which
stretched from end to end across his bedroom wall, that this
wasn't going to happen. I never wanted to be him. I just wanted
to be *me*, but from my eighth birthday on, AJ was the Top Dog
and I was the Little Dog who drank out of the toilet.

Ambition is a strange thing. How does one suddenly *get*
something one never had in the first place?

I sigh. "What'd you have in mind?"

"You need a job."

Before I say something along the lines of *I object, Your Honor!*,
she gestures at the crowd of people enjoying their drinks. "Look
around you, Bax. You need a healthy environment where you can
learn, provide a valuable service, and use the people skills I just
know you have."

I raise an eyebrow. "Serving overpriced caffeinated beverages
to college students is a valuable service?"

"Don't knock caffeine. Without it, the world would collapse."

Can't fault that logic. "And what makes you think this place
would hire a guy with a checkered past and no previous
experience?"

Her motherly look morphs into a wolfish smile. "I have some
pull with the owner. Come on."

We're up next, so we approach the counter. For the first time,
I notice the man working the register. He's tall, broad-shouldered,
around thirty, with light brown hair and a friendly smile. His eyes

light up in recognition when he sees Sheila. "Hey, pretty lady! Long time no see! Where've you been keeping yourself?"

The tension drains from Sheila's shoulders, and she slips into the kind of routine conversation that longtime friends have. "Oh, you know, same old, same old. Half my kids think I'm an angel, the other half think I'm the Devil."

His gaze turns on me for the first time. "Hello."

"Hi," I say.

"Bax, meet Austin, the owner and manager of this fine establishment," Sheila chimes in. "Austin, this is Bax."

He proffers his hand, which I take. Dude's got a grip like The Rock. "Nice to meet you, Bax," he says.

"Same here." I shoot a casual glance behind us to make sure our protracted conversation isn't holding up the line, but it's just us.

"Bax needs a job," Sheila says, getting right to the point.

"I see." Austin's smile diminishes. "First job?"

I nod. "Is that a problem?"

He shakes his head. "Not at all. We get a lot of first-timers here." He crouches down for a few seconds, and I hear rummaging sounds. He emerges with a pen and an application form, hands me both, and gestures at a table that just opened up. "Have a seat and start filling this out. I'll be along in a minute to ask you a few questions."

"Okay."

Austin graciously wipes down the table and even pulls out the chair for me. Man is polite, I'll give him that.

Filling out the application is a little surreal. I chuckle as I fill in the box asking me how long I've lived at my current address with "three hours." Irony turns to full-on embarrassment as I zoom right past the Previous Employment and Education sections, then grim finality when the only reference I can write down is Sheila. She is, literally, the only person I know. Well, there's Carl, but he wouldn't sign my stay of execution. I doubt Walrus Ted would vouch for me either.

I'm just about to sign my name when I notice a girl in a Hill O' Beans apron sitting at a table in the corner. Her fiery red hair is pulled back into a ponytail, flyaway strands curling behind her ears. Her brown eyes peek at me curiously over a pair of violet cat-eye glasses. She looks like a librarian, an image completed by the worn paperback she's holding in her left hand. Beneath her dark green apron is a navy-blue polo and khaki pants with frayed cuffs. Her cute little sneakers, black like my Converse, probably serve her well for being on her feet for hours at a time.

Her eyes blaze with curiosity, the corner of her mouth ticking up when our gazes meet. In the next instant, her face smooths into a look that I interpret as "You're applying for a job? Are you going to be the guy who helps me lift the heavy boxes or the douchebag who calls in sick even though you're not really sick and I get stuck with your shift?"

Austin appears, shoots a glance her way. "Piper, you almost done with your break? I have an interview, and I need you on the register."

Piper closes her book. "You got it, Boss," she says in a voice that, if I wasn't looking at the face it came out of, I might mistake for that of a twelve-year-old. I watch as she settles behind the counter, then turn to Austin, now sitting across from me.

"Let's take a look," he says. I hand him the application, and his eyebrows immediately go up. "Is that really your first name?"

And boom, all the blood rushes to my face again. "Yeah. It was my grandpa's name. Don't spread it around, okay? I've gone by 'Bax' since I was eleven."

"Not a problem." He returns his attention to the form, and a smile appears. "Three hours. Cute." I shift in my seat. "Oh..." His smile widens, and he looks up at me. "Happy birthday."

"Thanks."

He rapidly scans what little information I've given him, then places the application back in front of me. "So, let me see if I've got this straight," he says, folding his hands in front of him. "You turned eighteen today, moved into a new home, and now you're looking for a job."

"Yup." I sweep my eyes across the room. "Nice place you got here."

Austin beams with pride. "Thanks. It's been a lot of work, but I finally got it to where it needs to be. You like coffee?"

"I guess. Never really had anything fancy." I take a hearty whiff, enjoying the spicy fragrances that permeate the place. "Smells awesome, though. Anything would be better than the sludge I had to drink back at the ha..." I catch myself. "At the house I used to live in."

He adopts a stern expression. "Let me be blunt, Bax. I know about your...situation."

I gulp. Just how much did Sheila tell this guy? "You do?"

"Well, not that much. I know you've been in some trouble." He relaxes a little. "Hey, I was a teenager once. Thing is, eventually you have to grow up. Sheila speaks very highly of you, and I think very highly of her. She says you need a fresh start, and if that's truly what you want, then I respect that. For that reason, I'm going to take a chance on you."

I damn near faint. "Just like that?"

The smile returns. "One of the benefits of being the boss *and* the owner."

"Do I have to call you 'sir?'" I ask, leaning back in my chair.

He looks horrified at the question. "You do that, and I'll fire you on the spot."

"Gotcha."

"My name is Austin," he says. "If I'm in a bad mood, which I'd like to think is almost never, you can call me 'Mr. Wagner.' Or 'Boss,' if you're more comfortable with that."

I nod.

"I'm not a hardass, but I have zero tolerance for bullshit. When you're on the clock, I expect you to work. No showing up hungover or high, no thirty-minute smoke breaks, no locking yourself in the restroom to play Candy Crush."

His mention of alcohol stings a little, and for a second, I picture Mom passed out on the sofa, clutching an empty bottle of gin. I cover up my flashback with a laugh. "I don't drink, smoke, or do drugs, and I have no idea what Candy Crush is."

"Seriously?"

"Seriously."

"Well then..." He presses his palms together and bows like a Zen master. "Welcome to Hill O' Beans. The next pay period begins on October 1st, which is next Wednesday. That gives you five days to get settled in your new place. Is that okay?"

"Sounds fine. I could come in earlier if you want. It's not like I have anything else going on." Which is kind of sad, actually.

"I appreciate the offer, Bax, but Wednesday is when I need you. Be here at five sharp to start your training, young Padawan."

Huh. He likes *Star Wars*. Another point in his favor...wait, what? "Five *a.m.*?"

"Don't keep me waiting." He beckons to someone over my shoulder. A few moments later, Sheila appears at our table.

"So...how'd it go?" she asks. She's bouncing on the balls of her feet, like a little kid waiting in line to see Santa Claus.

Austin gestures toward me like a game show announcer. "Meet our new barista."

Sheila smiles so widely, her eyes crinkle into half-moons. Oh, God, woman, please don't cry.

The gushing I expect instead fizzles into a sincere, "Congratulations, Bax."

For like the fifth time today, I'm overwhelmed. Over the years, I've learned to keep my emotions in check, but today it's been so much, so fast. I swallow down a mini-gush of my own and rise to my feet. Austin stands as well, and we shake hands. I wince again. I'll be favoring my left hand for the rest of the day.

Note to self—do *not* arm-wrestle Austin.

I turn to Sheila. "Shall we go?"

She fishes her car keys out of her purse. "Here. You can wait in the car. I need a few minutes."

"Actually...would it be cool if I checked out the cell phone place next door?"

"Okay."

I move to leave, but Austin stops me. "One last thing...if you could get a haircut before you report for work, that would be great. I don't mean to be strict, but appearances matter, you know?"

I smile. "It's on my to do-list."

"Great." He points out the window. "Four doors down is a barber shop. Go there, ask for Nico. Tell him I sent you."

"Will do." I nod goodbye, and head for the door.

I'm halfway there when my heart literally stops, and my mouth flops open like a dying fish. Entering the coffee shop is the most stunningly gorgeous girl I have ever seen in my life. Dark blonde hair, crystal blue eyes, skin that perfect shade between pink and pale. A few freckles dust her nose. Are you *kidding me*? Oh my freaking God, I *love* girls who rock the freckles.

My feet turn to cement blocks, and I pray that the mountain of beans I ate for lunch doesn't choose this moment to return.

It takes a tremendous effort to shift my gaze away as she walks by Bax the Fish-Faced Doofus. I meet Freckle Girl's eyes, just for a second. She gives me a flirtatious smile and a wink, and my insides dissolve into goo.

Is she a regular? Holy hottie, I hope she's a regular.

If she's here, that means she likes coffee. I wonder what her usual is. Does she have a usual? I bet she has a usual. I need to learn it. So I can make it for her. Every. Single. Day.

She winked at me. You don't wink at total strangers unless there's something there, right? Does that mean we have a thing?

Piper is all smiles as she takes Freckle Girl's order. I throw a bucket of cold water on my raging hormones, and force my eyes to find something else, *anything else*, besides her butt—stop staring, you tool! You're an employee now! Do not creep out the customers!—to focus on. I zone in on the TV bolted near the ceiling above the register. It looks like the five o'clock news has started, and the top story is...

Oh, man.

A girl, missing for a week, has been found. Not alive. They flash a picture of her on the screen, and I cringe. She can't be more than ten.

I turn away, my buzz officially harshed, and head out the door.

INTERLUDE

"So that's him," Austin says, watching through the window as his newest employee disappears down the sidewalk. "The kid you've been going on about for the last two years."

"That's him." Sheila dabs at her eyes with a napkin. "God, I'm a mess."

Austin crosses his arms, fixing her with a stony glare.

"What?" she demands.

"He doesn't know, does he." It's a statement, not a question. "He doesn't know any of it."

Sheila matches his frown. "No. And you're not going to tell him."

He lets out an exasperated sigh. "I hate secrets. It's so middle school."

"Austin—"

"I won't say a word, I promise. But he's gonna find out eventually."

"I know. That's why he'll need a support system."

Austin leans in. "I understand your attachment to this kid, but you're not his mother. And he's not..."

"He's not what?" Sheila asks through gritted teeth. "Say it."

"He's not Anthony."

"I know that," she hisses. "This isn't about that. It's about Jeremy. I owe him."

They have a long, unspoken conversation. Austin smiles, and the tension evaporates between them.

"How's Daniel?" she asks, the cordial smile locked back in place.

Austin gives a tight smirk. "He's fine."

"How long have you two been together now?"

"Three years this Christmas."

Sheila stands. "Tell him I said hi." She makes a move toward the door.

"Aunt Sheila?"

She looks at him expectantly.

"Just to be clear...every kid deserves a break, and I'm all for giving him one. But I have a business to run. There's a drawer in my office with twenty applications filled out by kids who have high school diplomas and *don't* have criminal records. If he mouths off, or steals my inventory, or blows off his shifts, I will fire his ass in a hot second."

"I expect no less."

He stands and gives her a friendly hug followed by a peck on the cheek. "Danny and I cook dinner every Sunday night. You're always welcome to join us."

"I may take you up on that. Love you."

"Love you too."

CHAPTER FOUR

T*hump.*

I rouse from sleep, lifting my head an inch and turning toward my new alarm clock, which reads 10:48 a.m. It takes a full five seconds for me to register that I'm not at Asterly anymore, even though I'd spent hours last night celebrating that fact, an occasion just as joyous as *finally* turning eighteen. For a minute beyond that, my panicky brain wonders if Carl has tracked me down in order to torture me with another snap inspection. That's totally something he'd do.

I listen for the sound again. It doesn't come, so I sigh and lay back onto my awesome pillow—quite possibly the softest thing in the universe—reveling in the quiet.

I had gotten so caught up in the events of yesterday that it wasn't until I broke in my new shower—I practically squealed in delight when I realized I didn't have to share a bathroom with another living soul for the first time *ever*—that it really hit me how much my life had changed in one short day. More specifically, it was when I massaged the rough patch of skin that had been hidden underneath the ankle bracelet for the last eight months. The constant reminder of my innumerable failures was gone. In its place was a new home, a new job, a new *path.*

After years of moving from one person's shit-list to another, I was free. *Free.* No more shakedowns, body searches, or metal detectors. No hostile glances from my pissed-off housemates or baleful sneers from Carl. No gunshots or police sirens that could be right next door or five blocks away. No pounding on my door at sunrise to get my ass out of bed.

Nothing but...silence.

It was beautiful.

And freakin' terrifying. So terrifying, in fact, that after two hours of tossing and turning, I resorted to playing on the brand-new Galaxy I bought at the store next to Hill O' Beans. With no TV or gaming system yet, I was up till stupid o'clock last night playing Candy Crush. Blame the app store, it was front and center and my idiot brain just had to see what Austin was talking about. Fair point—that shit is *addictive.* I'm not sure if I spent six hours playing it or if it was just four and the rest was me having a high-res dream about kicking over pieces of candy while some deep, masculine voice said "Sweet!" every time I knocked a bunch off the board.

I reach for the phone sitting on my new end table, confirming that it's off and fully charged.

Thump.

What the hell?

I throw on a clean tee and a new pair of jeans, forgoing my Converse for a pair of flip-flops. Wiping the crud from my eyes, I rake a hand through my hair and head for the living room.

I peek through the spyhole thingy in my front door, wondering if I have a visitor. I see nothing.

Shrugging it off, I move to the kitchen. There's nothing left of the pizza I ordered last night but a few crumbs, so I snag a box of strawberry Pop-Tarts from a cabinet, where it currently occupies a shelf by itself. The pastries fall out as I fumble to remove the foil wrapper. They break apart on the counter, exposing the fruity inside like strawberry veins. I'm too lazy to wait the thirty seconds of microwave cooking time, so I start chowing down.

Thump!

Whoa, that was loud. Sounded like an angry bull attempting to break through my front wall.

Curious and annoyed—mostly annoyed—I step through my front door and nearly get a soccer ball right in the junk. The thing ricochets off my thigh, rolls five feet, then dies on the grass where the sidewalk meets the lawn. I lean down and grab it, then look up to meet the eyes of three girls staring up at me with wide, fearful expressions.

Judging by their height and clothes, I'm guessing they're around nine or ten. Two of them slowly back away like I'm going to go all wild grizzly bear on them. The one in the middle, the smallest of the group, stands her ground.

I take a moment to study her. Her dark brown hair is tied in a braid that pulls over her right shoulder with a neon orange elastic tie at the end. It's a lot warmer today than it was yesterday, which explains the bright orange board shorts and the white Wonder Woman tee she's wearing. And then there are her eyes. I've heard of girls having huge, doe eyes before, but these have to be the doe-iest. Starving puppies have nothing on this girl.

She whispers an awed "wow" under her breath. And she's staring at me like I'm a superhero or a rock star or some uber-celebrity. Which...huh?

I smile and hold the ball out. "Uh, is this yours?"

She exchanges a backward glance with her friends, who shrug. Then she steps forward, her face apologetic. "Um...yeah. Sorry about the noise. We were having a contest for who could bounce the ball off your door the hardest." She gingerly takes the ball from me. "We didn't think anyone was home. No one's lived there since Mrs. Peterson moved out."

I scratch the back of my neck. "I, uh, just moved in yesterday."

Her button nose scrunches. "I didn't see a van."

"Didn't really need one. Don't have a lot of stuff."

The tallest of her friends, sporting a tan complexion and wire-frame glasses, chimes in. "Trina, the ball?"

She shoots them a *don't embarrass me* glare. "Just a minute! He's our neighbor!" She turns back to me with a sigh. "Sorry. I'm Trina, and these are my friends, Cheyanne and Crescent."

Cheyanne, dark-skinned and round-faced, smiles. Crescent, the bespectacled one, still looks undecided as to where I fall on the Creep-O-Meter.

My eyebrows raise. "Those are some...interesting names."

Trina smiles like I just paid her the biggest compliment ever. "Thanks."

Crescent holds out her hands, and Trina tosses her the ball. Both Crescent and Cheyanne nod goodbye and dash off, kicking the ball around. Three other kids appear out of nowhere and join the fun.

Trina faces me again. "My name's actually Katrina, but I don't like being called that because of the hurricane."

"I totally get that."

She steps closer. This girl is so adorable it almost hurts to look at her. "What's your name?"

"Bax."

A smirk tugs at her lips. "*Bax?* That's..."

"Interesting?"

"Weird."

I chuckle. "It comes from my last name, Baxter."

Her mouth opens in a silent *ahhh.* "What's your first name?"

"You ask a lot of questions."

She lifts one shoulder in a half-shrug and brushes her long bangs behind her ear. "I'm a kid. It's what we do."

"Fair enough. My first name is...too embarrassing to say out loud."

She looks past me. "You'd better close your door. You don't want to get in trouble with your parents. My mom *hates* it when I do that."

My gaze falls to my flip-flops. "No parents. Just me."

"Really?"

"Really really."

Sadness flashes through her eyes, followed by a hopeful glint. "Well, if you need a friend, I'm right next door."

My brow furrows. "You want to be *my* friend?"

She folds her arms. "Only if you pass the Trina Test."

"What's the Trina Test?"

"You'll see," she says with a catty grin.

"Trina!" comes a voice from behind me.

I turn to see a woman, I'm guessing in her early thirties, scrutinizing me from the doorway ten yards from mine. Her dark, shoulder-length hair frames a face that closely resembles Trina's, and her arms are crossed over a stained white apron.

I wasn't lying when I told Sheila I liked kids. Truth is, I've had little experience dealing with them, especially girls half my age. The last thing I want to do is piss off some helicopter mother with the local precinct on speed-dial by coming three inches too close to her child.

On the other hand, I'm part of this community now, and I don't want the neighborhood kids to start referring to me as the Jerk From Unit 24. That's a grapevine I don't want to test.

"Hey, Mom," Trina beams and runs over to her, beckoning for me to follow.

I amble over, breaking out my most disarming smile. I catch a whiff of something wafting through Trina's front door. Something *awesome.*

"Who's this?" Trina's mom asks, her tone wary but not unfriendly. She, like Trina, gives me the once-over in a way I can only interpret as muted reverence. Have these two never seen a teenage guy before?

"It's okay, Mom, this is our new neighbor." Trina gestures to my front door, which is still ajar. "His name is Bax."

"Hi," I say, extending a hand.

"Gina Forrester." She returns the handshake. "Nice to meet you."

Trina and Gina? Did I just step into a sitcom? There are really families whose names rhyme? "You too. Your daughter was just about to give me the Trina Test."

Gina's eyes flick to Trina. "You're giving him the Trina Test?" Her mouth twitches with a smile. She tucks a strand of her dark hair behind her ear, her eyes intent on Trina.

I frown. "Uh, should I be worried? What happens to people who fail the Trina Test?"

The catty smile, apparently a Forrester family trait, appears on Gina's face. "Let's just say it's in your best interest not to."

Oooookay.

"First question," Trina says, striking a pose like an English professor. "Do you prefer chocolate or vanilla?"

I raise my eyebrows at Gina. She raises hers right back and nods. Girl is serious. "Uh, chocolate?"

Trina smiles. Guess I got that one right.

"Second question...cats or dogs?"

"That's an easy one. Dogs. By a mile." I turn to Gina. "Does this place allow pets? I don't remember that being one of the Ted Commandments."

Gina chuckles. "They're allowed, but only if you pay the deposit. You have to pick up after them, don't let them run free, and make sure they don't wake the neighbors."

Got it. Filing that away.

Trina clears her throat, drawing my attention. She hits me with a scowl that actually intimidates me. This girl does not mess around.

"Final question," she says, stretching each syllable out. "*Lord of the Rings* or *Harry Potter*?"

Hmmm. That's a toughie. I find myself wanting to pass this silly test, but which one do I choose? Girls love *Harry*, right? She's probably got a Gryffindor sweater in her closet and a jar of Bertie Bott's Every Flavor Beans in her sock drawer. I should lie and say I'm a Potterhead, but that glare is like sodium pentothal. "I love 'em both, but I gotta say *Lord of the Rings*."

I wait five, ten, fifteen seconds for the shoe to drop, during which Trina just stares at me. She doesn't even blink. Finally, she breaks into a huge, thousand-watt grin. "Three for three. You pass."

Wait, what? She's a Tolkienist?

Mind. Blown.

The soccer ball comes skittering across the lawn at us. Trina stops it with her foot as Cheyanne runs up. "Hey, Trina! Crescent's mom is taking us out for pizza! Wanna come?"

Trina turns her pleading stare on her mom. "Can I, Mom?"

"Go ahead," Gina says. "Just be back by two."

"Okay!" Trina faces me and holds out her hand. For the first time, I notice a charm bracelet encircling her wrist. "Welcome to Arbor Vista, Bax."

I lean over and grasp her hand, shaking it firmly. The loose bracelet slides down and makes contact with my fingertips.

A wave of happiness washes over me. I stick out my hand, bouncing with glee as the white-haired old lady fastens the bracelet around my wrist. The fit is perfect—not too loose, not too tight. I swivel my wrist around, watching the little flowers dance and jingle.

"I love it!" I squeal. "I promise to wear it every—"

Trina removes her hand from mine and gives me a playful smile. Then, she and Cheyanne bound away, disappearing into a unit about fifty yards down.

I straighten up, blinking rapidly. I stare at my hand, front and back. It's my eighteen-year-old hand again.

What in the world just happened?

I turn to see Gina staring at me, her brow furrowed. "Are you okay?" she asks.

I try to recall the memory—was that what it was?—that just forced itself into my skull, but the image is already starting to blur and fade.

Where did it come from? Was I hallucinating?

Candy Crush is so getting deleted. Less than a day and it's already scrambling my brain.

"Um, yeah," I say. "Just spaced out for a sec."

"Mmm." She glances at my still-open door. "Did I hear you say you're all by yourself?"

"I know. Weird, huh?"

"Not many kids your age getting their own place." She steps toward me. "You sure you're alright? You look a little freaked out."

I take a deep, cleansing breath. "It's been a crazy twenty-four hours."

"First time on your own?"

"Yeah."

"Ever?"

"Yup."

She gestures toward her front door. "Have you eaten today?"

As if on cue, the smell from within Gina's house intensifies, and my hunger skyrockets. "No, why?" I decide not to bring up the Pop Tarts. Cardboard has more flavor.

"I'm a chef, and I'm testing out a new recipe. Care to be my guinea pig?" She flashes a smile that's pretty darn attractive for an older woman. That alone would probably have convinced me even if the smell weren't already sending me into sensory overload.

After eight long months mired in a sea of discipline and negative reinforcement, this sudden friendliness seems...strange. "You trust me inside your house? Just like that?"

"Like I said, I need a guinea pig," she replies. "Why? Are you untrustworthy?"

"Depends on who you ask."

She laughs. "Well, you passed the Trina Test, so that's one point in your favor. Come on in, I'll give you a good meal in exchange for your life's story."

I take a second to lock my front door and Gina leads me into her kitchen, which is considerably larger than mine. Good thing, too, because it looks like she's been busy. Every square inch of counter space is covered in cooking gear, ingredients, and a dozen notecards. Divine smells issue from a pair of saucepans simmering on the stove, and it looks like there's something in the oven as well. I turn away as she dons a pair of mitts, certain I'm drooling. I go googly-eyed when she pulls a roasting pan out and deposits it on a heat-rack on the counter.

A huge mound of beef, surrounded on all sides by small potatoes, onions, and carrots, greets me. But the sensory feast doesn't stop there. I smell garlic, vinegar, and something that I think is black pepper. It's intoxicating. I want to eat the smell, a lingering aroma that sets my stomach growling.

"What is that?" I ask, leaving out the "and did you make another for yourself?"

"Brisket," she says with a proud grin, "with my own special rub. I've been tweaking the recipe for weeks now. I think I've got it perfect, but I could use another opinion besides Trina's." She retrieves two plates from a cupboard, then breaks out a wicked-looking carving knife and sets to work.

We sit at her cozy dining table and chow down. The brisket is quite possibly the most delicious thing I've ever eaten. As I fork another heaping spoonful of veggies onto my plate, Gina explains that she's been chef-ing at a restaurant called Harrigan's for almost five years. Her boss is a great guy who has tasked her with coming up with new entrees and appetizers for possible consideration to add to the menu. She boasts that she's responsible for nearly a third of Harrigan's current available choices. I don't doubt it.

She watches with wry amusement as the last bite disappears down my gullet. I have to use my napkin to muffle the ensuing belch. When I've recovered enough to render my opinion, I'm able to sum it up in one short sentence. "Don't change a damn thing." This elicits a proud grin.

By the time my stomach settles, Gina and I are deep in conversation. I gloss over my familial woes and go right into my adventures in the foster system, including my various legal issues. She takes it all in, her eyes friendly and non-judgy. She returns the favor by briefly recounting her wild "party girl" years in New

Mexico, her doomed-to-fail marriage to the guy she'd mistaken for Mr. Right, and her move to Arizona. Her first few years here were tough, but she found a career in food that's allowed her to take care of herself and Trina, whom she calls "the cherry on the sundae of my life." Greeting-card-level cheesy, I know, but having met Trina, I can't argue.

Gina takes a pull on her can of iced tea. "So, now that you're all moved in, what are you going to do?"

I shrug. "Try not to get fired in my first week, I guess."

"New job, eh? Where?"

"Hill O' Beans, the coffee place across the street from GCC. Ever been there?"

"No, but I've driven by it a million times. I'm just not a coffee person, I guess."

"I'll see if I can get you an employee discount." I grin. "Least I can do after that feast."

She nods. "Maybe I'll take you up on that."

Gina stares at me for several seconds, unblinking, and again I have to wonder what the heck is going on. Trying to remain polite, I say, "Is there something in my teeth?"

She shakes her head and rolls her eyes at the ceiling. "Oh, Jeez, I'm sorry. I really don't mean to stare. It's just...you seem like an interesting guy. I think you'll fit right in here."

Interesting? I've been called worse, that's for sure. "Are there any other residents my age? Just curious."

"One or two, but I don't know them that well," she says. "If you're worried about the young 'uns causing mischief, I promise, they're all good kids. I'm sure they'd look up to someone like you."

Huh. Will have to think about that.

I throw a glance at the microwave clock while Gina transfers the leftovers to her ginormous fridge. It's almost noon. "Well, I hate to gorge and run, but I've still got a lot of stuff to do." I smooth my flyaway hair with one hand. "Starting with a haircut."

Gina removes her apron and hangs it on a hook near the stove.

"Do you own a car? I was out back a little while ago and didn't see one in your space."

I shake my head. "Haven't really worked out my transportation situation yet."

She nods. "Do you need a ride?"

"Nah. It's only a few minutes' walk to the barber shop. I could use the exercise." I smile. "Especially after that meal."

She holds a finger up like a light bulb just came on in her head. "How about a bike?"

"A bike?"

"Yeah. A ten-speed. When I first moved here, I rode it all the time. Haven't ridden in years, though, not since my chef job took over." She gestures to her back door, leading to the parking area behind the row of townhomes. "You can borrow it until you figure things out."

Holy jeepers. This woman is too nice.

I decide to play it humble. "Thanks, Gina, but I couldn't do that."

"Why not? It's in good shape, and you need something to get around on. Besides, if you damage it, I know where you live."

I feel myself welling up a little, but I cover it with a huge smile. I'd almost forgotten what it was like to have neighbors, let alone cool ones.

It's just past one when I push the bike into the strip mall's bike rack, gasping and wheezing. Crap, how'd I get so out of shape? I make a silent vow to make exercise a regular part of my day. I might even make Gina an offer on the bike. Regardless of the cramps I'll have later, it feels really good to ride.

I secure the bike with a lock and chain Gina also lent me, then walk to the shop four doors down from Hill O' Beans. I step into Snips n' Clips, expecting a packed waiting room based on the number of cars in the parking lot. However, the place is nearly empty. There's only one customer, a man getting a trim from a heavyset Hispanic lady in her late thirties. The jingling bell inside the door announces my presence, and a brown-skinned guy in tight jeans and an even tighter yellow tee with a faded pompadour and a pencil-thin mustache looks up from wiping off a vacant chair. He smiles so broadly I'm nearly blinded by the light bouncing off his mouthful of gleaming teeth.

"Helloooooo! Welcome to Snips n' Clips!" he drawls in a decidedly feminine voice, whipping the towel over his shoulder and sauntering over to me. "And not a moment too soon, from the looks of it," he adds with a wink.

The woman pauses in mid-snip, rolls her eyes, and returns to her work.

"Uh..." I pause, my throat suddenly dry. I've got nothing at all against gay people, but I've never met one so over-the-top gay as this guy. "I'm, uh, looking for Nico?"

The guy spreads his arms. "Well, darling, you found him!" He reaches out a hand, which I tentatively shake. "Who do I have to thank for my newest customer?"

I point in the general direction of Hill O' Beans. "Um, it was Austin. From the coffee shop."

"Oh, *reeeealllly*?" Nico gasps, fanning his face. "How's that tall glass of almond milk doing?"

I've already worked up a sweat, but I can feel my glands going into overdrive. "Uh, fine, I guess. He just hired me, told me to come see you."

Nico steps back, surveying me. He casts what I hope is a professional eye over my face, my clothes, and my unruly mop, no doubt wondering how to turn garbage into fine art. I take a moment to hope that Austin sent me here because Nico's good at his job and not as a joke.

His inspection concluded, Nico gestures toward the chair he just finished wiping down and grabs an apron off the counter. Swallowing my apprehension, I take a seat. He throws a light blue body-cover over me, clasping it around my neck. I feel his hands lightly brush my hair.

He meets my gaze in the mirror. "So, tell me..." He raises a perfectly styled eyebrow. "What's your name?"

"Bax."

The grin returns. "I like it! Tell me, Bax, what is it you want your hair to say?"

I purse my lips. I probably should have thought about this before I stepped through the door.

Nico places his hands on my shoulders, and my whole body goes rigid. He obviously feels the tense vibes emanating from me and laughs.

"Relax, little man, I'm not hitting on you," he scoffs. "One, you're too young for me. Two, I knew you were hetero the moment you walked in. And three, I have a type, and you're not it." He pats my shoulder, and I feel like a total tool for my knee-jerk reaction.

I shoot Nico an apologetic smile, and my brain finally lets my mouth answer his question. "Uh, I just want to look good, I guess."

"For all those college girls, *sí*?"

Freckle Girl's face flashes through my mind, and I nod.

Nico laughs, picks up a spray bottle and a comb, and faces me. "Well, strap in, *amigo*, I'm bringing Sexy Bax!"

I struggle to keep my face neutral. This guy is growing on me.

The heavyset woman, who has finished with her customer and bid him goodbye, slams the register drawer shut with a resounding clang. "Pay no attention to my brother," she says to me. "He's not as funny as he thinks he is."

Nico leans in close to my ear. "Pay no attention to my sister. She has no sense of humor."

Ah. Siblings. That explains the antagonism.

"Izzy, bring me the pomade, would ya? I'm gonna turn our young friend here into a lady-killer." He grins again, and I'm tempted to ask what kind of toothpaste he uses. His teeth are *that* shiny.

Izzy grumbles and chugs off. I hear a muttered curse as the back door swings shut and am thankful I don't speak enough Spanish to be able to translate it. I suspect it's nothing complimentary.

Over the next hour, several customers come through the door, as well as a lady who Nico introduces as his Aunt Rita. She dons an apron and nods appreciatively at her nephew's work.

Finally, when it feels like my scalp can't take any more, Nico whips the oversized bib off my body with a flourish and a hearty "Voila!"

I gawk at the mirror, looking at a total stranger. This morning, my hair was somewhere between "coma patient" and "hobo." Now, it's...I don't have a word to describe it other than *frickin' cool!* Okay, that's two words.

My unkempt light-brown tangles are gone. Nico took at least half the length off the top, and the rest is swept back and to the side in a...quiff, I think it's called. With a little expertly placed gel, Nico textured it so it looks like it has some body, though the sides are tapered.

"Really brings out your eyes," Nico says, beaming.

I'm still staring, transfixed, at my reflection. "You think so?"

"Oh, honey, trust me, you got some serious Brown Steel going there," he says.

I chuckle and flash a comical Zoolander stare at him. He laughs.

I turn to Rita and Izzy, watching me have my moment from a discreet distance. "What do you guys think?"

Rita grins, and even Izzy's surliness slips for a few seconds. "Total lady killer," Rita says.

Nico just earned himself a big tip.

I'm eighteen. Not a kid anymore. I'm a *man* now. A damn good-looking one.

Sexy Bax.

CHAPTER FIVE

On Monday, Sheila picks me up at the townhouse for one final shopping jaunt. She spends five whole minutes gushing over my new 'do, and then we go out and I buy myself an entertainment system, including a 42-inch high-def smart TV and a brand-new Xbox/Blu-Ray/DVR. Between my Netflix app and this cool multiplayer game called Roblox that Gina told me Trina was into, I don't even look at the clock until midnight.

I sleep well into the morning and make a mental note to hit the sack early given my pre-dawn start. The last thing I want to do is come into my first day of work looking like an extra from *The Walking Dead*.

When the elementary and middle schools let out for the day and the lawn fills up with frolicking youngsters, I decide to join the fun. A smiling Trina vouches for me as she introduces me to all the kids I didn't meet before. Some are wary, most are friendly, and when I volunteer to be the impromptu goalie in the soccerball kick-around, they let me have it with both barrels. Who knew second-graders could kick so hard?

By dinnertime, I'm utterly exhausted but happier than I've been in forever. It hasn't been all that long since I was a kid. God knows I've been accused of behaving like an eight-year-old on more than one occasion in the last couple of years—including by a prosecuting attorney—but the ability to lose myself in the innocence of play is something I thought I'd never get back. Having ten laughing kids dog-pile on you may sound unpleasant, but if nothing else, it helped chill my anxiety about my impending career as a barista.

I say goodbye to Trina and the Arbor Vista gang, grab a quick shower, and am in bed by ten.

Look at me go.

Five o'clock sucks.

I yawn as I walk into Hill O' Beans, bumping into not one but two chairs on my way to the counter. I'm thankful Austin left the front door unlocked, or I'd have face-planted right into it.

Austin, fresh as a daisy despite the early hour—damn him—gawps at Nico's handiwork and smiles. I put on an apron, pin my brand-new personalized nametag to it, and training begins.

October, Austin explains, is Pumpkin Spice Latte season, so the first thing I learn is how to make Hill O' Beans' version of a PSL. I've heard of these things, and how college students gulp them down like there's money at the bottom of the cup, but I've never had one. It's a pretty complex procedure, and I struggle to maintain my concentration. After a couple of stifled yawns, Austin pours me a cup of black coffee, which I down in two gulps. Oh, man. Even the plain stuff tastes awesome. Suck it, Carl.

For the next forty-five minutes, I attempt to duplicate Austin's process of brewing, mixing, whisking, and steaming the myriad ingredients together in the right proportions. I even learn how to hold the whipped cream can correctly to top the thing off, dust the finished product with cinnamon flakes, and hey hey, I've created my very first thousand-calorie pick-me-up.

The shop opens at seven sharp, by which time two more

employees have shown up for their shifts. I am introduced to Imani, a diminutive, slightly chubby African-American girl with braided hair and a smile that rivals Nico's in brilliance, and Sierra, a pretty, slender Asian girl with short, purple-highlighted hair. Both welcome me to the Hill O' Beans family.

And then customers start pouring in. Holy crap, do they. When Austin said the pace would be fast, he wasn't kidding.

Austin, Imani, and Sierra proceed to work the morning coffee crowd like a well-oiled machine while I stumble around with all the grace of a hippo doing ballet. After my third collision with Austin, he assigns me to PSL duty before I cause an electrical fire.

It's almost eleven when the rush finally stops. I damn near collapse where I stand, my heart racing. I wipe away a thin sheen of sweat covering my face and glare at the ceiling fans, which seem to be working but must be distributing the air flow to everywhere but the PSL station. I hate you, fans.

"Not bad, rookie," Imani singsongs at me, patting my arm as she toddles off to the back room to get more muffins for the display case. I scowl at her retreating back. Not one of her hairs is out of place, and her white polo is completely wrinkle-free. I'd stamp my foot in jealousy if I could feel my legs.

Austin hands a customer his order and turns to me, all smiles. "Good job, Bax."

"Really?" I say, incredulous. "I messed up, like, five times. I kept waiting for you to can my ass."

He laughs. "I've found that the best way to test an employee's mettle is to throw them in the deep end right from the get-go. Either they'll sink, or they'll swim. It got a little rocky for a while, but you weathered the storm." He smiles again, and the knots in my stomach loosen. Dude's not only a good boss but a good guy. One more thing I need to thank Sheila for.

"So this is as stormy as it gets?"

"Well, you still have a lot to learn. I won't overwhelm you further by making you memorize all the recipes on your first day."

"Thank you," I say sincerely.

42

"But part of your job will involve unglamorous stuff. You know, stocking ingredients, sweeping floors, wiping the tables..." He tilts his head toward the restrooms. "...scrubbing the toilets."

I grimace and flash puppy-dog eyes at him. "Awww, Boss..."

He sighs, then shakes his head. "Fine, I won't task you with that today, but only today." He wags a stern finger at me. "*Everyone* shares duties here. Even I get down and dirty when I have to."

Whew. "Can I go on break now?"

"Sure, take a load off. Grab some water and a muffin, and in fifteen minutes, Sierra will train you on the register." He slaps me on the back, and I wince. That's gonna leave a mark.

I grab a sippy cup and a blueberry muffin, fill the cup with cold water, and fall into a chair near a table in the back, aahing in relief when a blast of cool air hits me. I glance up at the fans and mouth a silent thank you to them. Sorry I got angry before, guys. Let's never fight again. We're cool. Heh.

My eyes close as I let the fans show me their love. I don't know how long I sit there before a girl's voice wakes me from my cool-air coma.

"First day, huh?" Wry amusement plays across Piper's face as she peers over her cat-eye glasses at me.

"That obvious?"

"Just a little." She grins, and I can't help but return it. Her cheeks redden as she dumps a backpack on the floor and sits across from me. "I'm Piper."

"Bax. Nice to meet you." I straighten up, facing her. "When does your shift start?"

"Noon. Thought I'd get some reading done." Her eyes pass over the half-empty shop, then return to me. "You a student too?"

What do I tell her? If I lie, she'll ask me what I'm studying, followed by more questions, and I'm not savvy enough to bullshit my way through that conversation. On the other hand, if I say no, then I'd have to tell her about my dropping out of high school so I could dive headlong into the downward spiral that led me to an ankle bracelet and Carl's two-story kingdom.

Sigh. Brain hurting.

"Nope," I say. "Just plugging myself into the machine that is the workforce of America."

This earns another grin. I brace myself for more probing questions, but they don't come.

Piper unzips her backpack and pulls out two books. One is a thick textbook on anthropology, the other is the paperback I saw her reading during my interview. I angle my head to read the title —*The Moving Finger* by Agatha Christie. It looks old and well-read. I feel like I know the author's name from somewhere, but recognition dances just out of reach.

"Is that a good book?"

Her brow furrows. "The textbook or the novel?"

"Uh, the novel, I guess."

The cat-eye glasses slide down her nose as a grin spreads across her face. "Yeah. I love old mystery novels, especially Agatha. She was a pioneer in her field. Did you know she's the best-selling author of all time?"

"Even more than Stephen King?"

She scoffs. "Agatha spits on Stephen King."

I decide right then and there that I like Piper.

"Whoa. Harsh," I say. "Is anthropology your major?"

"It is. I've always been fascinated by societies and cultures."

"That's...interesting."

Her eyes flicker with an emotion I can't place, and she drops her chin, pushing her glasses back up her nose. Hmm. Wonder what Retro Girl is hiding.

I absently swig the last of my water, ball up the muffin wrapper in my fist, and stand. "Well, nice to meet you. I'll try not to run over you, but the way my day is going, I make no promises."

She gives a slight nod, opens her novel, and begins to read.

Sierra tries to teach me how to run the register, but it's pretty high-tech. You'd think they'd go out of their way to make their point-of-sale system dummy-friendly, but no. The lunch rush hits not long after, but it isn't as hectic as before, thank God. I'm relegated back to PSL duty, where I end up punching out a couple dozen more. Seriously, do these things have narcotics in them? By the time the clock hits one, my second wind is nearly spent, and the ache in my legs has returned.

I turn to the muted television above the register. The local news is showing the funeral of that kidnapped girl found on Friday. My stomach turns. I watch the girl's distraught parents shove past the female reporter and brush the cameraman, tilting the angle. Jeez, the nerve. Their child is barely in the ground, and you want a scoop? *Bitch.*

"Tears my heart out," Austin says.

I'm so distracted, I hadn't seen him approach. "Yeah, it totally sucks. They have any idea who did it?"

He shakes his head. "This is the third dead girl in a year. Whoever this psycho is, he's careful."

"The *third*?" Holy shit. A serial killer? Of children? Still at large? Just when you think the world can't get more fucked up…

Austin glares at me. "Don't you watch the news?"

"The news wasn't a popular show at the halfway house."

"Ah. Right."

"You've been following the story?"

"A friend of mine is involved in it."

I narrow my eyes. "Involved how?"

A jingle comes from the door, signaling another customer. I've come to loathe that sound in my brief time at Hill O' Beans, so much so that I don't turn to look any more. I did that thirty times this morning, hoping Freckle Girl would appear, but she didn't.

"You can ask her yourself," Austin says, answering my question.

I face the door, and my jaw drops open.

It's not Freckle Girl. Not even close.

Officer Natalie Rojas. Five feet, five inches of bad Karma.

And this week was going so well.

Even though she's dressed in a toned-down gray blazer, a white dress shirt, and dark slacks instead of the black uniform I remember her wearing during our previous encounters, I recognize her immediately. And despite my new haircut and Hill O' Beans apron, the recognition is mutual. The stone-shattering frown is a dead giveaway.

"Mr. Baxter."

She says it in a whisper, but the impact feels like she shouted it through a bullhorn. My gaze goes to the holstered gun at her side, and I gulp even though she doesn't make a move for it.

"Officer," I say, my voice cracking.

"It's Detective now."

Aaaand she got promoted. Ain't that just ducky.

Austin's eyes flick back and forth between us. "Do you two know each other?"

I'm unable to avert my eyes from Detective Rojas's Medusa-like stare, praying that I won't turn into a Bax statue right behind the counter. My voice box has shut down completely. Even her ponytail looks pissed.

"You could say that," she answers for me. "I busted this kid's punk ass several times. The last time was, what, New Year's?"

My paralysis fades just enough to nod and stare at my shoes. Even though I'm six inches taller, this lady intimidates the hell out of me. Compared to her, Carl is as scary as a pouncing kitten.

I flash back to the last time I saw her. It was in a courtroom, where she was testifying about all the stupid shit I got caught doing, and oh, what a list it was. Underage drinking, public intoxication, destruction of property. Then there was the cherry on top of the crap sundae—assaulting a police officer.

I tap my foot, willing the earth to open up and swallow me whole. Anything to get me out of that woman's death-glare.

"What happened?" Austin asks.

Her caramel skin flushes with anger. "He gave me a fat lip is what he did."

Austin's mouth falls open, and he points at me. "That was *him*?"

I look up to see that, yes, I am now the center of attention. Every staff member and customer is staring straight at me. "I was drunk," the mouse inside my throat squeaks. "I said I was sorry."

"You're sorry you got caught." Detective Rojas crosses her arms. "You're lucky you got a lenient judge. I'd have sentenced you to a lot more than eight months at a halfway house."

The stare-off continues, and just when I think I'm going to spontaneously combust, Austin swoops in to save my butt. "Look, Nat..."

'Nat?' What the actual hell?

"...I'm sure Bax is sorry for what he did," Austin finishes.

I nod vigorously.

"Whatever he's done in the past, according to the law, he's paid his debt to society." He puts a brotherly hand on my arm. "We all did stupid things at that age."

She turns her glare upon my savior, who, unbelievably, doesn't even flinch. "I doubt you took a swing at a cop, Austin."

'Austin?' '*Nat?*'

Great. Juuuuust great. My boss is buds with the woman who hauled my ass to jail. Twice.

Welp, it was fun while it lasted. With a resigned sigh, I begin undoing my apron.

"Hold up, Bax," Austin says, staying my hand. To Detective Rojas he says, "Nat, we go back a long way, right?"

Her face softens. I think. I've never actually seen her in anything but Terminator-mode. "Yeah."

"There was a time when I was heading down a pretty dark path," Austin continues. "If someone hadn't taken a chance on me, I wouldn't be where I am now." He puts a firm hand on my shoulder. "I've only started to get to know Bax, but I believe he has potential."

I think I want to kiss this guy. That's not weird, right?

The two of them stare it down for a few moments, and then she relaxes. "It's your business, Austin. Just take my advice and keep your eye on this one." She turns her laser beams back on me, and I avert my eyes again.

Austin moves to the register and starts ringing up Detective Rojas's order. "Bax, another PSL. Make this one your best yet."

Gee, no pressure.

I step away to pull myself together and crank out another latte, resisting the urge to put something totally not in the recipe in it.

Meanwhile, Austin and "Nat" have shifted the conversation away from me. Curious, I listen in.

"So...do I want to know how your day is going?" Austin asks.

"No," Detective Rojas grunts.

"That bad?"

"I want to find this guy and rip him apart with my bare hands."

Oh, man. She's investigating the dead girls' murders? That's intense. And it sounds like it isn't going well. No wonder she's so surly. I'd probably be stressed out too.

"Anything I can do to help?" Austin queries.

I watch Detective Rojas out of the corner of my eye. I see something I've never seen before...pain. This case, in all its ugliness, has affected her deeply. Maybe I misjudged her.

"Just keep me caffeinated," she says.

I spray a dollop of whipped cream on top of the newly concocted beverage, sprinkle on some cinnamon flakes and, in a moment of brilliance, slip in a cinnamon stick. According to Sierra, it gives the drink a bit of an edge. I slap the plastic lid on, grab a napkin, and lay them in front of Detective Rojas.

She eyes me skeptically for a few moments, then takes a wary sip. I watch her face for any flicker of approval or disgust, but I get neither. She gives a perfunctory nod, turns on her heels, and heads out the door.

My entire body slumps. Thank God I didn't pee myself.

I catch Austin staring at me. "You *hit* her?" he whisper-hisses.

"I was drunk." Is the room spinning, or is that just the fans? Stupid fans. "How do you two...?"

"We went to high school together."

Of course they did.

"Hey," Austin says in his "gentle boss" voice. "Nat's okay. Just don't get on her bad side."

"Pretty sure I'm already there."

"Yeah," he admits. "You wanna know how you get on her good side?"

I stare blankly.

"Don't break the law."

No shit.

Three more customers stroll through the door. Austin orders Imani to cover the register before turning to me. "I think you've had enough for one day. Empty the garbage bins, and you can go home. Dumpster's in the alley behind the shop. Use the back door."

I nod again. I move to walk away, but Austin stops me. "You did good today, Bax."

"Thanks, Boss."

I get about two steps before I run into Sierra and Piper, who are staring at me. Piper is grinning from ear to ear.

"Daaaayyumm," Sierra says, quirking an eyebrow. I can't quite tell if she thinks my act of drunken idiocy is impressive or moronic.

Piper chooses this moment to break into song. "Bad boys, bad boys, what'cha gonna do? What'cha gonna do when they come for you?"

"Cuuuute," I drawl. As digs go, that one's not bad. The more I get to know Piper, the more I like her.

Both girls laugh, but it's more playful than mocking. I smile back.

The ache in my leg muscles intensifies as I collect the full-to-the-brim garbage bags from each of the three bins and haul them through the shop's service entrance. I'm about to make the thirty-yard walk to the dumpster when I notice something strange.

Parked right next to the dumpster is a van with tinted windows. It's long and white and seems to be idling. I squint, searching for a sticker or a logo on the side, but there's nothing. All I see through the windshield is the faint shape of someone in the driver's seat. As I make my slow approach, the man—I assume it's a man—lowers the window and tosses a garbage bag out through it. It hits the rim of the dumpster and falls to the asphalt. He utters a curse as he opens the door and moves to step out.

"Hey," I yell. "Don't worry, I'll get it. I got a full load any—"

The man, upon hearing my voice, immediately slams the door shut. A second later, he guns the engine. I try to get a look at the guy as he zooms by, but he's already rolled up the window. He hits the street, peels to the right with a screech of tire rubber, and is gone.

Jeez, seriously? What's that guy's problem? Does he think I'm going to call the cops on him for littering?

I wonder what Detective Rojas would do if she were here. Probably chase him through three states.

I fling my burden into the open dumpster, then reach for the bag the asshat threw away. Standing as far away from it as I can—I mean, who knows where this guy's shit has been—I pick it up. The bag gets caught on a piece of jagged metal protruding from the dumpster, ripping it apart and spilling its contents all over the ground.

I glance skyward, shaking my fist at the man upstairs. Yeah, I know I'm being an ungrateful jerk given all the great stuff that happened this weekend, but today He's really pushing my buttons. I just want to get home, grab a shower, sack out on the couch, and lose myself in one of several first-person shooter games that I bought.

Thankfully, the contents of the bag are nothing but clothes. I poke the pile with my shoe, then crouch down for a better look.

They're children's clothes, something a little girl would wear. There's a white Moana T-shirt, a pair of blue jeans, socks, and pink sneaks with little hearts drawn on them in black Sharpie. They appear to be clean, with no visible stains, holes, or tears in the fabric. Why would someone throw them out? And why would he drive like a bat out of hell rather than be caught ditching them?

Sighing, I reach for the T-shirt. My fingers make contact, and something hard punches me right in the brain.

A cool breeze blows my hair into my face, and I shove my hands deeper into my pockets. I look up at the nearest street sign as I walk by it. 64th Avenue. Two more minutes, and I'll be home.

A loud scrape sounds from behind me. Before I can turn around, a hand clamps over my mouth. I try to cry out, but only a muffled squeal escapes. I thrash my legs, but they find nothing but air.

Omigodomigodomigodhelpmehelpmehelpme...I'm being kidnapped! Mommy! Daddy! Help me!

I'm in a strange room. All I see is a mattress, bare walls, a curtained-off area in the corner, and a tiny window too high for me to reach. I scream and scream, but no one answers.

What's going on? OmigodomigodwhereamI?

Hard, powerful hands lift me up. I kick, bite, but he's too strong. Something jabs into my neck, and—

Darkness.

Chapter Six

"Bax? Bax!"

A frantic voice registers in my brain a second before the smell hits me. This is immediately followed by the realization that my hair and forehead are wet, tiny pebbles and mud particles are clinging to my cheeks, and I have one mother of a headache.

I stir, largely thanks to someone's hand jostling my shoulder.

"Bax! Oh my God, what happened? Are you okay?"

I want to tell this person that I am the polar frickin' opposite of okay, but the stab of pain in my head crushes my reply. Instead, I let out a groan like I just woke up with a blistering hangover. Which is kind of what this feels like, minus the part where I actually, you know, got drunk.

"M'okay," I slur, pushing myself up. Nasty-ass water drips from my head back into the pothole where I face-planted. I shudder, not because of the smell, which is nauseating, but at the notion that if I had hit the ground a foot to the left, I might have literally drowned in three inches of water.

A pair of hands guide me into a sitting position. I open my eyes, and the light of day stabs me in the skull. I raise a hand to shield myself from the glare, searching for an object to focus on. I find one. Two, actually—a familiar-looking pair of black sneakers, poking out from the frayed cuffs of their wearer's khaki pants. "P-Piper?"

"Yeah, it's me. What happened?" Her tone bears so much genuine concern that I feel the vibes coming off her. I take a half-moment to appreciate that Piper would care so much about the welfare of a guy she just met.

I sit up, my back against the dumpster, not caring about the germs I might be accumulating. The fog lifts from my mind as my most recent memories return. The other half of my brain scrambles to find a better reason for my passing out in a dirty alley beyond "I fainted." Ideas pinball around my head, and I choose the one that seems the least lame. "Um, there was this van, and, uh..."

"Oh my God!" Piper says again, crouching next to me. "Did it hit you? Is anything broken?"

I look into her kind brown eyes, which at the moment are not hidden behind her glasses. "Don't think so," I say, mentally cataloguing every place my body is hurting, which all seem to be localized around my head. "I guess it missed me."

She breathes a sigh of relief. "Can you stand?"

I nod, holding out my hand. She takes it, and with a strength belying her diminutive frame, hauls me up. A wave of dizziness crashes over me, so I brace myself against the dumpster. I swat away several members of a gang of flies having a major party over the Hill O' Beans garbage. Ew. I hope I won't need a tetanus shot after this.

My gaze falls to the pile of clothes at my feet, next to the shredded trash bag, and my heart freezes. Moana smiles up at me from the front of the T-shirt, and clarity hits me like a brick to the face.

It was real. What I saw...somehow, was real.

But it wasn't me. How could it be? I was never snatched off the street, imprisoned in a room by some perv and then jabbed in the neck with a needle. I've had bad nights, many of which included periods of lost time, but nothing like that. And the thoughts that invaded my head...they weren't mine either. It was a child. A girl, I think. Terrified. Alone.

I feel the blood drain from my face.

Could that guy in the van have been...*him*? The killer the cops are looking for?

Nah. Can't be. That man, according to Austin, has killed three girls while thwarting every attempt by the cops to find him. He wouldn't be so clumsy as to throw evidence away in a coffee shop dumpster, would he?

And most importantly, how the fuck did I see what I just saw?

Something's going on. Something crazy. Something awful.

No. My life is normal now. *Normal!*

I let Piper lead me back into the shop, where Austin sits me down in that nice cool spot where I can bask in the fans' good graces. Piper relays to the rest of the team that I was nearly run over and fell on my noggin diving out of the way, an utter lie that I have no reason to refute.

After informing me that I was in the alley for nearly fifteen minutes—prompting another gasp—Austin peppers me with questions, which does nothing to make my headache go away. The Zip-loc full of ice that he hands me, however, is a godsend. I press it to my aching temple, letting the numbness seep into my head. I chase it down with two extra-strength aspirin, courtesy of the boss-man.

"I'm okay," I tell Austin, who signals for Piper and Sierra to tend to the line of customers and stop gawking. "I've had much worse, believe me."

"Not on my watch, you haven't." He takes the seat opposite me. "You want me to call the police? You should file a report, at least."

I picture Detective Rojas taking my statement, mumbling "Yeah, we'll get right on that," and then laughing as she drives away.

"What's the point?" I ask. "It was a van. A white van. No logos, no signage, nothing."

"You didn't get the license plate?"

I shake my head, wince, and slap the ice bag back on my skull.

He straightens up, hands on hips. "You sure you don't need a doctor? There's an Urgent Care right up the street and—"

"I'm fine!" I shout, louder than I mean to. I exhale in regret. "I'm fine," I say at a much softer volume.

"Okay. I'll go clock you out. Feel free to rest up until you're feeling better, and if you need a ride home, just ask."

I nod. My head feels heavy. Hope I don't have a concussion. "Thanks, Boss."

I sit, listening to the low rumble of conversation from the customers, the whir of the fan-blades slicing the air, and the jingle of the bell above the door. I crack open my eyelids several times, hoping against hope that Freckle Girl will add a ray of beautiful sunshine to my otherwise dreary day, but she's a no-show.

I spend thirty minutes vaguely aware of the comings and goings of the late afternoon crowd. When the pain in my face recedes to a dull throb, I finally have enough energy to make my way home. Both Piper and Austin convey their sentiments and tell me to take it easy. I thank them again.

I amble back to the tiny space near the walk-in freezer designated for employee's belongings and miscellaneous stuff, behind which is a long row of coat-hooks. I undo my apron with a groan and hang it up, hoping my next workday won't be so traumatic.

My eyes fall on a nearby shelf, upon which a half-empty box of trash bags sits.

A terrifying thought rushes through my mind.

The clothes. The guy tried to toss them, but I interrupted him. If I leave them there, he might come back for them. Then he'll dispose of them, and any chance I might have to figure out just what the hell happened to me goes away too.

Maybe that's for the best. That...whatever that was, was the scariest shit that's ever happened to me. If I touch the clothes again, will the same thing happen?

Am I going crazy? Or is it something else?

I eye the box of trash bags again.

Aww, man...

I grit my teeth, resisting the urge to hurl the remote across the room.

Ever since returning to Casa de Bax, I've been scouring the network channels, hoping to pick up a story on the news about the creepo I'm all but convinced is the man I interrupted, all while trying to ignore the trash bag sitting ominously on the carpet at the foot of the sofa. Epic fail on both counts. Thank God the aspirin is doing its job.

I grab a Coke from the fridge, hoping the caffeine will keep me wired despite the exhaustion pulling my body toward a lying position. I just know if I nod off, it'll be midnight before I wake up again.

I force myself to remain awake during sixty minutes of boringness that passes for local news. By five o'clock, I'm well versed on freeway closures, a sanitation workers' strike, the rehab status of the Cardinals' twenty-million-a-year running back who sprained his ankle in preseason, and the death of some former Congressman who looks old enough to have served in the Lincoln administration.

Just when I'm about to call it quits, an African-American woman with a severe expression kicks off the six o'clock news.

"Our top story tonight...the Phoenix Police Department, in conjunction with the FBI, has formed a task force to track down the Disney Princess Killer, believed to be responsible for the murders of at least three preteen girls in the Metro area. We now go live to Stuart Sellers at this afternoon's press conference at the Central Precinct."

The camera shifts to a dark-haired reporter standing in front of a police station, a semi-genuine look of concern wrinkling his forehead. *"Thank you, Linda. The body of ten-year-old Sarah Blankenship, a fifth-grade student at Desert View Middle School, was discovered last Friday in Saguaro Municipal Park, after disappearing eight days earlier on her way home from school. According to a statement just released by the county medical examiner, the girl was not abused or violated..."*

Thank heaven for that.

"...though she was wearing clothes, including a Little Mermaid *T-shirt, that her parents, Michael and Jessica Blankenship, claim was not hers. Cause of death has been confirmed as asphyxiation. Further details have been withheld for investigative purposes. The Blankenships have declined any further interviews at this time."*

Then a trio of pictures flashes on the screen—the killer's three confirmed victims. All look to be about the same age, with long, straight brown hair, brown eyes, and tan complexions.

Their names etch themselves into my memory. Mia Sachs. Jordan Clark. Sarah Blankenship.

My eyes start to burn, both from fatigue and righteous anger.

This asshole is stealing innocent kids from their families. Imprisoning them. Killing them. Dumping their bodies like broken dolls. He's done it three times. He's sure to do it again. People like that don't stop until they're captured or killed.

I turn the volume down on the TV to zero as the camera cuts to a husky-looking police captain with thinning hair and a Fu Manchu mustache talking into the reporter's microphone. I casually reach down for the trash bag but pull my hand back, fear turning my blood to ice.

When I touched the clothes before, it felt like a knife stabbing me in the brain. What's to say that won't happen again?

There's got to be a safer way to put my theory to the test.

And then it hits me.

I rap twice on the door. This is followed by a mad rush of footsteps and a girlish "Who is it?" that puts a smile on my face.

"It's Bax."

The door flies open to reveal Trina's adorable grin. "Bax! Hey!" She gives a knowing nod to Cheyanne, standing right behind her with a less pronounced smile, before returning her focus to me. "What's up?"

"I wanted to talk to your mom. Is she home?"

Trina shakes her head. "She usually gets home at 5:30. You can wait for her in here if you want." Her tiny little eyebrows raise expectantly, and she gives me the grade-school equivalent of a seductive smile.

Oh my God. Is Trina *flirting* with me?

"Uh, sure." She steps aside to let me pass, and I follow them back to the living room, where it looks like Trina and Cheyanne are deep in another round of Roblox. I smile. I honestly couldn't remember any girls I knew being into video games when I was a kid. Guess times have changed.

The two of them sit on the floor in front of the gaming system while I flop down on their thick, pillowy couch. The cushion gives a few inches under my butt, and I have to hang onto the armrest lest the thing swallow me up. Both girls giggle.

"Did you get a haircut?" Cheyanne asks, her dark eyes twinkling.

"Of course he did, silly," Trina interjects. "Looks awesome." She bats her eyelashes at me.

Oh, yeah. She's totally crushing on me. I race from flattered to terrified and back again in the blink of an eye.

"Thanks," I say.

Both girls stare awkwardly at me for a few more moments, then at each other. Then Trina shrugs, and they resume their RPG world-building.

I dig out my phone and pretend to be engrossed in my miniscule list of available apps. After a few seconds, when I'm confident neither girl is watching, I peek my head up. Trina is sitting at an angle to the TV, so I'm able to get a good look at her hands without craning my neck. Sure enough, the charm bracelet she wore on Friday still rings her wrist.

"So, uh," I mumble, "your parents are okay with you two being here all by yourselves?"

"Yeah, they're cool," Trina replies without turning my way. "I only have to wait an hour or so between when school gets out and Mom gets home."

"What if she has to work late?"

"Then I stay over at Crescent's."

Cheyanne adds, "But Crescent has soccer practice Mondays and Wednesdays, and my house is crazy loud with my two baby brothers, so my mom lets me keep Trina company till her mom gets off work."

I smile. I've only been at Arbor Vista for a few days, and I'm already feeling the sense of community. "You two been friends a long time?"

"Since we were kids," Trina says.

Cheyanne giggles, her milk chocolate cheeks flushing. "Um, we still are kids, ya doof."

Trina rolls her eyes and slugs her friend softly in the arm. "You know what I mean."

"Yup," I say. "Must be nice to have a best friend living only a few yards away."

"Yeah, but it sucks going to different schools," Cheyanne says.

"Different schools?"

She gives me a *duh* look. "Me and Crescent are in fifth grade. Middle school. Trina's still across the street, stuck in elementary school."

"Only for one more year," Trina adds. She puts her controller down and stands, flashing her wet puppy dog eyes at me. "Why don't you live with your parents?"

"Trina!" Cheyanne hisses under her breath. "You can't ask him that!"

"It's all right," I say. "Your mom already knows, so you might as well too." I take a deep breath. "My dad was in the army. He was killed in Afghanistan a few years ago."

"Awww, I'm sorry." Genuine sadness creases Trina's tiny features as she sits on the couch next to me. "I never really knew my dad. Mom says he was a real jerkweed, so I guess I'm better off."

I chuckle. Hearing the mild insult come out of Trina's nine-year-old mouth makes it almost sound endearing.

"What about your mom?" Cheyanne asks.

I think of Mom, and AJ, and my mouth pauses halfway open. Probably better to not bring up my brother. That's a bottomless pit of soul-crushing tragedy no child should have to listen to. "After Dad died..." I sigh heavily. "She got really sad. Depressed. She wasn't as strong as he was, so when she lost him, she kind of lost herself." I sigh again, meeting Trina's gaze. "I kind of got lost too."

Trina's head droops. "That's so sad." Then, like a switch has been thrown, she brightens. "But you're okay now, right? You've got a job, a house, and the coolest neighbors ever!"

I grin. "Can't argue with that." I hold out my fist, and she wastes no time bumping it.

And...go.

"That's a cool bracelet," I say, gesturing. I'm not just blowing smoke. It *is* cool, a ring of small interlocking circles. Five tiny flower designs dangle from it, each in a different color.

Trina's smile broadens. "You like it?" She holds out her hand at arm's length, swishing the flowers back and forth.

"Yeah, it's cool. May I see it?"

Cheyanne snorts. "If you're asking her to take it off, don't bother. She doesn't even take it off for P.E. She probably wears it in the shower."

"I do not, Chey!" Trina barks back. "I just like it, okay?"

I leap on Trina's moment of distraction, lean forward, and grasp her gently by the wrist. My fingertips brush the metal of the bracelet, and—

A wave of happiness washes over me. I stick out my hand, bouncing with glee as the white-haired old lady fastens the bracelet around my wrist. The fit is perfect—not too loose, not too tight. I swivel my wrist around, watching the little flowers dance and jingle.

"I love it!" I squeal. "I promise to wear it every day!"

A smile creases her serene, wrinkled face. "Happy birthday, Kitty Kat," she says.

"Thanks, Great-Grandma!"

I lean forward for a hug, feeling her arms wrap around me. "You're so welcome," she whispers in my ear.

I plant a kiss on her cheek. Her skin feels strange, not like kissing Mom's cheek. It's almost like kissing paper. Is Great-Grandma Rose sick?

Nah. She's fine. She'll be around forev—

The image blinks out as fast as it came when Trina bolts off the couch and disappears into the next room. I shake my head slightly, and just like that, I'm back in the...present? Yeah, I'll go with that. It might be my imagination, but the room feels ten degrees colder than it did a minute ago.

When this happened on Friday, I waved it off.

I can't deny it any longer.

Something is *very* freaking wrong with me.

I'm vaguely aware of a door closing, followed by the noisiest, gushiest hug I've ever heard. I catch Cheyanne rolling her eyes at her friend's shameless display of parental love. This tiny, insignificant gesture calms me, gives me something real to focus on.

Mother and daughter glide into view, arms around each other, and an exhausted smile cracks onto Gina's face. "Hey Bax, hey Cheyanne."

I give a casual wave, hiding my turmoil as best I can. "Hey, Gina."

"Hey, Ms. Forrester," Cheyanne says.

Gina kicks her shoes off, hangs her purse on a hook near the front door, and faces me again. Her dark hair is pulled back in a ponytail and although she looks tired, her eyes are bright. "So how was your first day of work?"

Oh, it was awesome, up till my reunion with the one person who hates my guts more than Carl, my nearly getting run over by a guy who just might be a serial killer, and getting knocked unconscious by something so bizarre I don't even have the words to describe it.

I stand up, faking nonchalance like a pro. "It was fine."

"How's the bike working out?"

Ah, right, the other reason I came over. "It's awesome. I was actually hoping to make you an offer on it."

Gina yawns. "I'm sure we can come to a..." Her brow furrows. "What happened to your face?"

I turn away, my hand going to the small scratches on my cheek. "Slipped and fell. At work. My bad."

"Wow, I didn't even see that," Trina adds. "Does it hurt?"

"A little. Two more aspirin and an ice pack, and I'll be fine."

"You sure?" Gina asks.

"Yeah."

I say goodbye to Cheyanne, who promises to return tomorrow for more Roblox-ing. Gina sets to preparing dinner while Trina, at her mom's instruction, heads to her room to do her homework. Honestly, I don't know how Gina does it. If I spent forty-plus hours a week preparing other people's food, the last thing I'd want to do is slave over a hot stove when I got home. She laughs dryly when I tell her as much.

"What can I say? I love to cook," she says. "Sure, it'd be easy to give in and get take-out all the time, but that feels like a cop-out. Besides, I've read about what prolonged exposure to fast food does to kids. I refuse to let Trina fall into that trap."

I nod. "You let her go for pizza, though?"

"That's different. Crescent's mother always takes them to Romano's. Their food is really good. And speaking of food, you'll be happy to know that brisket recipe you sampled is now on Harrigan's dinner menu." She beams with pride.

"That's awesome!" I gush. "What'll be your next creation?"

"I have some ideas. I'll keep you posted."

"Please do." I stare at the nearest wall, trying to come up with a plausible way to segue to my next question. Unable to find one, I go for the direct approach. "Trina was just showing me her charm bracelet. She really seems to love it."

Jeez, that was clumsy.

Gina, however, doesn't call me on the abrupt change of subject, focused as she is on her cooking. "Yeah, she does. I think she even wears it in the shower."

A miffed voice comes from down the hall. "I do not!"

I fight hard to suppress a laugh. Girl's apparently got rabbit ears. "Did you make it for her?"

Gina smiles. "Oh, God, no. Arts and crafts are so not my thing. It was a gift from my grandmother for her eighth birthday."

"That's cool," I say. "Never got to meet either of my grand-mothers. They both died before I was born."

Her face falls. "That's too bad. Grandmothers are awesome."

"I did have my grandpa, though. At least, until I was twelve. So that's something."

She looks up, meets my gaze. "Trina and I try to go back to Albuquerque a couple of times a year." She sighs. "My folks love their grandbaby."

My brow furrows. I definitely detected an undercurrent of weariness in her tone. "But?"

Gina twists a few knobs on the stove, wipes her hands on a towel, and approaches me. "Don't get me wrong, I love my parents. Thing is, they're kind of old-fashioned. To put it simply, they don't like the idea of Trina growing up without a positive male role model. I keep reminding them that she attends a great school, lives in a great neighborhood, and has wonderful friends. She's a terrific student, and is, I think, as happy as a nine-year-old can be. I make more than enough to provide for her, and yet..." She leans against the counter with a heavy sigh. "I'm sorry, I shouldn't be dumping all this on you."

I look into Gina's eyes. Though I've only known her for a couple of days, I've developed a deep respect for her. I wasn't sure how, or even if, I was going to make friends outside the system I've been buried in for the last two years. I certainly wouldn't have imagined I'd be living in a nice neighborhood, one door down from two people that I clicked with. It feels good.

"It's okay," I say. "No one's ever accused me of being a positive anything, but..." I shrug. "If you ever feel overwhelmed, I'm right next door."

She smiles, and for a hot, naughty second, I wonder if she's into younger guys. Then I come to my senses and pull my mind out of the gutter.

"I appreciate that, Bax," she says. "More than you know. But you're eighteen. Your new life has only just started. I have no doubt it's going to take you to some interesting places."

Already there, lady.

She wanders off toward the hallway leading to her and Trina's bedrooms and pauses halfway down. She beckons me over. Her eyes lock on a framed portrait hanging on the wall.

"Like my grandmother, God rest her soul, always used to say, life is a journey that must be traveled no matter how bad the roads are."

I grin, my gaze falling on the picture. Within the frame are four women, clad in lovely, elegant dresses. Their eyes shine and their perfectly made-up faces all bear wide smiles, especially Trina, who can't be more than six. Her blue dress with a matching huge bow in her hair is the cutest thing ever. The family resemblance between all four is obvious.

"Four generations of Forrester women in one photo," Gina confirms, pointing at each face in turn. "Myself, Trina, my mother Pamela, and Grandma Rose."

I focus on the matriarch of the family, and my heart skips a beat.

The face from my vision stares back at me from the photo.

Holy fuckballs.

CHAPTER SEVEN

Day Two at Hill O' Beans proves far less grueling. The pain in my head has succumbed to the aspirin, thank God. By the time I ride home on my bike—which I can now legally call mine after paying Gina fifty bucks for it—I've learned how to make a macchiato, a frappucino, and a black eye, which is tastier than it sounds.

Late in the afternoon, I park myself on the couch and skim through the news programs, hoping for a break in the DP Killer case, but there's nothing. Unable to stand the ominous glare of the trash bag—I swear that thing is judging me—I toss it into an empty closet, then contemplate my next move.

I stare into space, reviewing the facts as I know them, which isn't much. When I touch certain objects, I get a picture in my head that seems to be associated with those objects. I touched Trina's bracelet and saw her great-grandmother. To be more accurate, I relived Trina's memory of receiving the bracelet from Great-Grandma Rose. It was a happy, pleasant memory, one that has stuck with Trina even though it was more than a year ago. What I find particularly interesting is that I wasn't just seeing and hearing the memory, I was feeling it. Living it, like it was happening to me.

On the other hand, touching Sarah's clothes—I'm assuming that's who they belonged to until I learn differently—brought forth memories that were the exact opposite of pleasant. The fear, shock, and pants-wetting terror that girl experienced...it felt like ants were crawling all over my body. Ants dipped in ice.

I mute the TV and stare at my hands.

Come on. Things like this don't just...*happen* to people.

Unless they do and they just don't talk about it. Yeah, that makes sense. The line between reality and madness gets a little blurry when it comes to supernatural shit like this.

But why didn't this ever happen to me before? It only started on Saturday...

The day after I turned eighteen.

There's no freaking way that's a coincidence.

Okay, that's something. Arbitrary, but something.

But...I've touched dozens of things since I got out of Asterly. Nothing set me off except Sarah's shirt and Trina's bracelet. What do those two things have in common?

Well, they both belonged to young girls. Trina has attached a powerful, emotional memory to that bracelet. And if the clothes were what Sarah was wearing when she was kidnapped...well it doesn't get much more emotional than that.

There's a word for what I can do. There has to be. I just need to find what that word is. That will eliminate the what. Then I'll tackle the why, which should be about as easy as pile-driving King Kong.

Saturday morning brings good news from Austin. With most of my preliminary training out of the way—"the rest will come in time, young Padawan" he Yodas at me—I don't need to come in before sunup anymore. So yay, two extra hours of sleep.

I finally meet Lucas, who according to Piper only works Fridays, Saturdays, and Mondays. Dude's in his early twenties and built like a linebacker, which fits because he apparently was one in high school, but a knee injury in his senior year caused him to lose a promising scholarship. Which sucks so hard that I instantly feel for the guy, but he waves it off like it's no big whoop. He smiles at all the customers while he works the register, giving not-so-subtle winks to the college girls who seem to be in awe of his impressive musculature. Add in his blond hair and light blue eyes and girls nearly drool when they step up to the counter.

The place is half-full—not bad for a Saturday. Lucas tells me that GCC does weekend classes to help accommodate those students who work full-time, which is why Austin keeps the place open. Over the course of the morning, Lucas and I get into a lengthy discussion about who the best Batman was. He staunchly argued for Michael Keaton, but I'm stuck on Christian Bale.

"Bale had a great supporting cast," Lucas argues. "Freeman, Caine, Oldman...Bale's like the eighth-most-talented actor in the movie."

"Oh, so Jack Nicholson's chopped liver?" I retort.

"Not at all. All I'm saying is, Keaton was miles better at being Bruce Wayne."

"I'll give him a quarter-mile," I say after a moment's pondering. "He gets a full mile over Affleck. Let's not even talk about Clooney."

Lucas holds his nose in a *pee-eww* gesture. "On that, we agree. Nothing against George personally, but I hope he shit-canned his agent for bringing him that role."

"Agreed," Sierra says, joining the conversation. "As long as George is robbing casinos with Brad and Matt, he's cool with me."

Where have these people been all my life?

I spend all day Sunday catching up on sleep, which is a good thing because Monday is hellaciously busy, so busy that I'm not able to shoot the breeze with my new coworkers. People are a little more subdued and/or testy that the weekend is over, which Austin says is perfectly normal. Most people get their drinks to go. The coffee gods smile upon me as I don't have one single mishap, spill, or botched order. All hail me.

My one o'clock break on Tuesday finds me back at my usual table. Despite the cooling temperatures outside, the wave of cold air propelled by the overhead fans feels awesome. I've gotten more used to being on my feet for several hours, so I chalk my current fatigue up to stress more than physical exhaustion. Unfortunately, no amount of witty banter about pop culture can keep the knot in my stomach away indefinitely.

I close my eyes, hoping for the hundredth time that the solution to my next-level-weird quandary will be written on the inside of my eyelids. Nope.

Ever since my revelation in Gina's hallway, I've racked my brain for a way to both explore my new ability without getting a head injury and help the cops without risking another felony charge. They could hit me with evidence tampering, impeding a federal investigation, or, worse, they could think I had something to do with the murders themselves. With my record and lack of character witnesses besides Sheila, no judge would believe me. Even worse, I'm eighteen now, which means a conviction will see me in the itchy orange jumpsuit Carl mentioned. No more kiddie jail for me. I could go to prison where, let's face it, I'd be someone's bitch within an hour. No thank you times a million.

But I can't do nothing. If another girl's body shows up on the news and I did jack-all to stop it...

I'm vaguely aware of someone setting a small Styrofoam cup directly in front of me. I get a whiff of something lemony yet spicy. I manage a weak smile as Piper sits across from me.

"How're you feeling?" she asks.

"Better." I point at the steaming liquid in front of me. "What's this?"

"Chai tea. Nothing better when you're stressing."

I hold the tiny cup under my nose. It smells really good. I've never been a tea drinker, like *ever*, so this should be interesting. I take a cautious sip. It warms me all the way down, and I feel my frazzled brain calm. "Wow."

She smiles. "First thing I learned when I started working here —coffee will get you through the day, but tea is what will get you through to tomorrow."

"I'll remember that. What do I owe you?"

She waves off my suggestion like it's a pesky gnat. "Drinks are free for employees. It's a privilege Austin lets us enjoy," she lowers her voice to mimic his husky baritone, *"as long as you don't abuse it."*

I laugh, but it's hollow, and avert my gaze out the window. I watch cars pull in and out of the parking lot for a good minute before I notice Piper's raised eyebrows.

"You always this much of a space case?"

I smile again, and this time I'm feeling it. This chai stuff is magic. "I plead the fifth, your honor."

She leans forward. "This is going to sound hella corny, but Hill O' Beans has kind of become my family in the five months I've been working here."

I take another sip. "You're right, that is corny. Sweet, but corny. Do you guys, like, hang out after work?"

"Sometimes." She points at Imani, ringing up another customer. "Imani, believe it or not, is a dancing machine."

My eyes widen. Did *not* see that coming. "Really?"

"Yup. Sierra," she nods at Sierra, wiping down the tables nearest the door, "is into kickboxing."

I laugh. "What about you? I know you love old mystery stories. What else you got in your bag of tricks?" I make a thoughtful face and snap my fingers. "I got it. Monster trucks."

She glares at me.

"Death metal?"

Her glare deepens, but a flicker of amusement ripples through her irises, encouraging me to make one more guess.

"Competitive eating?"

"You suck at this."

She's not wrong. I give a noncommittal grunt.

Piper rolls her shoulders and leans back in her chair, lifting the front two legs off the floor. A moment later, she bounces back down, a wistful expression crossing her face. "I wish I had time for a hobby. Between everything I have going on and squeezing in ten minutes of sleep a night, I barely have time for my boyfriend."

I deflate a little, and I'm not sure why. I just met Piper. I have no reason to think that she might not be spoken for. I guess a tiny portion of my brain was mulling over the possibility of asking Piper out.

Like it matters anyway. I spent the better part of a year around nothing but pissed-off dickheads. I haven't had a girlfriend since Ellie Nichols in my junior year, and that was less a relationship than a series of hookups. But I'm eighteen now. I'm a free man, with a place of my own, some spending cash, and a snazzy used ten-speed to get around on. Hrm. Better leave that last part out of any pickup line I might use.

Dammit, I've spaced out again. "I hear you," I say, trying to keep my face neutral. "Do I fit into this quaint little family?"

Austin appears from the back room, curling his fingers at me in a clear *break's over* gesture.

I stand, but she puts a hand on my arm. "That's for you to figure out," she says. "But if you're there for us, we'll be there for you."

With that, I return to my grind. Heh. Coffee joke.

After dumping the garbage—without incident, thankfully—I ask Austin if I can call it a day. He tells me to restock the bottled drinks in the display cooler and punch out, followed by a "See you tomorrow."

I grab a six-pack of water and a fistful of bottled teas from the back shelf and make my way to the front. I stop dead and damn near drop my burden on the floor when I notice who's standing at the counter, giving Piper her order.

Freckle Girl.

The rest of the room fades away as I zero in on her face. Piper says something I don't hear, but it must be hilarious because Freckle Girl breaks into a wide smile. A soft, feminine giggle escapes her mouth and I zone out completely. I picture her in my arms, staring into my eyes, smiling that same smile and laughing at one of my dumb jokes.

Oh my God, I have to meet this girl.

She has a large satchel slung over one shoulder of a faded grey tee with the school's logo and the words "GCC Athletics" over her left breast. The shirt looks well-worn and bears a few sweat stains, and I wonder if she just came from practicing whatever her sport of choice is. Her hair is slightly disheveled, but damn if she doesn't rock the messy look too.

Freckle Girl takes her cup and moves to a table next to the window, not noticing my bugging eyes following her. She sits down, by herself, takes a sip, and I note relief and relaxation settle over her features. Her eyes momentarily close and a soft smile curls the corners of her mouth.

A slight cramp in my shoulders reminds me that I'm still carrying an armload of beverages. Up yours, gravity.

I move around the counter to the three-tiered cooler right next to the register and shove the bottles into it without the slightest thought to making them look neat, all while sneaking peeks at Freckle Girl out of the corner of my eye. After taking another sip, she pulls a laptop from her satchel. Oblivious to my ogling, she tucks a stray strand of hair behind her ear before squaring her shoulders. Then she pops open her laptop and begins typing.

"Wanna put your tongue back in your mouth, Mr. Subtlety?" Piper's voice shatters my concentration.

I stand up quickly. Piper glares at me like I'm the creepy freak I've just realized I am. "Uh... yeah."

Her frown takes a few moments to drop away. "It's okay," she says, but I'm not sure she means it. She lowers her voice to just above a whisper. "Remember, you're here to serve the customers, not mentally undress them."

I feel my face redden. "I wasn't doing *that*." Much.

No. She's right.

"Sorry," I mumble. "It's just...being in a social environment is kinda new to me."

"Just don't let it happen again."

If Freckle Girl is a regular, that's gonna be tough.

I flash another quick glance her way. Her fingers dance over her keyboard, and I sigh in relief. After taking a few moments to front-face the bottles in the cooler, I move back behind the counter. "Question..." I pause, making my face as contrite as possible. "Does she come in a lot?"

Piper's eyes narrow. "A few times a week, usually around two."

"Does she always order the same thing?"

"Mocha chai latte. Why?"

I scan the wide chalkboard-type menu board filling the wall behind the register. "I don't know what that is. Is it on the menu and I'm just not seeing it?"

"It used to be, I think. Not many people order it, but Austin's policy is that if someone wants it and we have the ingredients, we go ahead and make it anyway."

I nod. "Are they hard to make?"

A catty smile creeps over her face. "Ohhhh, I get it. You want to impress Sydney with your mad ninja barista skills, huh?"

Sydney. Freckle Girl's name is Sydney. "Well, I mean, what if she comes by and orders it and you're in the back or something? I can't just, like, run back and get you because I can't make an MCL, right?"

Piper exhales and shoots a look at Sydney, who is now biting her lower lip, her eyebrows furrowed in thought as her eyes quickly scan whatever she's working on. "Fine, I'll teach you."

I brighten. "Thanks. Tomorrow?"

"Sure."

The bell above the door jingles, and Piper's jaw visibly tightens. I turn to see a light-skinned African-American guy approaching the register. He looks to be my age, though not as tall. From the thickness of his arms, it's a sure bet he works out. "Hey, babe," he says, totally ignoring me.

Piper gives a smile that she clearly isn't feeling. "Hey, Gavin."

"Can I talk to you?" he asks.

"I'm kinda working, Gav. I'm off in a couple of hours."

He sighs dramatically. "It'll just take a minute. I'm sure this guy can cover for you."

What do you know, I'm not invisible. Gavin Thickarms still hasn't so much as glanced at me.

"Actually, I was just about to punch out—" I say, but he cuts me off.

"Come on, dude," he says, *finally* meeting my gaze. "I just need a word with my girlfriend. A few more minutes isn't going to kill you."

Huh? *This* is Piper's boyfriend? Ten seconds in, and I already don't like the guy.

"Bax," Piper says, turning to me. "Would you mind? It's not like we're busy."

I look around the shop, where precisely three tables are occupied. Austin's doing paperwork in his office, Lucas has already gone home, and Sierra's not back from her lunch break yet.

I sigh. "Sure. Go ahead."

Gavin gives me a shit-eating grin before turning to Piper. "I'll see you outside."

"Okay." She undoes her apron, folds it up, and places it on the counter. "Be right back."

No other customers come through the door while I wait for Piper to return. She and Gavin are a few yards up the sidewalk, but I can still see them through the window. Gavin uses a lot of emphatic gestures when he talks, and Piper looks like she'd rather be anywhere else. I can't help but wonder what the story behind their relationship is.

"Hello?"

I turn to see Sydney standing right in front of me, her eyebrows raised. I'd been so engrossed in Piper's drama, I hadn't even seen Sydney move from her table. "Uh, hi. Welcome to Hill O' Beans, how may I help you?"

And the prize for Dumbest First Impression of All Time goes to (first name withheld for personal reasons) Baxter. Thank you, thank you.

She grins, clearly amused by my gaffe, but it's not a cruel smile. Her eyes flash with amusement as she pauses. Wait a minute, is she checking me out? "Um, could I possibly have a blueberry muffin? To go?"

Right. The customer service thing. On it.

I spring into action like a starter's gun just went off. Using a pair of tongs, I deftly scoop the largest, blueberriest muffin I can find in the display case, drop it in a small paper bag, and zip back to the register. "Here you go," I say, presenting her the bag like it's full of twenties.

"Thanks." She raises her head to meet my gaze. Her eyes are so blue I could fall into them.

I can't help but stare. Man, she's gorgeous. She's got this adorable little cleft in her chin that makes her even more—

"Dooooooo you wanna ring me up?" she drawls, pulling a debit card from her pocket and holding it out.

Shoot...me...now.

"Uh, sure." I take the card, ring up her order, and swipe it through. I hand it back to her along with her receipt. The smile still hasn't left her face. Guess she likes doofuses.

Wait? She likes doofuses? Hmmm.

"Well, see you around..." She glances at my nametag, her grin widening, then back at me. "Bax?"

She said my name. With wry amusement and a dash of I-am-intrigued.

I nod.

"Have a good day, Bax." With a wink to me, Sydney shoves

the muffin into her satchel and heads for the door. The violin serenade playing in my head swells to a fever pitch. With a soft jingle of the bell, she's gone.

My eyes fall to the counter, and I resist the urge to bang my face on it with concussive force.

Piper returns sans Gavin a few moments later. She does not look happy as she puts her apron back on. "Thanks again, Bax. You can go home now."

I crinkle my brow. "Everything all right?"

"Yeah." She reaches down, grabs a clean rag, and starts wiping down the back counter.

I want to ask more questions, but I doubt I'll get any answers. Not that I deserve any, as Piper and I are still in the getting-to-know-you phase. Despite being part of the Hill O' Beans "family," it'd be arrogant to call us friends at this point. It's clear she's going through some stuff, and it doesn't take a detective to figure out that Gavin is a prime reason for the weary look she's directing at the espresso machine.

"'Kay. See ya," I say, hoping to draw one last look from her.

She doesn't oblige but simply nods.

After clocking out, I head for the back room and hang my apron on my designated hook. That's right, I have my very own hook. Yay me. I brace my forehead against an overhead shelf as the stress slowly leaks from my body. My memory freeze-frames on Sydney's smile, but just as quickly, her face is replaced by Piper's. She's really good at hiding her deeper emotions, but I know from experience that that only works for so long. Something big is gnawing at her, and it's only a matter of time before it achieves critical mass. I want to help her, I do, but why on earth would she confide in me? I'm sure she has friends who have her back, and some of them are right here at Hill O' Beans.

I'm about to head out when I catch a fleeting glimpse of something shiny near the baseboards. I lean in for a closer look, and sure enough, a tiny metallic object is peeking out from behind a cardboard box full of window-cleaning supplies. I nudge the box upward with one hand and grasp the thing with the other and—

He guns the engine, and I raise my arms in exhilaration. The Chainsmokers' "Closer" blasts from the speakers, and I'm singing along. My boyfriend runs his fingers through his ash-blonde hair in that mega-cool way he always does, all while singing right along with me. His singing voice sucks, but there's no way I'll ever tell him that.

I look down again at the locket nestled between my breasts. His gift to me. I'm tempted to open it again, to see our smiling pictures, but I don't want to come off like some lovesick teenage girl. Which is what I totally am. God, I love this guy. I—

The object slips from my fingers, bouncing off the floor with a barely audible clink of metal.

It just happened again, didn't it?

I look behind me, sigh in relief when I confirm no one is in the room, and thank my lucky stars that my latest flash was of a pleasant memory. Otherwise, I'd be picking myself off the floor about now.

I grab a napkin from a half-empty package off another shelf, wad the thing up inside it, and shove it in my pocket.

I need to get a handle on this. Like, right now.

Time to do some research.

CHAPTER EIGHT

A nd by research, I mean "jot shit down on the notebook I bought at the ninety-nine-cent store and pray I don't have a seizure."

Yeah, this is where having a computer would help. Definitely the next thing on my "to purchase" list.

I carefully extract the balled-up napkin from my pocket and tip the object onto my coffee table without touching it. A heart-shaped pendant stares up at me, silver with a collage of smaller heart designs covering the front. There's a hinge on the left side, which tells me it's probably a locket, just as the memory indicated.

At a total guess, this belongs to Piper. The hands I saw grasping the locket in my flash were definitely Caucasian, which rules out Sierra and Imani. It could belong to a former employee who's long gone—I mean, who knows how long the thing's been sitting there—but if it was Piper...who was the guy? She definitely had the hots for the dude, who was most assuredly *not* Gavin. An ex, possibly? Maybe Blondie dumped her, and she threw the neck-lace in the corner in a fit of rage. No, the chain is intact, so maybe she just dropped it and it got kicked into the corner?

I open my ninety-nine-cent notebook to the first page and ready the pen I bought along with it. Then I bring up the clock app on my cell phone, the only thing I own that tells time to the second. I figure finding out just how long I zone out when *it* happens is a worthwhile piece of information. For all I know, there may be no rhyme or reason to this, as let's face it, I'm dealing with freaky shit that's not supposed to exist in the real world, but having something down on paper may give me a starting point.

I take a deep breath, letting my index finger hover directly over the chain.

Another breath. I lower my finger, barely grazing the cool metal of the chain.

Nothing.

Okay, wait. This makes a weird kind of sense. If objects are able to hold the memories of their owners, then it wouldn't be the chain Piper cared about, it would be the locket. To confirm this, I touch three more spots on the chain, with similar results. I gulp, take a deep breath, and contact the locket.

He guns the engine, and I raise my arms in exhilaration. The Chainsmokers' "Closer" blasts from the speakers, and I'm singing along. My guy runs his fingers through his ash-blonde hair in that mega-cool way he always does, all while singing right along with me. His singing voice sucks, but there's no way I'll ever tell him that.

I look down again at the locket nestled between my breasts. His gift to me. I'm tempted to open it again, to see our smiling pictures, but I don't want to come off like some lovesick teenage girl. Which is what I totally am. God, I love this guy. I still can't believe we're together. Three years of high school and no boy ever gave me the time of day. It took seventeen years for someone to see the girl—woman— beneath the retro clothes and goofy weirdness.

I giggle, which is more middle school than womanly, but I don't care. I'm in love. I'm in love with Jackson Turnbull. I want to run my fingers through his hair, down his chest and—

Oh, jeez. I so did not need *that* thought in my head.

I look down, surprised to realize that my finger is no longer touching my locket.

Did I move it unconsciously? Does this mean that I have the ability to stop this...*thing* whenever I want to? Something else to ponder.

This is so weird. I'm aware the thoughts that ran through my mind just now were not actually mine, but the emotions attached to those thoughts seem to be tripping whatever part of my brain controls said emotions. While touching the locket, I was still *me*, and yet, for a few brief seconds, I was also Piper. I was literally inside her head.

Determined to see this experiment through to the end, I let my palm hover over the locket for a few moments, then lower it onto the metal.

For the third time, I relieve Piper's memory about her off-key singalong. I get through her more wanton thoughts unscathed. I begin to wonder how much longer this memory will go on when the entire scene changes. It's a quick shift, as abrupt as changing channels on a TV. One second I'm in a car, singing, without a care in the world, and the next...

Oh, God.

A telltale beep of medical machines, the smell of disinfectant, none of it can drown out the ache in my heart. Jackson's broken, bandaged body lies, still as death, on the bed before me. I clutch the pendant in one hand, his fingers in my other. They're cool and stiff and I tighten my hold, praying that the heat from my skin will warm him even though I feel completely numb inside.

It's not fair. It's so not fair.

Gavin's arm settles around my shoulder. I know he's trying to be strong for me, but even so, he's barely holding it together. I avert my eyes from Jackson in time to see a tear roll down Gavin's cheek, and that starts another cascade from me.

My best friend, the boy I love, is in a coma, on full life-support. I've heard stories about people who have been known to come out of this state, but the percentage is horribly low.

His body is alive, but deep down I know...he's gone. Jackson is gone.

I slump back onto the sofa, my mind reeling as, once again, I find myself in my living room. Everything's just as I left it.

I suppress a shiver, and I feel rather than see every hair on my arms stand on end, my skin having broken out in gooseflesh.

According to my phone, I was...out? Yeah, that seems like an appropriate word. For just under a minute, I underwent a truly out-of-body experience. I make a notation in my notebook, along with my perceived drop in temperature.

I blow out a breath. The rawness of the experience fades from my body, calming the rush of adrenaline, but the memories themselves remain etched into my brain.

I stare at the locket sitting innocently on my coffee table. I feel a perverse sense of accomplishment at having learned so much in such a short time, but it's followed by a wave of crushing guilt because, in a very real way, I've invaded—violated—Piper's personal space.

With a yawn, I recline horizontally on the couch and stare up at the ceiling. The room is eerily quiet, broken only by the muffled cries of kids playing outside. It's only a couple of minutes before I sit up again, snatch the pen, and start scribbling my observations down.

My God. Poor Piper. In one touch, I understand her, know her so much better than I did before. She loved this guy, Jackson, in a way that I've never loved anything or anyone in my life. What's more, the love was returned. Inside that locket are tiny photos of both of them. I don't even need to open it up to confirm that. And then, something tragic happened—some kind of accident, I'm guessing, that put Jackson into a coma from which he probably never woke up. The fact that Gavin was in the hospital with her, comforting her, also speaks volumes.

Obviously, the three of them were close at some point not long ago. Piper and Jackson fell for each other, and when Jackson died—I mark an asterisk by that word—she sought solace in

Gavin's arms. I can totally relate to that. If I'd had someone that close to me when AJ died, maybe I wouldn't have turned to unbridled asshattery as an outlet.

I can only guess how long ago Jackson left the picture, but from the way Piper stiffened up in Gavin's presence, it's clear whatever friendship they shared before they became a couple has taken a few hits since then.

I grab a snack from the fridge and a spare bedsheet from the closet, then resume my seat to begin the next phase of experimentation. Swaddled in the sheet, I touch the locket again. The effect of "flashing" isn't as pronounced the second time around, which is a relief. I end up getting the same memories, the same emotional highs and lows as before, but this time, I feel slightly more detached. It's like I'm somehow now able to separate my thoughts from hers, making it easier to observe the smaller details without the heart-racing adrenaline spike. When I break contact, I discover that exactly the same number of seconds has elapsed as the first time. I jot that down with a little smiley face.

Over the next hour, I repeat the experiment four times. What stayed the same—the two memories kept me "out" for fifty-seven seconds, and there seemed to be no variation between one flash and the next. What was different—each successive time, I felt less freaked out by the experience, and the drop in body temp also lessened.

As I wrap the locket back up in the napkin, I have to wonder how something so obviously important to Piper ended up underneath the supply rack. If she dropped it without realizing it, why wouldn't she turn the place over looking for it? On the other hand, maybe in a fit of anger or grief she took it off and flung it away, unable to look at it because of the painful memories it dredged up. Yeah, that makes more sense. But then, why kick it into a corner when she could simply throw it into the dumpster?

This is how little I know about girls. And relationships. And people.

I should give it back to her. Definitely. If she doesn't want it, so be it, but if there's even the tiniest part of her that wants to hold on to what she and Jackson once had, that probably won't happen.

I flip on the news, which, in my new bizarro world, has become normal. I mute the TV when the talking heads discuss stuff I couldn't give two shits about. The way the news is presented these days, the way they cram as much stuff in as they can—and what isn't spoken by the monotone newscasters can be read by the text-scrawl along the bottom of the screen—makes me wonder how information will be disseminated by the time I reach forty.

Big assumption there, I know, at the speed at which I'm plummeting down the crazy hole.

After twenty minutes of boredom, I switch channels, and yay, there's actually something relevant to the DP Killer case. The governor made a public statement that all available resources are being dedicated to bringing the psycho to justice. Parents are cautioned to not let their children walk the streets unaccompanied for the foreseeable future and are advised against letting their kids dress in any Disney-related clothes. As to the investigation itself, no further information is given. Which means either the police have made no headway or any promising leads are being withheld from the media. Neither thought brings me any comfort.

My gaze goes to the closet down the hall. Inside, right where I left it, is the trash bag containing Sarah's clothes, which hasn't moved an inch since I threw it in there.

The universe chooses to torture me further as photos of the DP Killer's three victims appear on the screen. My eyes lock on Sarah's, and I can't push the Power button on the remote fast enough.

God...damn...it.

Dad always used to say, "What doesn't kill you makes you stronger." I know, it sounds like it came right off a poster at a weight-training gym, which is why I never gave it much thought until now.

With a resigned sigh, I fetch the Hefty bag from my hall closet and dump the contents onto the coffee table. The blue jeans, shirt, and socks land with barely a sound, but one of the sneakers bounces off and tumbles to the floor. I'm halfway to picking it up when I realize touching it bare-handed while standing would be as smart as sticking my tongue to a frozen flagpole.

I use a pair of dishrags to spread the clothes over the length of the coffee table. Without touching them, I conduct as thorough an inspection as I'm capable of. Honestly, if I didn't already know the sinister story behind them, I'd swear on a stack that there was nothing out of the ordinary. The Moana tee looks slightly faded from multiple washings, as do the jeans. There are a few dirt stains on the sneakers, but nothing that screams "serial killer victim." I'm grateful there's no underwear in the pile.

In a terrible moment of self-awareness, I realize I'm picking through the clothes of a preteen girl, which is skeevy enough. The fact that the girl is dead makes bile creep up my throat, and I feel like a total perv. Is this really the only way I can—

Wait just a damn minute.

Apart from the shoes, the clothes are clean. In fact, they're almost spotless. Bastard must've laundered them before dumping them. Austin was right—he's careful. It's doubtful even a police lab would find anyone's DNA other than Sarah's.

And, of course, mine.

I'm not a big believer in fate, or destiny or what have you, but the irony of this batshit crazy mess twists my face into a grim smile. Mr. DPK did everything he could to remove all physical evidence of his crime, but he couldn't wash off the—paraphysical? Yeah, I'll go with that—paraphysical evidence. And it happened to fall into the hands of a guy with the power to nail his ass.

One of the shirt's sleeves dangles off the edge of the table, only inches away.

This is gonna hurt, I just know it.

I don't want to do this.

I *have* to do this.

For Sarah. For AJ. For *me*.

A surge of adrenaline pounds through me as I wrap my fists around rumpled cotton.

A cool breeze blows my hair into my face and I shove my hands deeper into my pockets. I look up at the nearest street sign as I walk by it. 65th Avenue. Two more minutes, and I'll be home. I can't wait to FaceTime with Cassie. She's the coolest cousin ever.

I turn onto 65th Drive, breaking into a fast walk. That white van is parked next to the Brodsky's old place again. It's like the third time I've seen it. Why is it there? No one's lived in that house for months.

I've just passed by the van when a loud scraping makes me jump. The van door slides open, like super fast. I move to turn around, but before I can, a gloved hand clamps over my mouth.

I cry out, but only a muffled squeal escapes. I thrash out with my legs as I'm lifted off my feet.

Omigodomigod...Mommy! Daddy! Help me!

I'm pushed into the van and see something next to the back doors. I try to open my mouth, to scream, to bite his fingers, but then I feel a sharp prick in my neck, and—

I blink several times as the world comes back into focus. I stare at my hand, which is still gripping the cloth of the shirt.

That's weird. I know there are more memories attached to these clothes than just the kidnapping. Why did it stop halfway through?

I think about this as I struggle to regain my breath. My limbs feel like limp spaghetti and again, the room feels way colder than it did a minute ago. I pull the sheet around myself as tight as I can, and a wave of fatigue crashes over me.

That's it for one night, I think. I'll go to bed and mull over this new development in the morning.

Then the last of my strength fails, I topple into a horizontal position, and sleep claims me.

CHAPTER NINE

Being woken up by someone pounding on your door? Not fun.

First comes that sense of disorientation that starts the moment your body wakes up but your brain is slow to follow. Then, as your synapses start to fire, you realize someone with no regard for your sense of calm is doing everything they can to get your attention. Mom used to do that on those days when I wasn't feeling the whole "school" thing. Carl did it practically every day during my stay at Asterly, though I suspect he put a little more gusto into beating his apelike fists on my door than anyone else's, his petty revenge for all the digs I made at him.

I jolt upright on the couch, my eyes widening when I discover it's not only broad freaking daylight, but Sarah's clothes are still spread out on my coffee table.

Shit. Shit, shit, shit.

How many people know I live here? I doubt Carl does, and I haven't done anything that might incur the wrath of Walrus Ted. It's a school day, so it can't be Trina unless she's sick—and seriously Hulked out. My brain leaps to the conclusion that it's Detective Rojas who, thanks to her X-ray vision, has discovered that I've misappropriated evidence in a homicide, and the courtesy thump will now be followed by a S.W.A.T. team busting my door in. Hot on their heels will be a *Cops* camera crew.

I'm considering making a break out the back door when Sheila's voice derails my crazy train. "Bax? Are you in there?"

"Hang on a minute!" I snatch the Hefty bag from the floor. In my haste, I am a half-second from picking up the Moana tee when I yank my hand back. Damn, that would have been stupid. Using the dishrags, I shove Sarah's clothes into the bag and deposit it back in the hall closet.

Another thump. "Bax?"

"Yeah, coming!" I push a hand through my hair and stumble to the door.

The look of maternal concern on Sheila's face, cranked up to eleven, is both heartening and scary. It dials back to six when she sees me upright and semi-coherent, and her hands fly to her hips. "What the hell, Bax? You don't answer your cell? We've called you, like, ten times!"

I stare dumbly. "I, uh, fell asleep. Guess I forgot to recharge my phone." My eyes narrow. "Who's 'we?'"

"You missed your shift. Austin's been trying to reach you for two hours." Her concerned look morphs into a scolding glare. "When you didn't answer, he called me."

"And you just rushed over?"

"Well, yeah." Her posture finally relaxes. "He told me you almost got hit by a car on Wednesday, and that you were out cold in the alley for fifteen minutes."

Nuts.

"Sheila, I'm all right," I downplay it. "I had a headache for a few hours, but that's it. I just overslept is all. I'll call Austin and apologize." I step back inside, then face her again. "He didn't fire me, did he?"

She rolls her eyes. "No, he didn't fire you, but he's understandably worried. So am I." Under her breath she adds, "I was afraid this would happen."

Huh?

"I'm okay. Really."

"So you keep saying. But Austin thinks you should get checked out by a doctor. I agree with him."

"Oh, come on! How many times do I gotta say it? I...over...slept. People do it all the time!"

"But what if something's wrong with you and you don't even know it?"

I'm about a second away from losing my shit when I realize she has a valid point. There *is* something wrong with me. Not quite what she and Austin think is wrong, but wrong nonetheless. Maybe medical science can fill in some of the many, many blanks.

I deflate and blow out a heavy sigh. "Fine. I'll see a doctor."

Sheila blinks as if caught off guard by my unexpected relenting. "All right then. Put some shoes on, and I'll take you to the Urgent Care down the street. And for God's sake, zip up your fly."

It's going to be a lovely day.

Urgent Care, as it turns out, is not the place to go if you want to be examined by top-notch medical professionals. Every employee looks tired, stressed out, and utterly sick of dealing with sick people. It's like craving fine dining and ending up at Denny's.

A middle-aged doctor in a white lab coat who clearly wants to keep the assembly line moving gives me a whole two minutes of her time before she tells me I'm fine. She returns long enough to hand me a note that deems me healthy enough to work yet advises that I see my primary care physician should my symptoms return.

I fight the urge to say "I told you so" as I show the note to Sheila. Instead, I give her a semi-smug "Satisfied?"

She reads the note with wary eyes, which she then turns on me. "This says you should see your physician."

"And I would...if I had one."

"I can find you one if you want."

I feel my anger rising in my gut again. "Sheila, *enough*."

"If there's something wrong with you, you owe it to yourself to—"

I don't hear the rest because I'm storming out the Urgent Care's front door. I'm tempted to forego the ride home with Sheila in favor of an Uber rather than deal with her pseudo-mothering any more today, but the plaintive tone in her voice stops me halfway across the parking lot. "Bax, I'm sorry."

I stop, take a few deep breaths, then face her. "I'm not in the system anymore. Which means I'm not *your* problem anymore. I'm eighteen now. It's not your job to babysit me."

She marches up to me, her expression resolute. "Don't tell me my job. I've seen hundreds of kids determined to throw their lives away as carelessly and gruesomely as possible. They think no one cares, which gives them an excuse to keep destroying themselves. Every week I hear about this girl who died of a heroin overdose, or that boy who took a bullet in a gang shooting, or another boy who got sentenced to hard time for aggravated assault. I tried to help them, but I couldn't."

I feel the air leak from my righteous indignation. "So why do you do it?"

"Because *I care*."

My gaze falls to my shoes. My old friend shame clocks me in the face.

"You're right. You're not my responsibility," she continues. "But when you do what I do, you scratch and claw for every single win. This girl kicked her drug habit and is helping other kids do the same. This boy got his high school diploma and is studying online to become an engineer. It's news like this that keeps me going. True, most social workers give fewer shits than the kids they're supposed to be helping, but that's not how I roll."

"But where does it end?" I retort. "I know I owe you big time, but at what point do you chalk me up as a win and move on?"

"When I'm convinced you *are* a win."

I frown.

"I'll make it easy for you, Bax. If you tell me to piss off—and you're well within your rights to do so—I'll leave, and you'll never see me again. Is that what you want?"

I consider the notion, but only briefly. As much as I hate to admit it, there's no way in hell I'm ready to stand on my own two feet yet. Her overprotectiveness is still better than no protection at all, no matter how annoying it is. "No."

Sheila unlocks the Spark's doors, and I slip into the passenger seat. She slides her key into the ignition, then faces me. "I'll try to give you more space from now on. Cool?"

"Cool."

She turns the key, and the engine sputters to life. "I'll take you home now."

An idea bounces into my head. "Actually...can you spare another half hour?"

"Sure, what's up?"

"I need a laptop."

"A laptop?"

"Yeah, you know, one of those computers that sits on your lap." I grin, and the remaining tension between us dissolves.

Sheila gives a half-chuckle, half-growl. "I know what a laptop is, smartass. What do you need one for?"

I spread my arms. "Porn. Duh."

"Bax—"

My smile falters. "I need to connect, okay? For a long time, I didn't care about the world around me. I have a lot of catching up to do, and watching the news is boring as shit. Besides, I should have an email address, right? And a Twitter account?"

Sheila's brow furrows briefly, and she nods. "All right. I think there's a Best Buy not far from here. Let's go check it out." She shifts gears, and we pull out of the parking lot. "You're sure you're okay?"

Her confession has softened me up so much that I seriously consider telling her about my flashes, but something stops me.

"Yeah. I had a hell of a headache and some dizziness, but no biggie."

She throws a look at me that makes me believe she's not buying my BS, then changes the subject. "By the way, Austin texted me back while you were in with the doctor. He got someone to cover your shift tomorrow, so you have the day off. He'll see you at noon on Friday."

"Okay," I say with a placating smile. A day off sounds pretty good right now.

Sheila scrunches her brow at me, and again I wonder if she's still suspicious about the reason for my missing my shift. But why would she be? I haven't seen or spoken to her since my birthday, and I didn't start flashing until the day after. There's no way she could know about that.

I was afraid this would happen, she said.

What did she mean by that? Was she afraid I had gone on a drunken bender like the one that led to my arrest? Yeah, that must be it.

Right?

CHAPTER TEN

I climb out of bed on Thursday, refreshed and a little anxious. Determined to make the most of my day off, I open my brand-new laptop and watch it boot up. My mind returns to last night when I removed it from the box. I took a minute to admire its gleaming black casing, its aerodynamic design. Then, after the high from the new-computer smell wore off, I had to ask Trina to help me hook the damn thing up. She had me surfing the net in under five minutes.

Kids today, I'm telling ya.

The look of childish ecstasy when I thanked her was so pronounced that it simultaneously warmed my heart and made me nervous. Being the object of Trina's little-girl affections is adorable, but I hope she's not telling all her friends that she's having a "thing" with the eighteen-year-old next door. That could turn real ugly real fast. I hope a conversation with Gina to nip this crush in the bud won't be necessary.

Anyway, thanks to my tiny IT consultant, I now have an email address, a Facebook page, and an Instagram account. Maybe I haven't officially joined the 21st century, but I'm definitely looking through the window at it.

I pop open a Coke, put my feet up on my coffee table, and

begin the next phase of my research. I start with a Google search on the DP Killer case. There's quite a bit of information, and in a lot more detail than I got from the newscasts. Most of the news is pretty grim, and the soda turns sour in my stomach as I peruse the details regarding the abduction of, the subsequent search for, and the ultimate discovery of each victim. There are similarities between all three cases, like the girls' ages, complexions, and hair color. There's also the fact that they were all snatched while wearing a piece of clothing featuring a Disney princess, and that their bodies were found clad in a *Little Mermaid* tee that they'd been dressed in by the killer.

I heard somewhere that serial killers tend to be territorial. They stake out a particular area when trolling for victims, and rarely stray outside it. The DP Killer, however, does not fit this pattern.

In early February, at roughly the same time I was on trial for my various shenanigans, eleven-year-old Mia Sachs was taken while walking her dog in a park near her home in Chandler. The dog was found wandering alone that night, and Mia's body turned up a week later in the playground of an elementary school in the same area.

Ten weeks later, Jordan Clark disappeared on her way home from her elementary school in Avondale, on the complete opposite side of town. An amber alert turned up nothing, and no trace of her was found until her body was discovered under a tree in a half-finished housing development a mile from her home.

Just under two weeks ago, Sarah Blankenship took her school bus home but disappeared after being dropped off only three blocks away. A jogger called the cops after finding her corpse in a municipal park.

So...three victims, all preteen girls, taken from neighborhoods dozens of miles apart. All died from asphyxiation after being administered a large dose of hydrogen cyanide. Other than the puncture wounds on their necks, their bodies revealed no injuries, no violations. Wherever they were taken, they'd been fed, clothed, and given a warm place to sleep. Doctors and profilers brought in to consult had attributed a great many psychological and neurological disorders to the DPK, but what they all agreed on was that he was calculating, detail-oriented, and highly unlikely to stop.

I stare at the Hefty bag, now placed behind the sofa in a way that anyone entering through the front door wouldn't be able to see. After last night's experiment, there's no longer any doubt in my mind that the clothes I found belong to Sarah.

In the alley behind Hill O' Beans, all of Sarah's memories were thrust into my brain at once. I was completely unprepared, which is why the experience overwhelmed me to the point of knocking me unconscious. The few images I remembered after waking up were sketchy at best. The second time, while equally disturbing, hit me with the force of a Nerf bat rather than a sledgehammer. I can only surmise that the sheer power and rawness of the memories, combined with the fatigue of having worked a full shift, are what put my lights out for twelve hours, and caused me to sleep through all of Austin's and Sheila's texts.

I replay Sarah's abduction in my mind, fighting back a tide of anger.

He was waiting for her. He knew where she lived, when she got dropped off, and the best spot to grab her. He'd picked the perfect time—there had not been one single witness to the abduction. None of the articles I'd read mentioned a suspicious van, though it's possible that detail was withheld.

I lean back, staring at the ceiling. What do I do now?

I could touch the clothes again. Just like with Piper's locket, maybe the effects will be diminished with further flashes. But doing that could turn me into a woozy, slobbering mess for hours. Is that really my only recourse?

Then a crazy thought hits me—maybe if I retrace Sarah's steps, I could pick up something the cops missed.

Remote, yes, but worth a shot.

The street signs near Sarah's house that I saw in my vision were of Lone Butte and 65th Drive. A Google Maps inquiry reveals that intersection is only four miles away from Arbor Vista. But how to get there? Taking a cab to the scene of a kidnapping seems wrong on so many levels. And asking one of my new friends or co-workers for a ride would require an explanation that I'm not ready to give.

Which leaves just one option.

I step off the city bus, nod to the driver, and pull my ten-speed off the bike rack attached to the vehicle's front. I stop at a convenience store to buy a Snickers and a bottle of water, scarfing down the candy bar before I've climbed back on my bike. Then, using a GPS app I just downloaded on my cell, I pedal to Sarah's neighborhood.

A sense of unease and foreboding comes over me as the street sign I saw in my flash appears down the road. I brake to a halt, and my chest tightens.

Breathe, Bax. Remember why you're here.

The rapid *click* of the bike's gears sounds in my ears as I walk the final fifty yards to the intersection of Lone Butte and 65th Drive. It's a residential neighborhood, much like the one surrounding Arbor Vista. It's quiet, sleepy, the kind of street where you can live your whole life without anything noteworthy happening.

I lean my bike against the six-foot concrete wall that abuts the road, eying the street signs. On a hunch, I touch the metal pole beneath them, wondering if it contains any of Sarah's memories. I get nothing.

I amble down the sidewalk, and my déjà vu needle climbs into the yellow. It slams into the red when I reach the spot where the creep's van was parked. That's where I stop. I confirm that the house the guy waited in front of looks like it's been vacant for months, judging by the boarded-up windows and the rusty For Sale sign in the front yard.

I stare at the ground for I don't know how long, and it hits me what a dumbass idea this was. What was I expecting to find? The guy's driver's license? A road map with a big red arrow pointing to his serial killer lair and an invitation to swing by?

My frustration growing, I kneel down and brush my fingers on the exact spot where the van was parked. Nothing.

I've seen my share of cop shows, so I know evidence can often come in the tiniest forms—a cigarette butt, a scrap of paper, a broken shoelace. In desperation, I pick up every piece of trash I can find, and the only flash I get is of a little girl playing in the snow after touching a dust-covered child's mitten. Not exactly what I'm looking for.

While conducting my search, I barely register a handful of vehicles passing by without stopping. It isn't until I hear a slight screech of brakes that I realize a car has pulled up very close to me.

I look up, and my eyes widen in alarm. It's an unmarked police car.

Aaaaaand guess who's behind the wheel?

Fuck my life.

Detective Rojas kills the engine and steps out, her ever-present scowl aimed right at me. "Mr. Baxter."

I freeze. The Snickers turns to acid in my gut. "Detective."

She strides up to me in that authoritative way that says, "I've got a badge, and I will lay you out if you give me a reason to." She folds muscled arms across her chest, her brows knitting. "What are you doing here?" Her lips barely move.

What do I say? I suppose an abridged version of the truth is my best option. "I'm, uh, out for a bike ride. You know, enjoying some fresh air."

Her eyes narrow into slits, and she curls her thumbs into her belt. "Don't you need a *bike* for a bike ride?"

I point at the concrete wall thirty yards away. "It's over there. I can show you if you like."

She waves dismissively. "Cut the bullshit. Why are you *really* here?"

If there's one thing I've learned since my first brush with the law, it's that lying to cops is a bad idea. On the other hand, telling Detective Rojas the real reason I'm poking around the scene of a child abduction would probably land me in the loony bin.

Then I realize that, for once, I don't owe her an explanation, and my tone becomes insta-defensive. "I'm not doing anything. Besides, this is a public neighborhood."

"You're right." I swear this woman doesn't blink. "It *is* a public neighborhood, which happens to be miles away from *your* neighborhood."

I swallow hard. "And how would you know where I live? Have you been checking up on me?"

"Don't flatter yourself. Just answer my question—is this your neighborhood?"

"No. Like I said, I'm out for a ride. That's not against the law now, is it, *Detective*?"

She takes a menacing step forward, clearly unamused by my sass. "I watched you for a full minute before I pulled up. You weren't riding. You were barely walking. If I didn't know better, I'd say you were conducting a search."

My biting retort dies at the back of my throat.

She points at an off-white stucco house a hundred yards down 65th. "Do you know who lives in that house, Mr. Baxter?"

I shake my head, even though I know full well who does. Or did.

Her nostrils flare so hard I actually hear it. "I don't know why you're here, and honestly, I don't care. You may have Austin fooled, but not me."

Anger born of fear swells in my chest, and my voice returns in full force. "What is your problem, Detective? I screwed up, okay? Is that what you want to hear? I was an immature, juvenile asshole, okay?" I take two deep breaths before continuing. "But I'm trying to change. Why is that so hard for you to accept?"

"Because I think you're a punk. An arrogant little punk with no respect for anyone but himself. And in my experience, the only time people change is when they get worse."

For eight months, I've wondered, while drunk off my ass, how pissed off I could have been to have done something so monumentally stupid as to take a swing at a cop. Now I know. The urge to do it again is almost overpowering. Almost.

"You don't know me," I seethe. "You don't know anything about me."

A dry chuckle issues from her throat. "The hell I don't. You think because your father died and your mother hit the bottle, that gives you the right to shit on the world and everyone in it. You think you deserve special treatment because of the crap hand life dealt you. Well, guess what? You don't."

She draws herself up to her full height, which somehow makes me feel six inches shorter, and points at the Blankenship residence. "I'm going into that house. By the time I come out, you'd better be long gone. If I catch you loitering around here again, I'll reacquaint you with the back seat of my car. Is that clear?"

I nod, flashing as defiant a frown as I can manage.

With a huff, she climbs behind the wheel and drives the short distance to Sarah's house. We lock eyes one more time as she makes her way to the front door. Moments later, she disappears inside, and I let out a humongous breath.

What a *bitch*.

I'm about to head back to my bike when I notice a small boy, maybe eight or nine, watching me from the sidewalk in front of the house next door to the vacant one. A mop of curly black hair frames a round face bearing a curious expression. In a voice that somehow reminds me of a male version of Trina's, he says, "She's angry."

Keeping an eye out for Detective Rojas, I approach him, stopping a respectful distance away in case his mom is watching. "I noticed."

"My mom gets angry at my dad sometimes, even if he didn't

do anything wrong. My dad says when a girl is angry, there's nothing you can do to make them un-angry."

"Your dad's a smart man."

"She hasn't found the man who took Sarah, has she?"

I shake my head.

He tilts his head to one side. "Why are you here?"

"I want to catch the guy, too."

"You know Sarah?" he asks, puzzled.

Sarah's image, the one splashed all over the news, burns into my memory. "A little. Did you know her?"

He nods. "She was nice. She let me play with Lucy whenever she took her for a walk."

"Lucy?"

"Her puppy dog. A pit bull, I think. She sometimes brought me hot fudge sundaes from Dairy Queen. She loved those things."

I shoot a sidelong glance down the street. No sign of Detective Rojas.

Wait a minute. This kid knows his neighbors. I wonder if...

"What's your name?" I ask the boy.

"Brandon."

I hold my hand out. "Hi, Brandon. I'm Bax."

His face breaks into an adorable toothy grin. "That's a cool name."

"Thanks. Listen, Brandon, I need to ask you a couple of questions. Is that okay?"

Brandon's smile disappears, and he shoots a quick look back at his house. "I...guess."

"Are you outside a lot?"

"Uh huh. As long as I stay where my mom can see me, she doesn't freak out."

Fearing Brandon's mom might be watching me at this moment, I take two steps back, and gesture at the vacant house. "Do you know how long this house has been empty?"

He pauses for a few seconds, then answers. "Like a year, I think."

I feel my heartbeat quicken as I ask my next question. "Do you remember ever seeing a van parked right here?" I point at the curb.

"A van?"

"Yeah. Did you see anything like that? Like, right before Sarah was taken?"

He stares at the spot. "Uh huh. It was big and white. There was a man inside it."

My eyes nearly bug out of my head. "How many times did you see him?"

"I dunno, like two or three. He never got out, he just sat there. He caught me looking at him once, and I ran back inside."

"Did you see him on the day Sarah disappeared?"

He lets out a sigh. "No. I was sick."

"Have you seen the man since then?"

"No."

"When the cops came, did you tell anyone about him?"

His gaze falls to his shoes, and he gives another head shake. "That was the bad man, wasn't it?"

I kneel down to face him. "Brandon, you didn't know."

The poor kid looks up, a tear forming in his eye. "He took Sarah."

I lean closer, making him focus on me. "And if we don't stop him, he'll take someone else. We can't let that happen, right?"

"How?"

I raise up and point at Detective Rojas's car. "When that lady cop comes out, I want you to go up to her and tell her about the van. Tell her what the van looked like, the man, everything."

He fixes pleading eyes on me. "Why can't you do it?"

"Because I wasn't here."

"Then how'd you know there was a van?"

Whoops.

"I—I can't tell you that," I mumble. "And it doesn't matter. The cops need to know what you saw. And trust me, that lady cop will listen to you a lot more than she'll listen to me."

Brandon flicks his gaze from the police car to me and back again, his whole body quivering.

"Please, Brandon," I say in my most soothing "adult" voice. "You have to do it. For Sarah."

His little mouth flattens into a straight line. "Okay. I will."

I smile and hold out my pinky. "Promise?"

He curls his own pinky into mine, and he gives a weak smile. "Promise."

For once, luck is on my side. Neither Detective Rojas nor Brandon's mother emerges to have me arrested for being in a strange neighborhood questioning a small child. "I have to go. You can do it, Brandon. Just...please don't mention my name, okay?"

"Okay." He waves goodbye. "See ya, Bax."

A minute later, I'm on my bike, pedaling away at top speed.

So my first foray into private investigation didn't go quite as planned. I managed to piss off Detective Rojas *again*, and I didn't find anything I could use to help catch the psycho. I'm going to have to have another go at Sarah's clothes, an idea I'm not relishing. But, if nothing else, maybe Brandon can steer Detective Rojas onto another line of inquiry that will end up nailing Mr. DPK before he strikes again.

Hopefully.

CHAPTER ELEVEN

There's a nip in the air as I pull my ten-speed up to Hill O' Beans and jam it into the bike-rack near the front door. I'm glad I wore my jacket, as it looks like I might have to ride home in the rain. I pat the right-hand pocket, confirming the two items I stuck inside are still there.

I've just fastened the lock shut on my bike when someone bulldozes through the front door at a full clip. It's Gavin, who stomps out to the parking lot, climbs behind the wheel of a shiny black Lexus, and peels out. This time, I'm glad he didn't see me. I'm equally thankful the door remained on its hinges.

Jeez, what crawled up his ass and died?

I enter Hill O' Beans, scanning for Piper as I go. All I see are Austin and Lucas behind the counter and a few scattered customers enjoying their beverages.

"Bax," the boss-man greets me. "How are you feeling?"

"I'm okay," I say, pulling the doctor's note from my pocket and handing it to him. "Sorry I missed my shift. Guess I'm still getting used to this whole 'work schedule' thing."

Austin peruses the note, purses his lips, and hands it back to me. "It's all right. In the future, if you're unable to make your shift, please shoot me a text so I can make other arrangements, 'kay?"

"Sure thing." I slip behind the counter, fist-bump Lucas, and clock in. "Was that Piper's boyfriend I saw storming out of here just now?"

Lucas frowns, an expression I've never seen on him. "Yeah. Something's got that dude bent out of shape."

"What happened?"

"Piper ran into the back the second he walked in," Austin says. "Gavin demanded she come out. She wouldn't, so he asked again. Louder."

"And then we asked him to leave," Lucas says.

I nod. No matter how strong and amped-up Gavin is, taking on Austin and Lucas together would probably have ended badly for him. "Is Piper still in the back?"

"Yup. She's pretty upset right now," Austin says.

I move toward the inner door. "I'm gonna get an apron on. And see if she's okay."

"Just...don't push too hard, Bax. She's going through a lot right now."

Aren't we all.

The storage room/employee area is not large, so it doesn't take me long to locate Piper. She's standing, shoulders slumped and head down, facing the wall, using her arm to brace herself against one of the ingredient racks. She's breathing hard, and I wonder if this is an exercise she employs to keep her emotions reined in.

I watch her ponytail, several strands of which have come loose from its tie, bob up and down in time with her breathing.

"Please don't stare," she says. "I hate that."

My face flushes, I hastily move to the other side of the room, remove my jacket, and hang it on my hook before donning my apron. "Sorry. Are you—?"

She turns sharply, glaring at me. Her eyes narrow into slits behind her cat-eye glasses and her eyes spark, burning like embers. After a beat, she sighs and faces the wall again, some of her feistiness fleeing as she lowers her head once more. "I'm fine. I just need a few minutes, okay?"

My dislike of Gavin blossoms into full-on hatred. I know I don't know the full story, but whatever he's putting Piper through makes me want to kick his perfect teeth in. But that course of action would either land me in the E.R., jail, or both. Probably both. "That's cool. Take all the time you need."

I reach into my jacket pocket and remove the other item I brought with me, wrapped in several layers of Kleenex. With a slow, measured pace, I approach Piper and clear my throat. My eyes fall to my hand, which I hold out to her. "I found something the other day that I think belongs to you."

She faces me for the first time, and her brow furrows. "What makes you think that's mine? I can get Kleenex anywhere."

"No, it's what's inside. Don't worry, I didn't blow my nose or anything." I proffer the wadded-up ball of tissue to her. "Go on, take it."

Piper reaches for the Kleenex, uncertainty washing over her expression. While her eyes hold a flicker of annoyance, they also burn with curiosity. Her eyebrows lift as she unwraps the tissue, revealing a flash of silver. When the heart-shaped pendant is uncovered, she inhales sharply. "Oh...my...God."

If I needed any more proof that the necklace belonged to Piper, this was it. I inwardly pray that her next action won't be to make a heart-shaped dent in my forehead with it. "I found it on Tuesday, and I thought—"

With a muffled sob, Piper wraps her arms around my waist and presses her head against my chest. She holds on tight, like her life depends on it. "Thank you, Bax. Thank you so much." Her already high voice has risen to a mousy squeak, and it melts my heart.

Whatever reaction I was expecting, this far exceeds it. It's been a long time since a girl has held me like this. The fact that she's holding me out of gratitude and not because of a bad combination of hormones and alcohol makes it even better.

I feel warm. I feel tingly.

I feel something pressing against the inside of my fly.

Jeez, *really*?

I break the hug before Piper discovers my body's unintentional response to our sudden proximity. I'm sure my face is fifty shades of red right now.

"You're, uh, welcome." I turn my back so she doesn't see the embarrassing bulge in my jeans.

"Where did you find this?"

I point at the floor near the supply shelf in the far corner. "Right there. Below the spray cleaners."

She slumps against the rack, staring unblinking at the pendant. "I can't believe you found it. I clearly remember looking for it back here. I thought I'd lost it forever." She breaks into a sad smile as she opens the locket, staring at the pictures within. The look she gives at the sight of Jackson's face is as close to true love as I've ever seen.

"Can I ask you...?" I start, then my nerve falters.

Piper turns the locket around so I can see the pictures. The images are tiny, but I can tell Piper is a year or two younger than she is now. "You want to know who this is," she indicates Jackson. "And what I'm doing with Gavin."

"Yeah. What is that guy's deal? Austin said he was about two seconds from calling the cops on him."

What's left of her smile vanishes. "It's a long story."

"Well...if you ever feel like telling it, let me know. One of the cool things about not having friends is that you have tons of free time."

She chuckles. "If you're free later, I may take you up on that. It would be nice to get a guy's perspective on...*this*."

"You don't have other guy friends?"

"Not really."

"What about Austin and Lucas? Didn't you tell me Hill O' Beans was your family?"

She shuffles her feet like I just put her on the spot. "Lucas is nice, but he's not really the person you discuss your problems with. Austin's cool for an older guy, but he's also my boss. That would just be weird. But for some reason, I feel like I can talk to you."

Piper's memory about not being popular in high school flashes through my mind. Piper is definitely cute but not, like, glamorous. Combine that with her introverted personality and retro style, and the revelation that she doesn't have any close male friends makes more sense. Plus, Gavin seems like the jealous type, and I make a mental note to tread carefully.

"All right," I say. "Just say the word, and we can swap life stories."

A faint series of jingles heralds the arrival of a new crowd of customers. Piper shoves her fingers through her hair, smoothing it out and retying her ponytail. She wipes away her lingering tears and slaps me on the back. "Time to get to work, I think. And you're wrong about one thing."

"What?"

Her smile returns. "About not having any friends."

The Friday lunch crowd is steady. For the next ninety minutes, the four of us operate as a unit. It boggles my mind that only eight days ago, I was a loser with no marketable skills, and now I'm churning out five-dollar coffee drinks like I've been doing it for years. I'm still prone to the occasional mishap—I've singed my fingers on the various appliances at least a half dozen times since my training started—but for the first time, I feel like part of a team and not the klutz who drags everyone down.

A brisk rain starts to fall around two o'clock and steadily increases into a downpour after that. Before long, we're fresh out of paying customers, so Austin assigns me to—groan—toilet scrubbing duty. Just my luck, the Hill O' Beans men's room's last visitor was someone with severe intestinal issues and seriously bad aim. I'm tempted to ask if Austin has a Hazmat suit, but I suck it up and get to cleaning. The longest fifteen minutes of my life, and that's saying something. After that, Lucas and I get into a lengthy discussion about who the coolest Spider-Man villain is. I mean, seriously, *Electro*? Did this guy play without a helmet?

By four, the place is spotless, Lucas has gone home, and the rain is coming down in buckets. Austin slips away for a few minutes and returns with several pieces of baklava from the Middle Eastern bakery five doors down. He then encourages Piper and me to take our break before disappearing into his office.

I sip my chai tea and relax into what I've come to think of as *my* seat at the table against the back wall. Piper lays a small plate in front of me with a huge dessert piece on it, and I get a whiff of honey and walnuts. I forego the plastic fork, grab the thing with my bare hand, and bite off a chunk. It's scrumptious.

Piper sits across from me and forks a more civilized bite into her mouth. "Good, huh?"

"Delish," I say through my mouthful.

She grins. "The bakery owner, Mr. Khan, is the sweetest guy you'll ever meet. His eggplant wraps are the best in town."

"The wraps of Khan?" I chuckle. "That I must try."

Piper wads up a napkin and throws it at me. "Boo hiss."

I suppress the urge to yell "Khaaaaaaan!" in my best Shatner voice and instead take another bite. Through the window, a crackle of lightning lights up the horizon, followed by a clap of thunder. The parking lot is all but empty.

I'm savoring my last bite of baklava when Piper produces the necklace from her pocket, opens the locket, and lays it on the table. With a wistful sigh, she says, "His name was Jackson."

Okay, I guess we're doing this now.

"Good looking guy," I comment, and I mean it. Dude looked straight out of an Abercrombie & Fitch ad.

"I'm sure you're wondering how someone like him ended up with someone like...me."

I actually was wondering that, but saying it out loud would be a dickish thing to do. It's a valid point, though. I attended enough high school to know that pretty-boy jocks like Jackson tended to hang with cheerleaders and rich bitches, not bookish types like Piper.

I shrug.

"Guess I'd better start at the beginning." She drains her chai, then meets my gaze. "You know that girl in high school whose favorite thing in life is pointing out why you'll never be as good as her?" Piper adopts a mock-haughty tone. "You're such a loser. Why do you even bother coming to school? You should probably kill yourself."

I scoff. "Yeah, I knew a few girls like that."

"Chrissy Marsh. Thought she owned the world the day she started wearing a bra. I was her favorite target."

"I'm sorry."

"Whatever," she says with a nonchalance I don't quite buy. "I wasn't at school to socialize. I was there to get an education. Because of Chrissy and her cronies, I learned to be invisible. I practically lived in the library. I wanted to be the first McKinney to go to college."

This statement takes me aback. "Really? The first?"

"My family's not well-off," she admits. "My dad's a working stiff. Same goes for my two older brothers. A higher education was never really an option for them, but Dad wanted better for me. So did I. Unfortunately, the only way I could afford a good college without amassing a mountain of crushing student loans was to get a scholarship. From fifth grade on, I got nothing but A's."

Wow. I knew Piper was smart, but not like off-the-charts smart. How on earth did she end up slinging lattes and attending community college?

"Two years ago, I was in consideration for a full-ride scholarship to Penn State. I was so excited, even though it would mean being two thousand miles away from my family. Dad was so proud of me."

"What about your mom?"

"Died of cervical cancer when I was six."

Yikes.

She continues, "Anyway, I was told that one thing I needed to punch up my resume was extracurricular activities. I wasn't into sports, and I hated the idea of joining one of my school's dumb clubs. I've always loved animals, so I ended up volunteering at a local animal shelter. That's where I met..." Her eyes fall to the locket.

"Jackson worked there?" I ask.

"Yup. So did Gavin. They were best friends."

I nod. "Was it love at first sight?"

She shifts in her seat. "Oh God, no. I had them pegged from Day One. Rich boys, cruising through life, got their whole future all planned out. I figured I was so far beneath their notice, there was no point even trying to relate to them. I didn't talk to them at all for the first two weeks. I didn't even stop to wonder why two rich guys were working at an animal shelter, cleaning up dog poop and going home covered with fur." She sighs. "I must have come off like such a bitch."

"Don't beat yourself up," I say. "I probably would have jumped to the same conclusion."

"One day, this lady brought a wounded border collie in. He'd been hit by a car. His leg was broken, and he was bleeding badly. The vet on duty was performing surgery on another animal, so Jackson and Gavin sprang into action on their own."

"What did they do?"

"They laid the dog on a blanket. Jackson cleaned and bandaged the wound, and Gavin gave it a mild dose of painkiller. Then they stayed with it until the vet took over. It was incredible."

"Did the dog live?"

Piper nods. "They had to amputate his leg, but he pulled through. His owner was so happy she gave both guys hugs. So did the vet. Jackson actually cried."

Whoa.

"I caught up to them in the parking lot later that day. They were getting into Jackson's car—a Honda Civic, can you believe that?—and I told them how amazing they were for saving that dog's life. I probably sounded like a child, but they were cool. Then they invited me to go get a burger with them, and I accepted."

Piper stands, ducks behind the counter, pours herself another tea, and sits down again. "I was so wrong about them. They were rich, yes, but they were nice. They weren't snobby or judgmental. I'd never had guy-friends before, but soon after, I was part of their little group. It was awesome."

I make a move to pick up the locket, then pull my fingers back. "Then you started dating?"

She nods. "It was like a fairy tale. Like he was Prince Charming and I was Cinderella or something."

I smile, but her face takes a turn for the sad. "It shouldn't have worked. Two people couldn't be more different than Jackson and me. But for seven months, I had something in my life besides schoolwork. None of Chrissy's bullshit could touch me. I was happy."

I avert my gaze, knowing full well what's coming next.

"In March of this year, Jackson and Gavin and some of their friends were planning a trip down to Rocky Point. He invited me to come along. I had to beg my dad for permission. We were going to spend three days south of the border. Jackson promised it would be a blast." A tear forms at the corner of her eye. "The day before we were supposed to leave, this asshole in a Hummer ran a red light while texting. T-boned Jackson's car."

Piper's memory of sitting beside Jackson's comatose body steamrolls into my brain, and my guts clench. The sadness, the soul-crushing despair she felt at that moment is heart-rending, and one I can relate to.

I try to look shocked at her statement. "Shit."

She sinks into her seat. "Yeah."

I drum my fingers lightly on the table as I segue to the next part of the story. "And then Gavin stepped in?"

She shoots me a hairy eyeball, but it only lasts a moment. "It wasn't like that. Losing Jackson destroyed both of us. He was Gav's best friend since grade school. When he died..." She sighs. "Gavin's girlfriend at the time was this total skank named Amberlynn. She actually dumped him at Jackson's *funeral*. I mean, who does that?"

I wince. I don't care much for Gavin, but...wow, that's cold.

"All Gavin and I had was each other, you know? It wasn't until May that we started dating."

"I gather it's not going well."

Bravo, Admiral Obvious.

"You don't know the half of it." She leans forward like she's telling me a closely guarded secret, which she just might be. "Right after Jackson died, my dad developed health problems. We spent three months going in and out of doctors' offices, during which he couldn't work anymore."

Oh, man. "Did they find out what was wrong?"

Her expression becomes grim. "Yeah. It's called Guillain–Barré Syndrome. We caught it early enough so it could be treated, but Dad needs intense immune and physical therapy. Our insurance only covers so much and trying to get him on disability has been like pulling teeth."

Jesus H.

I've relived the total collapse of the Baxter family over and over in my head for the last year. I wouldn't have wished that stretch of life between my fifteenth and seventeenth birthdays on my worst enemy. I managed to convince myself that no one had it as bad as me.

I am such a self-centered prick.

"Damn," is all I can say.

A frustrated sigh escapes her mouth. "It might be months or years before Dad is well enough to work again, if it happens at all. One thing I knew for sure was that I couldn't be on the other side of the country while he recovered. So I pulled out of the scholarship program, and..." she points at the GCC campus across the street.

I stare at Piper, my chest tightening. This girl's gone through seven levels of hell, sacrificed so much, lost so much. And she just keeps going, like the freakin' Energizer Bunny. "Your brothers can't help out?"

"A little, but they have their own families to take care of. So...I asked Gavin for help." Her eyes fall to the table. "I didn't want to. We may be poor, but..."

"I understand."

She nods. "Because of Gavin, my dad's been able to get his regular treatments. And while he claims the money was a 'gift,'" she says using finger quotes, "it's become clear that he expects me to pay him back. Not in money, but in...other ways."

I scowl. "You mean, sex?"

"Yes. No. Kind of?" She meets my gaze again. "He's not a jerk about it. At least, he wasn't until recently. I started being his girlfriend because I thought it was what I needed to fill the hole after Jackson died. *Now*," she throws her hands up, "I'm his girlfriend because it's the least I can do after he helped my dad."

My dense brain finally connects the dots. "You don't love him."

"As a friend, yes. I've tried explaining that to him. But the more I pull back, the harder he pushes forward. If I break it off—and it looks like we're headed that way—he won't help me or my dad out anymore. But if I don't..."

I give her my most sympathetic look. "Talk about a rock and a hard place."

She scrutinizes her empty cup. "Yup."

"There's no one else you can turn to?"

"No. Jackson's friends tolerated me being with him, but they wouldn't help. I think his parents felt the same way. And the few people I know well enough to ask are just as bad off as my family is."

"What does your dad say?"

This brings a wisp of a smile to her face. "He's an eternal optimist, even now. He was a little sore that I scrapped my scholarship chances to stay with him, but he tells me every day that dropping out of school to work full time is not an option. That a promising future awaits me. You know, stuff dads are supposed to say. As for the money, he says God will take care of us, one way or another."

I reach over and pat her hand. "I hope it does. You deserve a break."

"Thanks."

"So this fight with Gavin...what was it about?"

"Same as always. He thinks I shouldn't be wasting my time working when I could be enjoying life with him. Like being in his company is a cure for all that sucks about life." She scoffs. "I just don't understand why he's hanging on so tight. Guys like him can get any girl they want and yet he's fixated on me. It'd be flattering if it weren't so..."

"Control freaky?" I offer.

She nods.

A light bulb goes on over my head. "That's probably it. He's never had to deal with rejection until now."

Piper stares at me for a good long while, then realization dawns. "That actually makes sense. Thanks, Bax."

"*De nada*," I smirk.

The corners of her lips tug upward. "What *is* your first name, anyway?"

I almost blurt it out. Almost. I'm so not used to having deep, personal conversations with anyone, much less a girl that I'm now realizing I have feelings for. Telling her my first name lays another brick in the foundation of...whatever we have. Then I realize with equal clarity that despite my conversion from delinquent waste of space to upstanding citizen, I haven't earned that kind of relationship. And she deserves so much better than me.

"I'd rather not say." I flash a cheeky grin. "'Cause then I'd have to kill you."

She sags a little, and her gaze drifts to out the window. "Okay."

God, I want to confide in Piper so badly. But dragging her into this mess with the DP Killer on top of the ten-ton pile of crap she's already dealing with is the worst thing I could do.

But what's the alternative? I'm in so far over my head it's not even funny. And while I dither, that psycho may be stalking some other preteen girl.

I have to tell Piper.

I can't tell Piper.

I have to.

I shouldn't.

Gaaaaaaah!

A thunderclap, much closer this time, crackles overhead, and for a second I swear I feel the whole building vibrate. The lights seem to dim, but that's probably my imagination.

Austin joins us in the dining area, apronless and with a resigned frown. He surveys the half-flooded parking lot, empty save for two cars, and runs a hand through his wavy brown hair. "Guys, I think we're gonna call it a day."

Piper and I both stand, toss our trash, and face him. "You sure?" Piper asks.

"I doubt anyone's going to brave this weather on a Friday night just for a cup of coffee. Go ahead and clock out."

"Okay. Thanks, Boss," I say.

In short order, we both punch out, exchange aprons for jackets, and meet Austin at the front door. "Bax, I know you're not far away, but I don't feel right sending you home in this," he says. As if on cue, lightning strobes the sky.

"I'll drive him," Piper says.

"You sure?"

She nods.

"Alrighty then." Austin ushers us out, activates the security alarm, and locks the door behind him. "Great job, guys. Stay safe, and I'll see you soon."

Ten minutes later, Piper pulls her silver Nissan Altima into my covered parking space at Arbor Vista. I breathe a sigh of relief that the power's still on.

I release the catch on my seatbelt and notice Piper staring at me with a gracious smile. "What?" I ask.

She palms the locket, which once again hangs around her neck. "Thanks again for returning this. It means more to me than you'll ever know."

"You're welcome." Then my mouth ignores my brain. "Do you want to come inside?"

Piper's eyes widen, and so do mine.

"I mean...no. Forget it," I waffle. "Scratch that. You're still technically with Gavin, and I don't want to—"

"Sure."

I do a double-take. "Really?"

"My dad's not expecting me home for another hour. I don't mind chilling here till then."

Well.

I place my hand on the door handle. "Won't Gavin kick my ass if he finds out?"

"No. Because he won't find out. And even if he does, I'm not going to let him tell me who I can be friends with."

"Fair enough." I gesture at my back door. "It's a nice place. I'm sure it's no Turnbull Manor, but I like it."

She laughs, then we both step out of the car. I haul my bike out of her trunk, unlock my door, and lead her inside. The slight odor of unwashed socks hits my nose, and I make a mental note to avail myself of Arbor Vista's laundry facilities tomorrow.

I roll my bike on top of several layers of old newspapers, pop the kickstand, and remove my coat. "You want something to drink? I got Coke, Mountain Dew, and bottled water."

She doesn't respond, and I'm suddenly unnerved by her silence. I turn to see her standing in the middle of my living room, staring at me with the most shocked expression I've ever seen.

Oh, God, what did I do now?

"Are you okay?" I ask, approaching tentatively.

"How'd you know his name?" she says in just above a whisper.

"What?"

"Jackson's last name...it was Turnbull. How'd you know that? Because I never said it."

Open mouth, insert foot, swallow up to shin. "I, uh..."

She takes three steps toward me, a vicious scowl materializing on her face. "Answer me, Bax! *How...did...you...know?*"

I gulp down a wad of spit and force myself to turn away. "You won't believe me."

Her hands go to her hips. "What does *that* mean?"

I feel her eyes on me, breaking down my defenses. Finally, I crumble. "There's something about me you don't know. That no one knows. It's weird and scary and I wouldn't blame you for thinking I'm crazy. Which is probably what I am. All I wanted was a fresh start and—"

She holds her palms out, interrupting my rant. "Bax, *stop*. Just tell me what the hell's going on."

I meet her unblinking gaze for several seconds, sigh in resignation, and gesture at the couch. "You may want to sit down for this."

Chapter Twelve

iper's face runs a gamut of expressions as, right there on my couch, I relay my epic saga.

First comes sympathy, as I give the thirty-second summary of the disintegration of my family dynamic. Next is wry amusement with a hint of disgust when I rehash the dumbest night of my life, which thanks to a charitable judge got me an eight-month stay at Asterly. It turns to hope when I recap the sheer awesomeness of my eighteenth birthday, which ended with me having a nice chunk of change, a townhome, and a job.

I ease into the spooky stuff by telling her about Trina, and the first flash I had when I touched her bracelet. I make the executive decision to save the worst for last and jump directly to the part where I found Piper's necklace. She's dubious at first, but when I explain in minute detail the memories I absorbed from the locket —from her and Jackson's off-key Chainsmokers rendition to the overpowering smell of disinfectant in Jackson's hospital room— she finally looks away, hurt pouring off her in waves.

I don't blame her for her reaction. I mean, how would I feel if my most emotional memories suddenly found their way into someone else's head?

"I'm sorry," I whisper, staring at the blank spot across the room where the wall meets the ceiling. "These are your memories. I have no right to them."

I hear her edge toward me, feel her touch my hand. I turn my head to face her, relieved to see her pained expression has melted away. "It's not your fault," she says with a gentleness that surprises me. Her eyes are full of compassion before her gaze drops to the locket around her neck. "You didn't ask for this...ability."

I notch a skeptical eyebrow. "You believe me, then?"

"Yes."

A two-ton weight lifts from my shoulders. This confession could have gone wrong in so many ways. That she would accept the notion that supernatural powers are not just the stuff of comic books from a guy she's known all of two weeks is nothing short of a miracle. "I'm glad. Surprised, but glad."

She gives a half-shrug. "I study cultures, remember? Every civilization from the Mayans to the ancient Egyptians to the Celts have legends that speak of...unique individuals with abilities that go beyond what people consider normal. Most historians dismiss these stories as products of superstitious minds to explain things they couldn't understand. I've always wondered...was *all* of it just fiction? What you can do proves that ESP exists." She breaks into a wide smile. "And that is *sooooo* cool."

I can't share in her enthusiasm, as much as I want to. "It'd be a lot cooler if I knew what it was called. And why I have it in the first place."

"You have no idea where this came from?"

"None at all. Believe me, I've thought non-stop about why my life has turned into an episode of *The X-Files*. There's no reason my brain should work this way. I've never had a concussion. I've never had surgery. The only thing I've ever done to my brain is kill a few cells with too much beer."

Her brow scrunches. "Could you have possibly...inherited it?"

My eyes narrow. When recovering from my first flash with Sarah's clothes, I considered this possibility but rejected it. If any member of my family had ESP, I would have known, right?

Right?

Yeah, maybe not. Between long bouts of moodiness and self-absorption, my mom could have been a Satanist sacrificing small animals in our backyard and I wouldn't have noticed.

"It's possible," I finally reply.

She points at my computer lying closed on my coffee table. "Can I borrow your laptop?"

"Go ahead."

Piper pulls the thing onto her lap, powers it up, and runs a quick Google search. Thirty seconds later, she turns the screen to face me. "Here you go. What you can do is called psychometry."

I roll the unfamiliar word over my tongue, then read what's on the screen. "Psychometry—the psychic ability to read the history of an object by touching it. Such impressions may be perceived in the form of images, sounds, smells, and even emotions." I lean back against the cushions, nodding. "Yeah, that's it all right."

One minor mystery solved. Many, many more to go.

"You called this 'weird and scary,'" she says. "And you're right, it is. I know you didn't ask to be psychometric, but you are. The way I see it, you have two choices. One: treat your ability like it's a gift instead of a curse. Try to hone it, shape it into something you can use to help people..."

"And two?"

The smirk returns. "Wear gloves for the rest of your life."

"Yeah, right," I scoff. "This is Phoenix. It's a hundred degrees eight months out of the year. That ain't happening."

"Well then—"

I hold a hand up. "Before you encourage me anymore, I have one more part of the story to tell you. The worst part. By a mile."

She falls silent, gently chewing her lower lip as she slouches against the two throw pillows on her side of the couch. She raises her eyebrows, asking a silent question.

I exhale. "How much do you know about the Disney Princess Killer?"

"Not much. Just what I've seen on the rare occasions that I watch the news. I know he's killed three girls and—" Her eyes double in size, and she slowly shakes her head. "No."

I fight to keep my tone even. "That day you found me in the alley behind Hill O' Beans? I saw him."

Her nostrils flare and her lips tremble. "You *saw* him?" she echoes, her volume increasing. "*You* saw the Disney Princess Killer. In the alley. Behind *our* coffee shop."

I nod, then go on to relay everything I remember from that initial encounter, from the white van to the horrible images of Sarah's abduction, imprisonment, and eventual murder. I put the exclamation point on the story when I retrieve the Hefty from my hall closet and dump it on the coffee table.

Piper jumps up and scoots away like the bag is full of live cobras. "Oh my God, Bax! Are you freaking kidding me?" She continues to back away, toward the door, like she's going to bolt at any moment.

"I wish I was."

"Those are a *dead girl's clothes*?"

I nod.

"And you brought it *here*? Are you freaking stupid?"

I bristle at her words. "Hey now—"

She points a sharp finger at the bag. "That is evidence, Bax! In a child's murder! You could go to jail, for Christ's sake!"

"I didn't know, okay?" I stand, raising my voice to match hers. "At first, I thought he was just some asshole dumping his trash! It wasn't until you woke me up that I thought it might have been him." I flump back on the couch. "I had no idea what happened to me. If I'd left the clothes there, I couldn't get answers. Not only that, but he might also have come back for them, and any chance we have to catch him goes right out the window."

"*We*?" she retorts, tugging on her hair in agitation.

Sadness and desperation claw through my chest, and I rake my hands through my scalp. "I have no one else to turn to, Piper. No one at all." A sob breaks through. "I can't do this alone."

She falls silent again, taken aback by my request.

"That monster is out there right now. He's killed three girls. It may be months, weeks, or days before he takes someone else. But he *will* do it. And the cops have no idea who he is. The guy leaves no traces." I gesture at the bag. "The clothes in there? They're spotless. Yes, I could turn them over to the police, but I'd bet a thousand bucks the only DNA they'd find would be mine."

Piper shambles back to the couch and resumes her seat, never taking her eyes off the Hefty. "You didn't kill those girls, Bax. You were at Asterly when Sarah was kidnapped. With an ankle bracelet, no less. That's a pretty solid alibi."

I shake my head. "You think that'll stop Detective Rojas from arresting me? You saw her. She hates my ass, and she'll use any excuse she can find to jam me up." I lean forward, grazing my fingers over the bag's plastic surface. "I'm involved, Piper. Whether I want to be or not."

"Bax—"

"I'll understand if you want out. You've got work, and school, and your dad, and Gavin to deal with. If you want to get in your car, drive home, and forget everything I just told you, I wouldn't blame you at all."

The silence that follows is interrupted by yet another ominous thunderclap. The timing is perfect, like God Himself had thrown the switch.

Piper stares into space for a few moments, then lifts her glasses to rub her eyes. "Why do you want to catch him?"

"Because I might be the only one who can."

Her expression hardens. "That doesn't answer my question. You could burn these clothes, or bury them, or toss them somewhere they'd never be found. You'd be free and clear."

Yes, I would.

And heaven help me, I've considered doing just that at least fifty times in the past week.

But there's being able to live with myself. To look at my reflection and not hate what I see.

"I can't."

"Why not?"

Cold, hard guilt turns to cement in my stomach. "Because I haven't done one damn thing right in my life since I turned ten. And I've done so much wrong. I want to...no, I *have* to even the score." I turn to her, my voice a raspy whisper. "Please, Piper. *Please.*"

She closes her eyes. I can practically see the wheels turning in her mind.

With a resigned sigh, she faces me again. "I'll help you, Bax."

I brighten. "You will?"

"I will, but know this...weird and scary is one thing, but this crosses the line into extreme danger. I want to catch this guy, but there's no way in hell I'm putting myself in the path of a serial killer. I love murder mysteries, but I'm not going to become a character in one. Are we clear?"

I blow out a breath. "Crystal."

"All right." She rises to her feet, and I do the same. "I understand the urgency of this, but keep in mind that I have a busy schedule. Whatever free time I can devote to this, I will."

"I appreciate that. Any chance we can meet up tomorrow to discuss our next move?"

"Afraid not. I'm driving my dad to Anthem to spend the day with my oldest brother and his family. I'll talk to you at work on Monday."

"Sure thing." I open the back door, pleased to see that the storm seems to be diminishing. "You okay getting home?"

"I'll be fine."

We stare at each other for a few awkward moments. I'm wondering what the best way to say goodbye is, and I think she's doing the same. A handshake would be lame given the graveness of what we're about to embark on, as would a fist-bump. A hug would feel a step too far, despite the embrace we shared earlier.

Finally, she makes the decision for both of us by stepping into me. The hug only lasts a couple of seconds, but it makes me feel so much better. Not because I was able to survive it without getting a woody, but because, for the first time in years, I don't feel quite so alone.

I give her a friendly wave, which she returns, as she pulls out of my parking space. When her car disappears from sight, I realize that I made the right choice. Well, technically, I was kind of forced into telling her the truth, but whatever.

The rain continues to lessen but it doesn't stop completely, so I order a pizza and spend the next few hours enjoying Season One of *Stranger Things* on Netflix. Right before I hit the sack, I watch the ten o'clock news hoping for any new developments in the DPK case. On the bright side, no more kids have disappeared. The downside is, the taskforce that has been assembled to nab the killer seems to have made no progress, judging by the non-answers various members give in their ten-second interview clips. No mention is made of a white van. Not that this means anything— yes, Brandon might have chickened out of approaching Detective Rojas, but it's equally likely a new lead like this would be kept from the media just in case the DPK is watching.

I throw the Hefty back in the closet before shuffling off to bed. I'm already dreading what comes next.

CHAPTER THIRTEEN

I'm greeted the next morning by an overcast sky and cool temperatures, so I avail myself of the opportunity to go shopping. I take an Uber to Wal-Mart to purchase a few items I didn't realize I'd need when I moved into my new bachelor pad—cleaning supplies. I know teenagers have a rep for being lazy and slovenly, but if my stint at Asterly taught me one thing, it's that cleaning up after oneself is a necessity. If I'm going to have company at my place on a regular basis—whether it be Piper or Trina or Sheila or, God willing, Sydney—I can't let it become a winter resort for roaches. That, and I think it was #3 on the list of Ted Commandments. By the time I return to Arbor Vista, I've acquired a new vacuum cleaner and three bags full of sponges, cloths, cleansers, and sprays. Mom would be proud. Hmm, maybe not. But *someone*'s mom would be.

I also bought a spiffy new coffee maker and all the ingredients I'll need to brew the perfect mocha chai latte. I actually did try an MCL the way Piper showed me, and it's really good. I never would have thought you could combine coffee and tea flavors into something awesome, but after my second sip, I convinced myself I could do it better. I've also convinced myself that I can put my own spin on it that will knock Sydney's socks off, and she'll be so impressed she'll ask me out.

Hey, I can dream, can't I?

So in between running my new Hoover over every square inch of carpet and wiping down every flat surface, I conduct my experiments. I pooled several recipe sites for ideas and was shocked at the sheer number of variations. One lady suggested hemp seeds —*WTF?*—while another recipe included cardamom, which I'd never heard of. I ended up raiding the spice aisle at the grocery store, though paprika was probably a bad choice.

My first five attempts were epic fails. One tasted like hot glue. Another smelled like burnt toast, and not in a good way. My best one featured raw cocoa, cinnamon, and a few drops of maple syrup. It tasted okay, but it looked like mop water with whipped cream floating on it.

One of my middle-school teachers once said that Thomas Edison failed over a thousand times when he was trying to invent the light bulb. I vow to pray nightly to the gods of coffee that I'll make a breakthrough long before that.

Five o'clock sees me sitting on one of two worn chairs in Arbor Vista's laundry room. I listen to the rhythmic drone of the tumble dryer, playing on my cell to pass the time. I think about shooting Piper a text to see how she's doing, but then reconsider. No matter what stirrings I have for her, I have to keep my hormones on ice from this point on. I've been in need of a good friend for a long time, and that she's willing to help me out of this bizarro mess speaks volumes about her character. So I can't be thinking with my little head when I'm with her, period.

While my fingers are busy crushing candy—don't judge me— I distract my brain by planning my next few practice lattes. I'm considering adding peppermint to the recipe. Or perhaps a dash of ginger. I wonder if Piper likes it spicy.

I mean Sydney.

Sydney!

Stupid brain...

"Bax?" Gina, smiling through the fatigue creasing her face, stands in the doorway.

I switch off my phone and straighten up. "Hey, Gina."

"Glad I caught you. I knocked on your door just now, but you weren't in."

I use my head to gesture at the dryer. "Doing laundry. What's up?"

"Well...I have another prospective entree in the oven, and..." Her cheeks redden slightly. "I was wondering if you wanted to join us for dinner."

The thought of tasting another Gina Forrester original has me salivating within seconds. "Really?"

She leans on the door frame. "I don't want to impose. I mean, if you have other plans..."

I spring to my feet, grinning like a six-year-old offered extra sprinkles on his sundae. "Gina, if whatever you're serving is as good as your brisket, it's not an imposition, it's a privilege. I mean, don't most people have to pay to eat your cooking?"

Her posture relaxes. "Yeah, I suppose so. I just get nervous when trying out something new. So you'll come?"

"Absolutely. When's good?"

She checks her watch. "How's an hour sound?"

"Like a plan."

"Great. See you there." With a congenial nod, she disappears down the sidewalk.

I gawp as I take a seat at the Forresters' dining table, set right in front of the L-shaped kitchen counter. The entree in question is something called a "paillard," a boneless chicken breast Gina has pounded flat, drizzled with a lemony black pepper sauce, and served with sliced red and yellow cherry tomatoes, shaved parmesan cheese, and a leafy green thing called arugula. It's beautiful on the plate, full of color and enticing smells. Whatever spices she's added make the chicken zesty and delicious. It's all I can do to keep from moaning in pure joy.

I glance sidelong at Trina, who tucks into her meal with far more decorum than me, though her face displays no less pleasure. She chews thoughtfully, like a judge on one of those television cooking competitions. After three bites, she renders her verdict. "I think you used a little too much garlic, Mom."

Gina takes her daughter's critique in stride. After another bite, she says, "You know, I think you're right. I also think I over-salted it a smidge. What do you think, Bax?"

They both face me, and I freeze in mid-chew. I'm so intent on enjoying the delicious food I forgot I was supposed to be gauging its restaurant-menu potential. I smirk, then swallow. "I honestly couldn't tell, but then, my mom wasn't much of a cook. I grew up on Spaghetti-Os and Beanee Weanee."

Gina's expression conveys understanding tinged with sympathy. Trina gives me a "Canned pasta? You poor, poor guy" head-shake.

"Regardless, you're welcome to remain part of my official tasting team," Gina says.

Trina dabs her mouth with a napkin. "Hey Bax, do you like Halloween?"

I meet her gaze, adopting my best classic Dracula voice. "I lohve Halloveen. It vas my favorite holiday ven I vas a boy." I bare my teeth, showing off imaginary fangs. "Why do you ask?"

"Every year, Arbor Vista has this awesome Halloween party in the activity center. Everyone gets all dressed up. There's snacks and games and music. It's so much fun."

It's impossible not to be infected by her doe-eyed enthusiasm. "Sounds cool."

"Oh, it is." Gina takes up the charge. "It's mostly for the kids, but it's also a great way to socialize with your neighbors and blow off some steam."

A hopeful twinkle appears in Trina's eyes. "So...you wanna come?"

At first, the thought of attending a party full of people I don't know strikes me as a bad idea. The last time I did that, I got roaringly drunk, took a swing at a certain lady cop, and woke up in the local precinct's drunk tank. Given that this party is unlikely to have an open bar or an eighteen-gallon beer keg, I probably won't meet the same fate this time. "When does it start?"

"Right around sunset," Gina replies.

I nod. "The coffee shop usually closes at seven on Fridays, so unless my boss has me working the afternoon shift, I should be off by then."

"Great!" Trina downs half her glass of water and gives a satisfied aah. "I'll start thinking of costumes for all of us right away."

I glance at Gina, who's beaming. "Two years ago, we went as dogs from *101 Dalmatians*," she says. "Last year, she was Snow White and I was the Wicked Queen. All Trina's ideas. We had a blast."

"Then I'm in." I fork the last bite into my mouth and fist-bump Trina, who gives a tiny squeal.

An audible buzz comes from the kitchen counter behind Gina. She reaches behind her, scoops up her cell phone, checks the caller ID, and answers it. "What's up, Ken?"

I lean toward Trina, lowering my voice to a whisper. "Ken?"

"Mom's boss," she whispers back.

Gina's cheerful demeanor dissolves away as she listens to the caller. "Come on, Ken, this is my first day off in eight days. Can't you find someone else?" Pause. "Yeah, yeah. Fine. Just...give me a few minutes to find someone to babysit Trina, and I'll be there." She pinches the bridge of her nose and expels a weary breath. "You owe me one. Actually, you owe me about twenty-five by now. See you in a bit." She ends the call and tosses the cell on the table. "Dang it to heck."

I suppress a chuckle.

"Mom doesn't like to swear in front of me," Trina explains. "I've told her I hear bad words at school all the time, so it's no big deal."

"Just because other kids swear doesn't mean I want you doing it. I have to set an example, right?"

Trina gives Gina the same "whatever, Mom" look that I used after every one of my own mother's many, many lectures. I fight back another laugh.

Gina stands, composing herself. "I'll call Mrs. Macias, see if you can stay over at Cheyanne's place till I get back."

"Can't I just stay here?" Trina begs. "I'll shoot Chey a text, I'm sure she'll come right over. I promise we'll lock the door and won't go anywhere."

"Sweetie, you're nine. Having you and Cheyanne stay here unsupervised for an hour after school is one thing, but it's dark now, and I don't know how long I'll be gone."

I rise, depositing my plate and silverware in the sink. "I'll watch her if you like. I mean, if you're okay with that."

Trina's joyous expression returns.

"You sure?" Gina checks her watch. "I don't know how long I'll be. It may be one hour, it may be three."

I spread my arms wide. "I got nothing else going on."

Her olive skin flushes, and her mouth curls into a gracious smile. "Bax, you are a lifesaver. I'll compensate you for your time, of course."

"Not a problem. My fee is one amazing dinner. Which you've already paid me." I grin.

She nods, then nips off to her bedroom, where I hear her drag a brush through her dark, medium-length hair. She emerges, car keys in hand, wearing a light, sand-colored coat, and flat-soled shoes. "I'll be back as soon as I can, pumpkin," she addresses Trina. "Don't give Bax a hard time, okay?"

"I won't, Mom," Trina replies.

Gina turns to me. "Make sure she's in bed by ten." She gives her daughter a rushed hug, then departs. A few moments later, the sound of her car's engine fades into the distance.

Trina and I have no sooner finished loading up the dishwasher and putting the pots in the sink to soak when Cheyanne drops by unannounced. Trina explains that this is not a rare occurrence, especially when her toddler brothers are acting up. "Which is most of the time," Cheyanne says with an eye-roll.

Within minutes, the two of them are parked on the living room carpet, engrossed in Roblox and making little-girl small talk. I sink into the couch and watch them have their fun.

My God, how my life has changed.

A couple of weeks ago, all I owned was a worn duffle bag full of old clothes and an itchy ankle bracelet. I lived in a house with a half-dozen other kids with severe anger issues, run by a man who needed happy pills just to upgrade to surly. The closest thing I had to a friend was Kyle, who barely talked and almost never looked me in the eye.

And now...I have a job. A home. Co-workers. Neighbors.

A goddamn superpower.

I see freaking dead people.

Not only that, I'm about to step into the ring with a serial killer who has eluded authorities for almost a year. I'll probably end up dead, or in prison. A lot of people would say I deserve that, and I'd have no grounds to argue.

Cheyanne's voice breaks into my introspection. "You'll never guess what happened in school on Friday."

Trina pauses the game. "What?"

"Right after lunch, Crescent and I went into the girls' restroom. Kaitlyn was in there with Brooklyn and Avery. She had a cigarette in her mouth."

Trina's eyes widen. So do mine.

"No way," she says.

"Yes way. She said she stole it from her mom's purse."

Jeez Louise. I mean, I picked up some bad habits early, but the thought of a middle-schooler lighting up in the girls' room infuriates me. "How old is this girl?"

Cheyanne faces me. "She's eleven."

"Eleven? And she was smoking?"

Her face scrunches. "I'm not sure. I don't think it was lit."

I exhale, unexpectedly relieved. "Good. Smoking's not cool."

"How would you know? Have you ever smoked?" Trina asks.

"I have. It totally sucked. Don't ever start."

Wow. Look at me, being the responsible adult. Maybe there's hope for me yet.

Cheyanne departs with a cheery wave after getting a text from her mom to come home. Gina still isn't back yet, so Trina pops one of her favorite movies into the DVD player. We spend the next ninety minutes watching *Wreck-It Ralph*, an animated movie I somehow missed when it first came out. I love it. I also can't help noticing the similarity in personalities between Trina and Vanellope. Both are spunky, precocious, and not afraid to voice their opinion. This makes me enjoy the film even more.

It's just past nine-thirty when the credits start rolling. Trina's mouth opens in an adorable yawn, and dang if those things aren't contagious. I suggest she start getting ready for bed, so she shuffles down the hall to brush her teeth. I flip channels, settling on a pro football game between two teams I couldn't care less about. I check the time on my phone again and wonder how much longer Gina will be.

Trina returns to the living room in a print tee that says "Let Me Sleep" and a pair of shorts covered in drawings of closed eyelids, and surprisingly without her charm bracelet. I'm unable to stifle a chuckle.

"What's so funny?" she says with a mock scowl.

"That may be the most adorable sleepwear I've ever seen."

She smiles, her face flushing. "Thanks." She eases back onto the couch next to me. "What did you wear to bed when you were my age?"

I grin. "What else? Spongebob."

She clutches her chest and laughs, and it's the single sweetest sound I've ever heard in my life. I join in, but it tapers off quickly as Trina edges closer to me, not the least bit shy about cozying up to a guy twice her age. We focus on the totally uninteresting football game and lapse into silence. I get a teensy bit alarmed when she leans against my shoulder and takes my hand, but it dissipates quickly. I fold a protective arm around her, and she looks up at me with those huge eyes. A wordless conversation passes between us, and in an instant, I understand.

I was worried Trina may be developing an unhealthy crush on me, but that's not it at all. What Gina said about her own parents believing Trina needed a male figure in her life was spot-on. Trina's had no one but her mom since she was a toddler, and from what I gather, Gina's been too busy with her food career to actively date anyone, which means Trina has no men in her life other than—presumably—her teachers, neighbors, and maybe a few relatives she rarely sees.

For years, I wondered how my life might have been different if my parents had given me a younger sibling. Maybe I would have been more responsible instead of lashing out at my big brother's perfection. And though she's never said so, I think Trina likes the idea of having a big brother.

She snuggles into me, closing her eyes. I mute the TV, and the room falls quiet. Minutes later, I hear tiny snores coming from my armpit. I smile again, staring down at this little pixie who has completely stolen my heart.

For one terrible second, I picture Trina in the clutches of that bastard. I imagine her eyes, devoid of life, staring unseeing at the sky above wherever he chooses to dump her body. I envision the horror on Gina's face when Detective Rojas knocks on her door with the most awful news a mother can hear.

No.

Not happening. Not to her. Not to anyone. Never again.

Trina shifts position, and I twist my body slightly to accommodate. Her head slumps onto my chest, and within moments, her low snore resumes.

The tightness in my chest eases, and a comforting warmth spreads through me.

I let my lids fall, concentrating on her rhythmic exhales. Contentment turns to fatigue, and then I nod off.

I'm jostled awake to see Gina next to me. Her expression conveys both exhaustion and happiness.

"Hey," I slur, sitting up. It takes me a few seconds to realize my little friend is nowhere in sight. "Where's Trina?"

"Put her to bed."

I stretch my back muscles, yawning again. "What time is it?"

"Ten-fifteen. What did you two do while I was away?"

"Trina and Cheyanne played Roblox for an hour, then we watched a movie. I guess we fell asleep."

"I'll say." Gina produces her phone, then shows me a pic she snapped of Trina and me, bundled together, zonked out, and mouths open.

A wave of embarrassment washes over me. "I wasn't touching her, I swear. I mean, I was, but not, you know, inappropriately. You can ask her if—"

Gina puts a hand on my arm, shushing me. "Calm down, Bax. If I were the least bit worried something like that would happen, I wouldn't have let you stay with her."

Her vote of confidence both calms and confuses me. "Thank you. That means a lot, but..."

"But what?"

I stare into her sincere brown eyes. "I'm eighteen. I live alone. I don't have a girlfriend. And I have a criminal record. Most people wouldn't trust me to look after their goldfish, let alone their nine-year-old daughter. Aren't I exactly the kind of person Trina *shouldn't* be hanging out with?"

Gina slumps into the couch, staring at the switched-off television. I don't interrupt her train of thought, because I'm dying to hear the answer.

"I've known some bad people in my life," she finally says. "Angry, scary people who don't care about anything but themselves. The kind of people I go out of my way to avoid and have taught Trina to do the same." She faces me. "You are *not* one of those people."

"I can give you the name of a police lady who would disagree."

She waves my comment away. "Cops see bad stuff every day. That would skew anyone's world-view."

Gina has a point. I might even sympathize with Detective Rojas if she wasn't such a bitch. "But what makes you so sure about me? *I'm* not even sure about me."

"Because I'm very good at reading people, that's why. You're a good person, Bax. A little broken, maybe, but nothing that can't be fixed with hard work and positive reinforcement." She grins. "Plus, you passed the Trina Test." I laugh, we both stand, and she leads me to the front door. "I'm sorry I was so late. Work was crazy busy for a Sunday night."

"No prob."

"Can I call on you in the future if I need a sitter on short notice?"

"Yeah."

Gina opens the door, then gives me a light shoulder-squeeze. "Then I will. Thanks again."

INTERLUDE

Gina watches her mysterious neighbor disappear into his house, then shuts the door. After scrubbing her pots and pans clean and storing them in their proper cabinets, she heads down the hall to Trina's room. She pushes the door open a crack, surprised to see her daughter still awake.

Trina, nestled under her thick blue comforter, throws a tired smile her way. "Don't worry, Mom, I'm going to sleep."

Gina eases into the room, sits on the edge of the bed and gently moves several strands of hair away from Trina's round face. "I know. Just wanted to check on you. How'd it go with you and Bax?"

"It went fine, I guess. He's really sweet, and funny. He doesn't talk down to me and Chey like most older kids do."

"I'm detecting a 'but.'"

"But..." Trina closes her eyes, exhales, then meets her mother's gaze. "He's so sad, Mom. He tries not to show it, but I can see it." The beginnings of tears sparkle at the corners of her eyes. "I wish I could just hug him and make all his sadness go away like you did with me when Great-Grandma Rose died."

"There are some things even hugs can't cure, sweetie. But they do help." Gina grasps her daughter's hand. "Did he tell you about his family?"

"A little. He said his dad died, and he and his mom don't really talk anymore."

Gina nods. "That's what he told me too."

"You've seen how bright he is, right?"

"Yes, sweetie. He may be the brightest person I've ever met."

"Do you think he's...special?"

"I do."

"Are we gonna tell him?"

Gina takes a moment to consider her answer. "When the time is right. Until then, all we can do is be his friends. I can already tell how much he cares for you."

A weak smile curls the corners of Trina's mouth. "Well, that's because I'm awesome."

"The awesomest." Gina leans over and kisses her daughter's forehead. "Sweet dreams, baby girl."

"'Night, Mom."

After changing into her pajamas, Gina switches off her light and slips beneath her own comforter. Despite her tiredness, it takes many minutes for sleep to come.

Chapter Fourteen

Under the light of a lava lamp I bought for cheap last week, I stare at the pile of Sarah's clothes, which once again covers my coffee table.

Years ago, I lived in a nice house, on a nice street. My family knew most of our neighbors. They got along with them. Everyone looked out for each other, trusted each other. It was the perfect setting most people think of when they picture the suburbs.

This memory brings back a torrent of others, rushing through my head like a flash flood. Mom. Dad. AJ. All of us together, living normal lives. These are immediately followed by images that scrape my brain like steel wool. Dad, clad in his desert-sand-colored camo fatigues, waving goodbye, heading for his second tour in Afghanistan. Mom collapsing into tears in front of the uniformed man on our doorstep five seconds after being delivered the news of Dad's death by an IED. The wail of the ambulance siren the night that AJ...

I'm not going there. I'm not going there. I'm. Not. Going. There.

I scan the room, taking in all the stuff I've acquired since being discharged from Asterly. Furnishings. Comforts. Luxuries.

Piper's friendship. Gina's trust. Trina's adoration.

I have all these things, and I haven't earned any of it.

I glance up at the ceiling, imagining some higher power peering down at me with a sardonic smirk. Yeah, right back at ya. I'm reading you loud and clear.

Gina was right—there are bad people in the world. One of them just happens to be a stone-cold killer whom I have the power to stop.

I will stop him. I will even the score. I will make myself worthy of what these people offer so freely.

I exhale deeply and set the alarm on my fully charged cell to maximum volume, then slip it under the coffee table where I won't be able to grab it without getting off the couch. Definitely not sleeping through another shift.

One more deep breath and I recline into a horizontal position. Then, after another hopeful glance at the ceiling, I snatch the jeans from the table and clutch them to my chest.

A cool breeze blows my hair into my face, and I shove my hands deeper into my pockets. I look up at the nearest street sign as I walk by it. 64th Avenue. Two more minutes, and I'll be home. I can't wait to FaceTime with Cassie. She's the coolest cousin ever.

Something's changed. This is my third time—or is it the fourth?—living this memory. It's just like with Piper's locket in that I feel more able to separate myself from it with each pass. The first time, I couldn't distinguish between my own thoughts and Sarah's. Now, it's like...I don't know. I'm still Sarah, but it's like I'm listening to her thoughts like they're coming through my cell phone.

I'm right there when Sarah walks past the van, and I brace myself for the inevitable spike of terror when the man grabs her, but it doesn't come. I feel the man's hand on her back, feel her legs thrash as she's lifted off her feet, see her hauled into the van, hear the door slide closed. But the only fear I feel is a slight twinge tugging at my brain.

Interesting.

In the split-second before the scene changes, I notice something that I barely noticed before—the back of the van is not empty. There's a long, thin duffle bag jammed against the rear doors, and it looks like the zipper is open. Inside, I catch a glimpse of three steel rods, several feet long and joined at the top by a plastic fastener. A moment later, the van disappears, and so does most of the light.

Dammit. That might have been a clue! Can I hit the rewind button?

Guess not.

I'm now in a room, roughly the size of my living room. I'm surrounded on all sides by bare concrete walls. The only things to look at are a small card table, a metal fold-up chair, and a curtained-off section in the corner where I can see a toilet and a makeshift shower stall. Light spills into the room through a tiny window, too high for me to reach. The only sound comes from air flowing through a vent at the top of the opposite wall, near the room's one and only door.

I recognize this room from my first flash, in the alley. I guess whatever part of my brain controls my ESP overloaded before I could relive the entire series of memories. This time, however, I seem to be not only holding it together but keeping my thoughts separate.

I look down at my hands—Sarah's hands—folded in her lap. I —she...damn, keeping this straight is exhausting—is sitting, cross-legged, on a mattress wedged into one corner of her prison. She's wearing the same jeans, socks, and shoes that I've become familiar with, though the tee she sports features The Little Mermaid and not Moana.

Sarah's thoughts break into my own. *I'm so tired of crying. I wish my mommy were here to hold me. I wish my daddy would come to save me.*

I wish anyone would save me.

I want to go home.

Every word cuts through me like a blade. I feel every ounce of her desperation, her despair. The knowledge that Sarah spent her last days on Earth in this abysmal place plunges the dagger even deeper.

I feel her fear turn to raw anger as she removes her shoes, rises, steps off the mattress, and strides purposefully toward the card table. Her feet make no noise as she pulls it, inch by inch, right below the window. She stops, looks toward the door, listening for any sound, but none comes. She then picks up the chair, lifting it high so that it sits atop the table, which wobbles under its weight.

Another glance at the door. So far so good.

I know what she's doing.

My heart sinks a little as she tries to haul herself onto the flimsy table, but to no avail. I feel her tears return. Then she turns her gaze upon her mattress, and she hits upon an idea.

Her dainty muscles strain as she drags the heavy thing, inch by inch, toward the table.

The mattress itself is fairly thin, frayed at the edges and with a couple of stains decorating its surface. She moves around, lifts one end, and promptly folds it in half. Then, before it can uncurl, she throws a rumpled quilt over it. Finally, she climbs her makeshift stepladder onto the table. which again vibrates with the added weight.

A scraping sound comes from somewhere behind the door. Movement.

Her eyes flick to the door, panic surging through her veins.

What do I do? I can't put all this back before he comes in!

I may only have one shot at this...

Sarah steps onto the chair, first one foot, then the other.

The doorknob twists.

Expelling a breath, Sarah turns around, raises up on her tiptoes, and peers out the window.

I see, through a tall metal fence comprised of vertical iron bars, a vast expanse of desert. No buildings, no people, nothing but an empty landscape dotted with occasional patches of scrub-brush and saguaro cacti. A "Private Property – No Trespassing" sign sticks out of the ground a few yards in front of a second fence, this one made of barbed wire.

"Ariel!"

The sound of the man's voice makes her start. Her foot slips, the chair shakes. The ramshackle construction collapses, and she topples to the side. Thankfully, she lands on the doubled-up mattress. The landing is soft, but it still drives the air from her lungs. The crash of the chair hitting concrete reverberates through the room.

Sarah buries her face in the mattress, her breath coming in shallow pants. She chokes back several sobs.

"Ariel," the man says in a scolding tone. "I warned you what would happen if you misbehaved."

She raises herself up on her hands, still not meeting his gaze. "Please let me go," she whimpers. "Please, mister. I just want to go home to my mommy and daddy. I won't tell anyone who you are, I promise." Hot tears stream down her face.

"But you *are* home, Ariel. You were gone for a long time, but I found you again. All you have to do is behave, and things can be as they were."

With a surge of adrenaline, Sarah pushes herself to her feet, and all her rage breaks free. "I keep telling you, I'm *not* Ariel! Why don't you believe me?" She looks around for something to throw at him, but there's nothing.

"I know you're upset, Ariel, but this can't—"

Finally, she looks up at him. Through a fog of tears, I get my first glimpse of his face.

Since learning of his existence, I've tried to imagine what face a killer of children would have. In every scenario, I imagined a monster—wild eyes, unkempt hair, scraggly beard, with a swastika carved into his forehead. Something that screams "psychopath" in big neon letters. But no. This guy looks completely, utterly ordinary.

If I had to guess, he's in his early forties. Short dark brown hair with occasional strands of gray fall from his scalp. Thin lips are set in a straight line below a pointy nose and pale blue eyes. He's wearing a white button-down dress shirt and brown slacks, like thousands of guys who just got home from the office. I don't see any tattoos, scars, or facial hair. Nothing at all stands out about him except for the cold, calculating glower he directs at poor Sarah.

"Stop calling me Ariel!" she explodes. "My name is Sarah! *Sarah*! I'm not your daughter!"

In a spurt of irrational anger, she rushes at him, pounding her little fists into his stomach, which is as high as she can reach. It's like punching a wall.

He lets her flail away at him, giving no reaction at all. After ten seconds that feel like five minutes, he grabs her wrists and wrenches them upward. She cries out, and her eyes lock onto his.

"No, you're not," he says in a voice so emotionless it sends a shiver up my spine. At least, I think it's my spine, but it could be Sarah's. "My daughter was well-behaved. Respectful. You're not her at all."

My heart turns to ice as she offers a plea. "So...you'll let me go?"

He straightens up, one hand still clamped around her wrist while his other disappears behind his back. With a low growl, he spins her around so she's facing the wall with the window, then his arm shifts to curl around her throat. She doesn't even have time to cry out when something sharp pricks her neck. Something cold pulses through her veins, and blackness seeps across her vision.

The last thing she—and I—hear before all goes dark is the man saying, "Yes, Sarah. I will let you go."

Little by little, the sensation of couch cushions beneath me returns. I drag my eyelids open, taking stock of my surroundings. The sunlight streaming through the window is replaced by the lamp illuminating my living room.

I wait for the inevitable chill to sweep over me, and it does. And goddamn it, I forgot to get the blanket to stop the icicles pressing into my skin. I try to rise, but an invisible weight keeps me pinned to the sofa. I can barely lift my head. I can barely feel my fingers.

Tears born from impotent anger prick my eyes. That poor, defenseless girl. She didn't stand a chance.

Then, somewhere deep inside me, a fire of triumph ignites, which partially succeeds in chasing away the frostbite.

I saw you, motherfucker. I saw your face.

My neck muscles turn to Jell-O, and my eyes close.

I think I'll sleep now.

CHAPTER FIFTEEN

My cell phone wakes me at nine sharp, and it's only then that my dumb brain finally registers today is Sunday, and I have no work to report to. I really have to get a handle on this sliding shift, which Austin tells me is part of the job. Accommodating every employee's personal and school schedules is a challenge for Austin, and as the only Hill O' Beans employee with no scholastic or family commitments, it's up to me to fill whatever gaps need filling.

I shoot Piper a text hinting at my monumental discovery—I'm a little too paranoid to just blurt out "Hey, guess what? I saw the DP Killer's face! Let's do lunch!"—but I get no response. Likewise, my second and third texts go unanswered. Rather than blow up her phone with repeated texts, I sit on the couch and begin the next phase of Operation Nail the Psycho. As I hoped, last night's flash didn't wipe me out like it did the previous time. I'm confident further visions will follow the same pattern as with Piper's locket.

First, I scour the Internet, hoping to find "Psychometry for Dummies," but come up empty. Most of what I find on ESP is highly suspect. There's not much based in actual science, probably because the majority of people believe every form of ESP that has a word attached to it is a load of bullcrap. There is little that is helpful, which means I'm going to have to write my own manual.

To that end, I spend several hours revisiting Sarah's memories by touching her clothes. As with Piper's locket, the drop in temperature and the induced fatigue lessens with each pass.

I try grasping different articles of clothing. The Moana tee only shows me the kidnapping—which makes sense, since from that point on Sarah was probably forced to wear the *Little Mermaid* shirt she was found in—and the flashes I get with her shoes end the second she takes them off. Her jeans and socks give me the greatest volume of memories, but nothing I haven't already seen. I jot down every detail in my notebook just in case it's a viable clue.

By the fifth time through, the emotional rushes I got from Sarah's fear and anger barely have any effect on me. I'm able to view the memories with a more detached eye. This makes observation a lot easier, though it's tough to suppress my own rage when I stare into the killer's face.

On my eighth go-round, something else happens. The images become fuzzy, and the voices are muffled like I have pillows over my ears.

On the tenth try, every image is so blurry I can't make out any details, and both Sarah's thoughts and her spoken words are garbled beyond recognition.

Even though continuing on from that point turns out to be a waste of time, I do it anyway, to see how many more times it will take before the magic runs out. Sure enough, at two o'clock, I grasp the leg of Sarah's jeans and nothing happens. I repeat the process on every item of clothing, with similar results.

I sit back on my couch, staring into space. The window into Sarah's mind has closed. Her voice, which reached out to me from beyond the grave, has been silenced, probably forever.

My stomach growls, and I realize I have a sudden craving for ice cream. As luck would have it, there's a Dairy Queen a mile away. The skies are clear, so I decide to go have a hot fudge sundae in Sarah's memory. And maybe a burger. And fries.

With a regretful sigh, I throw the clothes into the Hefty and deposit them back in my closet. Then I grab my jacket and keys and head out the door.

Austin hits me with some bad news when I report for work on Monday. Apparently, Piper's dad had to be admitted to a hospital in Anthem—over twenty miles away—after experiencing breathing problems.

From what she told Austin, he's doing better but will need to be closely monitored for a while. Her brother Joe and his wife agreed to take that duty, but Piper will be spending her time outside classes today packing two suitcases full of her dad's stuff so he can settle comfortably into Joe's guest bedroom.

"Damn," I say.

Austin, Lucas, and Sierra nod sympathetically.

"Did she tell you anything else?"

"Only that she'd be back tomorrow, and that I'll have to cut back on her hours until she and her family decide what to do next. She said, quote, 'we may have to make some drastic choices soon,' unquote."

Three guys wearing construction helmets and safety vests come through the door, so we take our positions and get to work. While I whip up two frappucinos and another PSL, I listen in on the conversation the guys have with Austin. I learn that Trina's school's gymnasium has been in the remodeling stages for several weeks and is nearing completion. That'll make her happy. Girl's got energy for days.

My mood turns sour as I contemplate what I'm going to do next. It sucks hard that Piper had to have a family crisis *now* of all times. I mean, yes, obviously her dad comes first. It's good that she won't have to be his sole caretaker while he recuperates, but between worrying about him, her classes, and earning a paycheck, how much time will she now have to devote to our investigation? Guilt-tripping her into helping me would be such an asshole thing to do. No. For the next few days at least, I'll have to settle for as much of Piper's help as she's capable of giving.

I saw the DP Killer's face. Great. Now what? If I had an hour with a police sketch artist, I know we could come up with a spot-on likeness. Of course, that description would have to come with a plausible lie as to exactly *how* I saw his face, and I've been unable to come up with one. Not one that wouldn't result in me incurring Detective Rojas' wrath again, anyway. It's a shame that I have no artistic talent of my own. I just hope I can identify him before the memory fades.

I could turn Sarah's clothes over to the cops, something I've repeatedly kicked myself for not doing the moment I found them. But all that would probably do is implicate me, and I'd end up in a locked room for God knows how long.

At home, I continue to scour the news programs and the Internet for something positive, but all I get is a big bucket o' nothing.

On my lunch break the following day, I grab one of the three tables outside the taqueria fifty yards down from the coffee shop. Austin warned me that the place—cringingly called Ay Caramba! —failed a health inspection a few years ago but has improved since. The green chili burrito I bite into is decent if a little undercooked.

I'm about to send Piper a text when her car pulls up along the curb right next to me. Her power windows lower, revealing her bemused smirk. "Thought that was you," she says.

"Join me?" I offer.

"Sure."

After parking and placing her order, she flumps down in the seat next to me with an audible grunt.

"So...how's it going?" I ask. Stupid question, I know, but there's really no good way to ask how the last couple of days have been for her.

"A little better," she says. "Things got scary for a while, but Dad's breathing on his own again."

"That's good. Is he settled into your brother's house?"

She nods, hiding her face behind her hand. "He's always been strong. Seeing him like this..."

There's nothing I can say to soothe this kind of pain, so I remain silent. If I were in her position, the last thing I'd want is people bombarding me with forced sympathy.

Piper's spirits pick up a little when a server brings out her order. Fish tacos. Wish I'd ordered those instead. After her first bite, she actually smiles. I take this as a cue to change the subject. "Did you read my texts?"

"I did," she says between chews. "I'm sorry I never answered them, but...you understand."

"Yeah."

She lowers her voice. "Did you *really* see his face?"

"Clear as day. Saw a couple of other things, too. I took as many notes as I could, but...do you think you'll have some free time tomorrow to get together? You're off, right?"

She takes another bite, then chases it down with a gulp of soda. "I am, but I don't think I can spare the time. I have two essays to write and a test to cram for. Plus, Dad asked me to bring him some of his favorite books to read, so I have to go back to Anthem. I can probably squeeze in an hour or two on Thursday, though."

"Works for me. What about Gavin?"

She makes a disgusted noise.

"That bad?"

"I told him in no uncertain terms that between Dad, school, and work, I'd call him when I could. But that, apparently, isn't good enough for him. I've let his last ten messages go to voicemail."

I give her a sympathetic pat on the arm. Looks like the end is nigh for their relationship. I can't say I'm sorry, because I'm not. She doesn't need the headache...except that it now raises the question of how she's going to pay for her dad's medical bills and therapy.

It occurs to me that I can help her out. I haven't gotten around to frittering away what's in my bank account, and God knows I don't need a whole lot.

I worry, though, that my offer might be taken the wrong way. She had to swallow a lot of pride to accept Gavin's help, and look how that turned out. There's every chance she won't welcome my assistance, and the last thing I want to do is make it awkward between us when I need her the most.

On the other hand, she's not exactly rife with options. And her dad's bills aren't going to stop coming.

"You'll pull through this, Piper," I say with more reassurance than I'm feeling. "So will your dad."

"Speaking of dads..." She fixes me with a serious look, then lowers her voice. "Have you given any more thought to the possibility that you inherited your ESP from your parents?"

"A little. The sad truth is, if...*this* was passed on to me, there's only one person I can ask about it."

She swallows hard. "Your mom."

"Yeah." I grimace. "Talk about getting crushed by two tons of irony."

"Do you know where she lives?"

"Not exactly." I stare at my half-eaten burrito, which I haven't touched since Piper drove up. "But I know someone who does."

"Okay."

Piper polishes off the rest of her lunch. The thought of coming face-to-face with Mom again has made it impossible for me to take another bite. I stand up, toss it in the trash, and smile at Piper. "Come on, then. Let's go spread some caffeinated joy."

She scowls at me, but there's a visible playfulness behind it. "Screw joy. Let 'em make their own damn lattes."

I laugh. "You're so mean."

"No. I'm sleep-deprived and cranky and ready to lob grenades at people."

"Yowch. You need a spa day, stat."

"Ohhhh, if only." She holds out her arm, and I haul her into a standing position. "Let's go."

I've gotten pretty good at making roughly ninety percent of the beverages that grace the Hill O' Beans menu board, so much so that I don't even need my full brain to crank them out. After the lunch rush ends, Austin tasks Piper with cleaning both sides of the windows, then heads to the back room to log and unpack several boxes that were delivered an hour ago. He leaves me to man the helm. There's not much going on, so while I idly run a rag over the counter, my thoughts turn once again to my parents.

Seriously...could either of them have had this bizarre ability and passed it down to me? Try as I might, I am unable to picture my superpower as having come from Mom. I spent two years watching her drink herself into a stupor and hating myself for not only not trying to stop it but because I was the root cause of it. After nearly a decade of not being good enough for her, I just couldn't bring myself to care.

And Dad...what do I really know about him? He was in the Army. He did two tours in Afghanistan. I think he had achieved the rank of captain when he was killed, which is high enough on the food chain that he didn't have to slog through mud or barbed wire or whatever it is grunts on the frontlines do.

I never cared why or how he died. What did it matter? He was gone, and my remaining parent cursed the day I was born. But now, I can only wonder if there were things about his "job" that he chose not to share with his family.

"Hello?"

I turn to see Sydney standing by the register, smiling at me. She's wearing a burnt orange cardigan that hugs her body in a way that I hope I'll get to someday. I smile back, casting a glance out the window. Piper transfers the bottle of Windex to her other hand before shooting me a smile and a thumbs-up. I note that, for the first time, Sydney's presence isn't causing me to shift into Fish-Faced Doofus mode. Somehow, Piper's approval of my pursuit of Sydney is giving me the shot of confidence I need.

"Hey there." I approach her. "How's it going?"

"Going alright." She eyes my nametag again. "Bax. That is such a cool name. Sounds like a hero from a sci-fi story."

I laugh. "Thanks. And your name sounds like...a city in Australia."

Sydney laughs, and my body goes all tingly.

My face flushing, I turn away. "The usual?" She nods, and I set to concocting a run-of-the-mill mocha chai latte. "You really love this stuff, huh? I've never seen you order anything else."

She shrugs. "What can I say? I'm picky about what I put in my body."

Down, boy.

"Besides, once you find something perfect," she continues, "why would you want anything else?"

I whip up and fasten a lid on her drink in short order, placing it on the counter in front of her. "Fair point." I tilt my head to the side. "What would you say if I told you I could make it better?"

She lifts a skeptical eyebrow. "I'd say you're a big, fat, stinking liar."

I raise my hands in surrender. "Whoa. Harsh."

Sydney hands me her debit card, which I run through the scanner. "I'm just saying, if you think you can improve on perfection, you're either super-overconfident or the best barista on the planet."

My mouth curls into a smirk. "That sounds like a challenge. Shall we make it a bet?"

She crosses her arms and surveys me. I love the curious way she's staring at me. It's like I've finally caught her attention. "You're on."

Oh, hell yeah.

"Here are my terms," she says. "If what you serve me isn't to my liking, then the drink is on you. Along with one muffin of my choosing."

"Done." I like this girl. I mean, really like her. I can't wait to get to know her. "But you have to be honest. If you love it, you can't lie and say you don't."

She takes a sip of her latte and beams at me. "I would never do that."

Confidence swells in my chest. "And if...*when* I win, you agree to go out with me. Time, place, and duration to be determined later."

She holds the cup up with one hand and points to it with the other. "You make me something better than this, I'll have your child."

My eyes triple in size, and my heart stops beating.

Her expression morphs into an adorably evil smirk. "That was a joke."

I gulp. "Yeah. I totally knew that."

"Well then." She takes another sip and slowly runs her tongue over her lips. "See you tomorrow." With that, she turns on her heels and sashays out the door.

Oh, you little tease.

Piper reenters the shop with a jingle of the bell, approaching me with raised eyebrows. "So...how'd it go?"

I feel my chest swell. "It is *so* on."

CHAPTER SIXTEEN

D espite my best efforts to distract myself with Xbox, Netflix, and two more hours of mocha chai latte wizardry, I spend the better part of Wednesday morning pondering the origins of my fantastical ability. In the end, I can only conclude that Piper was right.

I wish like hell it wasn't true. Not because finding out I could be the latest in a long line of psychometric people—psychometrists?—would shock me, but because my mother is the only person in the world who can confirm it.

According to Sheila, Mom lives in Prescott Valley, a full ninety minutes' drive away. Too far to ride on a bike. I could hire an Uber, but I have to believe there's a way to get there without involving a complete stranger. Do people still go Greyhound?

I search the Internet phone directory for Mom's address but am unable to find anyone named Amy Baxter within fifty miles of Prescott Valley. I don't know her boyfriend Dwayne's last name, so that's a dead end too.

After showering, shaving, and dressing for work, I shoot Sheila a text.

Me: I need you to get something for me.

The response comes less than a minute later.

Sheila: What is it?
Me: My mom's address.

I half-expect to be confronted with a line of outraged emojis. All I get is silence. After a minute, I wonder if she's going to answer at all. Finally, I get:

Sheila: WHY?

All caps. Subtle.

Me: Rather not say. Do u have it?

I wait thirty seconds for the reply.

Sheila: Yes.

Me: Can u text it to me?

Sheila: Have to find it first. Not in office at moment. You working today?

Me: Closing shift. Off at seven.

Sheila: I'll come by at seven, then.

Me: OK. L8R.

My Spidey-sense is tingling. Guess I'd better brace myself for another of Sheila's lectures.

Yay.

Anyone who's ever lived in Phoenix knows October weather is annoyingly unpredictable. Any given day, you could get wet and miserable, hot and muggy, cool and pleasant, or warm and gusty. Some days you get all of the above. Like today, when the clouds are zipping around without a clue where they should go.

I tell Austin about my bet with Sydney, and he gives me a wry smirk.

"I'm sure you've realized by now that people, especially coffee drinkers, are stubborn," he says. "Once they've found their 'usual,' It takes an act of God for them to try anything else. And Sydney is as stubborn as they come." He claps me on the shoulder. "But hey, I applaud your entrepreneurial spirit. If you can find something to change *that* girl's mind, let me know. I'll add it to the menu."

I do a double-take. "For reals?"

"Subject to managerial approval, of course."

"Naturally."

I spend the next hour watching Austin take inventory, tapping numbers and notes on his iPad. He informs me that he gets most of his ingredients from a restaurant wholesaler that services the western Phoenix metro area. He then adds that his contact—one of the wholesaler's higher-ups—is an old buddy from business school. Apparently, Austin introduced the guy to his wife, which earned Hill O' Beans a five percent discount. Which...wow.

Learning how to do inventory also gave me a better idea of just what I have to work with in case I decide to make beverage crafting a "thing" beyond trying to score a date with Sydney. Austin tells me if I require something that isn't available, there are any number of specialty shops nearby where he can go. He's even allotted part of his monthly budget for "optional extras," as long as they aren't too expensive or funky.

The Hill O' Beans recipe for an MCL is pretty basic, containing chai tea, cocoa powder, condensed milk, cinnamon, ground cloves, and hot water. Sydney, without fail, asks for just a pinch of black pepper to be added. I don't get crazy with my first attempt, replacing the cloves with cardamom. She's not displeased, but says the taste, while pleasant, is not better than her usual. I shrug, scoop a huge cranberry muffin into a bag, and watch her wink as she strolls out the door.

One other thing I discover is that Sydney loves volleyball. I had no idea community colleges participated in extramural sports, but they apparently do. Sydney's been a volleyball enthusiast since middle school, so she was a shoo-in when she tried out for GCC's team. I might have to catch my future girlfriend in action some time.

By seven o'clock, darkness has fallen on the strip mall and the last few customers are ushered out the door by a grinning Austin. I'm in the process of upending the chairs and placing them on top of the tables when I spy Sheila walking up. Austin, completing his count of the money in the till, smiles. He locks the register and lets her in. The two share a hug, then engage in a brief whispered conversation.

My brow furrows. I never asked Austin or Sheila exactly how they know each other, but now I can't help but wonder what their story is. It's obvious they're close, and not in a way that suggests they're a couple.

Sheila's smile disappears as they approach. Austin shoots odd glances at both of us and says, "Take all the time you need. I'll be in my office." Then he disappears through the inner door.

She stares at me, maternal concern radiating from her. "How are you doing, Bax?"

"I'm fine."

"No more headaches?"

"Nope." I gesture at the table in the middle of the dining area, replace the chairs on the floor, and we sit down. I can already feel a lecture coming, so I don't waste time with small talk. "Did you bring it?"

She nods. "Dare I ask again why you want it?"

A dozen responses rush through my head, from half-truths to utter lies, and I discard them all. Instead, I opt for deflecting the question. "She's my mom. Do I need another reason?"

A stony glare accompanies her reply. "Considering this is the woman who devalued and belittled you for nearly half of your life, yes. Unless, of course, you're planning on doing something violent. That's not what you have in mind, is it?"

I match her frown. "No. Jesus, Sheila! I just want to talk to her, that's all."

She pulls a folded piece of paper from her jacket pocket. "You could call her."

I reach for the paper, but she doesn't hand it over. "She'd just hang up."

"Yes, she would, which would be preferable to driving a hundred miles only to have the door slammed in your face."

I consider this for a moment. She's right, of course. But I need answers, and the questions I have aren't the kind you ask over the phone. "I'll take that risk," I say, holding my hand out.

And she *still* doesn't give it to me. "Please, Bax. If my opinion means anything to you, listen to it now. I've seen dozens of kids confront abusive parents, before they're ready and against my advice. They think it'll give them closure, but all it does is open every wound they have. And that...*woman*," she practically spits the word out, "cares about nothing but her booze."

"It's been a year since I've seen her. Maybe she's changed." I hear myself saying it and not believing a word of it. That can't be good.

"No. She hasn't."

My brow scrunches. "How would you know? You've never met her."

"The hell I haven't. The day before your court hearing, I drove up and saw her."

"You did?"

"Yeah. It was ten o'clock in the morning, and she was already shit-faced. I begged her, just *once*, to be a mother to you. You know what she did? She threw a bottle at my head."

My jaw drops.

"She's a selfish, self-absorbed beast of a woman." Sheila sweeps her arm across the room. "You're making great strides toward rebuilding your life. You're eighteen, and you don't need her approval."

"I never said I wanted her approval," I retort, my volume rising. "I'm not going up there to make nice." I hold out my palm again.

Tense seconds pass. Her shoulders slump, and she slaps the paper into my hand. "Then why?"

I shove the address into my pocket. "That's *my* business."

As if I'd pressed a button, Sheila rises, looming over me. "No.

You don't get to brush me off like that. I am the *only* person who's looked out for you for the last two years. *Tell...me...why*."

Her statement sends waves of guilt through me, and just for a moment, I consider revealing my secret to Sheila. Again, I hesitate. But why? Why did I feel comfortable confiding in Piper, a girl I've known only a couple of weeks, and not the woman who's been more of a mother to me than my own mom ever was?

And why do I still have this nagging suspicion Sheila knows more than she's letting on?

"I have questions only she can answer, okay?" I snap.

"About your father?"

The scrape of my chair on the tile floor rends the air as I slide backwards, a thousand snakes writhing in my gut. I rise shakily to my feet, steadying myself against another table. "How'd you know that?"

She doesn't even blink. "That's not important."

My mind accelerates to Ludicrous Speed. Ever since Sheila became my case worker, I've wondered why she insists on being so involved in my life, and my rehabilitation. At first, I figured it was because she was good at her job and treated all her kids the same. But she's put way more time into me than is probably normal.

And suddenly, it all clicks into place. "You knew him. You knew my dad."

Her face becomes a stoic mask.

I wait for her to deny my accusation. She doesn't.

A sharp pain crashes through my head, making me dizzy. "You lied to me. You've been lying this whole time." I slump back in my chair, unable to look at her anymore.

"I never lied to you, Bax." Her voice trembles. "I just didn't see the need to—"

Anger bursts from me like an erupting geyser. "Who are you, Sheila? What were you to him? Old girlfriend? Mistress?" I stand, fists clenched. "Was he doing you on the side, is that it?"

Sheila takes a half-step back, her eyes ablaze. "It wasn't like that. Your father was a good man. The best man I've ever—"

"I don't give a fuck!" I take a menacing step forward, forcing her back even though there's still a table between us. "This...*condition* that I have. You know what it is, don't you?"

She nods.

"I got it from him, didn't I?"

Another nod.

My legs wobble, and I grip the table to keep from collapsing. "All this time, you knew this was coming, and you didn't say shit."

"I didn't know for certain," she quavers. "I hoped it wouldn't affect you. All I wanted was to make sure you were okay. That's all I've ever wanted."

Tears prick at my eyes as the weight of her betrayal hits me like a semi. Almost two years, we've known each other. She knew this would happen to me, or at least suspected. The headaches, the blackouts, the soul-crushing darkness of Sarah's final days...I had no warning. None at all. Maybe Sheila couldn't have stopped my *gift* from blossoming like a mushroom cloud, but even the tiniest word of caution might have helped me deal with it. But no. She kept it all to herself.

I'm so angry I want to pick up this table and throw it through the window. Thankfully, the little voice in my head telling me not to commit yet another felony is loud enough that I hear it.

I face Sheila, rage pulsing through my veins. "Get out."

"Bax—"

I pound my fists on the table. "Didn't hear me?" Sobs crack my voice. "Piss off, and never call me again!"

Rapid breaths escaping her throat, she backs toward the door, her gaze never leaving mine. Finally, she turns away. She fumbles with the lock, taking several awkward seconds to get it open. Then she vanishes into the night. I follow her silhouette out to the parking lot and watch as, seconds later, the Spark vanishes from sight.

I bury my face in my hands, forcing the tears back.

Screw her. Screw people. Screw this whole goddamn world.

The lock clicks back into place, and I look up to see Austin staring at me. His expression is one of both concern and repressed anger.

"That was uncalled for," he says in his "gentle boss" voice.

I want to stand, but the strength has left my body. "Are we gonna have a problem now?"

He shakes his head. "No. I'm just saying you didn't need to do that to her."

Frustration continues to simmer in my gut. Austin can probably pound my face into mulch, but I'm so numb, I doubt I'd even feel it. "I'm not in the mood for a lecture, okay? So if you're gonna fire me, just do it. I don't care."

His jaw tightens, and his arm muscles flex. "I get that you're pissed, Bax, but don't take whatever's going on between you and Sheila out on me."

"Why not? You two are friends, which means you're going to take her side anyway."

He closes the distance, then sits in the chair across from me. "She's not just my friend, she's my aunt."

My eyes widen at this revelation, and I throw up my hands. "Even more reason you'd take her side."

"Don't jump to conclusions. I love her dearly, but that doesn't mean I agreed with her decision to keep you in the dark."

What the actual...? "She told you too? Does everyone know my life's story?"

"No. She only told me. And not very much." I rise to my feet, but Austin gestures for me to remain seated. "Please, stay," he says.

"Why? So you can tell me what a dick I'm being?"

"So you can get answers. I think it's time you finally got some."

Whether it's from exhaustion or morbid curiosity, I slump back in my chair. More words form in my throat, but I can't get them out.

"First," Austin says, "let me state for the record that I agree with you. She shouldn't have kept this secret."

"Whatever."

He points out the window, at the parking space previously occupied by Sheila's Spark. "That woman has the biggest heart of anyone I've ever met. And she's suffered more tragedy than you could possibly know."

I click my tongue. "The reason I don't know is because she never talks about herself. And believe me, I've asked."

A thin smile creeps over his face. "But why, though? Most kids in your situation are so wrapped up in their own problems they don't give two shits about other people's. Why do you?" He pauses dramatically, then continues. "It's because you care too."

He's got me there. Damn him. "But she lied to me, like adults always do. They think they're protecting us from what a sucky world this is, but all they do is make it worse." I avert my gaze. "You don't know what it's like to have someone who's supposed to care about you betray you like that."

He folds his arms across his broad chest. "As a matter of fact, I do. So does she."

I quirk an eyebrow. "Really?"

Austin pushes a hand through his hair. "When Sheila was your age, believe it or not, she was a lot like you. A real troublemaker."

What the huh?

He's got to be kidding. Sheila, with her frumpy clothes and her tiny car and her limp hairdo, a troublemaker? "No way."

Austin nods. "She grew up in an ultra-conservative, traditional household. Her father was all about propriety. Discipline. The illusion of perfection. Unlike her big brother—my father—she never cared much for following the rules. All through high school, her relationship with her folks got more and more strained. The day she graduated, she wanted nothing more to do with them, nor they her.

"She had it all figured out, you see. She'd hooked up with this rich asshole, and together they lived the high life...wild parties, fast cars, booze, drugs—"

"*Sheila?*" I gasp.

"Yup. Two years after she married the guy—Greg, what a prizewinner he was—she found out she was pregnant."

I gasp again. "Sheila has a kid?"

"A son. Anthony." His brow crinkles. "For whatever reason, the news that she was going to be a mother knocked some sense into her. By the time Anthony was born, she'd gotten herself clean. Greg, the bastard, had already moved on to his next conquest."

"Did she leave him?" I ask, noting how my outrage seems to have dissipated.

"To go where? She had no job, no money, and only a high-school education. Her parents had disowned her. The only person who supported her at all was my father, and that was more out of a sense of obligation than brotherly love. He gave her a place to stay, but that was the extent of his generosity."

Austin gives a weak smile. "I loved having her around. She was fun...not like my father, who married a 'traditional' girl just like Grandpa did. Sometimes she would take Anthony and me to the park, or out for ice cream. She loved kids so much.

"Anyway, after a few years of trying to salvage her marriage, she finally filed for divorce. Greg didn't give a damn about her or Anthony, but he wouldn't just let them both go—his ego wouldn't allow it. His lawyer, whose car cost more than this place earns in a year, eviscerated her in open court. All she got was visitation rights, two weekends a month."

"That blows," I interject.

"Five years later, she had a job, her own apartment, and was earning a degree in social work. She was determined to prove to a judge that she could provide a better home than her deadbeat ex. Unfortunately, she never got the chance."

I blanch.

He wipes his eyes with the back of his hand. "As I said, Greg wanted nothing to do with Anthony. Whenever he had the boy, Greg would hand him over to servants or nannies or whatever.

One night, he threw a party for his girlfriend's birthday that would've made the ancient Romans proud. So while he was busy doing shots off her naked tits in the jacuzzi, Anthony snuck into their bedroom, where he...found Greg's private coke stash."

A boulder drops into my stomach. "He OD'd?"

Austin's expression turns rock-hard. "Yup. Twelve years old and gone."

I lower my gaze to the table. "Holy shit."

"Yeah."

"Greg didn't get away with it, did he?"

"No. First, he claimed Anthony got the drugs at school. When *that* didn't work, he tried to lay all the blame on the nanny. The jury didn't buy a word of it." Austin's frown deepens. "All through the trial, he never once showed any remorse over his kid's death, so the judge gave him the max. Sentenced the fucker to fifty years. I hope he rots in hell."

"And...Sheila?"

"Anthony's death totally destroyed her. She begged her parents to take her back, and you know what her father said? 'People always get what's coming to them.' Then he slammed the door in her face. Her own brother, who had become just like his old man, also turned his back on her."

Austin's face falls. "She considered ending it all. Who could blame her?"

"What stopped her?"

"She found a support group for people who had lost loved ones. It didn't seem to help at first, but then she met a man who changed her life. His name was Jeremy Baxter."

I bolt upright in my chair. "My dad?"

He nods. "He had just gotten back from his first tour in Afghanistan. He went to the group with an army buddy whose daughter had just died of leukemia. I'm not sure how he and Sheila became friends, but that's how it started."

Austin leans forward, resting his arms on the table. "Before you ask...no, they were never romantically involved. Despite the strain his absence put on his marriage, he was devoted to his wife. And to his boys."

I turn my head to stare out the window. "Did my mom know about her?"

"I have no idea. All I know is, because of Jeremy and the support group, she found her footing again. She got her bachelor's degree, and her career as a social worker began. She's devoted every moment since to helping troubled teens. She calls it her 'penance,' so more kids don't end up like Anthony." He flashes a sardonic grin. "Imagine her surprise when *your* file crossed her desk."

I lean back, staring up at the row of mini-chandeliers dangling from the ceiling. This explains a lot. Actually, it explains everything. Almost. "Why didn't she tell me?" I mutter.

"She would have. Eventually. I can only ask you to believe that. I've been listening to her gush about you since you two first met. She goes on and on about what a great kid you are and how much she wants to help turn you around. She'd give her soul to see that happen."

Well, don't I feel like an asshole.

"And as for her connection to your dad...that's one monster of a secret to just drop on a kid. She wanted to make sure you were in the right headspace first." Austin shifts in his chair. "Don't be too hard on her. She loved your father, and by extension, she loves you too. You're just like him, or so she says."

I quirk an eyebrow at this. "My dad was a soldier. A hero. I'm nothing like him."

A paternal look comes over his face. "You're intelligent, compassionate, and are willing to learn new things. Even I see that." He grins. "You're also a total smartass. It's a trait I value, and one you apparently inherited from your old man."

Huh.

I lower my eyes to meet his. "Did she tell you about my brother?"

"Only that he died in an accident. And that your mother blamed you for it."

And rightly so. "Did she tell you anything else about my dad? About me?"

He shakes his head. "Nope. That's pretty much it."

A wave of fatigue crashes over me. I feel like I could sleep for days. "So what do I do now?"

"Same as you've been doing," he replies with a warm smile. "Stay out of trouble. Make friends. Make a good living. Live a happy, normal life."

Normal? Yeah, no. That train left the station weeks ago.

Rather than rebut his answer, I change the subject. "You told Detective Rojas you were headed down a 'dark path' when you were a kid."

"I was."

"Were you in trouble with the law?"

He sighs. "Not with the law, but I struggled with depression. A lot."

"How come?"

"I told you, my parents, like my grandparents, are total tight-asses. When I came out to them my junior year of high school... well, let's just say it didn't go like I'd hoped."

My eyebrows raise. "You're *gay*?"

"I am. And it was Sheila who taught me to be strong. How to deal with the rejection and the bullying and the assholes who can't resist pointing out how unmanly it is for a man to love other men." His mouth flattens into a straight line. "It's because of her, and a select group of friends—like Natalie—who couldn't care less who I date, that I'm the person I am today."

"Good for you, Austin," I say sincerely.

"So...do you still plan to go see your mom?"

All I can do is shrug. "I don't know. I have a lot to process right now."

"Will you apologize to Sheila?"

"Different question, same answer."

"Fair enough."

We both stand and place the chairs on the table. I clock out, retrieve my jacket, and he unlocks the front door for me. "You okay getting home?"

"Yeah. Never got around to sweeping the floors, though."

"I'll take care of it."

"Thanks, Boss."

"No problem. See you tomorrow." He pulls the door open.

I pause, then face him. "You're really gay?"

"You sound surprised."

"I am, a little." I scratch the back of my neck. "I haven't known many gay people, and the few I've met are like...well, Nico."

Austin rolls his eyes. "Oh. *That* guy."

"I think he has a crush on you," I tease.

"I'm sure he does." He places a hand on my shoulder. "Let me tell you something about Mr. Nico Suave...he's great with hair. With relationships? Not so much. He's a total player. And besides, I've been involved with someone for almost three years now."

For the first time all night, I crack a grin. "Is there a place around here where I can get my gaydar fixed?"

He gives me a gentle shove out the door. "Get out of here."

CHAPTER SEVENTEEN

I consider calling in sick on Saturday—not because I'm under the weather, but because last night drained my reserves so much, I doubt I could muster up the energy to make lattes or smile at customers. I'm so distracted, I might put drain cleaner in someone's macchiato. Which would suck for all parties concerned.

I'm not even in the mood to kick the ball around with the Arbor Vista gang. After two minutes of lurching like a zombie while the crowd of kids chases the soccer ball all over the lawn, I decide to sit on my stoop and stare vacuously into space. I have no doubt I resemble the juvenile delinquent senior citizens talk about on bingo nights.

Trina pulls Cheyanne and Crescent aside. The trio engages in a whispered conversation, peppered with occasional glances in my direction. They then disappear into Cheyanne's house, right across the lawn from my unit. A few minutes later, they reappear and rush over to me. They're each carrying an ice cream cone, except Trina who has two.

With a flourish, Trina holds out a flat-bottomed cone topped by a humongous scoop of mint chocolate chip ice cream.

I stare at it. "What's this for?"

"You were looking a little sad," Crescent says.

"So we decided to cheer you up," Cheyanne adds.

"'Cause it's impossible to be sad while eating ice cream," Trina finishes.

I take the cone, and I'm unable to stop the smile spreading across my face. "You guys rock, you know that?"

"So true," Cheyanne says with a grin.

With that, the trio sit down on the sidewalk in front of me. I take a tentative lick, and man, it's exactly what I need right now. Moments later, we've all lapsed into silence, enjoying our sweet treats.

If I could freeze this moment in time, I would. For a few blissful minutes, the drama with Sheila and the DP Killer and the psychometric crap melt away like mint chocolate chip ice cream in my mouth. Right now, I'm not a guy facing potentially life-altering decisions. I'm just one of the girls.

"Why did the teddy bear say no to ice cream?" Trina says, breaking the silence.

The question is directed at me. Judging by the coy grins on Cheyanne's and Crescent's faces, they already know the answer.

"I give up," I play along. "Why?"

"Because it was stuffed."

I facepalm. "Boo. That's *so* bad."

"How much does it cost for a pirate to get his ears pierced?" Crescent asks.

Apparently, the "silly joke" portion of our program has begun. "How much?" I ask.

"A buck an ear."

The girls try to hold back their giggles but fail. A guffaw escapes my throat as well. "Ba dum bum. That one was actually pretty clever."

Cheyanne swallows the last bite of her cone. "My turn! What do you call a dog magician?"

I notch an eyebrow in an attempt to look thoughtful. "No idea."

"A labracadabrador."

"Aargh!" I raise my voice to a comical, high-pitched squeak. "Somebody save me! I'm being joked to death!"

Trina laughs, then punches my arm. "Your turn."

"My turn?"

"Yeah," Crescent says. "We all told one, you have to tell one too."

I rack my brain, searching for a joke appropriate for young girls. It takes a while since most of the gags told at Asterly involved female body parts or the handling of said body parts.

Come on, Bax, you knew a million jokes when you were a kid. You must remember...ah.

"Got one," I announce. "What dinosaur had the best vocabulary?"

The trio exchange a glance, then shrug.

My face morphs into a *duh* expression. "The thesaurus!"

Their little eyes widen. Two seconds later, they erupt in laughter.

"That's the worst one I've ever heard," Trina says, clutching her sides.

"You laughed," I point out.

"Yeah, you totally did, Tri," Cheyanne says.

I clap the crumbs from my hand and stand up. "I have to go to work now. Thanks again for the ice cream."

Trina grins at me. "You're welcome. So...you're not sad anymore?"

Huh. I'm not. What do you know.

I shake my head. "Nope. Operation Cheer Bax Up was a complete success."

"Cool. Our work is done." Trina holds her fist out, and I bump it. I do the same to Cheyanne and Crescent. Then, with friendly waves, they vanish through Trina's doorway.

My God, those three. I wish I could bottle their carefree, little-girl joy. I'd call it Liquid Giggles and sell it online. I'd make millions.

As seems to be the norm for Thursdays, customers come through in spurts, practically in time with the rays of sunshine that poke through the thick clouds. Looks like it might rain again, which would dampen my already tenuous good mood. Austin is understanding enough not to mention Sheila or last night's blow-up. I'm sure she had her reasons for not letting me in on her connection to my dad, and maybe someday she'll let me know what those reasons are. But not now. My emotions are still too raw.

Sierra surprises me when she reaches into the bottom shelf of the display case and produces a plate filled with yummy-looking pancaky objects dusted in powdered sugar.

"What are these?" I ask, taking a whiff of the cinnamony aroma.

Piper, having finished her floor-sweeping duties, gasps in wide-eyed pleasure at the sight of Sierra's bounty. "You brought hotteoks?"

Sierra's face flushes, and I swear, the purple highlights in her hair start glowing. "Sure did."

"Hottie-what?" I ask.

"Hotteoks. They're a popular street food in Korea. My parents loved them growing up, so I was taught how to make them as a kid." With a beaming smile, she passes them out to me, Piper, Austin, and several customers enticed by the smell.

I cram one into my mouth, and jokingly profess my undying love for Sierra, earning me a punch in the arm. I swear, I've eaten better in the last few weeks than I have my entire life.

Piper wolfs down her hotteok like she hasn't eaten in weeks. A satisfied moan escapes her lips, and I swear I hear her eyes roll back into her head. She chews quickly, swallows, and proceeds to devour a second one with the same gusto. "Sierra, I totally love you."

Sierra laughs. "Yeah, I get that a lot." She snags a napkin from the counter and holds it out to Piper.

"I'm good, thanks."

"I'd take it." I fight back a chortle. "Unless you plan on wearing that powdered sugar for the rest of the day."

Piper's eyes widen as her fingers fly up to her cheeks and come away with a white smear. Mumbling under her breath, she takes the napkin and wipes her face clean. She then grabs a rag, heads for a table in the back whose occupants just left, and begins clearing it away. I help her.

"You still up for our research session after work?" I ask.

"Yeah. You closing today?"

"No, I'm only here till five. You can head right over when you're done here."

"Sounds like a..." She trails off, staring past me. Her jaw visibly tightens. "Oh, shit."

I turn to see Gavin stride nonchalantly in like he's just popping in for his usual caffeine injection. Instead, he walks straight past the counter and approaches us. Piper doesn't move to greet him. Throwing caution to the wind, I gallantly interpose myself between her and Gavin.

This is not the first time I've stood up to someone larger and more intimidating than myself. It happened quite often at Asterly, which was home to at least three thugs or bangers on any given day. Carl may have been a jerk, but he knew how to keep order. Asterly was two rungs above a crack house, but there were far, *far* worse places kids could be sent, as those who violated his zero-violence policy found out. Whenever someone got in my face, all I had to do was look him in the eye and dare him to take a swing for him to back down.

Here's hoping that strategy works again.

"You need to leave, dude," I say coolly. "Right now."

As before, he spares me only the slightest glance, though he does stop walking. He steps to the side, shooting an icy glare at Piper. "Baby, come on. I just want to talk."

Before she can answer, I move in front of him, blocking his

view. This gets his attention. He raises his head, scowling at me like I'm a mosquito he can swat away. Which I kinda am.

"I *said*, you need to leave," I repeat.

He bares his perfect teeth at me. "You need to get out of my way."

"Make me."

Just past Gavin, all of the current Hill O' Beans customers have stopped what they were doing and are watching us. One lady chooses to exercise caution by grabbing her coat and purse and ushering her two preteen children out the door.

Rather than raise his fist or try to bull past me, he says, "Really, Piper? This is how you want to play it? Hiding behind this asshole?"

I feel red creep up my neck. Stay cool, Bax. You're on the side of righteousness this time. Don't make the first move. He's a pretty boy who's not going to stain his name with an assault charge.

"I'm the asshole?" I retort. "You're the one who can't seem to take a hint."

He meets my gaze again. "You have two seconds to move, jagoff, before I start breaking body parts."

"Leave him alone." Piper stands at my shoulder. "I told you before, Gavin, I don't want to talk to you. I don't want to hear from you. I'm going through a ton of shit right now, and all your drama is doing is *making it worse*." She says the last three words through gritted teeth.

"Come on, baby, you know how much I love—"

"Stop calling me that! I'm not your baby!" A muffled sob pushes past her lips, her breath devolving into shallow rasps. "You claim to love me, but you're making me miserable. I can't take any more of your *love*."

Gavin makes a face like he's been sucker punched. His response is just above a whisper. "You feel that way now. But you need me. You know you do. No one can be there for you like I can."

I look sidelong at Piper. Fear and indecision play over her face.

Time seems to stretch out. The air thickens. I place a comforting hand on her back and give her a silent nod. In a soft, squeaky whisper, she tells her former friend, "Go, Gavin. Don't call me again."

His brow knits into a scary frown. "Think about this, Piper. You're not just hurting yourself by cutting me out of your life."

I don't know what's worse—that this arrogant prick is using her father's debilitating condition to blackmail Piper, or that he thinks doing so is for her benefit.

"Sounds like she's thought about it plenty, Gavin," says Austin.

Gavin turns to see the boss-man's imposing figure standing several yards away. His expression is even stonier than the one he gave me last night after I lost my shit with Sheila, which I wouldn't have thought possible. He proffers the cell phone in his hand like it's a weapon.

"Just so you know, I'm on a first-name basis with one of Phoenix's finest." Austin puts the phone to his ear to drive home the point. "And she's about two minutes away. So you can either leave in your own car, *right now*, or you can leave in the back of hers. Choose. *Quickly.*"

He flashes his shit-eating grin at Austin. "We're just talking here, man. No law against that."

Austin's scowl turns deadly. "You are in *my* place of business. And I clearly heard you threaten one of my employees with bodily harm. So I'm going to ask you—for the *very* last time—to leave."

Gavin has a stare-down with Austin for a few moments, then his shoulders slump. He looks over his shoulder at Piper and gives a condescending headshake. "Fine. Have a nice life."

With a shrug, Gavin saunters past Austin and Sierra without glancing at either. Sierra's expression is ferocious, like she's prepared to open a can of whoop-ass on him. The jingle of the bell above the door signals his departure, and the tension evaporates from the room.

Austin taps his phone and pockets it before turning to the remaining customers. "I apologize for the disturbance, folks. I'd be more than happy to treat you all to free refills if you so desire."

This offer is met with smiles and nods.

"Sierra, will you...?"

"You got it, Boss." She nips behind the counter as the customers form a line to collect their freebies.

Piper sags against me like all the air has gone from her body. I wrap an arm around her shoulder, keeping her upright. She gazes into my eyes. The gracious smile she gives me makes my chest swell with pride.

"You okay?" I ask.

"I think so," Piper replies. "Just glad the melodrama is finally over."

"Thanks for the backup, Boss."

"No problem," Austin says.

I quirk an eyebrow at him. "Did you seriously just hang up on Detective Rojas?"

He pulls out his phone, waggling it at me. "What, this? I was calling my voicemail."

I stifle a laugh.

"I figured the last thing a kid like that would want was a run-in with the law. Sounded convincing, though, didn't it?"

Piper laughs, engaging Austin in a light embrace. "You rock, Mr. Wagner."

Hugging your boss? I guess I can get behind that. We are a 'family' here at Hill O' Beans, after all.

Austin steps back, then faces me. "Did I hear you say you two have something planned after work?"

"Yeah. It's kind of a...study session."

For some reason, Austin doesn't call me on the fact that I'm not actually in school. Instead, he checks his watch. "Tell you what, Bax...I think Sierra and I can handle it from here, so after you throw the garbage, you and Piper can take off. I'll give you both credit for the full shift."

My eyes widen. I wonder for a second if he's making this generous offer as a way to get me to patch things up with Sheila but dismiss the notion. I risked life and limb standing up to Gavin, so I don't even think about turning Austin down. "You got it."

"Boss of the Year," Piper adds.

Austin winks, then joins Sierra behind the counter.

I head for the nearest receptacle and haul out the extra-large trash bag. "Be right back."

"Don't touch anything strange," Piper teases. "I'm not picking your ass up again."

"Quiet, you."

CHAPTER EIGHTEEN

The short trip from Hill O' Beans to my place is silent and tense. The classless douchebag part of me—every guy has one—wonders if I should ask Piper out, now that she's available and all, especially if this thing with Sydney doesn't pan out. Thankfully, I keep my toolish side submerged.

I flip on a series of lights upon entering, shrug off my jacket, and make a beeline for the kitchen. "I'm fixing myself an MCL," I tell her. "You want one too?"

"An MCL?" she asks, brows furrowed. "Haven't you had enough of the smell of coffee for one day?"

I switch on the coffee maker and shoot her a wry grin. "In the interest of full disclosure, this is more than just a friendly gesture on my part. I kind of need your help."

"Oh?"

"I made a bet with Sydney. She agreed to go out with me if I improve on Hill O' Beans' recipe."

Her stifled chuckle comes out as a snort. "Good luck. That girl's as stubborn as my Nana."

"That's where you come in. You've got a lot more experience in this field." I retrieve a handful of clean mugs from the cupboard. "Plus, you've known Sydney much longer than I have."

An emotion I can't pinpoint flashes through her eyes, and her mouth flattens into a straight line. "'Known' is a loose description. I'm her barista, not her BFF. She's friendly and all, but we've never had a conversation longer than thirty seconds." She approaches as I retrieve various ingredients from my shelf. "Did you really buy all this just to win a silly bet?"

"No." I draw out the word.

She folds her arms across her chest.

"Okay, sort of. But it's more than that. I want to create something...unique. Something no one's done before."

Her face relaxes. "I respect that. And I suppose if a date with a hot volleyball player is what it takes to inspire creativity, then I respect that too."

"Well, it wasn't just her who inspired me. Gina, the lady who lives next door, is a chef at Harrigan's. She's been using me as a guinea pig to try out her last couple of inventions." I pat my stomach. "And she's really good at her job."

Piper nods. "Okay then. Show me what you got."

To make this a truly blind taste test, I send her to the couch before I set to work. I decide to take advantage of her presence by creating three possible bet-winners at once. Within minutes, the pleasant aromas of chocolate and chai fill my kitchen.

"Smells good," she says. "Do you mind if I look through your notes?"

Right. I forgot I left my notebook on the coffee table. "Go ahead. If you can read my chicken-scratch, that is."

"I'll manage. You should see my dad's handwriting. It's like reading Sanskrit."

I pause in my stirring. "San-what?"

"Just make with the damn lattes."

Wow, someone's on edge. I would've thought kicking Gavin to the curb would ease some of the tension, but I guess she's already moved past that and onto worrying about her family's financial woes. I can only imagine what the "drastic choices" she and her family will have to make are. They may have to sublease their house, maybe even sell it.

With a sigh, I gather up the three mugs, set them on my tiny dining table, and have a seat. "Here you go."

She does a quick visual inspection of the mugs' contents before sitting down opposite me. "Sheesh, you don't do anything halfway, do you?"

I shrug. "That, and I don't like to lose."

She picks up the first one, taking a hearty whiff. "Smells good. What'd you do?"

"Instead of black pepper, I added a spoonful of caramel syrup and a dash of sea salt."

She blows on it and takes a cautious sip. Her eyebrows raise, then lower. "It's good, but way too sweet. With the cocoa powder, it's already got a fair amount of sugar in it, so you don't want to make it too overpowering."

"All right." I make a mental note to put it in the "adjust further" pile. "On to number two."

The sour face she makes after her next sip is all I need to see.

"Too spicy?" I ask.

Her lips curl into a frown. "That's an understatement. What'd you put in this?"

"Cayenne pepper. I read online that they add it to chocolate in Mexico. Thought I'd give it a go."

"Ugh, no." She grabs a napkin from the side of the table and wipes her mouth. "Austin tried making a version of a dirty latte this past summer. Didn't work. It's really hard to get the balance right."

"Hrm." I grimace, then push the last mug toward her. "Third time's the charm."

She wraps her hands around the mug. "Only a teenage guy tries this hard to score a date."

"I told you, it's not just—"

"Yeah, yeah," she says with pronounced flippancy.

Do I detect a note of jealousy, or is that my imagination?

What is not my imagination is the smile that washes across her face after taking a sip from my final attempt. I wait for her to comment. She doesn't. Instead, she downs a second, much heartier gulp. By the time the mug hits the table again, her eyes are closed, and her mouth is open with an audible *aah*.

I lean forward in anticipation. "So?"

She drains the mug and faces me. "It's heavenly. What am I tasting?"

"You'll laugh."

"I won't."

"Promise?"

"I promise I'll punch you if you don't tell me."

I hold my hands up in surrender. "Well, as good as the cocoa powder Hill O' Beans uses is, it's a little too...refined for me. So I decided to replace it with something more ordinary."

"Which is...?"

"Nesquik."

Her eyes widen. "You're kidding."

"Nope."

A chuckle bursts out, but she reins it in before it blossoms into a belly laugh. "Nesquik? Seriously?" Her gaze flicks from me to the empty mug and back. "How on earth did you come up with that idea?"

I lean back with a smug smile. "I drank about two gazillion glasses of chocolate milk as a kid. It's probably my blood type by now."

Her smile still hasn't diminished. "If this doesn't get you a date with Sydney, nothing will."

"And you're...okay with that?"

She swigs the last few drops, then dabs her mouth with the napkin. "You're young, hot, and single. Beyond that, it's not my place to offer dating advice."

Piper thinks I'm hot? Hmmm...

I shake my head. After a year of state-forced celibacy, I should have expected this. My hormones must be slamming around my body like a pissed-off gorilla in a cage. I need to find a release before my brain explodes.

Like a hobby that doesn't involve chasing serial killers.

"So anyway." I switch on a couple more lights, then we sit on opposite sides of the sofa.

"Yes," she says, scanning the opened notebook on my coffee table. "I've gone over some of your notes, but just so I know I'm getting the whole picture, maybe you'd better start at the beginning." She picks up a pen and the notebook, flips to an empty page, and looks expectantly at me.

I stare for a few seconds at the TV on the other side of the room, gathering my thoughts. It's off, but I swear I can see Sarah's face staring out at me from the screen, along with Mia's and Jordan's. Two more deep exhales, and I lay out the entire vision, which I'd forced myself to endure a dozen times. I can't stop the shudder that dances up my spine when I relate Sarah's final moments.

"He sucked her into his sick little fantasy," I whisper, still staring vacantly at the television. "When she wouldn't play along anymore, he just got rid of her. Like her life meant nothing."

Piper's hand on my shoulder calms my racing thoughts, as does the determination in her eyes. "We're going to get him, Bax."

I stand and move to the kitchen. "I need some of that chai tea."

By the time I return, having drained half the mug of tea I hastily prepared, I feel strangely... cleansed. As morbid as this experience is, it feels good to have someone willing to share my burden.

"Okay." Piper taps her pencil on the armrest. "Before we really get into this, let's review what we know about the DP Killer. He kidnaps preteen girls right off the street, keeps them prisoner, and then kills them."

"That about covers it," I say glumly. "I take it you've been reading up on him?"

"As much as I can. It's true most serial killers and sexual

predators have a 'type,' and the DPK is no different. The three girls were between nine and eleven years old, with tan skin, brown hair, and wearing an article of clothing featuring a Disney princess."

"But he's not kidnapping them for…" I feel my stomach turn, "…sexual reasons."

"His one redeeming quality," she snorts. "Plus, all three girls turned up wearing a *Little Mermaid* T-shirt that he obviously dressed them in."

"And now we know why."

"Yes, but we'll talk about that in a minute. From what the news reports have said, he's left no evidence that might lead the cops to figure out who he is…no DNA, footprints, et cetera. He's also been lucky enough to not be caught on video. There wasn't one single eyewitness to the kidnappings or to the dumpings." She leans forward. "We need to think like cops."

Detective Rojas' vicious scowl imprints itself in my mind's eye. "Why would we do that? Cops are idiots. It's no wonder they're all choking on this guy's dust."

Piper glares at me like she's about to leap to the PPD's defense but lets my comment slide. "They have access to sophisticated lab equipment, national databases, and forensic resources."

"That won't stop the DPK from killing again."

"No, it won't." She puts the notebook down, rises, and starts pacing around the room. "The first thing the cops probably did was make a list of everyone whose M.O. fits the DPK killings. Mia and Jordan were killed months ago, and yet no arrests were made. We can probably assume he's not in the system."

"That makes sense."

She turns to me, her forefinger pressed to the skin beneath her nose. "But thanks to you—and Sarah, of course—we know things about him the cops don't. That's where we need to concentrate our efforts."

I nod in admiration. "Betcha never thought all those Agatha Christie novels would come in handy like this."

"True, that." She sits again, grabs my mug, and drains the remnants. "Okay. Let's start with the van. I think it's safe to say the one from your vision is the same one you saw in the alley, am I right?"

I consider this. "I guess so. I mean, I saw it from the front while Sarah saw it from behind, but it has to be the same van. Unless he has a whole fleet of them."

"Let's hope not." She turns to the page in the notebook where she made some of her own notes. "I don't suppose Sarah saw the license plate?"

"I thought of that. Unfortunately, if there's a way for me to hit the pause button on a vision, I haven't learned it yet. I could only see what Sarah saw, and unless she was looking directly at something, I couldn't see it clearly. And she never looked at the license plate."

"Course not. That would've been too easy." Piper sighs, then pulls my laptop toward her. She boots it up and opens a browser window. "This object Sarah saw in the back of the van. You described it as," she scans the notebook, "'three metal rods fastened together at one end.'"

"Right. What do you think it could be?"

In the Google search engine, she types the word "tripod." This brings up a slew of images of three-legged stands, many of which have cameras attached to the tops. "Was it something like this?" she asks.

I turn the laptop toward me and click on one image, enlarging the picture. "Yeah. You think our guy could be a photographer?"

"It's possible. Did Sarah see any other camera equipment?"

"Afraid not. The duffle bag looked pretty full, but this was the only thing I could make out."

She scribbles in the notebook. "If he's a freelance photographer, he probably takes pictures all over town, maybe all over the state. That explains why his victims were taken from such a wide area."

Yes, it does, but something doesn't quite add up. It takes a full minute of brainstorming before I realize what it is. "There's got to be more to it than that. He finds these girls, somehow. He discovers where they live, where they go to school. He knows exactly when and where to grab them—when they're alone and no one's watching. You can't get all that information in one day. He had to have stalked them before making his move."

She sags into the couch. "That may be the most disturbing aspect of all this. In this day and age, when everyone is suspicious and paranoid and hypervigilant, how could a creep like the DPK follow a little girl around for days without being noticed?"

I scrub my hand over my face. "Because he doesn't look like a creep. I'm telling you, the guy is completely nondescript. If you saw his face in a crowd, you'd forget it a second later. He counts on that. He's really good at making people ignore him."

"How ironic. Everyone's looking for him, but no one sees him."

"I've seen him." The steel in my voice surprises me.

"I know, Bax. But we need a name to go with that face."

"Not to mention an address. Assuming he even has one, out in the middle of nowhere."

Her brow scrunches. "You really saw *nothing* but desert through his window?"

"Nope, nada. The only thing between his house and the wide-open desert were a couple of fences."

"What about grass? Did he have a lawn?"

I think for a moment. "A little bit, I guess. What are you getting at?"

She edges up to me, so close that I can see a gleam in her eyes. "I told you my brothers work construction, right?"

I nod.

"My oldest brother, Joe, has done a lot of work for a housing developer that just loves building high-end neighborhoods on the outskirts of town. Many of them have desert views."

"Why build all the way out there?"

"Because within city limits, there's not much in the way of

new real estate. A lot of people, especially seniors, prefer to live in brand-new houses in places with less traffic, noise, and smog, yet still close enough to enjoy the luxuries of big-city life."

"And you think the DP Killer lives in one of these neighborhoods?"

"It's certainly possible. You don't find many houses with basements in this part of town, that's for sure."

I grin, and softly punch her arm. "You're really good at this."

She accepts the compliment with a smile. "Thanks. We're a long way from doing our victory dance, but at least we've kinda-sorta narrowed down the who and the where. The biggest question of all, though, is...why? What's driving him to kidnap and kill these girls?"

An idea strikes me. "The man said, 'You were gone for a long time, but I found you again.' Then, before he killed Sarah, he said, 'My daughter was well-behaved. You're not her at all.' He had to have had a daughter, named Ariel. What if...what if she went missing, and it drove him crazy?"

She picks up on my train of thought. "You think he's kidnapping these girls to replace his missing daughter? That makes a sick kind of sense." Her face falls. "But I'm sure the cops would've thought of that. The *Little Mermaid* reference is a dead giveaway."

I roll my eyes. "Cops are—"

She cuts me off with a huff. "Idiots. Yeah, you said that already. I understand why you're not fond of police officers, Bax, but you can't blame them for what happened to you. You brought most of that on yourself."

Her comment stings. She's right, of course. It wasn't cops who made me stop caring about myself or about the broken path I was heading down. It wasn't cops who made me spend half my days pounding back beer like a frat boy on spring break. All cops did was remind me what a pathetic piece of shit I was.

The only time people change is when they get worse. Detective Rojas said that to my face. When she looks at me, she sees a worthless punk, and that's all she'll ever see. It doesn't matter that I have my own place, a steady job, and have been stone-cold sober for almost a year. She and her colleagues on the force will never give me the benefit of the doubt. Ever.

My musings are interrupted by a soft buzz. Piper pulls her cell from her pocket. Stress lines crinkle her forehead as she reads the caller ID. With a grimace, she answers. "Yeah, Joe, what is it?"

I watch as she pinches her nose in obvious frustration. I'm guessing it's not good news.

"No, I'm not at home. I'm heading back there now." A pause, and then her volume increases. "It's none of your business where I am. I'll bring it over tomorrow. Good night." With that, she ends the call and leans forward, her elbows on her knees. She takes several deep breaths, not meeting my gaze.

"Everything okay?" I ask, realizing how dumb the question is.

"Yeah. Apparently, the cushions in Joe's guest bedroom don't give my father the proper neck support. Dad asked me to bring him the orthopedic pillow from his bedroom. Yay, another forty-mile round trip."

I make a sympathetic face as we rise to our feet. "Total rando question...when's your birthday?"

"December third. Why?"

"'Cause you're totally getting that spa day."

Piper's grin widens, and she steps into me. Our arms wrap around each other in maybe the most heartfelt hug I've ever experienced, even more than when I gave her back her locket. In only a few short weeks, she and I have become close friends. She's had my back, and I'll have hers for as long as she needs me to. I'll see her through this shitstorm, one way or another.

We separate and, whew, my man-parts chose not to embarrass me this time. "See you tomorrow?"

She nods.

"Anything you want me to do in the meantime?"

"Yes. Check out local missing child websites. Try to find out if any girls named Ariel have gone missing in the last few years. Start in Phoenix and work your way outward. Any information you find might lead us to her father."

I shoot a glance at my laptop, already dreading the task. But it has to be done. "How about you?"

"I'm going to research photographers. No matter what he's done, he still has to work. Odds are there's a profile page of him somewhere. I'll try to find it, using the description you gave me."

"Anything else?"

She points at the coffee mugs still on my dining table. "Think of a name for that awesome drink. If you can convince Austin to put it on the menu, there'll be customers lined up around the block for it."

Possible names, each one sillier than the last, race through my mind as Piper and I share goodbye waves. I watch through the blinds as her car pulls away.

Chapter Nineteen

The first thing I do after Piper leaves is run a Google search for any local girls named Ariel who went missing in the last few years. Links to several news stories appear, but none of the featured girls are close to the DP Killer's "type." After that, I comb through several databases dedicated to missing persons. The sheer number of children who disappear every year is staggering, and with each innocent face that flashes across my screen, the more depressed I get.

Where could all these children have gone? They can't possibly have *all* been kidnapped. But then, no one just disappears off the face of the earth if everything is hunky-dory.

After two frustrating, fruitless hours and hundreds of photos later, I slam my laptop cover down and press my palms to my eyes.

"Shit," I shout at the walls, who thankfully don't respond.

One thing has become crystal clear since Piper and I began our impromptu investigation—I suck. At pretty much everything.

Unlike most teens, I've spent almost no time online. In school, I would roll my eyes as I watched nearly everyone walk from class to class with their eyes glued to their phones, tapping out texts or taking selfies. I was like, "Really? Is your life so interesting that you have to chronicle every single second of it?" I didn't need a social media profile to know where the action was. My slacker friends and I knew where to score beer and which girls liked to drink it with us. Nothing else mattered.

Basically, what I know about the Internet could fit inside the navel of a Barbie doll. What sucks even more is how reliant on Piper I am to do all the heavy lifting in this partnership. I briefly consider asking Trina to join my investigative team, but Gina would have my head in a chafing dish if I did that, and rightly so.

It's nice and temperate outside, so I decide to go for a post-sunset bike ride. I succeed in clearing my head, and the exercise does me a world of good. I end up at the supermarket where I purchase a few groceries, including a large container of Nesquik. By the time I hit the sack, I've practiced making my version of an MCL so much that I could do it in my sleep. I look forward to the expression on Sydney's face as she concedes defeat.

I wake prematurely the next morning to the chorus of Lil Pump's "Boss" blaring from my cell, which is the ringtone I've assigned to Austin. I'm scheduled to close today, so the fact that he's calling me at...crap, seven a.m.? That can't be good.

I snatch the phone and answer it. "'Sup, Austin?"

"Hey, Bax." Seriously, how does this guy sound so freaking fresh this early in the morning? "Did I wake you?"

"Yes."

"Hm. Sorry, but I need you to come in now. Imani's down with the flu. It's just Lucas and me at the moment, and we're getting slammed. I need help, and you're all I got."

With a groan, I swing my legs out of bed. "I'll be there in ten minutes."

"Thanks, Bax." He ends the call.

I'm met with total chaos when I step through Hill O' Beans front door. Austin is at the register, doing his best to calm the caffeine-deprived crowd while Lucas throws together coffee orders like a man possessed. The look Austin shoots me clearly says for me to get an apron on and my ass in gear.

The next three hours are a frenetic yet awe-inspiring exercise in teamwork. The three of us don't engage in small talk, filling order after order as the stream of customers refuses to abate. The only time our momentum breaks is when I have to zip to the back to get more pumpkin spice and soy milk.

Thirty...damn...PSL's.

I barely register the jingle of the bell as the final customer of the morning rush departs. Only a few diehards on laptops populate the place. All I can do is shuffle to that magic spot in the dining area where the fans show me the most love. I pull a chair over, flop into it, spread my arms wide, and face the ceiling like I'm Andy Dufresne having just escaped from Shawshank Prison.

"That was brutal." Austin puts a tall cup of ice water in front of me, then slips into the chair across from mine.

"I'll say." I swig half the cup and feel ten times better. "I've never seen a rush that big. Is there a statewide coffee shortage that I didn't hear about?"

"Not quite. Have you heard of Java Luvva?"

"Nope."

"It's another coffee joint on the other side of the GCC campus. They do a fair amount of business, as you might expect."

"Java Luvva?" I scrunch my brow. "Jeez, that's awful. Who came up with that name?"

"The owner, Sam. He and I have had our share of run-ins since I opened Hill O' Beans. He even threatened me once. I told him there was more than enough business for both of us, but he wouldn't have it. To listen to him, you'd think I was snatching food right out of his kids' mouths. Guy's a total drama queen."

"So what happened?" I smirk. "Did he finally realize he couldn't beat you and close up shop?"

He laughs. "That would be poetic, but no. Apparently, he had a small electrical fire yesterday, and it set off his sprinkler system.

He'll likely be closed for a week or three while his insurance company assesses the damages."

"What a shame."

"I know, right?" He downs his own cup of water. "Anyway, people need their coffee. Maybe we can convert a few of Sam's customer base to our cause while his doors are closed."

The bell jingles again, and I turn weary eyes to the entrance. In an instant, I'm out of my chair and greeting the latest customer. "Gina!"

My awesome neighbor sees me and smiles. She's wearing her immaculate chef's clothes, so I assume she's on her way to work. "Hey, Bax." She looks around the establishment with an approving nod. "Nice place you got here."

"Thank you." Austin flashes a charming grin as he joins us. "I take it you two know each other?"

"She lives next door to me," I explain. "Gina, meet Austin, the king of the Hill. Austin, this is Gina, Harrigan's chef extraordinaire."

The two shake hands. "Harrigan's, eh? Love their prime rib," the boss-man says.

Gina beams with pride. "One of my signature dishes."

I nudge his shoulder. "You should try her brisket. You will cry actual tears."

She laughs, giving me a one-armed hug. "I love this kid!"

Austin chuckles. "Now I'm intrigued. My boyfriend and I will have to dine there again sometime. Is this your first visit to Hill O' Beans?"

"It is," Gina affirms. "I drive by it every day, though. I've just never been much of a coffee enthusiast."

"So what brings you by today?"

She gestures at me. "This guy, for one. But mostly because I slept like crap last night and need a pick-me-up before I spend six hours in a hot kitchen."

Austin waves at Lucas, silently watching us from behind the register. "Lucas, one espresso, double shot, for the nice lady."

"You got it, Boss," Lucas says, then heads for the espresso machine. Moments later, a telltale whooshing sound fills the room. As if on cue, four more customers enter.

Austin greets them, then faces me. "When this rush ends, Bax, I'll need your help to do some decorating. I want to Halloween this place up real good."

"All right."

"So nice to meet you, Gina." Austin gives a gentlemanly bow. "Drop by anytime."

"I may just do that," she replies.

Another smile, and he steps behind the counter again.

Gina pays for her coffee, shooting Lucas an appreciative look. "Wow, some good-looking guys on staff here. I'm surprised this place isn't packed."

"You should have been here an hour ago," Lucas says. "New York subway cars are less crowded."

She takes a sip from her cup, closes her eyes, and aahs. "Oh em gee, I needed that."

I shoot Lucas a thumbs-up on a job well done, which he returns. "I've been meaning to ask, Gina...has Trina decided on our Halloween costumes yet?"

"She has. It's not a common theme, but it's cool. You'll love it. I'll probably pick them up this weekend."

I lean back, arms folded. "Do I get a hint?"

"Sorry. Sworn to secrecy." She winks, then heads for the door. "Catch you later."

Java Luvva's loss continues to be our gain as customers parade in and out with barely a break in the action. Sierra arrives to lighten the workload at one o'clock, giving Austin and me enough breathing room to retrieve several large boxes from his car that are full to the brim with decorations.

Lucas and I string fake cobwebs up, down, and across every

wall and dangle rubber spiders from the chandeliers. Austin sets up the high-tech gizmos, including the life-size vampire statue that drawls "*Velcome*" in a spooky baritone whenever someone enters. The best fake plastic jack-o-lanterns money can buy grin from the countertops, and a skeleton with a Hill O' Beans tee is fastened to the wall above my usual table.

By two-thirty, the transformation is complete. Several regulars gape at the abrupt change in decor, and one lady in her sixties jumps at the disembodied vampire voice. It's all I can do to keep from laughing when, not ten minutes later, Detective Rojas's hand goes right to her gun when she gets the same greeting. Not in the mood to be the recipient of her laser-glare, I opt to hide in the restroom while Austin does damage control.

I want to find joy in her torment, but it doesn't come. The newscasts continue to be empty of any positive developments, and if Detective Rojas's face is any indication, she hasn't slept much.

Business picks up again soon after. I clock out when a bleary-eyed Piper arrives for her half-shift. She reports, rather gloomily, that her search for the killer's photographer profile yielded no results. She then tells me she'll devote more time to our investigation on Saturday, and I vow to do the same.

I wake up early the next morning so I can get a few more hours of searching in before work. I expand my search for Ariel to include the neighboring states, then move up the west coast. Nothing. I call Piper at ten, hoping she has better news. She, too, came up goose eggs. I'm beginning to see why Detective Rojas is so pissed off all the time.

"I can't help thinking we're on the wrong track," Piper confesses.

No shit, I almost say. "Any ideas?"

She doesn't respond, which answers my question.

"Me neither. Well, maybe one," I add.

"Which is?"

"That Ariel's not missing. She's dead."

Piper jumps on my train of thought. "And her father couldn't deal with it, so he drowned himself in denial until he could find a replacement for her."

"Exactly."

She exhales. "Worth a shot."

"I'll search again when I get off work. Talk to you soon."

"Good luck."

The weekend crowd is steady, and six hours fly by uneventfully.

I'm about to clock out when Lucas asks me if I can help him run an errand. His live-in girlfriend, Kelly, wants to liven up their backyard by planting a couple of trees and some flowers, so he's heading to Home Depot to get some gardening stuff. I tell him my thumb is whatever the opposite of green is, but he assures me I'm only there for extra muscle. He then tells me there's a free dinner at Wing Stop in it for me if I help out. I take a millisecond to agree.

I scoff as Lucas and I push two full shopping carts into the long line at the cash register, one of which is taken up by an unassembled outdoor swinging love seat. Seriously? There's, like, six people waiting for checkout and they can't open a second register? You'd think in a store the size of a high school football stadium, there'd be more than one cashier on duty.

"This blows," Lucas grumbles, echoing my thoughts.

"No kidding. You got everything you need?"

"Let's see." He takes a quick inventory, probably comparing it to his mental checklist. "Gardening gloves, shovel, trowel, pruning shears, eight bags of soil, the marigold, the daffodil, the canna lily, and of course the love seat...yeah, it's a start."

"You must love this girl."

He flashes a knowing smile. "Love isn't a strong enough word for how I feel about Kelly. She's the kind of girl my grandma used to call 'a keeper.'"

"Do tell."

A storm rages in his blue eyes. "I made all-state in my junior year of high school. Going into my senior year, I was being recruited by over a dozen universities, including half the Pac-12. I had it all lined up...college, maybe a shot at the pros." He shakes his head. "Then in the second game, some sasquatch trips over his own teammate and falls on my knee. Even over the roar of the crowd, I heard the ligaments pop."

I wince.

"And that was it. My whole future blown away in the blink of an eye."

"You couldn't have surgery? Tons of athletes do that, don't they?"

"Yeah, they do. Unfortunately, when you're an unsigned seventeen-year-old kid, that burden falls on your parents. They paid for the treatment, of course, but it set them back a lot. I tried so hard to get back into playing form, but I was never the same. Certainly not good enough to play college ball."

Damn.

"You know what the worst part of the whole experience was? Not the injury. Not the surgery. Not the months of rehab. It was the look on all my teammates' faces. The guys I trained with, who called me 'brother' from the time I first put on pads, were looking at me like I was damaged goods. Those that *would* look at me."

Lucas stares into space, no doubt reliving every painful memory. I spare him the rest of the recap by skipping to the end. "And how does your girlfriend fit into this?"

A wisp of a smile plays over his face. "We had only just started dating when I was injured. I fully expected her to drift away like all my so-called friends did. I mean, why would a gorgeous girl like that shackle herself to a guy with no future in football? During my many, many bouts of self-pity, I begged her to leave me, to find someone else. But she didn't. She was there for every appointment, every scan, all the way to the end. And five years later, she still finds reasons to stick around."

The contentment, the earnestness in his expression floors me. The thought of someone showing me that level of support, of love, is so foreign to me that I can barely grasp the concept.

"You're right, she is a keeper," I say, lightly punching Lucas's arm.

It's not that I grew up totally unloved. When I was a kid—and when he was around—Dad was a great dad, and AJ never lorded his status as Mom's favorite over me. Sticking by someone after they hit rock bottom is...

Exactly what Sheila's been doing since my first brush with the law.

Shit.

I rehash our confrontation again in my mind. Now that I've had a few days to cool off, I realize what an asshole I was to her. Could she have been honest with me from the start? Yes. If she'd told me the day we'd met that she was an old friend of Dad's and that I would one day develop ESP...well, I'm not sure what I would've done. Blown her off, probably. I certainly wouldn't have put any stock in her claim.

I think about shooting Sheila an apologetic text when a guy in a puffy green jacket with a few days' worth of graying stubble shambles into line behind us. At the same moment, Lucas's turn at the register is up, so while the cashier is scanning his haul, I let my eyes wander to a familiar object poking out of the man's cart. A tripod.

My brain scrambles to find an explanation as to why Home Depot would sell photography equipment but comes up empty.

The man must see my wide-eyed scrutiny as he says in a not-unfriendly voice, "You okay there, son?"

I feel my face redden, like I've just been caught doing something skeevy. "Uh, yeah. I was just, uh..." Think, dingus, think! "Is, uh, is that a tripod?"

I expect the guy's eyes to narrow in suspicion at the strange teenage boy poking his nose into his business. Instead, he breaks into a smile. "Sure is. My old one broke. Got twenty years out of it."

"Are you a photographer?"

He chuckles, like I just asked the dumbest question ever. "Not in the conventional sense, though I do spend a great deal of time looking through a lens. I'm a land surveyor."

A bolt of lightning strikes my brain, and I wonder if I just hit upon one doozy of a clue.

Trying to keep my enthusiasm from showing, I press on. "What exactly is that?"

"Basically, I use a device called a theodolite to collect data on undeveloped properties or sites to determine their legal boundaries."

I stare blankly.

He continues to delight in my ignorance. "What's your interest, anyway? Thinking of becoming a surveyor?"

I smile, feigning interest. "Maybe. Do they make a lot of money?"

"If you're good at it, you can pull in 70K a year."

Seventy *thousand*? A year? "Wow. That's...a lot."

He sticks out his hand. "I'm Rod."

I grasp his palm and shake it. "Bax."

"Pleasure to meet you, Bax. It's nice to see a young fella such as yourself taking an interest in what I do. My own boys couldn't give a rat's ass."

Lucas pushes one cart away from the register, gesturing to the other in a clear sign that it's time to get a move on.

I give Rod a cheery wave and a thank you as I follow Lucas through the sliding doors. My fellow barista doesn't speak until we reach his pickup, and we start transferring his purchases to the truck's bed. "What was that all about? You really interested in becoming a surveyor?" he asks.

"Nah." I place two flowerpots against the wall and brace them with one of the bags of soil. "Just keeping my options open."

As I climb into the passenger seat, my mind is awhirl with excitement.

Maybe this is the clue we've been missing. I can't wait to run my next Google search.

But first, wings. Lots of wings.

CHAPTER TWENTY

I stare, goggle-eyed, at the screen of my laptop, which displays the picture of a dead man. Except that he's not dead. He's very much alive. And killing little girls.

My fingers feel numb as I speed-dial Piper's number. The discovery of the DP Killer's identity has sapped my strength so completely, I don't even have the energy to raise my cell to my ear, so I put it on speaker before she can answer.

After the fourth ring, I despair that my moment of triumph will be cut short when I'm shunted to her voicemail, but sigh in relief when a weary, "Bax?" drifts up from my palm.

"Hey." I want to just blurt out my monumental findings, but rein it in. "You busy?"

"Not really. Went back to Joe's house this morning, then to the GCC library. Been cramming all day, hoped to catch up on sleep tonight."

"How's your dad doing?"

"Better, I guess. Joe says the new pain meds are helping him sleep, so that's good." She sighs. "That's this month. No idea what we're gonna do next month."

And so begins the epic fallout of Piper's breakup with Gavin. Crap.

The offer to contribute some money to her cause is halfway out of my mouth when I hesitate. As much as I want to help, I remember the promise I made to myself that I would stay out of Piper's business until she specifically asks for my aid.

Feeling slightly insensitive at changing the subject, I say, "I, um, I have news."

"What is it?"

I tap a key on my laptop, and the screen saver disappears to reveal the DP Killer's face again. "I found him, Piper. I found our guy."

She draws in a breath so sharp it echoes around the room. "You...what? How?"

"Remember that tripod I saw?" I slump back into the sofa, my eyes never leaving the image on the screen. "I ran into a guy at Home Depot who was buying one just like it. He wasn't a photographer, he was a surveyor. I did another search, hoping to find a land surveyor who lost a daughter named Ariel, and bingo. The killer's name is Harold Crane."

A mad rush of movement follows, including several grunted exhales and a distinct jingle of car keys. "I'll be right over," she pants. "Have a Nesquik MCL in the largest mug you have waiting for me."

Ten minutes later, Piper's car pulls into my parking space. I open the back door and she blows right past me, straight to the couch where my laptop and a steaming hot latte await.

I don't say anything, instead letting her fuel her adrenaline rush with some extra caffeine. I can't help but think that when she crashes, she's gonna crash *hard*.

She stares at the killer's picture, which fills the screen. "This is him?"

I slide onto the couch next to her. "Yup."

"This is huge, Bax."

"I know."

She gestures at the laptop. "Jeez. When you said he looked ordinary, you weren't kidding. So what's this guy's story?"

I back-shift from the photo to the article I found on my final Google search. "Three years ago, a seven-year-old girl from Medford, Oregon slipped, hit her head, and fell into her backyard pool. By the time her mother found her, it was too late."

"Let me guess...her name was Ariel."

"Correct. To say the girl was a Disney enthusiast would be an understatement. Her mom, Clarissa, was an Olympic-level swimmer who had the nickname 'The Little Mermaid' because of her love of water and of the Disney movie. So, when she had a daughter, naturally, she named the girl Ariel."

"And Ariel died of drowning." Piper sighs. "God has a sick sense of humor sometimes."

I can't disagree. I'm living proof of that statement. "Clarissa blamed herself for the tragedy," I continue. "Six months after the funeral, she overdosed on sleeping pills."

Piper takes another gulp from the mug, and her face creases into a frown. "And I thought my life was messed up."

"Yeah."

"Are you absolutely sure Harold is the man Sarah saw?"

"A hundred percent. The photo's a little indistinct and grainy, but it's definitely him."

She removes her glasses and scrubs her hand over her eyes before replacing them. "Then I don't understand. How on earth did this guy not appear on the task force's radar?"

I switch browser windows and bring up the second article I found with his name in it. "Because he's dead. Officially, anyway."

"Dead?"

"Not long after Clarissa died, local authorities found Harold's car on a bridge overlooking the Klamath River. He left a suicide note on the dashboard saying he couldn't go on without his family."

"I'm guessing they never found his body."

"Nope. They recovered a few scraps of clothing, some blood whose DNA matched his, but no corpse. It was the dead of winter, and the water was near freezing. Experts declared no one could have survived both the fall and the river. His death was ruled a suicide, and that was the end of it."

"So he faked his death and moved to our neck of the woods." She scoffs. "Lucky us."

I can't stand looking at Harold's face anymore, so I close the browser window and snap the laptop shut. "What do we do now?"

Her response is a gaping yawn.

"You want another latte?"

Piper shakes her head, and yawns again. "No. I need sleep. My brain is totally fried." She tries to use her hands to push herself up, but they give way and she falls back to the couch. She tries again, with similar results. Finally, she leans her head on the armrest, eyes closed.

Called it.

"Look, if you want to sack out here, it's cool. You can even take the bed if you want. The sheets are clean and everything. I'll sleep on the couch."

She kicks her shoes off and pulls her legs onto the sofa, then buries her face in the largest of my throw pillows. "Here is fine. Wake me up by seven, 'kay?"

"Sure thing."

Piper's eyes open into slits, and her lips curl into a tired smile. "You're sweet."

The compliment turns to liquid warmth in my chest. I don't remember ever being called that before. "Yeah, too much of me will send you into diabetic shock."

Facepalm. Why couldn't my ESP have come with the ability to not say whatever stupid shit comes into my brain? "I mean, uh, thanks," I say. "Sleep well."

Her eyes close again. "Ya done good, dude."

A grin forms. "Score one for Baxter and McKinney, Psychic Gumshoes."

I wait for a reply, but it doesn't come. A lock of red hair falls indifferently over her face, and she makes no move to brush it away. Moments later, her soft snores fill the room.

I switch on the small lamp and kill the overhead lights, plunging my living room into dimness. I then retrieve a clean sheet from the hall closet and drape it over Piper's sleeping frame. Finally, I remove her glasses and place them on the coffee table. She stirs briefly, grasping the cloth and pulling it around her, but doesn't wake.

I spend the next few minutes standing over my fridge, staring at my assortment of canned and bottled beverages. Water, sodas, fruit juices, even a couple of energy drinks. But no beer.

God, I could use one right now. It would take the edge off, help me unravel this ginormous ball of stress that's been tangling up my insides since the day I left Asterly. What sucks is, I'd have to risk buying it myself at the local supermarket and pray I get an employee apathetic enough not to card me.

Then I picture Detective Rojas' face, smiling at me from the other side of a wall of prison bars, and the notion vanishes from my brain. I am *not* proving that bitch right about me.

And there's no way in the fiery hells I'm letting Piper down now.

I grab a Mountain Dew and a cinnamon roll, retrieve my earbuds from my pocket, plug them into my phone, and sit down at the dining table. I spend a few wistful moments staring at my houseguest, this amazing girl who, against all odds, has kept my crazy train from derailing.

Rather than give into the temptation to fire up my gaming system and spend the next few hours shredding CGI zombies, I head for my bedroom, snacks in hand.

With the lilting strains of Korn's "Here to Stay" pelting my eardrums, I stare up at the ceiling, reliving the day's events. A smile pushes through, and I pump both fists in triumph.

Thank you, Rod. Thank you, Piper.

You're going *down*, Harold.

I place two fresh mugs of French roast and a bowl of cereal on the kitchen table, making just enough noise that Piper's eyes flutter open. She lifts her head, shoots a glance at the sunlight filtering in around the closed blinds, then meets my gaze.

"What time is it?" she slurs, reaching for her glasses and sliding them on.

"Almost seven," I say. "How're you doing?"

"I'm good." She sits up straight, sweeps her hair back, and smooths out the wrinkles in her sweatshirt. "I love your couch. Now I know where to come if I get insomnia."

She means it as a joke, but I find the thought of Piper and me sleeping under the same roof on a regular basis very appealing.

Jeez, Bax. Stop being such a douche. She just got out of a horrible relationship. I'm sure starting another one is the last thing on her mind right now. And we've got much bigger fish to fry.

"Wasn't sure if you had time for breakfast, so I prepared something simple," I say.

She walks over to the kitchen table and grins as she zeroes in on the mug of coffee. She then scans the contents of the bowl with a raised eyebrow. "Cap'n Crunch? Really? What are you, seven?"

I feign annoyance. "Hey now. I will stand for no mockery of my beloved Captain in my house."

"Whoa, sorry. Didn't realize you two had a thing," she jokes, standing from the couch and stretching.

I hand her the coffee, watch her take a grateful sip. "Yeah, the Cap and I go way back. What was your overly-sugared breakfast choice as a kid?"

"Frosted Flakes, of course. They're grrrrrrrreat!"

I laugh and gesture for her to take a seat. "Nice."

We sit in silence as she slurps down her coffee, followed by a few bites of cereal. I pass the time by activating my laptop, then grimace when Harold's face reappears on the screen. "You have time to talk, or do you gotta jet?"

Piper checks her phone and breathes a sigh of relief at the lack of new texts and missed calls. "I can spare you a few minutes. Now that Dad's out of danger, Gavin's out of my life, and I'm nice and coffeed up, my brain is finally working again."

I pick up my own mug and take a swig. It surprises me how good I've become at making coffee. I only wish I'd had all this knowledge during my stay at Asterly. Suck it, Carl.

"I've been thinking about our next move," I say. "I don't know if there's a public listing of local surveyors on the Internet, but I'll have a look."

"Good idea, but remember that Harold faked his own death. Even if he is still making a living as a surveyor, odds are he's doing it under a different name."

"Right. Beyond that, I'm open to suggestions."

She ponders this for a few moments, staring into her coffee between sips. After setting the mug down, she opens another browser window and does a Google search. I watch as the phone number for the federal task force's tip line pops up. A banner across the top shows that a reward of $75,000 has been offered for anyone who provides information leading directly to the DP Killer's capture.

Whoa.

"Here's what you do," Piper says. "You write down all the pertinent facts, call this number, and tell the cops everything you know."

I groan. "You sure that's our only play?"

She shoots me a *duh* expression. "What else can we do? We're eighteen, and not equipped to take down a stone-cold killer. I'm happy to help, but as I told you before, I'm not risking my life for this. We've done all we can. It's time to let the professionals finish what we started."

I stare at my phone, running my thumbs over its surface. "I hear you, but...what if they trace the call back to me? They can do that, you know. The last thing I want is some cop showing up asking how I got this information."

"So call from a payphone, and don't leave your name."

"Seriously? A payphone? Those still exist?"

She rolls her eyes. "Jeez, you need to get out more. Go to any convenience store, and you'll find one. Though you may have to check a few to find one that works."

I run this scenario through my mind. It makes sense. Plus, if I disguise my voice and wear a hoodie and shades in case there are any cameras around...

Sheesh. Paranoid much?

"All right. I'll do it." I sigh in dread. "Can't believe I'm actually calling the cops on purpose."

She pats my shoulder. "It's the right thing to do, Bax."

"How many tips do you figure they get?"

"Dozens, maybe hundreds. But they still have to follow each lead. Just be sure to mention the van. If that kid you met really did tell Detective Rojas about it, then your tip will give that fact extra weight."

Yes, it would. Here's hoping the cops are smart enough to make the connection.

I grab the pen and notebook from the coffee table, flip to an empty page, and begin jotting everything down.

Piper checks her phone again, exhales, then stands up. "I have to go. Gotta grab a shower and a change of clothes. I have a mountain of chores and errands to do, then back to studying."

I stand as well, then lead her to the back door. "All right. I'll see you tomorrow. Thanks for all your help."

She smiles. "You know, I never did thank you before...for standing up to Gavin. That was brave of you."

"We're a family at H.O.B., right? Families have to stick together."

"Yes, they do."

I hold open the back door for her with an evil smirk. "When you shower, make sure you get that booger out of your hair."

Her eyes widen, and she frantically searches her red tresses for it, muttering, "Oh, shit, oh shit..."

I give her ten seconds before I whisper, "Gotcha."

Piper levels a glare at me that could punch through a brick wall, then slugs me semi-softly in the stomach. "You are a butt-hole, you know that?"

I hold my hands up in surrender. "That's me. The sweet, brave butthole."

Her expression softens. "Let me know how the phone call goes. See ya."

I close the door behind her and return to the couch. By the time the sound of the Altima's engine fades away, I'm deep into writing my part of what should prove a very interesting phone call.

Chapter Twenty-One

Somewhere between finishing my script and leaving the house to find an appropriate payphone, I get it in my head that an entire squadron of cop cars will descend on me within seconds of dialing the hotline. Yes, I know giving info to the police, anonymous or otherwise, is not a crime, but if there's one thing I've learned from TV, it's that Big Brother is always watching.

So, I scrap the payphone idea and instead bike to the Best Buy a mile away with the intention of buying a prepaid cell. Then I catch sight of the burly security guy eyeing everyone who passes in and out of the sliding double doors, and I pedal right on by, heading instead for the Burger King a couple hundred yards away.

Great. I can now add "basket case" to my resume. Woo hoo.

A couple of rough-looking teens with pencil-thin mustaches glower at me as I slide into the adjacent booth. I wonder for a second if they're former residents of Asterly, but they don't look familiar. I give them a congenial "wassup" nod and turn my attention to my breakfast sandwich.

After two bites and a handful of oversalted tater tots, my eyes lock on the 7-Eleven across the street. My eyebrows raise when I spot a thing that just might be a payphone right next to the Redbox kiosk.

Crap. What to do. I have to make the call from somewhere. Any location I might choose would come with some risk, but...

Come on, Bax. Suck it up and grow a pair.

Thirty minutes and several refills of my extra-large Coke later, I inhale deeply and step outside. I opt to leave my bike in the BK bike rack and cross the street on foot, reasoning that if the convenience store has an external camera, a guy on a bike would stand out more than a random pedestrian.

My hood pulled tight over my head, I amble to the phone. No one pays me any attention except a homeless guy who mutters under his breath at me. His glassy-eyed stare, unkempt facial hair, and foul stench make me thankful that even at my lowest, I never sank into a personal abyss that deep.

Focusing on the reason I'm here, I pick up the payphone's receiver in one hand while digging the notebook out of my hoodie pocket with the other. I flip to the page where I wrote the hotline number and the script, shove three quarters into the coin slot, and start pressing numbers.

It rings three times before a female voice answers, "Federal Task Force Hotline. This is Officer Wanda Harris. To whom am I speaking?"

I exhale again. I look to the generic pseudonym I created just in case I was asked to identify myself. "My name is Scott. I have information about the Disney Princess Killer."

A tense pause, then, "I see. Before we continue, I must inform you that willingly providing false information to federal law enforcement is a prosecutable offense."

Shit. It is? Or is that just something they say to scare off the prank callers?

Doesn't matter. My info is solid, regardless of how I got it. "I understand."

"Do I have your permission to record this conversation?"

"Uh, I guess," I say, lowering my voice to a not-at-all-guilty level.

"All right. What is the nature of the information you wish to disclose?"

And...go.

"I know who he is."

I wait for a sign that Officer Harris is impressed by my statement but get nothing. No doubt she's heard those exact words umpteen times since the hotline was created.

"Please continue," she says.

After confirming no one is within earshot, I place my finger on the notebook, running down the list of facts about the DP Killer one by one. Speaking lowly but clearly, I say, "His name is Harold Crane, formerly of Medford, Oregon. He's in his forties, with short, dark brown hair and pale blue eyes. No facial hair, no scars, no tattoos. He might be working as a land surveyor, and he lives in a house with a desert view. He is kidnapping these girls to replace his dead daughter, Ariel. That's why he dresses them up in *Little Mermaid* T-shirts."

Wow. I think I actually got that all out in one breath.

"I see," Officer Harris says with more than a tinge of skepticism. "That's a lot of information, Scott, and quite specific. May I ask how you obtained it?"

I grit my teeth and push through the nerves churning in my gut. "I'd...rather not say. But it's the truth. Officer Harris, can you promise me you'll follow up on this lead and not just dismiss it?"

There's a long pause, and my brain kicks into full paranoia mode. She's tracing the call, I just know it. I have to end this. Now.

"Scott, I can assure you, all tangible leads are followed up on. May I have your contact information in case we—"

The receiver makes a dramatic *thunk* as I hang up, cutting Officer Harris off.

My heart thundering in my chest and my eyes glued to the

ground, I cross the street again and retrieve my bike. I don't stop pedaling until I'm a half-mile away.

I did it.

Please, cops, feds, whoever the entire city is counting on to nail this sicko, do your fucking jobs.

I'm not in the best of moods when I report for work on Monday. I spent last night scouring every Internet news wire, watching every network and cable news program, anticipating the breaking story that the DP Killer had been apprehended and the reign of terror he held over this city was over. But there was nothing. A brief conversation with Piper, who again assured me I did the right thing, does little to convince me. I spewed muttered curses at my bedroom ceiling for an hour before I finally fell asleep.

I spelled it out for them. In plain English. And they *still* couldn't find him.

Cops are idiots.

The one piece of good news is that Imani is over her flu. Between her, Austin, and Lucas, they handled the morning rush like pros. The mood is festive and jovial, and I catch more than a few GCC students taking selfies with Hobula the fake vampire. Lucas and I spend the morning firing *Deadpool* quotes at each other, which draws both chuckles and eye-rolls from assorted patrons. The black cloud over my head thins but doesn't disperse.

It's not until Sydney comes in for her usual MCL that I realize I forgot to bring my secret ingredient. She smiles flirtatiously when I hand over her order, which turns into a semi-serious frown when I assure her my victory is at hand.

"Is that so?" she says, taking a sip of her usual. "Do I get a hint as to what you've cooked up in your secret coffee laboratory?"

"Not even a little one," I say, resolute. "In fact, I'm so sure I'm going to win, I'm already thinking of restaurants I might take you."

"Hmm. I don't remember specifically agreeing to go out with you if you won."

I lean forward, undaunted. "No, you said you'd have my kid."

Her face goes deep crimson. "You know that was a joke, right?"

"Of course. But if we're renegotiating terms, then a nice dinner would be a great start to whatever torrid love affair may follow."

This gets a laugh. "Fair enough. Will this be a dress-up-nice date or a hang-out-casual date?"

"Oh, definitely the first one." I feel my own cheeks flush. "Though I may need a ride."

Sydney takes another sip, shoots me a wink, then turns away. "You gotta win the bet first, Baxy. Which you haven't yet. See you soon."

Baxy. She's already got a pet name for me. Me like.

I can't help but watch her butt wiggle as it saunters out the door...which then turns into a big bucket o' karma when Piper walks in moments later. She gives me a cheery nod and a slight wave, then heads for the back room.

Two girls. I like two girls. I wonder if...

No. Stop it. What Piper and I have goes way beyond sex or mutual attraction or whatever lame excuse I had to waste time with the party girls I used to hook up with. We're friends, and I'm not going to let my libido ruin it.

Traffic is pretty consistent throughout the afternoon, including the construction crew remodeling the gymnasium at Trina's school. Austin engages them in conversation, and I eavesdrop as I fix their orders. The job is apparently one day away from completion, meaning the kids can start using it once it passes a final safety inspection. Austin sends them on their way with a friendly smile.

"Hey Boss," I say, wiping down a nearby table. "Are we allowed to dress up in costume if we're working on Halloween?"

"Of course." Austin beams. "Last year I came as Professor

Snape from *Harry Potter*. It was awesome. Still haven't decided what I'm doing this year. How about you?"

"Gina's daughter Trina is picking out our outfits this year. They're supposed to have a common theme, but they haven't told me what it is yet." I grimace. "I hope it's not *My Little Pony*."

Piper grins. "I'd pay actual money to see you dressed up as Pinkie Pie."

Austin chuckles, then glances at the clock next to the television, which reads a quarter to five. "Bax, you're free to go as soon as you restock the beverages."

"All right," I say.

I make my way to the back, Piper right behind me.

"No news, I gather?" she whispers.

"Nope. I've been racking my brains trying to think of something else we can do. Short of calling the FBI directly, I got nothing." I feel somewhat empty saying it, like there's more I can do, more I should have done. Again, I kick myself for not turning Sarah's clothes over to the proper authorities and wonder exactly how I'm going to get rid of them. Throwing them away would be too cold-hearted, like I'm trashing Sarah's memory. Donate them to Goodwill? Maybe.

"Me either," she says. "We'll keep watching the news, see if anything changes."

I nod, grab a six-pack of water in each hand, and head to the counter. No new customers have come in, and Austin is busy doing a cash drop from the register. I've just started placing the water bottles in the display case when Austin's cell rings.

"Hey, darling," he answers.

Must be his boyfriend. Austin calls him 'darling.' That's so cute.

"I know, I forgot to buy pasta last night. I promise I'll pick some up on the way h—"

He trails off, and the sudden silence worries me. I meet his gaze, disturbed by the faraway look in his eyes. His normally cheerful expression has become haunted.

Uh-oh.

"Yeah," he whispers, barely loud enough for me to hear. "I'll check it out now. Thanks, Danny." He hangs up, snatches the remote off the back counter, and turns the TV on. The picture coalesces immediately on the face of a reporter, whose lips are moving with forced urgency. I stand up, and my eyes lock on the caption at the bottom of the screen:

PHOENIX GIRL ABDUCTED — DISNEY PRINCESS KILLER SUSPECTED

Fuck.

Then I focus on the reporter, and the buildings in the background, and my heart drops into my shoes. It's a school.

Trina's school.

No no no no.

As if reading my mind, Austin turns the volume up, and the reporter's strained voice fills the room. Every Hill O' Beans customer and employee is now watching the screen with guarded terror.

"—on her way home from a friend's house," the reporter says. "It is not known at this time whether the missing girl was wearing an article of Disney-related clothing, or if her disappearance has anything to do with the man known as the Disney Princess Killer. However, based on the similarity in age, skin color, and hair color between her and the previous three victims, investigators cannot rule out this possibility. All we know at this time is that police have cordoned off the area and are beginning their investigation."

Then the picture changes, and my blood turns to ice. On the screen is the entrance to Arbor Vista Townhomes.

Panic floods my brain so much that I no longer hear the reporter's voice. I watch the screen, trying to make out faces within the crowd of residents milling around, each bearing a horrified expression. Off to the side, I see Crescent, bawling her eyes out as she hugs her mother.

Trina. Oh, God, no.

I don't think. I don't speak. I don't even remove my apron. I just race out the front door.

I reach Arbor Vista's front entrance five agonizing minutes later. Three police cars, their lights flashing, dominate the guest parking lot. A quarter-mile up the street are a half-dozen more. Traffic has been blocked in both directions, and crime-scene tape stretches all the way across the road. As I watch, a CSI truck passes through the barricade. The back doors open, and four men and women exit carrying armloads of gear.

I punch the code for the walk-in gate, wheel my bike in, and let it drop to the grass. In front of me, dozens of residents cluster together in small groups, murmuring amongst themselves or keeping a close watch on their children. I see most of the Arbor Vista Gang—Rodrigo, Omar, Maribel, siblings Tanisha and Tyjuan.

My breath, already ragged from the sprint home, quickens further as I cast desperate eyes over the length of the lawn, looking for my nine-year-old buddy.

"Trina," I call, but only a hoarse croak emerges.

No. This is not happening. Not now. Not to her.

"Trina!" I call again. One of my neighbors, an elderly Hispanic lady named Celeste, hears my plaintive cry and points at Gina's door, which is wide open. I acknowledge her with a grateful nod and rush the last thirty yards.

I am almost to her doorstep when a tiny figure slams into my waist, wrapping its arms around me. Choked sobs drift up as Trina buries her face in my apron.

A palpable wave of relief crashes over me. I drop to one knee and hug her as hard as I can without crushing her. "You're all right," I whisper. "When I saw the news, I thought for sure—"

She stares at me, her huge eyes puffy and red. She sniffles hard, and soft whimpers are all that come out of her mouth.

I look up to see Gina standing in her threshold. Her expression matches Austin's, one of disbelief and dread.

"Gina, what's happened?" I ask.

Then my brain does the math. I know why Trina's so upset. One of her friends has been taken. One of her best friends. It's not Crescent, which can only mean...

Gina finishes my thought. "It's Cheyanne. She's disappeared."

Chapter Twenty-Two

I ease myself away from Trina, fighting back the urge to vomit as I slump onto the concrete sidewalk, my palms jammed against my eyes.

Why, God? Why did you pick *me*, of all people, to sort out this mess? What were you thinking?

Oh, I know why. My great-grandfather was a war hero. My grandfather was a war hero. Dad was a war hero. And AJ...I'm sure he would have served his country with distinction and valor. If he had lived.

If I hadn't killed him.

Images flash through my mind. AJ's body, clad in a pristine black suit, lying face-up in the open casket during his memorial service. Mom, dabbing her eyes with her sodden hanky and shooting hate-filled, accusatory glares at me.

You took him from me, you fucking bastard, she'd said. *You took the only thing I had left in this world.*

Tears well up in me as I relive Sarah's terror. The same terror Cheyanne is probably feeling right now.

All because I couldn't stop it from happening. Because I'm not a hero. I'm a stupid, ignorant loser who thought he could make things right.

Ha. "Right." What a crock.

Three little girls are dead. I couldn't have done anything to help them. But if Cheyanne—sweet, funny, adorable Cheyanne—dies because I was too dumb to figure it all out in time...that's on me.

I become aware of Gina kneeling beside me, her hand on my shoulder. Trina has taken a seat on my other side, still quietly sobbing.

"Bax?" Gina says in my ear.

"What...what happened?" I ask. "Does anyone know?"

"Cheyanne usually comes home right after school, but not today. She went to her friend Lily's house a few blocks away because they're working on a history project together. They think she was taken on her way home, at around 4:15."

I turn to Trina, who meets my gaze. "Was she..." I gulp. "Was she wearing something with a Disney princess on it?"

Trina's brow scrunches, then she shakes her head. "She has a sweatshirt with the two girls from *Frozen* on the back, but she hasn't worn it in weeks."

A glimmer of hope ignites inside me. If she wasn't wearing a piece of Disney clothing, then maybe it wasn't Harold who took her. Maybe she wasn't even kidnapped.

I shoot a hopeful glance at the entrance, praying Cheyanne will walk through and tell all the cops and news crews that it was just a big misunderstanding.

Yeah, right.

"I don't get it," I say, almost to myself. "He only takes girls who wear Disney princesses."

"That's right," Gina says. "But after the last girl's body was found...what was her name again?"

"Sarah," I reply automatically.

"Yes. After Sarah was found, I had a chat with some of the parents who have kids going to Arbor Vista Elementary and Arbor Vista Middle School. They all agreed that, until that man was caught, it would be safer that no one wears anything Disney-related."

My head spins as everything I thought I knew about the DPK starts to crumble. "I don't get it. Why would he take Cheyanne if she wasn't—"

"Mr. Baxter. Don't you turn up in the darndest places."

I lift my head to see a pair of legs, clad in dark dress slacks, ten feet away. I dare not lift it higher, because I can't possibly look *her* in the eyes right now.

Piper was wrong. This thing I have isn't a gift. It's a curse, one I brought on myself. The Man Upstairs, in all his wisdom, let me have the illusion of security, of forgiveness, of...*happiness?* For almost a month, I fooled myself into believing I could turn my disaster of a life around. That I could use my power to do good.

What kind of fucked-up divine entity would sacrifice a ten-year-old girl to prove how wrong I was?

I'm about to utter the foulest, most blasphemous curse I know when Detective Rojas speaks again. "On your feet. *Now.*"

I haul myself up. Gina and Trina stand with me. Their gazes waver from me to the angry cop trying to roast me with her laser-glare.

Even though my insides have turned to tapioca, I'm able to stare back without combusting. "I'm here because I live here. That's my unit right over there." I wag a finger at my front door.

She hooks her thumbs into her belt and takes a step toward me. "Where exactly were you between four o'clock and four-thirty today, Mr. Baxter?"

Before I can answer, Gina comes to my defense. "You can't possibly think Bax had anything to do with this!"

Detective Rojas turns her scowl upon Gina. "I'm asking the questions here, Miss. Do not interrupt me."

"I was at work," I say, bile creeping up my throat. "Since ten this morning. Call Austin, he'll tell you."

"Oh, I will. Are you acquainted with the missing girl, Cheyanne Macias?"

"Yes." On my left, Trina slips her hand into mine. "She's my friend."

Detective Rojas' glare deepens. "Your *friend*? You're making friends with little girls? Is that what you're into now?"

"Now just a damn minute." A hard edge tinges Gina's voice. "I know what you're implying, and it's disgusting. I don't care if you are a cop, I'm not going to stand here and let you paint Bax as a pedophile. That's not who he is."

Detective Rojas' expression turns to one of bemusement. "Look, Miss..."

"Forrester. *Ms.* Forrester."

"Ms. Forrester, are you aware that your new neighbor has a criminal record?"

Gina places her hands on her hips. "Yes, I am. He told me all about the stupid teenage stuff he got sentenced for. And you know what? I don't care. I wasn't a saint at that age either, but that doesn't make me a serial killer any more than it does Bax."

My breath catches. I think I seriously love Gina right now.

Great. Make it three girls.

"He's a good person," Trina chimes in, still sniffling. "He wouldn't hurt Cheyanne in a million, billion years."

Detective Rojas holds her hands up, silencing both of them. Once again, her stony glare falls upon me. "Let's assume I buy that you being neighbors with the latest kidnap victim is a coincidence. That still doesn't explain what you were doing outside Sarah's house. So I'm going to ask again...why were you there?"

Gina turns surprised eyes to me. "You went to the dead girl's neighborhood?"

This gets the attention of several of my neighbors, all of whom furrow their brows at me. I can't look at any of them, so I stare at my shoes and nod dumbly.

"He didn't tell you that, did he, Ms. Forrester?" The smugness in Detective Rojas' voice makes me want to punch her. Again. I swear this woman brings out the worst in me.

Somehow, though, I keep my ire under control. "I was investigating."

She snorts. "Investigating? You are an arrogant little prick, aren't you?"

This time, Gina doesn't leap to my defense. All I can do is mouth, "I was just trying to help."

"And what on God's green earth makes you think we need your help?"

"Because you haven't found him yet!" I pull a stupid amount of bravery out of nowhere as my eyes bore into hers. "If you had, we wouldn't be having this conversation, would we? I wanted to find something you missed. Something I could shove in your face."

Detective Rojas takes another step toward me. Barely two feet separate us now. "This isn't an episode of *Scooby-Doo*, you jackass. And it isn't a pissing contest, either. A little girl's life is at stake, so if you have anything to tell me, now's the time."

I almost blurt it all out. Harold. Ariel. The van. The basement. Sarah's clothes. Every single thing I learned since my ability first manifested. But something stops me.

Maybe it's the fact that I told a cop everything I know earlier today. Maybe it's the fact that Detective Rojas is but one search warrant away from having probable cause to arrest me. Maybe it's that she wouldn't believe a word I say anyway.

No, I take it back. I know what stops me from spilling my guts. It hits me in a moment of clarity so pure it nearly knocks me backwards.

This is why I got this crazy superpower. It wasn't to help the cops catch the DP Killer. It was to stop him myself. To save Cheyanne.

A life for a life.

"No," I utter. "I got nothing to say to you."

I feel Trina squeeze my hand, a gesture I return. "Please, Officer," she whispers. "Find my best friend. Please."

One look into Trina's doe eyes is enough to dissipate Detective Rojas' righteous indignation. She plasters the fakest reassuring smile I'm sure she's capable of on her face and says, "We'll do our best. I promise."

My stomach still hasn't stopped churning, so I take my leave of Gina and Trina without another word. I dig in my pocket for my house key, which I shove into the lock without delicacy. The accusatory scowls of my neighbors follow me in as I lock the door behind me.

Despite my utter lack of appetite, I force a few spoonfuls of microwave mac and cheese into my mouth and wash it down with a full can of Coke. If nothing else, the combination of carbs and carbonation in my stomach make me feel something other than the pitched battle going on inside my mind.

It's funny that, after eighteen years, it took something as batshit crazy as ESP to make me believe in a higher power. Yeah, I know I inherited my ability from dear old Dad, but that my first steps toward taking back my life coincided with finding Sarah's clothes...no. There's no way that's random. Because if it is, this episode will end with me failing again. I could live with that. I've been a failure most of my life. What I can't live with is the knowledge that Harold Goddamn Crane spirited away one of my new friends right out from under my nose. That unless the cops make a breakthrough—and *soon*—Cheyanne will be just another funeral captured on the five o'clock news.

Harold's picture, that of a grieving father, once again dominates my laptop screen. It'd be so easy to feel sorry for him. To lose one's child has to be the worst feeling ever. And then his wife killed herself, piling heartache on top of heartache.

Grief does terrible things to people. It turned me into a delinquent, Mom into a boozehound, and Harold into a psychopath.

Yeah. Life sucks.

I picture Cheyanne, regaining consciousness in Harold's basement. She'll be terrified, scream for help, cry her eyes out. Then he'll come in and expect her to play her part in his sick little drama.

Cheyanne's smart. She may not know Harold's story, but it won't be hard to figure out once he starts calling her "Ariel." If she plays along, it could buy her a few days. But eventually, she'll grow tired and impatient, demand he release her, and then...

A rap on the door jolts me out of my reverie. Gentle, not an angry thump. That means it's probably not Detective Rojas, back with a search warrant. It's been a couple of hours since the cops left, and the only positive development I've gleaned from tonight's news is that, for the first time, someone was found who witnessed the abduction. Some old guy walking his dog apparently saw Cheyanne being forced into a white van but was too far away to get the license plate. By the time he'd dug out his cell phone, they were long gone.

I move to the door. "Who is it?"

"It's Gina," says a muffled voice.

"And Trina," says another.

I open the door to see them standing on either side of my bicycle, which Gina holds by the handlebars. Trina's not crying anymore. She's probably all out of tears.

"You left this by the entrance," Gina says. "Thought you might want it back."

I smile in spite of myself. With a grateful nod, I relieve her of her burden. To avoid leaving tracks on my carpet, I hoist the bike up and carry it across the living room, depositing it on the newspapers. When I turn around, Trina is already several feet inside the door.

"Can we come in?" Gina asks.

"Are you sure you still want to be seen with me?"

Her brow scrunches into a frown. "What's *that* supposed to mean?"

"You saw what Detective Rojas did. Now everyone's looking at me like I'm in league with the DP Ki...the man who took

Cheyanne." I notice Trina visibly shudder. "By morning, they'll probably petition Ted to have me evicted."

Gina closes the door and faces me. "They won't."

"What makes you so—"

"They're scared, Bax. Their...*our* quiet little community has been disrupted in the worst possible way, and they're looking for someone to blame. What that cop did, outing you in front of them, was wrong."

I slump onto my couch, grateful that my laptop's screensaver has engaged, hiding Harold's picture. "Arbor Vista is a great place," I say glumly, "but I don't belong here."

Trina's mouth presses into a flat line. "That's bullcrap."

My eyes widen. The swear word coming out of Trina's mouth almost makes me laugh.

Gina shoots her daughter a reproachful glare but doesn't call Trina on the profanity. "She's right. You think because you raised a little teenage hell, that makes you unworthy of being part of this community?"

I nod.

Gina slides onto the sofa next to me, and Trina takes the cushion on my other side. "I've been here five years, Bax, so let me tell you a little something about Arbor Vista," Gina says. "Everyone here has issues, baggage, skeletons in their closets." She points toward my front door. "Mrs. Muncie in Unit 17? Twenty years ago, she was a heroin addict." Her finger moves several degrees to the left. "Mr. Zapata in 29? Did hard time for armed robbery." She points again. "You know Gabriel, the ten-year-old four units down from you? His mom, Sally, had him when she was fifteen. Her parents demanded she have an abortion. When she wouldn't, they kicked her out."

Holy shit.

Gina takes my hand in hers. "People make mistakes, Bax. You, me, everyone. You learn, you grow, you move on. I love every one of these people, warts and all. That's what a community *is*. You're as much a part of it as any of them, if only you'd get your head out of your butt and see it."

I want to believe her, maybe more than I've ever wanted to believe anything. But no matter what sins my neighbors may have piled up in their lives, I doubt any of them have another person's death on their hands.

Memories of that terrible night flood my mind, and then the tears start. One is snaking down my face before I even realize it. The next thing I know, Gina's arms are around me, and I'm sobbing into her shoulder. I feel Trina's small hand on my back.

I sniffle and make incoherent sounds for a few seconds, then out it comes. "I haven't told you everything about myself."

"I know," Gina soothes in my ear. "I've already figured it out. Both of us have."

What the huh?

I straighten up, meeting her eyes. "Really?"

"You have an ability. Something no one else can do. Am I right?"

Her deduction astounds me so much that my imminent confession regarding my part in AJ's death freezes and dies in the back of my throat. My mouth flops open and shut like a dying fish as my gaze flicks from mother to daughter and back again. I can't even muster up the brain power to bark out a half-assed denial. I finally stammer a shell-shocked, "H-how'd you know that?"

Gina takes my hand again, then smiles. "Because we have them, too."

Say *WHAT?*

In a voice way too mature for a fourth grader, Trina adds, "You didn't think you were the only one, did you?"

Mind...blown.

Chapter Twenty-Three

A thousand questions swirl around my mind, but I'm unable to speak even one of them aloud.

I stare at Gina's face, then Trina's, the full weight of their confession hitting me like a cartoon anvil dropped on my head.

There are others. Others like me.

Dumbass. Of course there are. How could I not have realized that before? Am I really stupid enough to believe that my family was the only one in the world who was...is there even a word for it? Gifted? Cursed? Whackadoodle?

And how is it the existence of people like me—like *us*—still remains the stuff of comic books and spooky movies?

I realize Gina is still gripping my hand. The concern, the absolute sincerity in her expression calms me, if only a little. I concentrate on her features—warm chocolate eyes, tan skin, full cheekbones. She's actually quite hot. If only she wasn't nearly twice my age...

Focus, dipshit!

After several deep inhales, I'm able to form syllables again. "So...you guys have ESP too?"

Gina nods. "When did you find out you were..."

"Special?" Trina finishes.

Special. Yeah, I guess that works as well as any.

"Funny you should ask," I say. "It was the day you and I met."

Gina's eyebrows shoot up into her hairline. "Really?"

I turn to Trina. "Remember when we shook hands?"

"Yeah," she says.

"I touched your bracelet, just for a second." I point to it, once again encircling her wrist. "When I did, I saw your great-grandmother, Rose."

She moves her arm in front of her face, scrutinizing her prized possession. "Wow, that's really cool. What else did you see?"

"I relived your memory of Rose giving you the bracelet. You were so happy." I reach over and lightly tap her nose. "She called you Kitty Kat."

Trina blushes.

"You're psychometric," Gina says, drawing my attention. "I've heard people with that ability exist, but I've never met any. In fact, you're the first person I've ever met outside my family who is..."

"Special?"

"Yes."

"How many of us are there?" I ask, my curiosity dial now cranked up to eleven.

"From what my mother and grandmother told me, the percentage of people whose brains work...shall we say, *differently* from other people's is very low. Only one person in every fifty thousand is like us. That's a total guess, though, as most people who discover their abilities go out of their way to keep it a secret."

Yeah, that figures.

"Are you guys psychometric too?" I ask.

"No. We're aurapaths," Gina answers, as matter-of-factly as if she'd admitted she and Trina were Democrats or vegetarians or Episcopalians.

"Aura-what?"

Gina opens her mouth, then closes it again. She averts her

gaze, staring across the room. Finally, she mutters, "This may take a while to explain. I don't suppose you have any tea?"

"Is chai okay?"

Her lips curl into a wry smirk. "You drink chai?"

"Don't sound so surprised. I work in a coffee shop, you know." I go on to explain my desire to create a unique beverage worthy of adding to Hill O' Beans menu board, leaving out the part about my bet with Sydney. "I've put my own spin on a mocha chai latte that I hope will impress Austin. I just have to come up with a name for it."

Gina chuckles. "Sounds terrific, but I try to avoid caffeine this late in the day."

I stand. "Fair enough. One hot chai coming up. Hot chocolate okay, Trina?"

Trina nods.

It takes me a few minutes to brew up two steaming mugs of chai and a hot chocolate, and then Gina proceeds to tell me everything she left out of that first conversation we had over brisket. She explains that her and Trina's power—like mine, an inherited trait—is the ability to read people's auras.

Keeping the words simple so I can understand them, she explains that all living creatures generate an energy field on wavelengths that practical science is unable to detect. Things like memories, thoughts, emotions, everything that makes up a person's psyche, help generate this field, which can manifest in a wide variety of colors and levels of intensity.

I recall something Gina told me before. "You said you were good at reading people. Is this what you meant?"

"It is."

"So...you can tell good people from bad?"

She takes a sip from her tea. "It's not quite *that* simple. People's auras can change slightly depending on their moods, their circumstances. Good people can have bad days, and bad people can have good days. Being able to read another person's heart? That takes years of practice."

I'm almost afraid to ask the next question. "What...what does my aura tell you?" My nerve falters, and I cover it up by staring at the floor.

Trina sets her mug down on the end table, pulls her legs onto the couch, and adopts a kneeling position so she can look me square in the eye. "You're bright. In fact, your aura is the brightest I've ever seen."

"Bright? Is that...a good thing?"

Gina's expression becomes almost reverent, much like the first time we spoke. "It's not a *good* thing, Bax. It's the best thing."

Wow. Did not see *that* coming.

I feel my eyes glaze over as I process this latest ten-megaton bombshell. A dozen possible explanations zoom through my brain, each more ridiculous than the one before it.

Though my thermostat is set at a level most would call "toasty," my legs start to shiver. I push down on them with my hands before they start tapping out a drum beat on my carpet.

Nothing makes sense anymore. Nothing at all.

"It can't be true," I whisper.

"I assure you, it is," Gina says. "Even now, the energy you give off is so radiant that it takes a lot of concentration not to be blinded by it."

"But you're also very blue," Trina says. "I mean, your aura is."

"Blue?" I ask. "You mean, like, sad?"

"Exactly," Gina confirms. "That's where the term comes from." Her voice becomes soft, maternal. "I gather something terrible happened to you, something that affected you on a profoundly deep level. I will say this...you hide your pain well. But your aura doesn't lie."

I feel a pang of embarrassment. These two can read me like an open book printed in a ridiculously large font. I tug at my fingers, wondering if I should spill my darkest secret, but a little voice tells me not to. I can't dump that on Trina when her best friend is in the hands of a killer.

No doubt sensing my turmoil, Gina says, "Was it when your father died?"

I shake my head. "No. It was...something else. Something worse."

"It's all right. You don't have to tell me if you don't want to. But if you need someone to talk to, and I mean *ever*, I'm here."

I fix her with a puzzled stare. "Why are you so nice to me?"

She flinches as if taken aback by the question. "I'm nice to everyone. At least, I like to think I am."

"It's more than that. You invited me into your home even though you'd only just met me. You let me babysit Trina even though you knew about my sketchy past." I shoot a glance Trina's way, earning a sad smile. "You stood up for me in front of Detective Rojas. That's more than just being nice."

Gina lets out a deep sigh. "When I was a little girl, my grandmother told me all about what it means to be an aurapath, to be able to see deep into a person's soul with just one glance. It sounded so cool at the time, like magic. I had huge dreams about how I could use my gift to help mankind. Stuff like that."

"I was like that when I found out I could read auras too," Trina says.

"How old were you when you...?" I ask.

"Five."

"Huh?" I face Gina. "My power didn't kick in until, literally, the day after I turned eighteen. How is it Trina started so young?"

"Because every person's brain is different," she replies. "And every version of ESP is different. I'm sorry I don't have a better explanation than that."

"What was it like for you?"

Gina slumps back into the couch. "Once the glamor wore off and I discovered how scary the world outside my door is, I took what my mom and grandmother had to say a lot more seriously, to sharpen my skills, to focus. I couldn't use my gift frivolously, and neither could I reveal it to anyone, not even my closest friends. The lesson that took me the longest to learn was that being special didn't make me superior to anyone else.

"By the time I finished college, I learned that the line between good and evil is a lot thinner than I could have ever realized, as well as the heavy price for ignoring my instincts."

Not sure I want to hear the story behind that sentence.

She puts a hand on my shoulder. "Grandma Rose told me about people like you, those with an aura so bright it's like angels were surrounding you. She said if we're lucky, we'll come across such a person in our lifetime, and if we do, it's our duty to support them in any way we can. I thought it was just a fairy tale… until I walked out my front door and saw you talking to Trina."

"It's not that I don't believe you," I stammer. "What I don't understand is why it's that way. I'm a screw-up, always have been. I'm selfish, obnoxious, unreliable—"

Gina's face breaks into a warm grin. "In other words, you're human." She edges closer to me so that our legs are touching. "You have the potential to do so much good, Bax. I may not know you well, but even I see that. You just need to be around people who believe in you. Most importantly, you need to believe in yourself."

I feel some of her words sink in, and my last stubborn defenses crumble.

Over the next ten minutes, I return the favor and reveal everything I've experienced since I moved into Arbor Vista. I tell them about the DP Killer, from the moment I caught him tossing evidence to my confiding in Piper to my phone call to the hotline this morning. By the time I finish, I feel despair creep back in. "I wanted to catch him. Not just to show up Detective Rojas, but to stop him from killing another little girl. I risked my freedom to pursue this, and I thought I was helping. I know the guy's name, his face, what he drives, what he does for a living. And he took Cheyanne anyway. Because I failed."

Trina's arms wrap around me. "It wasn't your fault."

I think of all the time I wasted between discovering my ability and today. All the things I should have done differently. Instead of slinging lattes, I could have been doing research. I could have taken Piper into my confidence sooner than I did. Maybe If I'd called the hotline one day earlier, the cops would've found him, and Cheyanne wouldn't be in mortal danger.

Yeah. That and a quarter will get me a gumball.

A buzzing sound shakes me out of self-pity mode. Gina grunts and winces when she checks the caller ID. "Crud."

"Is it Grandma Pam?" Trina asks.

Gina nods, then takes the call. "Hi, Mom."

I can't make out any words on the other end, but from the tone, Gina's mother doesn't sound happy.

"Yes, it's true. Trina's fine. A little shaken, but...no, Mom." She pinches the bridge of her nose. "That's not necessary. I assure you, we're perfectly...The police are on it, okay? Not only that... what?" She lowers the phone, closes her eyes, and mouths a curse word I'm grateful she didn't say aloud. "Hang on a minute. No. I said hang on, okay?" Gina hits the Hold button and makes an exasperated face.

"Dare I ask?" I say.

She shakes the cell like she wants to throw it against the wall. "My mother saw the story about Cheyanne on CNN. She wants Trina and me on the next plane to Albuquerque."

Trina's mouth forms a perfect O. "Oh, no. I am *not* leaving town! If...*when* they find Cheyanne, she's gonna need me."

Gina stands. "Relax, sweetie, we're not going anywhere. I need a few minutes to talk Mom down, so I'll take this next door."

"Can I stay with Bax?" Trina asks. I nod, indicating my permission.

"Okay. I'll be right back. And if I'm not, just come home soon."

"Sure thing."

With a final reassuring smile, Gina leaves.

"So..." Trina says after an awkward silence. "What do we do

now?"

That's the million-dollar question, for which I have no answer.

My eyes return to the blank laptop screen, and a germ of an idea forms. It's a long shot, but at this point, I'll take it. I lean forward, running my fingers across the mouse pad. Given what I'm about to do, I'm suddenly glad Gina's no longer in the room. "Trina, I need you to look at a picture for me." The screensaver vanishes, and Harold's picture once again appears.

Trina edges forward on the couch cushion, bringing her face closer for a better look. Neither of us speaks for many long moments. She turns the laptop toward her, then leans even nearer. A tiny gasp escapes her lips. "I know him," she whispers. "I mean, I've seen him before."

"At your school?"

She nods. "He was there several times, looking through this weird-looking camera-thing at our gym. Me and the other kids were told to leave him and the rest of the construction guys alone." She shudders. "I didn't want to go anywhere near him."

I think I know the answer, but I ask anyway. "Why?"

"His aura is dark. Like, scary dark." She sniffles again. "Now he's got Cheyanne."

Lowering my voice, I say, "This is very important, Trina. When was the first time you saw him?"

She faces me, her brow scrunched. "It was about a month ago, I think. A few days before the construction started."

"And how many times did you see him after that?"

She shrugs. "I dunno, like three or four."

I grimace. The monster I, and a zillion cops, are looking for was less than a mile away several times, and no one had a clue. "Did you see him today?"

Trina shakes her head. "Believe me, I would have noticed. Someone with an aura that dark stands out. If he was at the school today, it wasn't because he was there to take pictures or whatever."

A glimmer of hope grows in my brain. "When was the last time you did see him?"

She looks at her fingers, counting them off. "It was Friday, so four days ago."

"Did you see him leave?"

"Kind of. When school got out, I saw him in the parking lot, leaning on his car. He had a clipboard in his hands, but he wasn't looking at it. He was watching all the kids walking by."

Another piece clicks into place. Harold was looking for Cheyanne. His next victim, who he'd already picked out.

Wait...what? "His car? He wasn't leaning on a van?"

"No, it was a car. A dark blue one."

"And you're sure the car was his?"

She scowls. "Positive. I waited outside the middle school for Cheyanne and Crescent for like ten minutes. The three of us walked home together like we always do. Halfway between school and here, the blue car drove by us. It was definitely him driving. He slowed down for a second to look at us, then he drove off. I remember saying what a creep I thought he was."

The bastard has another vehicle. One the cops probably don't know about.

Tears well in Trina's eyes. "I'm so stupid. When I heard Cheyanne was kidnapped...I was just so shocked. I never thought..." Her fists clench and unclench, and she squirms in her seat.

"Hey." I slip off the couch and kneel in front of her, placing my hands on her knees to steady her. "You couldn't have known it was him."

"D-do you think I should tell the cops?"

"Definitely. As soon as you get home, tell your mom. You can call them together. Tell them about Harold, and his car. They'll probably ask you to come to the nearest precinct to give a statement, or they may send an officer by. Just make sure you don't use Harold's name, or you'll have to explain how you know it."

She nods slowly. "Okay."

"I don't suppose you know what kind of car it was?"

Her lips pull into a frown. "Sorry. It looks kinda like the Chevy that Crescent's mom drives, but I could be wrong."

I feel my breath quicken. This thing ain't over yet. "One last question, Trina. Is the construction on your gym done?"

She nods. "Pretty much. It was supposed to end today, but there's still a lot of stuff that needs to be picked up. I think they'll come get that tomorrow."

I envelop Trina in a light hug. "You are amazing, you know that?"

After the horrendous day we've both had, her tiny chuckle warms my heart. "Well, duh."

Our embrace is interrupted by a knock on my back door, followed by a familiar voice. "Bax?"

"Who's that?" Trina asks, glancing furtively at the door.

"A friend."

I've no sooner swung the door open when Piper steps into me. "Oh, God, Bax, I'm so sorry."

I hold her tight, pressing my cheek to the top of her head. "So am I."

"I should've spent more time on this," she sobs, facing me. Her distraught expression is heartbreaking.

"Stop," I soothe. "We couldn't have known he'd strike again so soon."

The words are meant to allay Piper's guilt, but I'm still beating myself up over the exact same thing. Hypocrisy, thy name is Bax.

"Ahem." Trina, arms crossed, stares at us bemusedly from the couch.

"Oh." Piper steps away from me, smoothing out the wrinkles in her thick brown sweater. "Sorry. Didn't realize you had company." She plasters a smile on her face and approaches Trina, hand outstretched. "Hi. I'm Piper. You must be Trina."

"Yeah." Trina accepts the handshake but doesn't return the smile. "He's told you about me?"

"Only good things."

"Hmm." My little friend eyes my coworker up and down. "Are you two, like, dating or something?"

Is it my imagination, or does Trina sound a teensy bit jealous?

"No," Piper says. "We're just friends."

Trina's scowl remains, and I find myself getting annoyed. The last thing I want tonight is for two members of my support group to get off on the wrong foot over a non-issue. "Put your claws away, *Kitty Kat*. Piper's cool, I promise."

Trina turns her glare upon me, our moment of mild triumph apparently behind us. I swear, little girls and their mood swings... "Maybe she is," she says. "But she has to pass the Trina Test before I agree."

Piper shoots me an *is she serious?* look.

Hoping to get this over with quickly, I shrug and say, "Just go with it."

"First question," Trina says without preamble. "Do you prefer chocolate or vanilla?"

I consider giving Piper a visual cue so she can pass this childish test, but Trina's too sharp to not pick up on it. I can only watch and hope as Piper answers, "Uh, chocolate, I guess."

Trina nods in approval. "Second question...cats or dogs?"

Piper, trooper that she is, places her purse on the coffee table and takes the far end of the couch. "Dogs, definitely. When I was your age, my black lab was my best friend."

A slight grin appears on Trina's face. "Final question...*Lord of the Rings* or *Harry Potter*?"

Piper turns to me. "You weren't kidding, were you?"

"Nope," I say, shouting *Lord of the Rings* at her as loud as I can inside my mind. I have no idea what will happen if Piper answers wrong, and I hope Trina doesn't decide to hate on Piper just because we hugged each other.

"And your answer is...?" Trina says.

Piper spreads her arms. "*Harry*, of course. House Ravenclaw all the way!"

Crap.

I wait long seconds for Trina to give my coworker the bad news. Then Trina grins and holds out her fist. "You pass."

Piper bumps Trina's fist, and the two share a smile.

What the what? I answered *Lord of the Rings*! Didn't I?

Whatever. As long as they're cool, that's all that matters right now.

"Is Austin pissed at me?" I ask Piper. "I know I left work in kind of a hurry."

"Yes, you did, and no, he's not. In fact, he vouched for you when Detective Rojas came by Hill O' Beans. So did I."

Bitch actually checked out my alibi. Color me surprised.

"Thanks for having my back," I say.

"Just returning the favor. I don't suppose there's any news?"

"About Cheyanne? I'm afraid not."

"But we figured something else out about Harold," Trina says.

Piper's mouth falls open. "You told her his name?"

"I had to. It's her best friend." I hold my hands up in a defensive posture. "She also knows about...me. So does her mother. They know everything."

Piper stands quickly, then moves over to me before whispering, "And you trust them?"

"Yes," I say, loud enough for Trina to hear. "As much as I trust you. Which is a lot."

She turns to Trina. "I know you and Bax are friends, but this is a *really* big secret. Are you sure you'll be able to—"

"I can keep a secret," Trina says with pronounced indignance. "Not all girls are blabbermouths."

Piper looks at me, then at Trina, then exhales. "All right then."

Trina's phone dings. She pulls it from her pocket, scans a text, then nods. "Thank God. Mom talked Grandma into letting us stay." She stands. "I gotta go." Without warning, she wraps her arms around my waist. "We have to find her, Bax."

I return the hug, a knot twisting in my stomach. "We will."

She smiles weakly up at Piper. "Nice to meet you."

"You too."

"Remember to tell the cops only what we discussed," I admonish Trina.

"I will. Talk to you soon." With that, she rushes home.

While I'm disposing of the remnants of the tea in the sink, I fill Piper in on my conversation with Trina, leaving out the revelation that my next-door neighbors are aurapaths. Letting that little factoid slip would be a 6.8 on the Richter scale of stupid.

"So he has another car." Piper stifles a yawn, then rubs her eyes.

"Yup. Assuming the cops take Trina's statement seriously, it may lead them directly to Harold's door."

"What if it doesn't?" Piper quavers. "I know I said I didn't want to get personally involved, but we can't just sit back and wait for the cops to..." She trails off, and her entire expression changes. I practically see the light bulb come on over her head. A sly grin materializes.

"Well, don't keep me in suspense," I prod.

"I have an idea. It's the mother of all longshots, but if it works, we might just be able to end this."

Adrenaline courses through my veins. "Is it risky?"

"Yes."

"Dangerous?"

"Yes."

"Like, we-might-get-killed dangerous?"

Her smile melts away. "You're not helping."

"Sorry."

"But our only other option is to sit and wait. And I suck at that."

I punch a fist into my open palm with a resounding smack. "Let's do it."

Chapter Twenty-Four

W hat's more suspicious than two teenagers staking out an elementary school from a car parked not thirty yards from the spot where a kid was abducted less than a day before?

Answer—nothing.

Thank God for tinted windows.

"How about some tunes?" I ask Piper, who's slouched in the driver's seat.

"No. We can't have any distractions," she says.

"Fine." I heave a dramatic sigh. "Just wanted to break up the monotony. We've been here for hours."

She pierces me with a determined glare. "And we may be here for several more. But the alternative is giving up. Which ain't happening."

I nod. She's taken Cheyanne's kidnapping hard, almost as hard as me. I guess in her mind, she turned our investigation into one of her sleuth stories. If it weren't for the fact that three sets of parents had to bury their preteen daughters, I might even be caught up in the thrill of it all. But Piper's right—Cheyanne needs all the help she can get, and we can't let boredom win out.

Based on the plan we hashed out last night, she'd picked me

up just before eight o'clock this morning. We drove all of five hundred yards, choosing an empty spot along 57th Avenue for our stakeout. Since then, we've watched hundreds of parents escort their kids to both the elementary and middle schools, though I suspect an even greater number of children were forced to stay home today. All that remains of the police presence that blanketed the area last night is one section of curb across the street surrounded by crime scene tape and one patrol car that seems to be making a circuitous route every half hour or so. The only person who's noticed Piper and me is a burly rent-a-cop no doubt brought in by the school district for extra security. He gave us the hairy eyeball but didn't ask us to leave.

Yeah. *Now* they bring in extra help. As Grandpa used to say, talk about locking the stable door after the horse has gone.

So far I've managed to keep my reservations about this last-ditch plan silent—honestly, it sounded so much better in my living room—but as the silence grows uncomfortable, I can't keep them in any longer. "You really think Harold's going to show up for work today? The guy may be a wacko, but he's smart. Coming back would be like stepping into the lion's den."

"Maybe you're right," Piper concedes. "Like I said, it's a longshot. But he's a surveyor, right? Most of them are independent contractors. They sign a deal to take measurements before, during, and after construction. If he doesn't perform his duties, he doesn't get paid."

"I get that. But he's wreaked havoc on this city, and the cops are under a shit-ton of pressure to bring him in, dead or alive. He's a cold-blooded sonofabitch, but I can't see him risking certain death just for a paycheck."

She slurps some melted ice from her soda cup, the last remnants of our drive-thru breakfast. "Bear with me here. Harold is nothing if not meticulous. I have to believe that extends to his work habits. He's gone undetected this long by being invisible, by reporting to work, doing his job, and not drawing attention. Shirking his duties would look suspicious."

"He could call in sick."

"Yeah, he could. Maybe we are just wasting our time. He could come back to finish tomorrow, or Friday. But if Trina's right and the construction is done, I'm betting the state or the school district or whoever hired Harold will only give him so long to submit the final measurements before they ask someone else to do it."

"Those are some pretty big assumptions," I say.

"I know."

"Speaking of calling in sick, are you gonna text Austin you're not coming in today?"

Piper runs her thumbs across the casing of her switched-off phone, then glances at the clock, which reads ten minutes past noon. "I guess I'll have to."

With a sigh, she activates it and shoots boss-man a text.

Piper: Austin - just heard from Joe. Dad's sick again. Have to be there for him. Will try to be back tomorrow. Sorry.

With that, she turns her phone off and drops it into the compartment between the seats. "Shit."

"Yeah."

My own phone buzzes with a text from Austin, asking me if I can cover for Piper. I respond with a half-baked story about spending time with one of my old drinking buddies on the other side of town. Not sure if he buys it, but he doesn't pressure me.

"Shit," I say.

"Yeah," Piper responds.

"Austin's a great boss. I hate lying to him, but I can't exactly say, 'Hey, can't make it in, we're going after a child murderer,' can I?"

"Nope."

"Duck."

We scrunch down in our seats just as the police car coasts by at five miles per hour. It doesn't slow down, which means the cop behind the wheel didn't see us. Again.

"Any more trouble with Gavin?" I ask after the patrol car turns a corner.

"No. Guess it finally sank in. Took him long enough." She sighs, and tugs at the folds of her sweater. "Guys can be such assholes sometimes."

I feign annoyance. "Hey, I resemble that remark."

She smiles. "You're not an asshole."

"You wouldn't say that if you'd met me a couple of years ago. I couldn't have been more of a jerk if I'd taken classes for it."

Piper straightens up, then leans against the driver's-side window. "I guess both of us have grown up a lot since then."

Word.

"It's not always going to be like this, you know," she says.

"What won't?"

She spreads her arms as wide as she can in the cramped space. "Everything. I have to believe that a time will come when we'll be able to assert some control over our lives. To make our own decisions. To do what we want to do and not what we *have* to do."

I gaze out the windshield, focusing on the construction crew's pickup trucks that pulled into the elementary school parking lot an hour ago, right around the time the kids' recess period started. "There's always gonna be rules. Usually written by someone else."

"I don't have a problem with rules. But life should be more than that."

I fold my arms and quirk an eyebrow at her.

"What?" she asks.

"Are you always this existential, or is philosophy an elective course you're taking?"

She punches me playfully in the arm, and I see the twinkle return to her eyes. "I should have warned you. I tend to get introspective when I'm sitting in a parked car with a clairvoyant while waiting for a serial killer."

I chuckle, but it dies quickly. So many things I want to say to Piper clog my brain. How she's the greatest friend I've ever had. How she's smart and selfless and amazing and beautiful.

How I wish I wasn't completely the wrong guy for her.

My chest constricts, and guilt washes over me. "I'm sorry. I shouldn't have dragged you into this mess. It was wrong and boneheaded and...I'm sorry."

She takes my hand and gives it a squeeze. "Make good on that spa day, and you can consider yourself forgiven."

Seven brawny guys in white coveralls and orange vests, laden with gear or carrying ladders, emerge into Arbor Vista Elementary's parking lot, making their way for the row of pickups. Piper and I watch as they proceed to secure or stow their equipment inside their vehicles. Most of them go back for more. The whole process takes several round trips. By two-thirty, all but one of the pickups has left. The straggler, who I guess is the crew's foreman, produces a clipboard, scribbles on a few sheets of paper attached to it, and hands it to a chubby guy in a fugly suit with a professorial beard. The bearded guy signs the paper, hands the clipboard back, and bids the foreman adieu. Seconds later, the pickup peels out of the parking lot, in the direction of Hill O' Beans.

"Well, that's that," I say. "Trina's gym is open for business, but there's no sign of our guy."

Piper smacks the steering wheel with her palm. "Dammit. I guess I was wrong about...wait a sec, who's that?"

I squint in the direction of her pointing finger. In front of the administrative building stands another man, talking to Fugly Suit. He's not wearing coveralls or a vest. Rather, he's dressed in tan slacks and a crisp white button-down shirt. A black baseball cap tops his head, and his eyes are covered by sunglasses.

But it's what's in his hand that gets my attention. A theodolite. In his other hand is a duffle bag.

"Holy shit," I whisper. "It's him."

Piper gulps. "He's wearing shades. Are you sure?"

I whip out my cell phone, switch on the camera app, and zoom in as close as I can. Trying to keep my hand from shaking, I snap a couple of pics. Despite the coolness of the car, beads of sweat trickle down my neck.

I show Piper the picture, which is slightly blurry, but it perfectly frames the man's face. "Same nose, same mouth. Same shirt, same slacks. And that's the same duffle bag Sarah saw in the back of the van. It's him."

A mixture of fear and triumph flashes through Piper's eyes. "He came. Jeez, the balls on this guy ..."

"But how?" I puzzle aloud. "We have a perfect view of every car that came into both schools' parking lots. There hasn't been a single white van or a blue Chevy."

Before she can answer, the man places the duffle on the ground and shakes Fugly Suit's hand. The two men share a friendly farewell, then Fugly Suit vanishes inside the administrative building. Harold —please, Lord, let it be Harold—pulls a fob from his pocket, clicks it, and the trunk of a red Ford Taurus rises of its own accord. Moments later, the duffle bag and theodolite are inside the trunk.

"What the hell? A red car too?" I mutter. "How many vehicles does this guy have?"

"I don't know." In one fluid movement, Piper slides her seat belt over her torso and locks it in place. Then she twists the key, and the Altima's engine turns over. "Any sign of that cop car?"

I crane my neck, scanning every inch of street I can see. "Nope."

Fifty yards away, Harold slips behind the Taurus's wheel and slams the door shut.

"What are we gonna do? He's about to leave!" I say.

Piper closes her eyes, utters what sounds like a short prayer, then shifts the gear into Drive. "Only one thing we can do." She shoots me an evil grin. "Buckle up, Bax. The game is afoot."

Oh, goody.

Turns out tracking a moving car from another moving car while you're making every effort not to be seen by the driver of said moving car is not as easy as they make it look on TV. Screw you, Hollywood.

Piper handles her little economy car like a pro. She somehow manages to keep the Taurus within sight while maintaining a discreet distance, a task helped by the approximately ten billion cars that congest the streets of Phoenix. I swear, it seems half the city's roads are under construction at any given time. Never thought I'd be thankful for that.

Harold, for his part, gives no indication that he's aware he's picked up a tail. Which, granted, means nothing. I have no reason to believe he might be armed with anything deadlier than a syringe full of poison, but that's pure wishful thinking on my part.

Any hopes I had that Harold would head straight back to his house—or wherever the hell he's stashed Cheyenne—are dashed as he pulls the Taurus into the parking lot of a small mom-and-pop diner. Guess even serial killers have to eat.

After another hour's wait, he emerges. From the diner, we follow him to a discount clothing outlet, a toy store, and now a supermarket.

"Jesus H. Is he *ever* going home?" Piper grumbles, killing the Altima's engine again as Harold exits his vehicle to run his latest errand.

I give voice to the gnawing fear eating a hole in my gut. "Do you think he knows we're here?"

"I hope not." She pops open the compartment between the seats and roots around for a few seconds, producing a pencil and a piece of scrap paper. "Wait here."

"Where do you think you're going?" I ask, my eyes glued to the store entrance. "What if he sees you?"

"Relax. He doesn't know me from Adam, remember? Besides, he'll be in there for a while."

"How do you know?"

She gestures at the plethora of cars crammed into the parking lot. "There's gotta be hundreds of customers in there, which means there's gonna be a line. I'll only be a minute."

My partner strolls, casual as you please, up to Harold's car, conveniently parked next to one of those metal racks where shoppers deposit their empty carts. She makes like she's going to pull a cart out, then pauses. She scribbles something down on the paper, then pulls out her phone and snaps a pic.

"Learn anything?" I ask when she rejoins me.

"Sure did," she says. "The car isn't his. It's a rental."

I furrow my brow. "How can you tell?"

"There's a sticker with a barcode in the window. Rental car agencies use those for easy check-in and check-out."

"And you know that how?"

She sighs. "Remember that trip to Mexico Jackson and I were going to take with his friends? I was with him when he rented the van. Every car in the rental lot had one of those stickers."

"Wow." I shake my head. "This guy knows all the tricks. Wanna bet that blue Chevy Trina saw was also a rental?"

"Safe assumption. He probably only uses the van on those days when he..." She grimaces. "You know."

"Yeah."

"Anyway, I wrote down the license plate and took a picture of the rental sticker."

I turn back to the supermarket entrance. Still no sign of Harold. "Do you think we should call the police now?"

"And tell them what? All we have on him is that he resembles a guy who died three years ago under mysterious circumstances, a thousand miles from here."

I feel a flush creep up my neck. "But it's him!"

"I know that. But we only have one shot at this. We have no clue where he lives, or where he's keeping Cheyanne. Tomorrow he might be driving a different car, surveying another site on the other side of town." She frowns at me. "I'll try not to lose him, but if he gives us the slip, we'll have no other choice but to inform the police."

"Okay then." I check the car's tiny clock, which reads 4:15. Something else occurs to me. "If he really does live out in the sticks, it might be dark by the time we get there. And there won't be a ton of traffic to hide behind either. Sooner or later he's gonna notice the same Nissan's been tailgating him since he left the school."

"Maybe. Maybe not. Look at what he's done. He evades a citywide manhunt and kidnaps another girl like it's just another day at the office. Then he has the balls to return to the *very same* neighborhood the next day and finish his work assignment. He's confident in his ability to evade every cop in this city. Two teenagers are the last thing he'd expect."

Hrm.

The sun is just above the western horizon when Harold exits the supermarket, pushing a cart laden with bags, a small square cake, and a half-dozen pre-inflated balloons with "Happy Birthday" written on them in huge, festive letters. Harold transfers the cake to the passenger seat and shoves the rest in the back, then we're on the road again.

"You saw the balloons?" I ask as we run into another clutch of traffic.

"Uh huh. One guess who they're for."

I adjust the seat to a slightly more reclining position. "Ariel would be ten today, I guess. Unbelievable that one little girl's accidental death could destroy so many lives."

"He won't be destroying anything else."

Piper says it with such resolve that I actually believe her.

Eventually, the logjam of cars thins out and Harold turns the Taurus north on 99th Avenue. A row of distant mountains grows ever closer as the traffic lights become fewer and farther between. Piper maintains her distance, and I continue to hope that our quiet pursuit will remain undetected. Every mile we travel brings us closer to twilight and reinforces that belief.

"You're good on gas?" I ask, breaking the protracted silence.

"Filled it up this morning," she says. "And now that it's

getting dark, I'm going to turn my headlights on. Between that and the balloons obscuring his rearview, he won't be able to see us."

Here's hoping.

Piper decelerates as Harold turns off the main road and onto the first of a series of undulating two-lane streets. I feel the onset of panic when the Taurus disappears from sight a couple of times, then heave a sigh of relief when we pick up his trail again.

A huge decorative wall bearing the words "Copper Mesa Estates," proudly displayed beyond a lush stone fountain illuminated by bright halogen lights, greets us around the next corner. Piper slams on the brakes, causing me to pitch forward slightly. It takes me a moment to realize why.

Just ahead of us is a wide security gate, through the bars of which I spot the Taurus disappear around yet another corner.

"Dammit," I grunt. "We lost him."

"Don't sweat it," Piper says. "It's a gated community. This is probably the only way in. Which means we're close."

I focus on the few houses I can see on the other side of the gate. They're large and luxurious, many of them two-story affairs that look like they could comfortably house a large family and still have plenty of elbow room. I'd stop short of calling them mansions, but I'm sure it would take a bank account with at least seven figures in it to live here.

"You were right," I say. "This is a nice neighborhood. Remote, quiet, respectable. You could cook crystal meth in your basement, and no one would even suspect."

Piper shoots me a skeptical glance.

"Just sayin'," I finish. "So what do we do? Wait for someone else to enter and follow them in?"

Her reply doesn't come. That's when I see the guard, who exits a structure next to the entry gate and approaches us. He's huge, with a stocky build and a head so square it looks like he stepped out of a Minecraft game. The scowl he directs at us is severe enough to melt the Altima's engine block. He makes a circular motion with his finger, an indication for Piper to lower her window. She obeys.

"Visiting someone or making a delivery?" he says in a clipped voice. The man's ugly face and donut gut make me believe he washed out of cop school and took this job so he could get paid to sit on his ass while taking advantage of every opportunity to throw his considerable weight around.

"Uh, neither," Piper says with a disarming smile. "We're um, seniors, and we're, uh, doing a fundraiser for our high school band so we can compete in nationals."

Wow. Did she make that up on the spot? This girl never ceases to amaze me.

The guard, sadly, isn't biting. "No soliciting allowed here. Shove off."

"Please, sir. With budget cuts, our school is unable to—"

Mr. Squarehead leans down, giving us a full view of his bull-dog-like face. I catch a whiff of garlic as he sneers at us. "I don't like repeating myself. Shove off right now, girlie, or I'll detain you."

Piper recoils from the man's stinky breath, scrunching her nose.

"Relax, Deputy Dog," I say, unable to contain the sass, "we're leaving. Go gnaw on a milk-bone or something."

The guard opens his mouth to bark out a rebuttal, but Piper cuts him off by rolling up her window and throwing the Altima into reverse. Seconds later, Mr. Crankypants is a hundred yards behind us.

The road we're on leads into several more neighborhoods, not as swanky as Copper Mesa but still high-end and thankfully not gated. Piper finds a stretch of curb, pulls over, and kills the engine before turning to me with an annoyed smirk. "I guess oral hygiene isn't a requirement for security positions in this part of town," she says. "Bleargh." She fans the air, which still has a garlicky stench. It doesn't help, so she rolls down all four windows.

"So now what?" I ask.

"Give me a minute." She activates her phone and does some quick tapping.

I lean in. "Is that Google Maps?"

"Yeah." A few more taps, and the picture changes to that of a website. "Copper Mesa Estates. One hundred and thirty-five homes spread over twenty acres. The land was purchased eight years ago, and the first ten homes were completed less than a year later. There are still a handful of lots that are on the market, as the houses have yet to be completed."

"A hundred and thirty-five?" I ask, incredulous. "Even if we could get in, how can we search that many houses without getting caught?"

"It won't be that many. Remember, the view outside his basement window is nothing but desert." She smiles, then switches back to the map. "Which means his house has to be on the northern perimeter. That narrows it down to about a dozen addresses."

"Any ideas about getting in?"

She shuts the phone off and faces me. "Maybe. But we need to take a few minutes to formulate a plan. Whatever we end up doing, it'll have to be after dark."

"I think I saw a sandwich place about a mile back up the road."

"Sold."

Thanks to our old friend Google, Piper and I determine our entry point to Copper Mesa over pastrami hoagies—an exit gate on the western side of the complex. The good news is that it's more than a half-mile from the guard gate and Carl's long-lost brother, and that it exits onto a street close to several other neighborhoods. The bad news is that the exit gate is very well lit...and in full view of a security camera.

And then there's the spike strip that will shred Piper's tires if she attempts to drive in unnoticed.

"Well, crap," I say.

Piper grunts in response.

"We could scale the wall."

She points. "You mean that wall? The eight-foot-high monster with the barbed wire on top? Good luck, Peter Parker."

Now it's my turn to grunt. "Where are the guys from *Ocean's Eleven* when you need them?"

"Not here." Piper restarts the car, then moves it to a spot along the curb a hundred yards up the road, out of the camera's line of sight. Phone in hand, she grabs her jacket from the backseat, then we leave the Altima behind. Night has fallen, and there's a definite nip in the air, so I zip up my jacket and pull on my gloves.

As we walk toward the exit gate, Piper slips her hand into mine, catching me off guard. "In case anyone's watching," she says. "We're just two kids out for a walk."

I squeeze her hand, noting the look of trepidation on her face. She's scared shitless, and I gotta admit, I am too. But we've come too far to turn back now.

The exit gate, now thirty yards away, remains obstinately closed. The security camera, attached to a pole on the other side of the huge wall, stares down at it like it's daring us to enter.

We slow our pace, then stop before we enter the camera's field of view. Selling the illusion that Piper and I are a couple, I pull her into my arms. She doesn't resist. I think both of us could use some comfort right now, given the epically foolhardy thing we're about to do.

"Bax?" she quavers. Her arms tighten around me. God, this feels good.

"Yes?"

"What the hell are we doing here?"

I pull back slightly, pressing my forehead to hers. "Stopping a killer. Saving a little girl."

Her eyes close behind her cat-eye glasses, and she swallows several times. Her breath is warm on my face and smells faintly of pastrami. I find myself staring, captivated by our proximity.

I want to reach out, to caress her cheek, to say something romantic, all that mushy stuff I never had to bother with in my previous relationships. To show her what she means to me, and what her friendship has done for me.

I can't, though. Now would be the wrongest time in the history of ever for that.

Maybe someday, there'll be a right time. Assuming I don't end up in prison. Or dead.

The faint hum of moving metal and the scrape of wheels on asphalt meets our ears. We both turn to see the exit gate sliding slowly open. Any second now, a car will drive through it, giving us our window of opportunity.

"This is it," I say.

"Once we go through that gate, we're breaking the law," she whispers. "My dad's gonna kill me."

Better him than Harold, I almost say. "I can go alone if—"

"No. I'm coming with you."

Our arms around each other, we resume our stroll along the sidewalk. The gate, now half-open, is twenty yards away.

Time stretches out. The gate slides all the way open.

A black Mercedes eases through, high beams on full blare. It merges onto the street, then zooms past us without slowing down.

The gate starts to close.

"Let's go," Piper says. "For Cheyanne."

"For Cheyanne."

Lowering our heads to avoid looking at the camera, we break into a sprint and charge through the open gate.

Chapter Twenty-Five

Piper and I race a good hundred yards before we risk a glance behind us. No alarm bells, no flashing sirens, no team of Special Forces dudes leaping from the shadows armed with automatic weapons. I'm a little surprised—I mean, it's not like we just broke into the Pentagon, but still.

On the off chance no one spotted us sneaking in, we resume our stroll around Copper Mesa, once again joining hands to enhance the illusion that we totally belong there. Not that there's anyone we need to convince of this, as the only person we see in the first five minutes is some guy hosing down his driveway. Piper waves in greeting but is ignored. Guess Copper Mesa isn't the close-knit community Arbor Vista is. Wonder how they'd feel if they knew who one of their neighbors is.

Hopefully, by this time tomorrow, they will.

We turn a corner and find ourselves looking down a long, straight stretch of road. Green signs designate numerous side-streets all the way down. I take a moment to admire the splendor of the houses we pass, with their vaulted roofs and three-car garages and lawns that have been manicured so precisely you'd think the President was dropping by for a visit. Even the lamps that provide much of the illumination are fancy schmancy.

And then there are the security cameras, which look to be attached to every fourth lamppost. Piper and I spot one at the same time, its lens focused right on us.

"Nuts," I breathe.

"Keep walking," she says. "Eyes on the road."

"What if Deputy Dog sees us?"

"Then he sees us. I'm fairly certain we can outrun him before he shoots us."

I honestly can't tell if she's joking.

"Maybe we should split up," I suggest, pointing. "If that map you showed me is right, Harold's house has to be at the end of one of these four streets."

"Good idea." She faces me. "Stick to the shadows, don't look at any more cameras, and if you find his house, text me right away. I'll do the same."

I nod and gesture at the nearest street. "I'll take the first two, you take the other two."

"All right."

We grasp hands once again, sharing a wordless conversation. Again, I have the urge to plant a kiss on her lips, but fear stops me. Either she'd pull away, or she'd let it happen. I'm not sure which would be worse in the long run.

Piper and I part company as I cross the empty street to scope out the three houses at the end of the cul-de-sac. I shoot a glance over my shoulder halfway down, to find Piper has already disappeared from sight.

Most of the houses are fairly well-lit, and I'm suddenly thankful it's not Christmas season yet—this looks like the kind of neighborhood where every resident goes overboard trying to make their houses as sparkly as possible. There's only one streetlamp, which I avoid as much as I can without being obvious about it.

One of the three houses that might be Harold's is completely dark. I check that one out first. The garage is large enough to fit two cars, but the only vehicle I see is a light red SUV with a bumper sticker that reads "My Child Is An Honor Student At

Copper Bluff Elementary School." Several plastic toys are scattered across the lawn.

Either this isn't Harold's place, or it's the best damn disguise in history.

Taking care not to trip any motion sensors that might be affixed to the house, I crouch down next to the SUV and scope out the other two houses on my list. The shrill cry of a wailing baby issues from the next house over, which eliminates that one from contention. The third house is a gigantic two-story with shuttered windows and a small fountain of a dolphin near the front door. I peek up at one of the upper windows, which thanks to a bright overhead light I can see inside. I catch sight of what appears to be a preteen girl, walking back and forth across her room.

My brief hope that this might be Cheyanne is dashed when she turns around, and I see a cell phone stuck to her ear. Plus, the girl's complexion is much lighter than my missing friend's.

Without another word, I stand and walk back the way I came. I make a vow to be more careful. If that girl had seen me skulking outside like some pervy peeper, I'd be in even more trouble.

I head for the second of the four streets. There's no sign of Piper or of Deputy Dog, so I shoot her a quick text.

Me: First street down. No luck.

Seconds later, the reply comes.

Piper: Same here. Checking last street now.

The second cul-de-sac proves a bust as well. All three residences that could have been DPK HQ are eliminated in quick order when it's revealed that all of their garages have their doors open and not one is occupied by a white van or a Ford Taurus.

I'm about to shoot Piper another text when I see a car drive past me across the T-junction. It has the word "Security" prominently displayed on the side, and I bet I know who's behind the wheel.

I freeze, preparing to book it in the opposite direction, but whew, the car drives right by without stopping.

I palm my phone and am halfway from sending Piper a warning text when it rings. I answer on the first ring.

"Bax!" Excitement and dread lace Piper's voice. "I found it. I found Harold's house."

This barely registers with me as I feel my adrenaline spike. "Piper, listen! A security car just drove by and…"

As I watch, the car makes a left turn down the fourth street.

"He's on to you!" I stammer. "Get out of there!"

"I can't! It's a dead-end street! There's nowhere to go!" I hear her breath quicken. "Oh, shit, there he is."

Not fair. So not fair.

"Piper, just run. Maybe he can't catch you."

"It's too late."

In the background, a crusty voice shouts, "You there! Stay where you are!"

"Okay! Don't shoot!"

'Don't shoot?' Is that asshole holding a gun on her?

Piper froze. Of course she did. She's never broken the law before. She's probably never been in any kind of trouble at all. She doesn't have the fight-or-flight response delinquents like me have. And now she's gone and gotten herself caught.

"I gotta go," Piper whispers. "His address is 32038 North Shadow Trail Circle. Call the cops. *Don't get caught.*"

My response comes out as a whimper. "Piper—"

And then, silence as the call ends.

Crap. Crap shit fuck shit crap.

It's a full five minutes before the security car appears again. By that time, I've found a hiding spot behind one of many fat-trunked palm trees that line the road. It moves, slowly and deliberately, its driver no doubt searching for me. If it was Deputy Dog who nabbed Piper, then he'll be looking for me too. Piper won't give me up. I know this in my heart.

God, I hope I haven't just ruined her life.

Thoughts race through my mind as the car continues its snail's pace.

We could have come back tomorrow, staked out the entrance until Harold left, then found a way to approach his house from the desert side. That might have been easier, and much safer. Assuming, of course, that Cheyanne lives through the night.

No. I can't think like that. And it doesn't matter anyway. We made our play, and now it's down to me.

Finally, the car's engine fades away. I risk a peek around the tree and see it disappear around the bend. I picture Piper in the back seat, her head down, contemplating what a criminal record will mean for her and cursing the stupidity of this plan. I consider sending another text but dismiss it when I realize Deputy Dog probably confiscated her phone.

I'm alone. In every sense of the word.

Stop wallowing. You have a job to do, and because of Piper, now you can do it.

Hmm. With Deputy Douche out of the security office, maybe that means the monitors are unmanned. Or maybe not, but I have to chance it.

At a brisk pace, I move down the sidewalk, keeping a close eye on every camera I can see and making sure not to show my face to any of them. Two minutes later, I hang a left on Shadow Trail Circle and breathe a sigh of relief when I see a cul-de-sac much darker than the ones I just searched. It takes only a moment to discern why—several houses on this street are still under construction.

Skeletal wooden frames of incomplete homes greet me as I make my trek down the road. Piles of lumber and heavy equipment decorate the front yards, two of which have "Sold" signs staked to them.

For the first time since we entered the property, I feel a twinge of hope. There are no cameras keeping vigil on this street, which means I can stick close to the half-finished houses and not be noticed. To that end, I scoot off the sidewalk and duck behind a six-foot brick wall that separates this lot from its neighbor.

I poke my head out, scanning the end of the cul-de-sac. There, only thirty yards away, clearly visible despite the dim light, is a medium-sized one-story house that looks considerably smaller than all the other ones I've seen tonight. On the driveway are two vehicles.

A red Ford Taurus and a green van.

Wait...*green*?

Of course. The news reported that the DPK was seen shoving Cheyanne into a white van, so he went and repainted it.

Think you're clever, do you, Harold? We'll just see about that.

Several lights are on, but I don't see any movement inside the house. It's been an hour since he got home, which means Ariel's "birthday party" is likely underway or is about to be.

I sit there, on a mound of packed dirt, listening to the slight breeze blowing through Copper Mesa. Other than that, there's no sound at all. I shift position when I feel the cold penetrate my jeans and dig out my phone again. I stare at it, another plan falling into place inside my head. I wish I had time to think of a better one, but I can't stay here indefinitely. For all I know, Deputy Dog will call the cops in to do a sweep of the complex. Which actually wouldn't be such a bad thing, but I need to give them context. If Harold sees a kaleidoscope of flashing blue and red lights outside his window, he might decide to dispose of Cheyanne.

On my cell's screen, I bring up an Internet search window and find the number for the hotline. Quickly rehearsing what I'm going to say this time, I press the Call button.

After two rings, a male voice answers. "Federal Task Force Hotline. Officer Shoemaker speaking. Do you have information pertaining to the Disney Princess Killer?"

I exhale. "Yes."

"Before we begin, I must inform you that willingly providing false—"

"Yes, yes," I interrupt. "I know the drill. I called you guys yesterday."

"I see." Officer Shoemaker's tone turns to one of curiosity.

"Do I have your permission to record this conversation, Mister...Baxter?"

He knows my name? How does he—

Because I'm calling from my own phone, dumbass.

Oh well. That doesn't really matter now, does it?

"Go ahead," I concede.

"All right." Silence reigns for a few tense seconds before he continues, "You are now being recorded. What information do you wish to provide?"

"Quite a bit, actually." If not for the cold and my frazzled nerves, I'd probably be gloating. "I can start with his home address."

"His...home address." Officer Shoemaker says, clearly not buying it.

"Yeah. It's 32038 North Shadow Trail Circle, Copper Mesa Estates. He currently has two vehicles—the white van which he uses to kidnap the girls, which he's just painted green, and a rented red Ford Taurus, license plate HCG3429. I don't know what name he's using now, but he used to be called Harold Crane."

I wait several tense seconds for the officer to speak again. He doesn't. "Hello?"

"I'm here," he finally says. "May I ask how you know all this?"

"Because I followed him. I'm outside his house right now."

I hear the clack of a tapped keyboard, and then, "Hold on one moment."

Hold on? What in the world could he possibly be—

"Mr. Baxter?" It's a female's voice. A very familiar one.

How can my luck possibly be this bad? I mean, *how*?

"Detective Rojas," I mumble.

"Mr. Baxter," she repeats. I imagine her clenching her teeth and suppressing the urge to turn into She-Hulk. "I don't know what game you're playing, but it ends now. You are trespassing on private property, which is a Class Three felony. In addition to paying a heavy fine, you will—"

Rage pumping through my veins, I release my inner John McClane. "Go ahead. Fine me. Come the fuck down here and arrest me. I don't care! I gave you his name and his address. Do your goddamn job and save Cheyanne!"

I end the call and resist the temptation to smash the phone against the wall. Instead, I drop it into my lap and take several deep breaths while I calm myself. Man, that felt good. If nothing else, I finally got the last word on Detective Bitchface.

I gave them everything I had. Twice. That should be enough, right?

They're on their way. They have to be. If they suspect I might be telling the truth at all, they'll come. If they don't, Detective Rojas will come so she can personally arrest me.

Of course, knowing her, she could hang me out to dry and simply wait for me to come home.

You have the potential to do so much good, Bax, Gina's words echo in my brain.

Maybe I do. But doing good shouldn't be this hard.

I wait five minutes for the cops to show up. They don't. So I wait for five more. Still nothing.

Fuck.

I have to do something.

And I know what that is.

I activate the camera app and switch it to Selfie Mode. There's hardly any light, so all I see on the screen is a vague outline of my face, barely enough to identify me. It'll have to do.

I swallow hard, then hit Record.

"Uh, hi," I say. "My name is Bernard Baxter. Yeah, that's right, Bernard. Go ahead and laugh. I was named after my grandfather, who was a Vietnam war vet, and..." I shake my head. Focus, man! "Anyway, if you're listening to this, it's because I'm dead. Some might say I had it coming. Mom sure would. Probably Detective Rojas too. The reason I'm recording this is because I need someone to understand what my life has been like the past few weeks. You see, I'm psychic."

I pause for a few moments, giving any potential viewer time for that revelation to sink in. "To be more accurate, I'm psychometric. I discovered this ability the day after I moved out of Asterly Halfway House and into Arbor Vista Townhomes. A few days later, when I started working at Hill O' Beans, I came across a man in a white van throwing trash into the dumpster."

I spend the next ten minutes relating every bit of craziness that's taken place since that fateful day. The temperature seems to drop even further as I finish up. "I know it's hard to believe. But it's all true. If you want...what's the word...corroboration, just ask Piper McKinney. She's been helping me deal with this, and I wouldn't have tracked down the DP Killer without her. She's risked her future by helping me, so please, go easy on her. She's a good person, maybe the best person I've ever known." A cold tear forms at my eye, and I wipe it away. "Uh, that's it, I guess."

My finger hovers over the Stop button, but something else occurs to me. "Oh, yeah. If I really am dead, then let this be my last will and...whatever word goes after that. I want all the money I still have coming to me divided two ways—fifty percent will go to Piper, and the other half is to be put into an educational fund for Trina Forrester. Piper, Trina, Gina, your support has been... amazing. You've made the last few weeks the best of my life. Same goes for everyone at Hill O' Beans."

My guts clench. Time to wrap this up before I bust out crying. "Sheila...I'm sorry. I'm so sorry. You've been like a mom to me, and I want you to know that I appreciate all the sacrifices you made for me. And as for my real mom...well, I can only say I'm sorry for the millionth time. I didn't want what happened to AJ to happen. He's dead, and it's my fault. I'd give anything for it to have been me and not him, but it didn't work out that way. Maybe you'll never forgive me, just like I haven't forgiven myself, but please know that I died trying to make things right."

I stop recording and turn my phone off. Then I place it on the dirt pile next to me. With luck, the police or a construction crew will find it. If not...oh well.

The street is empty and quiet as I emerge from hiding and stride up the walkway to Harold's front door. I cast a sidelong glance at the van, catching the distinctive smell of paint.

You're so good at covering your tracks, Harry. But not good enough.

I take several deep breaths as I approach the door. My hand is surprisingly still as I press the doorbell. A deep buzz sounds from behind the door, followed by footsteps.

Here we go. Three, two, one.

The door opens, and it's all I can do not to turn to stone as the Disney Princess Killer appears on the threshold. In a kitchen apron, no less.

"May I help you?" he asks in that emotionless tone I know so well.

"Uh, hi." I feel my face flush. Hopefully, he'll attribute that to the cold and not my jangling nerves. "Um, my dog got out this morning, and I'm looking for him. You haven't seen him, have you?"

Harold's brow furrows as he looks me up and down with those cold blue eyes. He neither frowns nor smiles, and it's impossible for me to tell whether he can see through my bullshit or not.

Then a terrifying thought hits me. What if he recognizes me from the alley? If he does, I'm worm food.

"I have not seen a dog," he says, his tone monotonous and robotic, the same voice he used when jabbing the needle into Sarah's neck. The memory chills my blood.

"Okay. Just checking with everyone, you know?" I say, an unwelcome tremor entering my voice.

One eyebrow raises. "I don't think I've seen you before. Where do you live?"

I turn sideways, pointing into the distance. "A few blocks away. Just moved in with my grandparents."

He nods. "I'm sorry I can't be more help. I hope you find him."

Harold makes to close the door, but I decide to play for time. "Smells good."

He narrows his eyes, then glances over his shoulder. "It's my daughter's birthday. I'm making her dinner. If you'll excuse me." With that, he shuts the door.

I turn and head down the walkway, my mind working at top speed. Okay. He didn't recognize me. That's good. He's cooking dinner for his daughter, which means Cheyanne is still alive. That's even better.

Just in case Harold is watching me through his kitchen curtains, I continue to the next occupied house like I'm making the rounds. I even go so far as to approach the door before I bolt to the left and into a patch of darkness in the house's side-yard. My heart thumps wildly in my chest as I listen for any sign of Harold. Nothing.

Keeping low, I skulk back to his driveway, making sure to stay out of view of any of the windows. I find myself next to the Taurus, and suddenly wish I had a switchblade I could jam into his tires. From there I move to the space between the Taurus and the van, and my heart stops when a loud scrape comes from my shoe.

I look down, panic rising. Dammit. I must have stepped on a pebble or something, and it got lodged in my sole.

He heard me. There's no way he didn't hear me. I am so dead.

I duck down behind the van. I can't even look, so I listen. For anything. The sound of a doorknob turning, floorboards creaking, anything to remind me just how big a mistake I made by coming to this awful place. I picture the man plowing through his doorway, with any of a variety of deadly weapons in his hands, ready to pick off the idiot with delusions of grandeur who thought he could tackle the boogeyman all by himself.

ESP. Why couldn't it have been super-strength or invisibility or something that would actually help me right now? But no, it had to be ESP.

Cheyanne's in there, probably scared shitless, and here I am, creeping around outside with no plan at all.

Oh, wait. Maybe if I can find a way into his backyard, I can signal Cheyanne through the basement window. Maybe if there's a way to open it from the outside, I can even get her the hell out of—

Scrape.

Was that me? No, it came from behind me.

Which can only mean...

Shit.

Something solid slams into my head, and all goes black.

Chapter Twenty-Six

Ow.

I feel something cold and hard pressing against my face. For an instant, I think I'm back in the alley behind Hill O' Beans. I wait patiently for clarity to return, for Piper to pull me up, to rouse me from this painful state between sleep and waking.

But something's different this time. There's no warmth from the sun, no smell of motor oil, no pebbles or dirt stuck to my face. Plus, there's a sound. The faint whir of circulating air. I'm inside a room.

My wrist won't move. What gives?

I decide to lift my head an inch. White-hot pain stabs my brain, nearly sending me into unconsciousness again.

Ow ow.

When the throb in my head recedes to a tolerable level, I crack my eyes open. Several yards in front of me is a set of chair legs. In front of them is a pair of human legs. A few feet above those is a face, which contains two watery blue eyes glaring down at me.

Definitely not the alley.

I try to sit up, but something cold bites into my wrist, jerking me backward. One glance confirms my fear—I'm handcuffed to a pipe.

"With the headache I imagine you have, I wouldn't recommend screaming," Harold says.

"Never...crossed...my mind," I mumble. I hoist myself into a sitting position, back to the wall, and get my first look at my surroundings.

I'm not in *a* room. I'm in *the room*. Harold's basement. The place where Mia, Jordan, and Sarah took their last breaths. It's just like I saw in Sarah's vision. The mattress in the corner, covered by an old quilt. My heart swells in relief when I see Cheyanne sitting on the mattress, clad in a *Little Mermaid* tee and with the most terrified expression I've ever seen. Her knees are pulled up to her chin, and dried tears ring her eyes.

"Let me explain what's going to happen." Harold's voice draws my attention. My eyes go straight to the kitchen knife in his hands. I can't help but wonder what he whacked me in the head with. "I caught you trespassing on my property. So I'm going to ask you some questions. I'd advise you not to lie when answering them. That would not end well for you."

"Wh-what do you want to know?"

"Let's start with your name."

For some stupid reason, I opt to ignore Harold's warning and tell a bald-faced lie. Not for me, but hopefully it will prompt Cheyanne not to call me by my name.

"Gavin," I say.

His jaw tightens, and his eyes grow even colder, if that's possible. "What did I just tell you about lying to me?"

Instead of backpedaling or apologizing, I plow on full speed. "I'm not! I swear! My name is Gavin!"

Harold tsk-tsks me like I'm a naughty child caught in a fib. He raises up slightly, reaches into his back pocket and pulls out a wallet. *My* wallet.

Fuck me. Why didn't I leave that in Piper's car? I am so getting a brain transplant if I get out of here.

"That's funny," Harold drawls. "Because the name on your bank card clearly says 'Bernard Baxter.' Would you care to try again?"

Cheyanne's eyes widen and her lips curl upward, but only for a second.

"I told you the truth," I say. "Do I look like a Bernard to you? I stole some old guy's wallet in line at a Jack in the Box this morning."

"You're a thief."

I nod.

He opens the wallet, examining its contents. "A hundred and seventeen dollars, a supermarket discount card...hmm. No ID." He tosses it nonchalantly at me, and it bounces off my chest.

"Not a good idea to carry ID when you're trolling for targets," I say.

Harold's frown deepens, and he points the knife at me. "You picked the wrong house to rob, boy."

I cringe against the wall, fear turning my insides to marshmallow. "Hey, man, nothing personal, okay? Just let me go, and you'll never see me again."

He continues as if I hadn't spoken. "People like you are what's wrong with society." The knife blade edges ever closer. "You take from honest, hard-working citizens and you give nothing back. Too bad for you I installed cameras on my roof as well as a system to alert me when someone comes within forty yards of my house."

Crap.

"Nice try with the 'lost dog' story. But I saw you the moment you ducked behind that wall. It'll be the last mistake you ever make."

Double crap.

"Please, Mister!" I raise my voice an octave, moving my free hand in front of my face. "I'm sorry, okay? I'm only seventeen! Please, just turn me into the cops! I'll go quietly, I promise!"

Harold edges off his seat, and for a second I think this is it. He's going to gut me like a fish with Cheyanne watching. I prepare to kick out at him. Maybe if I catch him on that sweet spot on the knee, I can get him to drop the knife and—

The hiss of water falling on a hot stove drifts into the room, and the knife halts its forward progress. Harold stands straight up, and it's like a switch has been thrown. He turns his back and heads for the door like he wasn't just about to murder me. With a glance at me over his shoulder, he addresses Cheyanne. "I must attend to our dinner, precious girl. I will be right back. Keep an eye on our...guest, will you please?"

Cheyanne, sitting rigidly still, nods but doesn't speak.

"Do *not* go near him. Do you understand?"

She nods again.

With a final look at me, he departs, closing the door behind him.

In an instant, she's off the mattress and halfway across the room. "Bax?"

I put a hand up, stopping her in her tracks. "Keep your voice down," I whisper. "And stay back."

"Bax?" she squeaks. "How did you—"

"No time to explain," I say with as much urgency as I can muster. "Are you all right?"

"I've been kidnapped! How do you think I am?"

Right. Stupid question. "Has he hurt you?"

"No." She steps back a few paces, staring at her socked feet. "But this guy's crazy. He keeps calling me Ariel. He made me change into *this*," she fists the hem of the *Little Mermaid* shirt. "I've told him over and over that I'm not his daughter, but he—"

"You need to stop," I interrupt. "No more arguing. That's what got the other three girls killed."

Cheyanne's chocolate skin pales. "Wh-what do I do?"

I cast a wary glance at the door, listening for any sign of footsteps. "Be Ariel. Be his daughter. As long as you do that, he won't hurt you."

She nods in understanding. "What about you? Please tell me you told *someone* I'm here."

Not wanting to cause her any additional alarm, I decide on a half-truth. "I did. The police are on their way. I gave them the address and info on his car. But they have to be careful, Chey. They have to figure out how to take Harold out before he can do the same to us."

"H-how long will it take?"

"I don't know. Just promise me you'll play the part for as long as you have to, okay?"

The sound of feet on floor meets my ears. Only seconds before Harold returns.

"Promise me," I hiss.

"I promise."

The knob turns, and the door opens. By the time Harold enters, Cheyanne is back on the mattress.

"Dinner's almost ready, Princess." He grabs the chair and slides it further away from me. "I've been considering your request to turn you over to the police, Gavin."

I brighten.

"Under different circumstances, I might consider it. But you invaded my privacy and scared my daughter Ariel half to death. On her birthday. I'm not predisposed toward leniency."

"Please, I'll do whatever you want," I whimper. "I'm sorry. I'm so sorry, Mister." I glance at Cheyanne. "I'm sorry, Ariel. I didn't mean to..." I trail off, devolving into a choked sob. I cover my eyes with my free arm.

"I, too, am sorry." His hand disappears into his pocket, and out comes...

A syringe.

"Don't think of this as punishment," he says with no more emotion than a freaking robot. "The way I see it, you are a miserable boy with a miserable life. What I'm doing is ending your misery, your suffering." He pulls the plastic safety tip off and flings it to the side. "I promise, you won't feel a thing. One little prick, and you'll go right to sleep."

Balls. He's gonna do it. Right in front of Cheyanne. What

kind of father who claims to love his daughter would murder another human being with her watching?

No. This isn't love. Whatever love Harold had for the real Ariel died with her. What's left is only the best approximation his twisted mind can produce.

Tears cloud my eyes, and the pain in my head intensifies. I'm backed into a corner, and the best defense I have would be clumsy with my hand shackled. Plus, I know how strong he is. Despite his mediocre features, he's no lightweight. I'd get maybe one weak punch in before he puts my lights out for good.

He darts forward, grabbing my arm in a vice-grip. I wince as he drags me toward him. "Don't struggle, Gavin. It'll only hurt more."

No. This isn't how it's supposed to end. If I'd died saving Cheyanne, I could go happy. But no. I couldn't save shit. I've failed again.

My voice abandons me as the needle-tip moves ever closer.

"Daddy, *stop*!"

Cheyanne's cry turns both of us into statues.

The tip stops, flush against the cloth of my jacket.

"What did you say?" Harold asks, incredulous.

"I said, stop." Cheyanne takes several tentative steps toward her faux father. "Please, Daddy, don't hurt him."

Still seemingly in shock at his daughter's change of heart, Harold utters, "I'm sorry, Ariel. It has to be done."

"You can't! It's my birthday! I'm ten today, right? If you hurt him it'll ruin it." Tears flow from her already puffy eyes. "Please, Daddy. I just want to enjoy it...with you."

How she said that without biting her tongue, I'll never know. Yeah, girl.

A proud smile spreads across Harold's face, and he turns to me. "My daughter, so compassionate. When she was old enough to walk, she wouldn't even step on an ant."

My heart threatens to explode. My gaze hasn't moved from

the needle, which is one layer of cloth from my skin. I close my eyes, awaiting death...or reprieve.

Harold releases me, and I sag to the ground, all strength gone from my limbs. It takes all I have to meet the eyes of my little savior and mouth "Thank you" at her.

"You made my favorite, right, Daddy?" She's smiling. My God, this girl.

"I sure did." Harold picks up the needle-cap, covers the tip with it, and slides the syringe back into his pocket. "Spaghetti and meatballs."

"Mmm mmm." She rubs her tummy.

Don't oversell it, Chey...

Harold gestures her through the door, and she obeys without another look at me. Several seconds later, I'm expelling forced breath after forced breath into an empty basement.

I sit there for I don't know how long. The throb in my skull has gotten worse. Whatever Harold clobbered me with did some damage, that's for sure. Part of me actually hopes I'll die from an aneurysm. It'd sure beat being sliced and diced by Mr. Father-of-the-Year.

The row of track lights on the ceiling glower at me. They're so harsh I can't look at them without the migraine making me blind. I have little range of movement because of the handcuff, which is snug around my wrist but not cutting off my circulation.

My thoughts turn to Piper, who is probably sitting in Copper Mesa's security office, wondering what the hell I'm up to. Of all the dumb things I've done in my life, dragging an amazing girl like her into this quagmire of awfulness is the dumbest—yes, even more than punching Detective Rojas. God, why couldn't that woman get off her high horse *just once* and listen to me?

Piper, if I don't make it out of this...find a way. Put all this craziness behind you and have a great life. Hopefully, my little contribution will help. Nobody I've ever met deserves it more.

I shouldn't sleep. That's the worst thing a guy with a head

injury can do. But damn, my eyelids are heavy. Spending half the day in a car after a night of only three hours shuteye does that.

Maybe I'll just close my eyes for a little while. Yeah.

"You've really gone and stepped in it now, *Bernard*."

I look up. There, eying me bemusedly from Harold's chair is... AJ.

Oh, come on. I *so* do not need this right now.

Did the whack on my noggin joggle the ESP part of my brain so much that my abilities changed? Maybe I'm hallucinating. That would be bad. The least alarming possibility is that I've gone completely looney tunes like that guy outside the convenience store.

AJ's just like I remember him—medium-length wavy dark hair, piercing brown eyes, and a strong chin. Well-defined muscles bulge beneath his gray tee. And that smile...I only saw it when he had something on me, a situation I hated, but it feels good to see it again. Though this is probably all in my head.

Yee-haw. My crazy train has driven off a cliff. Nothing for it but to ride to the inevitable wreck.

"Tell me something I don't know, *Amos*," I retort.

He winces. "Yeesh. Why couldn't our grandfather and great-grandfather have had cooler names?"

"Yeah. And why did Mom and Dad feel the need to force them on us?"

"You know why. 'Cause they were heroes."

"Just like you probably would have been if not for me."

AJ folds his arms across his chest. "That's why you're here, isn't it." It's not a question.

"No," I say defensively. "I'm here because the cops wouldn't believe me. And my friend was in danger."

His eyebrows raise. "Sneaking into a serial killer's house to save a little girl's life? Sounds pretty heroic to me."

Aargh. Damn his logic. "Shut up."

"Do you want to talk about what's going on inside that thick head of yours?"

I shift position. Crap, this floor is uncomfortable. "You came back from the dead just to psychoanalyze me?"

A frown creases his forehead. "Quit deflecting. You haven't talked about *that night* since it happened, not even to that state-appointed shrink."

I avert my gaze, unable to meet his ghostly glare. "What's there to talk about? I killed you."

"No, you didn't. It was an accident."

"That *I* caused."

"The police investigated. They determined you weren't at fault. But Mom, true to form, blamed you anyway."

I stare glumly at the wall. I'd kill for an aspirin right now.

"You have to stop, B," AJ says, drawing my eyes back to him. "You have to stop torturing yourself. If you don't, it's going to ruin you."

Anger flashes through me. "You think I did all this so Mom would be proud of me and we can be all lovey-dovey? Screw that. I don't give a shit what she thinks."

He spreads his arms wide. "And yet, here we are."

"Wonder what Mom will say when she hears about this. She'll probably be glad. The death of her beloved son has finally been avenged."

AJ tilts his head back and barks out a mirthless laugh. "Beloved? Are you effing kidding me? You think she loved me?"

I nod.

"Let me tell you something about our mother, B. I knew how messed up she was by the time I turned twelve.

"You know why I got into athletics? Because of Grandpa and Dad. Not her. All that praise she heaped on me? It was for *herself*, not me. Every game I won, every trophy I brought home convinced her she was a superior parent, something she bragged about to anyone who would listen. I hated it. What made me even sicker was that she used every one of my accomplishments as a club to beat you bloody with.

"I begged her to stop. So did Dad. But she wouldn't, of

course. And when Dad died..." AJ shakes his head, his expression sad. "I told you not to let her inside your head. That you were a great kid with more brains than I'd ever have. But you, unfortunately, are as pigheaded as she is. And you've gotten more so since my death."

Horrible memories, ones I've tried to forget but have relived a thousand times, resurface. "That night—"

"That night," he cuts me off, "I was pissed off as hell, and not thinking clearly. You remember how much I loved Stacy, right?"

"Yeah."

"When I found out what that asshole Brock did to her, I wanted to kill him. If you hadn't stopped me, I probably would have. At the very least, I would have messed him up real bad. And that would have been it for me."

"You don't know that."

"Do the math, little brother. I was a week away from turning eighteen. I'd have been arrested, tried, and convicted. I wouldn't have been sent to a halfway house, either." He leans back in the chair, and for a second, he looks ten years older. "Every good thing I ever did would have been forgotten. All people would remember about me is what I did that night. Even if I survived prison, my life would've been over. At least my death allowed everyone who really cared about me to remember me the way I want them to. And as for you..."

I can only watch as AJ stands and approaches me. Should I feel scared? What if he really is a ghost and not a hallucination? Brother or not, this is scary new territory for me.

Rather than yank my soul out through my nostrils, he sits down next to my outstretched feet. I want to reach out and touch him, insanely curious yet dreading what I'd find.

"Mom's been out of your life for two years, but you still let her use her mind games on you," he says in that warm brotherly tone that got me through more horrible nights than I can count. "I died. It sucked. For Mom, for you, for everybody. But you need to let it go. If not," he gestures at the door, "you might as well just let this psycho kill you right now."

I raise my left hand as far as it'll go, the metal of the handcuff clinking. "Not much I can do about it either way."

His crooked half-smile, the one that used to drive all the cheerleaders nuts, appears. "You're not gonna die here, B."

I do a double-take. "Wait just a damn minute...how do you know that? I don't even know that."

Oh my God.

It can't be. Can it?

"AJ...is it really you?"

"Who else will save your sorry ass?"

I feel a smile form. "Are you...a ghost?"

His face goes blank, and he holds his arms out toward me. Then he waggles his fingers, and his eyes go buggy. "Ooo-ooo-ooooooooo," he groans.

The smile widens. "Really?"

"Well, we are close to Halloween," he says through his grin.

"Come on, man, this is important."

He rises to his feet, becoming serious. "I know. But I can't give you *all* the answers. Some things you just have to figure out for yourself."

"You suck."

"I love you too."

This gets me right where it hurts. Sixteen years we had together, and I never once told him I loved him. Never once. We were brothers, family. Our love was implied. Like it is now. But I feel like a total scumbag anyway. Dammit, I miss him.

AJ tilts his head to one side like he's listening to something. I strain my ears as well. A strange sound forms. The whirring of helicopter blades.

A chopper! Is it the police?

It's faint, so I keep listening. It sounds high up. I live in a big city, so helicopters pass overhead all the time. I stare at the ceiling as if I could actually see the thing in the sky above. Seconds pass, and the sound moves from one side of the room to the other. Then it fades away completely.

"Stand up," AJ says. "You'll want to be ready."

Wincing and hugging the wall with my back, I clamber to my feet. Thankfully, the pipe I'm chained to is high enough off the ground that I can stand straight up. "Ready for what?"

He steps aside, giving me a clear view of the door. "You'll know."

From the gravity in his voice, I expect Harold to come barging through it at any moment. When he doesn't, I turn back to my brother, only to find I'm alone again.

Was that real?

Sigh. Another unanswered question.

Minutes pass. The throb dwindles to a more welcome dull ache, which makes concentrating on the door easier. I run through several scenarios of what I'll do when Harold comes to finish me off. Begging for mercy is not an option, so my best bet is probably to wait until he comes within range and kick him as hard as I can in the junk. Unless he's the T-1000, it may give me a chance to get the upper hand.

A faint rustle comes, but this time, it's not from outside the door. No, it came from outside...the window?

Because the light's on and night has fallen, I can't see anything from my spot in the corner. I wait for another sound, and it comes. I try to place it but am unable to.

The lights go out, plunging the basement into darkness.

I tense up, ready for anything. The total blackness is disconcerting, but before I can freak out, I hear another shuffle from outside the house.

Police? Feds? Jason Statham? I'll take any of the above.

A voice, amplified by a megaphone, blares from outside, but there are too many walls between the speaker and me to discern any words. This is followed by a mad rush of footsteps and someone pounding on wood.

The basement door flies open. Harold, with a flashlight in one hand and the other locked around Cheyanne's wrist, steps through. He turns the beam on me, and I shield my eyes.

"You! You little bastard!" With a grunt, he shoves Cheyanne away from him. She lands with a cry on the mattress. "You brought them here! You've ruined everything!" He steps menacingly toward me.

For some reason even I can't fathom, I raise up, square my shoulders, and show him my meanest glare. The pain in my head fades away as adrenaline kicks into high gear. "It's over, *Harold*."

He stops dead, and the flashlight clatters to the ground, casting weird shadows over my corner of the room. In the half-light, I can see the gobsmacked expression on his face, but it quickly morphs into a contemptuous sneer.

"Harold is dead." He pulls the syringe from his pocket and flicks the safety cap off. "And so are you."

Uh boy.

Time slows down, and a million things seem to happen at once.

"Run, Cheyanne!" I scream.

Harold lunges forward.

I brace myself, preparing to dodge even though I have nowhere to go.

He slams into me, crushing me against the wall, knocking the breath from me and multiplying my pain by five. In a moment of horror, I feel the needle tip penetrate my jacket and plunge into my arm.

Cheyanne screams.

I use the last of my flagging strength to push Harold off, but it's useless. I try half-assedly to kick him in the balls, but the attempt is feeble.

He reaches for the syringe's plunger, which will push enough poison into my veins to end me.

Weakness and fatigue permeate every muscle, and I feel my body going limp. My vision fades to a blurry white.

The last thing I hear before blackness swallows me is a muffled bang, followed by shattering glass.

CHAPTER TWENTY-SEVEN

Ow.

This is getting old.

Oval-shaped blurry globs that might be human faces peer down at me as I drift in and out of slumber. The pain in my skull is still there, which means I'm still among the living. On the other hand, if I'm dead and feeling *this* shitty, eternity's gonna suuuck.

I see my bare feet, poking out from the other side of a blanket. I wiggle my toes experimentally, and they obey. Words attached to certain objects bob into my mind. Gurney. Hallway. Nurses. Doctors. Hospital.

This leads to other, better words. Rescue. Medicine. Recovery.

Alive. That one's my favorite.

And...back to sleep.

I'm awakened by the soft clink of metal on metal. I crack my eyelids open to see a middle-aged, dark-haired woman in light blue scrubs exchanging an empty IV bag for a full one. She notices my vacant stare and smiles. "Hello."

"Where..."

"You're at North Phoenix Baptist Hospital," she informs me. "You looked a little rough when you came in, but you're going to be just fine."

I nod, smiling internally when I realize my head has stopped hurting. Yay for pain meds.

"Get some rest," she admonishes. "It's what you need right now."

"Thank you," I slur.

She points at a small remote lying on the bed next to me. "Just press the call button if you need anything." She breaks out in a warm smile. "And don't worry. You're in good hands, Bernard." With that, she leaves.

Bax. It's *Bax*, dammit.

Ahhh, never mind.

I become aware of a faint regular beeping, like an electronic heartbeat. My foggy brain jumps to the conclusion that it's a machine measuring my heart rate, and it brings me comfort. Then comes the sound of a door closing and the shuffle of footsteps. More than one person, I think, so it can't be the nurse who woke me an hour ago to check my vitals.

"So this is him," says a husky male voice.

"Yes, sir," says another. This one's younger, still deep but definitely female. And familiar.

"Thirty years on the force, I thought I'd seen everything," says the man.

I crack my eyelids open. To my left, sunlight shines through thick blinds. Across the room, a clock indicates it's just past eight.

The next thing I notice is that the skull-splitting pain is...gone. Well, not gone, but it's been reduced to an annoying tickle. I want to touch the spot where it hurts but think better of it. I'll let the pain meds—I assume that's what's pumping through the IV jammed into the crook of my elbow—do their work before I tempt fate.

I turn my head to see two people standing near the door. One of them is Detective Rojas. The other is a tall man with a Fu Manchu mustache. From the way she's listening intently and the way he's glowering down at her, I'm guessing he's her superior officer. A captain, I think. I know I've seen him somewhere—I mean, how many people have Fu Manchus anymore?—but I can't quite place it.

The captain notices me watching him, nods, then addresses Detective Rojas at a more audible level. "This boy is a hero, even if no one will know about it. Make certain he understands what's at stake."

"I will, sir," Detective Rojas says.

The big man checks his watch and dons his hat. "The press conference is in an hour. Join me at the precinct when you're done here. *Don't* screw this up."

"Yes, sir," she repeats with shocking humility.

With a final glance at me, he strides from the room.

I say nothing as Detective Rojas approaches. I spot a newspaper tucked under one arm and a plastic bag clutched in her other hand.

I sink into the pillow, bracing myself for what I'm sure is bad news. Her expression is unreadable. "Was that your boss?"

She grabs a chair from next to my bed, pulls it up, and sits. "It was."

"Are you in trouble?"

"Let's just say I'm not his favorite person right now."

Huh. I bet I'm the reason behind her chewing-out. Rather than press, I change the subject. "Harold? Cheyanne?"

Detective Rojas exhales, then meets my gaze. "He's dead. She's currently at Phoenix Children's Hospital, surrounded by family."

"Was she hurt?"

"Physically, no. Mentally and emotionally...well, children are resilient, but being kidnapped by a murderer is not something you just shrug off."

Yeah. Kid's gonna relive that nightmare for months. But it beats being dead.

I take a breath, holding my ribcage. "Do my friends know I'm here?"

"No one does," she says. "We thought it best in order to keep the press from finding you."

I frown. "Do they even know I'm alive?"

"They will. But first, we have a lot to talk about. Are you in pain right now?"

"Not really."

"Are you lucid enough to carry on an *adult* conversation?"

I ignore the underlying barb and nod.

She turns away, staring vacantly out the window. "I've been hard on you, Mr. Baxter."

My fists close around the folds of the blanket covering me. "You've been a raving bitch, Detective Rojas."

I wait for her eyes to flash a fiery red, for her brow to slope, for the scowl I know so well to materialize. All I get instead is a tightened jaw. "You're right, I have. And I'm sorry."

I tilt my head to one side. "Did your boss order you to say that?"

"No. This is all me."

I think hell just froze over.

"Do you know the number one reason cops stop being cops?" she asks.

"Having to wear all black in a hundred-and-ten-degree weather?"

"Stress." She pauses. "Most of my family are cops. From the age of seven, I was groomed for this life. By the time I joined the force, I was convinced I was tough enough to take anything the job could throw at me."

Epic fail, from the sound of things.

"When you're a cop, you see so much evil. All day, every day. Eventually, you wonder how much good there is left in the world. This case," her voice cracks, raw emotion leaking out, "pushed every single button I have."

I lie still, unsure how to respond.

"I tried the usual stuff to blow off steam—boxing, hiking, even yoga. Didn't work. My husband got the worst of it."

Detective Rojas is *married*? Funny Austin didn't mention that.

"It affected my job performance, and it nearly cost that little girl her life. And yours," she adds. "I know you can't stand me, but for what it's worth, I'm starting anger management counseling next week."

"Hrm," I grunt. Better late than never, I guess.

A protracted silence follows. She leans forward, a wry smirk playing over her lips. "So...psychic, huh?"

My jaw falls open, and my brain locks up. "How did you—"

She holds up the plastic bag. Inside is my cell phone.

I lean back against the pillow, and my fingers go to the numerous layers of bandages wrapped around my head. "You watched the video."

"Four times. Very edifying."

"And you believed it?"

Detective Rojas deposits the phone on the portable tray-table next to my bed, then edges closer. "Thousands of man-hours and millions of dollars were spent trying to nail that dirtbag. And two teenagers, with no resources beyond Google and Wikipedia, were able to not only identify the perp but track him to his house." She snorts. "ESP? Why the hell not?"

I throw her a disgruntled frown. "We shouldn't have *had* to track him. I called the hotline a full day before Cheyanne was taken. I told you his name, his profession, and about the white van. Why was that not enough for you to catch him?"

"Police work isn't like it is on TV, *Scott*." She grimaces, and I feel my face redden. "Hollywood has the ability to compress a months-long investigation into a sixty-minute program, skipping over the ninety-nine percent that viewers would find tedious. They have these snazzy supercomputers that process all the information and spit out the answer in two seconds. Doesn't work that way in real life. Whatever you may think of our methods, we did follow up on your lead—"

"Not fast enough," I interject. "Did it really not occur to you that he was attached to the construction crew across the street? The bastard showed up for work the *day after* he took Cheyanne, and the only people waiting for him were Piper and me." Frustration claws at my throat. "*Why weren't you there?*"

Rather than come back with a biting retort, she absorbs the inquiry without comment. Visible shame plays over her expression. When she answers, it's barely above a whisper. "Because as smart as we are, sometimes the bad guys are smarter."

"*That's* your answer?"

"That's *life*, Mr. Baxter. As I said, we followed your lead. And it led straight to a dead end."

A sour taste invades my mouth. "How is that possible?"

"Mr. Crane had more identities than I've had years on the force. The house he lived in, the van, the rental cars, even his surveyor's license—each of them was obtained with a different name, date of birth, social security number, and a bogus address."

I slam my eyes shut. "When I called you from outside his house..." I trail off, reliving that moment and how I'd cursed the woman sitting beside me now.

In a surprising move, she reaches out and touches my hand. I'm so shocked I don't flinch or pull away.

"I hadn't slept in thirty-six hours," she confesses. "Every failed lead made me angrier and angrier. Cheyanne disappearing and your junior league investigation put me over the top. Because of me, you nearly got yourself killed." She squeezes my hand. "Believe it or not, I was never out to 'get' you."

"You could've fooled me," I scoff. "So what finally changed your mind?"

A wisp of a smile appears. "Every criminal, no matter how careful or clever, always makes one mistake. Mr. Crane was no different."

"Oh?'

"The man had a different identity for every day of the week. But he never changed his phone number."

I blink, then shrug.

"We pulled the contracts for the car rentals, then determined the phone number was the same as on his surveyor's license application. When you gave us his home address, we pulled up the purchase agreement. Same phone number again."

My indignation gives way to laughter. "You got him because of his cell phone? That's freakin' brilliant. Your sharpshooter sure cut it close, though."

"I'll pass on your thanks." Detective Rojas tugs the newspaper from under her armpit, unfolds it, and hands it to me. "Here's a copy of this morning's paper."

Taking care not to bend my right arm lest I mess up my IV, I scan the headline: "DISNEY PRINCESS KILLER CAUGHT" appears in big block letters. The subheading below that reads, "Latest Victim Found Alive." There's a large color photo of Harold's house. Further down the page are head shots of Harold himself, along with Mia, Jordan, Sarah, Cheyanne, and...Piper.

"What you'll read here is a rather abridged version of the facts," she continues. "Piper McKinney was on her way to work when she spotted a suspicious man enter an unmarked white van identical to the one reported as possibly belonging to the Disney Princess Killer. She and a friend, an unidentified male, followed the van to his home. They called the police. Further investigation by the PPD into Ms. McKinney's suspicions proved justified. Police moved on the suspect's home at just past eight p.m. on Wednesday evening, resulting in the suspect's death and the rescue of Cheyanne Macias."

I place the newspaper on my lap. "You're right, that is abridged."

"That's just how the public likes it—simple and without any gray area."

"And Piper's on board with this?"

"Yes, and we have dropped her trespassing charge. Which brings us to you."

I narrow my eyes at her.

A hard edge tinges her voice. "Because of the contentious relationship you've had with the PPD in general, and me in particular, my superiors are worried that you may use this opportunity to score a little payback. You could tell the papers or blast on social media how we—I—dropped the ball on this case."

I tap my finger on the newspaper. "If this is the official story, why would they believe me?"

"They probably wouldn't. But there are people out there who love stories of cover-ups and police incompetence. If you found the right person, it could give the PPD a serious black eye."

I feel my face flush. "You *really* think I'd do that?"

She doesn't even blink. "If you'd asked me that question a few days ago, I'd have said 'yes.' In a heartbeat. Now?" She shrugs. "Jury's still out."

My gaze shifts out the window. I want to deny her claim, that I'm now above such things as petty revenge, but I'm not. Despite my self-professed rehabilitation and my efforts to live a respectable life, I'd drop the bomb on Detective Rojas in a hot second, collateral damage be damned.

But I don't want to be that guy again. Not now, not ever.

"Things have a way of coming out, you know," I whisper. "But you have my word, no one will hear about my part in this mess from me."

"You'll sign a paper to that effect?"

I nod, facing Detective Rojas again. "But there are already people who know I'm involved. Cheyanne, for one. Probably her parents, too."

"Cheyanne is due to be discharged tomorrow. She and her

family have been briefed on the situation. They, like Miss McKinney, have agreed to keep your part in this case a secret."

That's another one I owe Cheyanne.

"I have some other news," she says. "As a token of gratitude for your help, the PPD will be covering any medical expenses you may incur during your stay here."

My eyes widen. That's *huge*. Since I don't have insurance yet, the bills would have wiped out my little nest egg in one fell swoop. "That's awesome," I manage.

"And then there's the matter of the reward. I'm sure you know that a sizable cash payout was offered to whoever provided intel that directly led to the capture of the Disney Princess Killer."

I bolt upright, my heart racing. "Yeah. What is it, seventy-five thousand?"

She shakes her head. "It was upped to a hundred after Cheyanne was taken. You and Miss McKinney are entitled to a fifty-fifty share."

Holy shit.

Ho...ly...*shit*.

Giant dollar signs tattoo themselves on my brain, and for a few seconds, I lose my mind.

A car. I can get a car. Maybe not a Porsche or a Lambo, but something cool that'll turn Sydney into a quivering pile of jelly. Add that to the mostly unspent pile of cash I received on my birthday, and I won't have to work anymore. I can take up a hobby, like...well, something.

Then the page turns, and I picture Piper's face when she receives a check with all those zeroes. She won't wonder what to do with it. She'll know. She'll put enough aside to cover her schooling and use the rest to take care of her dad. I don't know how much his bills are, but I'm sure that much money would cover them for a while.

Yeah. A while.

She can do a lot with fifty thousand.

She can do more with a hundred.

"No," I state flatly.

Detective Rojas's brow furrows. "What do you mean, no?"

"No fifty-fifty. Give it all to her."

Her jaw drops. "Are you serious?"

"As a heart attack." Heh. Hospital joke. "She's trying to get a degree. Her dad is sick. She needs it. I don't. Give it to her."

The next look she gives me is so unexpected, I almost don't recognize it—admiration. From my nemesis.

What a week I'm having.

When the cat finally releases her tongue, she says, "You really have changed."

I flash my most charming smile. "I make a killer latte, too."

She laughs, and it's a pleasant sound. "There's really nothing you want from us? At all?"

I point at my phone, still in its baggie. "Can I have that back?"

"I'm afraid not. It's evidence. But we'll get you a new one."

"With Candy Crush, please. I have a feeling the next few days are going to be boring as shit."

"Done." She checks her watch, stands, and picks up my phone. "Captain Callahan's expecting me at the press conference, so I have to go. Anything else?"

A brilliant idea occurs to me. I'd pat myself on the back if I didn't have an IV jammed into my arm. "A spa day."

Five seconds pass, and she shakes her head. "I'm sorry, did you say, 'spa day?'"

"Someplace nice, classy, hopefully not too far away. And I'll need the Deluxe VIP Golden Pass or whatever they call it."

After trying to determine my motivation behind this request and failing, she shrugs. "Fine. One spa day, coming up."

"Not one. Six."

"*Six?*"

"Yup."

"Six spa days."

"Yup."

"Nobody on Earth is *that* tense, Mr. Baxter."

I chuckle. "They're not *all* for me. The second one is for a girl I hope to be dating real soon. Three are for friends, and the last one..." I spread my arms wide, "is for you."

Her expression changes again. Dammit, I wish I could take a picture of this.

"I've treated you like crap. I almost got you killed," she whispers. "Why would you do that?"

My jovial mood dims, replaced by resolve. "As a peace offering. I'm tired of fighting you, Detective. I'm trying to nail my life back together, and this petty feud of ours is frickin' exhausting. Can we *please* put it behind us and try not to hate each other?"

She considers this for several moments, then nods. "We can. Unfortunately, I can't accept a gift from you. It edges too close to bribery, which is frowned upon in my job."

My face falls. "Is it still a gift if I didn't pay for it?"

"It is."

"What about Christmas presents? Are you allowed to accept those?"

"You won't let this go, will you?"

I try a different tack. "Consider it part of your therapy to chill the hell out."

This earns a smile. "I'll run it by my captain." She retrieves her coat from a chair near the door, then faces me again. "I'll be back tomorrow with some paperwork for you to sign, along with your cell phone and your spa certificates. See you then, Mr. Baxter."

Her hand is on the knob when I say, "Bax."

"What?"

"For the love of God, will you call me Bax? The only other person who called me 'Mr. Baxter' was my third-grade teacher, Mrs. Cherkofsky. And I'm pretty sure she was a witch."

"A witch," she replies drolly.

"Yeah, she had a broom and everything. My friends call me Bax."

"We're not friends."

"We're not enemies either. That's close enough for me." I hold out my hand, hoping she'll cross the room and shake it.

She does, and smiles again.

But I just can't resist delaying her one more time. "Can I call you Nat?"

"No."

"Natster? Natanator? Nattress?"

"You do know I'm armed, right?"

"Oh, come on."

She pauses in the doorway and faces me again.

"We made a breakthrough today! Are you really going to make me keep calling you 'Detective?' It's so impersonal." She doesn't respond, so I offer another solution. "Can I call you Natalie, at least? Please?" I clasp my hands together like I'm begging, which I totally am.

"I will think about it." And with that, she's gone.

CHAPTER TWENTY-EIGHT

Not long after Natalie leaves, a man in a crisp white coat identifying himself as Dr. Singh gives me the news—which, unexpectedly, is not that bad. The blow I sustained caused a one-centimeter fracture in my skull and a mild concussion. When I was brought in, they were worried about intracranial bleeding, but that turned out not to be the case. They did, however, have to shave the back of my head to clean and stitch up the wound, ruining Nico's awesome work.

With nothing else to do, I watch the press conference on the tiny TV on the other side of the room. Captain Callahan is standing behind a woman identified as "Chief Maxine Travis." She does most of the talking, giving thanks to the "many, many people instrumental in bringing a killer to justice." Off to the side, I spot Piper, dressed more conservatively than I've ever seen. She looks so out of place, no doubt because she's never had a spotlight this bright on her before. She smiles and nods as her name is mentioned but doesn't field any questions. The telecast cuts off just as the Q&A part begins.

What's that saying? Everyone's famous for fifteen minutes? For Piper's sake, I hope this bizarre chapter of her life ends quickly and she can get back to her normal routine.

At just past two, a nurse helps me out of bed. She tells me I need to get my leg muscles going again. Plus, they need to determine whether I'm able to stand and walk without pain, dizziness, or nausea. The room tilts slightly the first time my feet hit the floor, but afterward, I'm able to walk like I've been doing it my whole life. Dr. Singh tells me I'll be taken off the IV and put on solid food the next day. He also tells me that if no complications arise, I might be able to go home in a week.

Detective Rojas returns the next morning with five envelopes from Desert Enchantment Day Spa—she declined one for herself on orders—and a new phone, the same model as my old one but with a new number. I sign some paperwork promising not to spill my guts about my part in the DPK case, and she spells out the consequences if I break that promise. Which are *scary*.

I love having a phone again, and spend an hour crushing candy while I eat my bland lunch. I make the unpleasant discovery that my Favorites list is all but empty, meaning I can't call Gina or text Piper about my current whereabouts and status. The only name that's been programmed in is Austin's, probably thanks to Natalie.

I wait until three o'clock before I make the call, hoping the afternoon rush is all but over. It rings three times before Austin answers. "Hello?"

"Hey, Boss."

"Bax?"

"It's me."

"Hey, everybody, it's Bax!" he says, I'm guessing, to whoever is currently occupying Hill O' Beans' dining area. A smattering of cheers and applause follow.

I love this guy.

"Oh my God, Bax, it's good to hear your voice. Nobody's told us anything. Even Piper didn't know where you were."

The mention of Piper's name makes me sit straight up. "Is she there?"

He pauses, then says in a low tone, "Bax...Piper's taking a leave of absence from Hill O' Beans, and from school."

The news should surprise me, but it doesn't. Piper is the Woman of the Hour. Every major network is probably clamoring to interview her. The fifteen minutes has begun.

"I see," I say glumly.

"How are you, Bax? I've called your cell, but there's been no answer."

"Yeah, I've been laid up in the hospital for a few days." I go on to explain my symptoms and prognosis but leave out the circumstances of my injury. I'm somewhat surprised when he doesn't press for answers.

"I'm just glad you're on the mend," he says. "Rest assured, your job is waiting for you when you're up to it. Just let me know when you're able to return. And make sure to bring a doctor's note clearing you."

"Will do. Listen, Austin...I need a favor. I had to get a new phone, and I lost everyone's numbers. I was hoping to get one of them from you, if that's okay."

"You got it, dude. Oh, and Sierra just told me there'll be a plate of hotteoks for you when you return."

This sets me salivating. Damn, I miss good food.

Austin continues, "So...whose number do you need?"

The clock creeps past five-thirty, the time Sheila told me she'd be here. Not that I'm worried...much. She gave no indication during our brief exchange of texts that she was still raw about the horrible things I said during our last conversation. Yesterday, I was able to bury the hatchet with Detective Rojas. Here's hoping I can do the same with Sheila.

I quickly tire of watching the door, so I climb out of bed and move to the window, which features an impressive view of the Phoenix skyline. I check for the tenth time that my hospital gown is tied in the back. Hard enough to look dignified in one of these things without your ass hanging out.

A hot-air balloon drifts through the air several miles away. I follow its progress until it disappears from sight. I consider shooting Sheila another text when a tentative knock comes from the door.

"Come in," I say.

Sheila pokes her head inside but doesn't enter all the way. The look she's giving me tells me she's not convinced I didn't bring her all the way out here just to read her the riot act again. When she sees the regret in my expression, she steps inside. "Bax?"

A million words threaten to come out at once, but all I can manage is a "Hey, Sheila."

She steps toward me, pausing halfway across the room. "My God, Bax. Are you all..." She trails off, her hand flying up to her mouth.

"I'm all right," I say, closing the distance between us. "Took a good knock to the head, but the doc says if I pass a couple more scans and the pain doesn't return, I can go home early next week."

Sheila reaches forward as if to touch my cheek but pulls back. "It's true. You took on a serial killer." Her maternal look morphs into a frown.

I remember thinking on several occasions that Sheila is telepathic. Given what I now know about ESP, I have to wonder if this is an actual likelihood. "Uh...I don't know what you're—"

She places her hands on her hips. "I'm not an idiot, Bax. A girl who just *happens* to be your coworker tracks down the Disney Princess Killer with the help of an unidentified male, and three days later, you—who just *happen* to be psychic—call me from a hospital not three miles from where the killer lived?"

"Um...yes." My cheeks flush, and I avert my eyes.

"Why would you do something so stupid?"

"I had to," I whisper. "A friend's life was at stake. There was no other way."

Her anger softens, and a smile creeps over her face. "Well, don't that beat all."

We lock eyes, and the apology I've put off for way too long breaks free. "I'm sorry, Sheila. For all that shit I said to you."

She exhales and pulls me into a gentle embrace. I wrap my arms around her, the lingering scent of her floral perfume filling my nostrils.

"I'm sorry too," she says into my ear. "For not telling you the truth before."

I break the hug. "Why didn't you?"

Her eyes find the floor as she gathers her thoughts. "When I first met you, you were so..."

"Effed up?"

"Lost. Your mother had really done a number on you, and between your stints in the foster system and the legal system, I decided you weren't ready to hear the truth. 'Someday,' I promised myself, 'someday I'll tell him.' Whenever I saw you after that, it never seemed to be the right time.

"A couple of months before your eighteenth birthday, when I told you about the inheritance your dad left you, it seemed to have a positive effect. You were determined to leave the childish behavior behind and start fresh. By then, though, I thought I'd crossed the line from 'too soon to tell you' to 'too late.' If I told you then, how could I justify not telling you before? Would you even believe me if I did?"

"Probably not, but you still should've tried." I don't want to sound harsh, but I probably do. "Any warning at all would've been helpful."

"You're right," she admits. "I made excuses, and it cost you. I'm sorry."

It's no use. I can't stay mad at her. "I'm sorry about Anthony."

Her eyes widen, then narrow. "Austin told you."

"Right after you left that night. It's awful that you had to go through that."

Her lips curl upward, and the last remaining tension dissolves from the room. "We're just a couple of sorry so-and-sos, aren't we?"

It feels like the right moment for another hug, and we give into it. "You saved a little girl's life," she says.

"Well, the cops helped too. And Piper." Then something else occurs to me. "But none of it would have been possible without you."

She faces me, confusion in her eyes. "What are you talking about? I had no idea you were involved in this nightmare until a few days ago."

"If it weren't for you, I wouldn't have gotten a job at Hill O' Beans, and I wouldn't have found the first clue that put me on the DP Killer's trail. If you hadn't gotten me into Arbor Vista, I wouldn't have found the final clues in time to save Cheyanne." I squeeze her arms. "After all the shit that's gone down in our lives, I think we both just pulled even."

This revelation seems to steal the breath from her lungs. "That's...wow," she croaks. "I suppose you're right." The gleam returns to her eyes. "Do you remember when I told you that when you do what I do, you scratch and claw for every win?"

I nod.

Her smile widens. "Congratulations, Bax. You're a win."

I step back and do the stupidest, dorkiest victory dance I can come up with. I finish it off with a clumsy pirouette and some jazz hands.

Sheila cracks up laughing. It makes my entire damn day. "You are *so* your father's kid."

I straighten up. "Will I see you again?"

"You're not getting rid of me that easy. I'll pop by every now and then. Promise." She wipes lingering tears from her eyes. "Ugh. I'm a mess."

"Yeah, but you rock the mess."

"Shut up."

"Just sayin' you need some 'me time' is all. To that end..." I retrieve a certificate and brochure from the pile and hand it to her.

The sheer elation that erupts on her face warms my heart, but it quickly melts away. "Bax, I...this is—"

"Way less than I owe you for all you've done for me," I say. "And besides, I insist."

The smile returns. "Well, if you *insist*." Her eyes light up as she continues to scan the brochure. "Ooh! Hot stone massage? That one's got my name all over it!"

She engulfs me in another huge hug. Neither of us speaks or moves for a long time.

This warm, fuzzy feeling I'm getting? I think I can get used to it.

CHAPTER TWENTY-NINE

After several more rounds of tests and scans, of being poked and prodded, of boredom and more boredom, Dr. Singh finally discharged me.

If I never set foot in another hospital, it'll be too soon.

My grip tightens on the complimentary hospital tote bag as the Uber driver pulls away and I tap in the entry code for Arbor Vista's walk-in gate.

It feels more than a little surreal coming home after all that's happened. I can only hope that Gina's assessment of Arbor Vista's general demeanor toward me is true and that my neighbors don't decide keeping me around is more trouble than it's worth.

Kids are flying up and down the length of the lawn, blowing off steam from a hard Monday of elementary and middle-school education. Most of the gang is there. I see Crescent kicking a ball around in the distance, but there's no sign of Trina. Or Cheyanne.

I take about ten steps when Maribel, an adorable six-year-old who lives two doors down from Cheyanne, spots me. She points her little finger and shouts, "It's Bax!"

The whole world stops dead. A dozen kids and six parental overseers simultaneously turn to stare at me.

I stand, frozen in place, my stomach clenching.

The heart attack I anticipate never comes as every child screams in glee and rushes me like I was Santa Claus with a sack full of goodies. Maribel reaches me first, hugging my knees so tight I'm unable to walk. Moments later, I'm surrounded, staring down at an ocean of toothy smiles. The grown-ups keep a safe distance away while I'm being mobbed.

"Uh, hey, everyone." I barely hear my own voice over the tumult.

Crescent gently pushes through the throng and faces me. "Are...are you okay?"

I nod, and she throws her arms around my waist. I stand there and let her.

"Get back, kids, give the man some room." Gina walks up, and the crowd parts to let her through. We stand face-to-face, palpable relief evident in her expression. "Everyone was so worried," she says, inducing a round of nods from the kids. "No one knew where you were. I called you twenty times. We didn't even know you were in the hospital until a few days ago."

I furrow my brow. "Who told you?"

"Austin. I went down to the coffee shop hoping someone there had news, and he obliged. He assured me you were doing well, which made all our days." She sweeps her arm to encompass the crowd.

"You told *everyone*?" I ask.

"Of course I did." A guilty look crosses Gina's face. "Oh. I shouldn't have done that, should I?"

I heave a sigh. Guess my involvement was too big to contain after all. Perhaps it's just as well. One enormous secret in my life is enough. "It's okay," I say, loud enough for all to hear. "Just...don't tell anyone *else*, all right?"

A chorus of apologetic nods follows.

"Where's Cheyanne?" I ask. "The cops told me she was released from the hospital days ago."

"That's right. The first thing she did when she got back was pound on your door. She was desperate to see you, to thank you. But no one knew how to reach you."

I crane my neck, searching the crowd for her, but she and her family are nowhere to be seen.

"She's not here, Bax," Gina says. "When she came home with her family, there were two camera crews waiting. They tried to follow her inside, but Ted wouldn't allow it." She smiles. "That guy never fails to surprise me."

Walrus Ted? Our property manager? Whoa. Color me shocked.

"Needless to say, Cheyanne's not quite ready to jump back into her life, so we suggested she and her family get away for a few days. After the crews left, they went to stay with relatives in Casa Grande."

"Will she be back in time for the Halloween party?" I ask.

"I have no idea. I hope so. So does Trina." She takes my hand. "Come on. I just bet you're aching for some real food. I think I've perfected my paillard recipe, and I'd love your opinion."

We make the slow trek to her unit. Along the way, I field thanks and well-wishes from my neighbors. Celeste comes up, rosary in hand, and recites a short prayer and a blessing for my continued recovery.

Wow. Like...wow. Only a few nights ago, I was sure these same people were going to tar and feather me. I really, really have a lot to learn about people.

Trina greets me in the doorway, tears pooling in her eyes. She steps back and lets me pass into the house. It's not until Gina closes the door that our joyful reunion commences. And it lasts a long, long time.

We move to the couch, where my little friend continues to cry happy tears on my shoulder. Gina says nothing as she heads for the kitchen, from which emanates maybe the most delicious smell I've ever experienced.

"You did it," Trina squeaks. "You saved her."

"With your help." We finally face each other, and I use my thumb to dry her tears.

A wobbly smile pushes through the raw emotion. I improve the picture by tucking her braid neatly over her shoulder. "Thanks," she whispers.

Dinner is served, and as I've come to expect when eating Gina's cooking, it's heaven on a plate. I can't remember what Big and Little Forrester said was wrong with the dish the first time I tried it, but whatever the problem was, it seems to have been fixed. Trina gives an enthusiastic thumbs-up two bites in, which I mirror.

Flavor. So. Much. Flavor.

Gina eyes me as she scoops more veggies onto her plate. "So, is hospital food still as bad as I remember it?"

I down my latest bite with some water. "Not all of it. The Jell-O was pretty good."

Trina laughs, and I wink at her.

"So what'd the doctor say?" Gina asks. "You're not going straight back to work, are you?"

"Not right away. Doc said to take it easy for a couple of days. If there are no complications or pain, I can return to light duty. Austin's cool with that. Honestly, it'll be good to chill for a while. I can explore this whole 'social media' thing I keep hearing about."

"Good idea. Gotta have a digital profile in this day and age."

"On another subject...any news about the Halloween costumes? I'm burning with curiosity."

"Picked them up a couple of days ago." Gina gestures down her hallway. "I promise, you're going to love what Trina picked out."

The unveiling happens the minute we finish our meal. She's right. I stare at my costume, draped over the couch, and beam at both of them. "It's perfect. They're all perfect. I love that mine includes the prosthetic hands." My gaze shifts to Gina's costume right next to it. "But yours is badass, Gina. Did the plastic space-gun come with the costume?"

"Nope," she admits. "Had to get that at the toy store. Wasn't easy to find, but I love going that extra mile for Trina."

"This is gonna be the best Halloween ever!" Trina says with infectious enthusiasm.

"Yeah," I agree. "I'm totally wearing that to Hill O' Beans on Friday. Minus the hands. It'll be hard to make lattes wearing those."

We clear the dinner table, load up the dishwasher, and fold up the costumes. I should probably head home now, but after spending a week in that hospital room with no one to talk to but doctors and nurses, I'm glad for the company. Gina fires up the DVD player and pops in *Zootopia*, another animated movie I somehow missed. It's awesome.

At eight-thirty, Trina is sent to her room to finish her home-work and get ready for bed. She reluctantly releases me and obliges.

Once Gina and I are alone, my whole mood changes. Light-hearted and carefree give way to serious and somber. I've been thinking long and hard about what I'm about to do since the night she revealed her and Trina's big secret to me, and my close encounter with AJ convinced me this was an issue I needed to deal with, *now*.

After sneaking a peek down the hall to confirm Trina's door is closed, I face Gina. "The last time we talked, you asked me what happened that made my aura so...well, blue."

She nods. "And you said it wasn't your father dying."

"That's right. It was what happened to my big brother AJ."

Her eyes widen. "You have a brother?"

"Not anymore." Even after two years, the words still leave a bitter taste in my mouth.

A gasp issues from her throat. "Oh, Bax."

"He was two years older than me. I know brothers close together in age are supposed to fight and hate each other, but it wasn't that way with us. He was a great big brother. With Dad gone for months at a time, he was the only one who protected me from Mom. He was always her favorite, you see—star athlete, golden boy, total winner at everything he ever did. And me..." I shrug. "She reminded me every single day what a disappointment I was."

Gina's face contorts into a scowl. I've clearly activated her maternal side.

"I was fifteen when Dad was killed. She'd fallen into depression and alcohol abuse before that, but when he died, she went completely off the rails. Because of Dad's life insurance, she had enough money to drink herself stupid every night. AJ tried to help her, but she wouldn't listen. For a year, we were pretty much left to fend for ourselves.

"I tried to muster up the energy for school every day, but I couldn't. I was failing most of my classes, barely squeaking by in others. I figured I'd just enter the workforce somehow and find a way out of that hellhole. And then..."

Gina takes my hand. I have her full attention.

"At the time AJ graduated, he was dating this girl named Stacy. He'd had a lot of girlfriends, of course, but he completely flipped over her. They were going to attend ASU together, maybe plan a future. Anyway, a few days after graduation, they were invited to a big party one of their friends was throwing at his parents' summer house in Prescott. AJ and Stacy had planned to go together, but Mom was being more difficult than usual, so he told her to go with one of her girlfriends. To make matters worse, AJ blew out a tire halfway there. He had to call for a tow truck, and he had to come back home.

"He tried calling Stacy the next morning, but she didn't answer. He was going out of his mind, texting all his friends who were there. Then he got the bad news—Stacy was found in one of the bedrooms, unconscious, with her skirt hiked up and her underwear around her ankles."

"Jesus," Gina whispers. "She was *raped*?"

I nod. "Stacy used to date this guy named Brock, but she dumped him when she found out what a douche nozzle he was. He never got over her. He was always doing creepy stalker shit around her. AJ even kicked his ass once. But the bastard never learned his lesson. According to three of their friends, Brock showed up uninvited after everyone had started drinking. He probably found a way to roofie her.

"AJ hauled ass in Mom's car all the way there. Stacy was taken to the nearest hospital, and they did a rape kit. They couldn't find any of Brock's DNA on her. Prick probably used a condom. Even worse, his rich parents provided an airtight alibi for him that was far more *reliable* than the sketchy testimony of a few drunk teens."

"So he got away with it?" Gina says through gritted teeth.

"Yup. I'd never seen AJ look so helpless. For two days, he didn't leave Stacy's side. She became withdrawn, hollowed out by the trauma. When AJ and her parents finally got her settled back in her own house, he decided to act."

I close my eyes and blow out a breath. Steady, Bax. Keep going.

"When he came home, he had this crazed look in his eyes that I'd never seen before. He grabbed a bottle of beer from the fridge and chugged it. I tried asking him what he was going to do, but he ignored me. Then he disappeared into Mom's room. She was passed out, as usual. When he came out, he was holding Dad's gun, which she kept in a box on the top shelf of the closet."

Gina shakes her head. She already knows what's coming.

"I don't know what made me get in his way. If Stacy were my girlfriend, I'd probably want to kill the asshole who hurt her myself. But I knew if AJ went through with it, I'd lose him. Forever. Then it'd be just Mom and me, and I didn't think I could survive that.

"He grabbed another beer and tried to bull past me, but I stood my ground. He told me to get out of his way, that this was personal and none of my business. But I wouldn't. He slammed the bottle on the floor, shattering it. I was afraid he would point the gun at me, but he just tried to shove me out of the way. He was much stronger than me, but somehow, I got leverage on him. I pushed him as hard as I could, and..." A choked sob forces its way through. "He slipped on the puddle of beer, and fell and...the broken glass went right into his..." I'm unable to finish the sentence.

Gina releases my hand, edges next to me, then pulls me into a hug. I feel her warmth, her support, wash over me. I never make it to full tears, but it takes a while to get my voice back.

"Mom woke up just as the paramedics were working on him. We all went to the hospital, but they couldn't save him. When we got the news, Mom let me have it. Both barrels, right there in the waiting room. How I'd done it on purpose because I was always jealous of him, that I did it just to get even with her. She called me every name in the book."

"But you weren't charged."

"No. The police determined it was an accident. Didn't stop Mom from blaming me." I slump against the cushions. "I left home after that. Dropped out of school, too. I had no other family. I spent the next year in and out of foster homes, mooching off some of my loser friends, living the slacker lifestyle, not giving a crap about anything or anyone. Then, right after New Year's, I got drunker than usual and decided to have fun smashing car windows. A certain lady cop showed up, and...well, you know the rest."

"You blamed yourself for AJ's death," Gina whispers.

Shame flushes my cheeks. "All this time, I was convinced that I really was guilty. But the truth is, I was going to lose him that night, one way or another. He would've killed Brock, and I would've blamed myself for not stopping him. Instead, AJ died." My breath quickens, and I suddenly feel faint.

"Easy now," she soothes. "In through the nose, out through the mouth."

I try this several times, and my heartbeat slows.

You know that cliché about a great weight lifting off your shoulders after confessing a deep, dark secret? Turns out it's true. The guilt, which had been pressing down on me, constricting my chest for two years, is gone.

I look up at the ceiling, imagining AJ staring down at me with that cockeyed grin, and smile. Thanks, big brother.

Gina edges away from me with an expression that I can't quite discern. Her head is tilted to one side, her brow furrowed. "Huh. Would you look at that."

"What?" I ask.

"Your aura. It's not blue anymore."

I push myself into an upright position. "It's not? What is it now?"

She leans one way, then the other, like she's getting a reading on me. "There is still a little blue, but there's a new color in the mix."

"Which is?"

"Pink."

"Pink?"

"Bright pink."

Great. I *am* turning into Pinkie Pie. "Is...is that good?"

She closes the distance between us and smiles. "It's very good. It means...you're happy."

"Really?" I say, dubious. "Just like that?"

"I told you, Bax, your aura doesn't lie." She taps her head knowingly.

Am I happy? Like, for real?

I have a life again. One far away from Mom's influence. I have a job, friends, a community that's accepted me. I have a superpower, and someone to help me figure it all out.

Yes. I am happy. Whaddaya know.

The biggest, stupidest grin spreads over my face, right before it opens in a gigantic yawn.

"Okay, kiddo, time for you to be getting home." Gina pulls

me to my feet. "Rest up, relax, and try not to think about anything abnormal for a while."

"Sounds like a plan. There is one more question I wanted to ask you, though."

"What is it?"

I cast another glance down the hall, toward Trina's room. "You once told me your parents didn't like the fact that Trina was growing up without a male role model. I'd like to fill that role. Be a big brother to her, like AJ was for me. If that's alright with you, of course."

Gina takes only two seconds to consider. "I'd love that, and I know she would too. She adores you, you know."

"Yeah, I know." I smile. "I may not be 'role model' material, but at least I can give her the benefit of my experience. Teach her to not make the same mistakes I did. Talk to her about evil things. Like boys. And drugs. But mostly boys."

She wags a finger at me. "I hope you know what you're getting yourself into. She's been all peaches and cream around you so far, but you haven't seen her when she's in 'stubborn child' mode. Trust me, you'll have your work cut out for you."

Meh. She's nine. How bad could it be?

I change the subject. "Will I be starting my Jedi training soon, then?"

She punches my shoulder and laughs. "Don't worry, I won't make you run through swamp mud with me on your back."

"Good to know." I pick up the tote bag, rifle through the ream of discharge paperwork, and find what I'm looking for. "I have something for you. Consider it payment in advance for my...education."

She opens the envelope, scans its contents. Her eyes grow huge, her gaze wavering from me to the certificate and back again. Her jaw falls open, and she points to it as if wondering whether it's real. I nod, and she exhales deeply. "Can I adopt you? Would that be weird? That would be weird. Never mind. Oh my." She wipes her eyes. "I'm going to love this. Thank you, Bax."

"You're welcome."

She claps me on the back and, after I scoop up my costume, she leads me to the door. "I should probably warn you—now that the residents of Arbor Vista have a great reason to ring your doorbell, they will. And some of them are old-school about rewarding acts of bravery or selflessness with food."

I lift an eyebrow. "How much food?"

"Let's just say you should probably clean out your fridge."

Ooookay. "Duly noted."

She opens the door and gives me another brief hug. "Welcome home."

I pause on the threshold. "One last thing...my name is Bernard."

A guffaw escapes, but she recovers quickly. "*Bernard*? That's really your name?"

"It was my grandpa's name. He was in Vietnam. Won the Silver Star."

She gives a light whistle.

"Now you see why I go by Bax. You let me in on your secret, and I didn't want to have any more from you."

"And I promise I'll keep this one, too. Under pain of death, if need be."

What are the odds of two psychics ending up next door to each other? Man Upstairs, I sense your hand in this. Thanks, Big Guy. I owe you.

She squeezes my shoulder. "Goodnight, Bax."

"Goodnight, Gina."

I feel her eyes follow me as I fumble my key into my door. Once inside, I toss my Halloween costume onto my sofa. From there, I head straight for the bedroom, shed my jacket and shoes, and collapse into bed.

CHAPTER THIRTY

Boy, Gina wasn't kidding.

The first knock on my door comes around ten o'clock on Tuesday morning. Celeste brings me a plastic-wrapped plate containing something she calls chilaquiles, which she claims is from a recipe passed down from her grandmother. I return her grin and let her bless me one more time before she heads back to her unit.

After that, the floodgates open as every stay-at-home mom in the complex pays me a visit. And they *all* bring food. Huarache, chile relleno, pozole, carnitas, flan, and some delicious-smelling empanadas. And then there are the tamales. Oh my God, the tamales. I have so many tamales stuffed into my freezer, I needed several strands of duct tape to keep the door closed. I'm overwhelmed. I mean, I know I'm eighteen with a blast-furnace metabolism, but it's gonna take me a month to get through all this food.

I wake up on Wednesday refreshed and completely pain-free. My energy level feels almost back to normal, and the prescription Dr. Singh gave me for pain meds still sits in my drawer next to Mom's address. I hope I'll never need either.

Austin and I have a brief texted conversation that ends with him scheduling me for a half-shift on Thursday, eleven to three. I won't have to do any heavy lifting or cleaning, which is fine by me. He also tells me he hired two new baristas to pick up the slack since Piper's going to be gone for a while. I can't help but wonder if, after a few months away, she really will be able to slide back into her old routine like nothing's happened. Boss-man graciously provides me with Piper's number before telling me he'll see me tomorrow.

After mucking about on Facebook for an hour, I shoot Piper a short text asking how she's doing. I want to include "I miss you" in the message, but don't want her to misinterpret it. I'm surprised when I get an immediate response:

Piper: You gonna be home this afternoon?

Me: Yeah.

Piper: Is it OK if I come by? Really need to speak to you.

My guts knot, but only for a moment. Calm down, Bax. She didn't say it was bad news.

Me: I'll be here all day.

Piper: OK. See you later.

I still haven't had my morning coffee, so I switch the machine on and scan the contents of my cupboard, looking for inspiration. There's every possibility Sydney will be there tomorrow, so getting in a couple more practice MCL's might be in order.

I've no sooner prepared two mugs and am about to sample them when a knock comes from the front door. I grunt, hoping it's not yet another neighbor fulfilling his or her quest to keep me from starving to death. One peek through the spyhole, however, shows a person who clearly doesn't live here.

The door swings open to reveal a guy in his late twenties and a dark blue polo with the words "Crime Lab" over the breast. Dude's a couple of inches taller than me, with short black hair and bearing a bemused expression.

He breaks our gaze to consult a clipboard he's holding in one hand. "Um, are you Mr. Baxter?"

"That's me," I say.

"Good morning." His tone is friendly, which puts me at ease. "CSI Olsen, Phoenix Crime Lab. I'm here to pick up some evidence I was told is in your possession."

Oh crap, Sarah's clothes. In all the excitement, I completely forgot I still had them. "Uh, yeah." I gesture him inside. "Come on in, I'll get it for you."

"Thanks." CSI Olsen walks past me, and I close the door behind him. I'm about to head for my hall closet when he takes a big sniff. "What is that? It smells wonderful."

"Mocha chai latte. Freshly made."

His eyebrows lift. "You make lattes in your home? That's intense."

"I work at a coffee shop," I explain. "I've been trying to come up with a drink that my boss can add to the menu."

"Really?" He points to the two mugs on the counter. "Would you mind? I could murder a cup of coffee right now."

Crime lab joke. Cute.

I hadn't planned on giving a complete stranger a blind taste test, but hey, his opinion is as valid as anyone's. I hand one mug to him and take a sip from the other. Just as I hoped, it's perfect. Judging by the look of pure bliss on CSI Olsen's face, he's on Team Bax.

"Dude, seriously, this is fantastic."

"Thanks. Be right back." I return moments later, Hefty bag in hand, and place it on my kitchen table. "I'm glad you're here. I gotta admit, I had no idea what I was going to do with these." I pry the bag open, getting one last look at Sarah's clothes. "May I ask what you're going to do with them?"

CSI Olsen takes another sip. "Analyze them, write a report that no one will read, and then probably return them to her family."

Works for me. I'll be happy to end this grisly chapter of my life once and for all.

He polishes off his latte and fixes me with a curious stare. "Do you mind if I ask you something, Mr. Baxter?"

"Uh, I guess not. And please, call me Bax."

He holds out his hand, which I shake. "Eddie. Nice to meet you."

"You too."

"Anyway, there's a rumor going around the lab that the DP Killer case was cracked because the police were tipped off by someone who is...psychic." His face reddens. "I was just wondering if it was true."

Alarm bells jangle in my brain, and my eyes narrow in suspicion. Could Detective Rojas be behind Eddie's sudden visit? Is she testing my ability to keep my promise? Maybe this guy is wearing a wire, and she's waiting for me to slip up...

Stop it, Bax. Get a grip. We talked about this, remember? You and Natalie made peace. Quit seeing the worst in people!

Even so, I can't break the rules just because I feel like it, either.

"I can't talk about it," I say with as much resolve as I can. "My name didn't appear in the news for a reason, and I'm not allowed to discuss that reason with anyone. The last thing I need is to make an enemy of Captain Callahan. That guy's a little intimidating, you know?"

He gives a dismissive wave. "Aah, he's not as bad as you might think. Sure, he comes off as a grump, but he's a pussycat once you get to know him."

I cock my head to one side. "And you know this how?"

Eddie smiles. "I married his daughter."

Whoa. "Seriously?"

He holds up his hand, showing off the gold band around his ring finger. "Just over a year ago. We're expecting our first child in April."

"Congrats."

"Thanks. Look, I don't want to get you in trouble. It's just that...I've been a fan of the paranormal for a long time, and I'm insanely curious. I mean, I've heard police departments all over the world consult psychics, but to actually meet one would be..."

He sways on his feet for a few moments, then holds up his hands. "Never mind. Forget I asked."

He makes to leave, but I stop him. "Hold up."

Maybe I'm just asking for trouble, but something about Eddie's request strikes me as genuine. Besides, if he's Captain Callahan's son-in-law, then telling him my secret would still be "keeping it in the family," so to speak.

Ah, what the hell. Just this once.

"Do you have anything on you that's personal? Something you associate with good memories?"

His eyes widen in anticipation. He pats his pockets, then his gaze falls to his wedding band. "Uh, just this, I guess."

"That should work." I move to my sofa, sit down, and point to my coffee table. "Please put the ring here."

Eddie obeys, then steps back. "You're sure you're cool with this?"

I flex my fingers and take several deep breaths. "As long as the memories are pleasant, yeah, it's cool."

"Really, man, this is awesome of you." He kneels down, and for a second, the ten-or-so-year gap between us shrinks to nothing.

I focus on the ring, lying flat on the table. I lean forward, centering myself, both index fingers hovering right above it.

You can do this, Bax. Just like Piper's locket and Trina's bracelet. Easy peasy.

My fingertips brush the metal, and—

The most amazing woman in the whole world smiles at me. Her freckly face flushes, and my heart misses a beat. I glance down, and she slips the band onto my finger. It fits perfectly, of course. She grips my hands in hers, which are just as soft and warm as when we were thirteen. God, that feels like a lifetime ago.

There's a sparkle in her eyes as we await the priest's final words, the ones that will cement the bond I've sought half my life. Both our breaths hitch in anticipation.

"And so, by the power vested in me by the state of Arizona, I now

pronounce you husband and wife," the priest says. "You may now kiss the bride."

You don't have to tell me twice.

I throw my arms around my beautiful wife, kissing her with everything I have. It's magical, just like I hope the next million kisses will be. Never in my life did I think I could be this happy, that after so many years apart we'd end up together. But it happened. Like it was destiny.

We break the kiss, but not the embrace. "I love you...Detective," I say.

"I love you too...Ethan." She chuckles softly, and I can't help but join her.

Wait a sec...'Ethan?'

The scene changes, and this time I'm more able to detach myself from Eddie's emotional state. I'm now on a raised platform peering out at a sea of smiling wedding guests. The bride, now sans veil, hoots and hollers up at me. Captain Callahan, looking sharp in his dress blues, joins in the applause. I raise my palms in front of me, showing off the ring on one hand and the microphone in the other.

"This next song goes out to the most beautiful woman in the whole world," Eddie says. "My wife, Kelsey Olsen."

The bride hollers again.

"I sang this song for you a long time ago, on a very memorable night. I have a feeling, though, that this night will end a little differently than that one did."

"It better!" says one of the bridesmaids, a petite blonde woman. Everyone laughs.

"This one's for you, baby," Eddie says.

Eddie turns to his left. Next to him on the stage is a dark-haired guy holding an electric guitar. His grin stretches from ear to ear as he says with a distinctly Irish accent, *"Just like old times, eh boss?"*

I pat my childhood friend on the shoulder. "I can't believe you're actually here, Baz."

"Are you kidding? I wouldn't have missed this for anything." He stands back, grasping the neck of the guitar. *"Let's rock this party!"*

Baz begins jamming on his instrument, a series of notes that I recognize immediately. I feel Eddie tap his foot and raise the microphone to his mouth. Once the opening riff concludes and the rest of the band has joined in, both he and Baz pump their fists in the air and sing, "Ai! Oh! Let's go! Ai! Oh! Let's go!"

The flash lasts through the entire two-minute song, during which Eddie never stops looking at his new wife. The sheer, unbridled joy coursing through his veins, the love he feels for this woman...it's breathtaking.

The song cuts out, and just like that, I'm back in my living room.

I blink several times and shake my head, dispelling the images and focusing on Eddie, watching me from across the room. I wait for the cold spell to hit, but it doesn't. Hmm.

"So?" Eddie's face lights up like he's about to cross something off his bucket list. "Did you see anything?"

"Yeah," I say. "Hope you don't mind my saying so, but your wife is mega-hot."

"You saw my wife? Like, actually saw her?" He's looking at me with such awe that it feels weird, much like the day Gina and Trina saw my aura for the first time.

"I sure did. You like girls who rock the freckles too, huh?"

"Oh, God, yes." Eddie gingerly takes a seat next to me, scoops up his ring, and slips it back on. "It was the first thing that attracted me to her when we were kids."

"You've known her that long?"

"Yeah." His mouth flattens into a thin line. "So, what did you see?"

"Two things," I explain. "I saw the actual moment you two became married. Then it was you and some guy with an Irish accent singing 'Blitzkrieg Bop' to the entire wedding party." I chuckle. "Nice job, by the way."

"Thanks. Baz was my best friend back in eighth grade. He flew all the way in from Boston. That night was the best night of my life."

I nod. Who knows if I'll ever take the plunge myself, but if I do, I hope my wedding night contains as many amazing memories as Eddie's.

"So...your wife's a detective? Guess that makes sense since her dad's a captain and all."

He smirks. "Actually, she's a middle school counselor."

"But you called her 'Detective.'"

"It was a nickname she had, years ago. It's kind of my pet name for her."

"Ah. And is 'Ethan' her pet name for you?"

Eddie's mouth drops open, and the blood leaves his face. "Holy shit. You heard her call me that?"

I point to his ring. "Technically, you heard her call you that. I just shared in the memory. Is that your middle name or something?"

He shuffles in his seat. "It's, uh, a long story." He checks his watch, then whistles. "Damn, look at the time. Gotta get this bag to the lab."

We rise together, he retrieves his clipboard and the Hefty, and I open the door for him. "Are you, um...are you going to be doing any more crime fighting?" he asks. "Just curious."

The question takes me aback. I honestly hadn't thought about it. I fell into this mad chase for the DP Killer by accident. Using my ability to help the police...well, stranger things have happened. I think. "Anything's possible, I guess."

He offers his hand, which I shake. "Thanks again for indulging me, Bax. That was, like, the coolest thing I've ever seen. If we ever get a chance to work together again, I promise I'll tell you my and Kelsey's story."

"Look, Eddie, I took a risk just now. I'd rather word of my little demonstration never got back to Detective Rojas. Or Captain Callahan."

He claps me on the shoulder and gives me a smile so authentic I instantly believe it. "Don't worry, Bax, what happened here will stay between us. Believe me when I say, I'm very good at keeping secrets."

I exhale in relief.

We exchange friendly waves as he heads for the guest parking lot.

That was interesting. Cool guy. And he gave me something else to think about.

Later that afternoon, I'm halfway through my plate of reheated huarache—which is phenomenal—when my phone rings. I see the caller ID and answer on the first ring.

"Piper?"

"Hey, Bax." Damn, it's good to hear her voice. "I'm outside the gate, but the entry code I used before isn't working."

Right. Ted changed it after the police came by the night Cheyanne was kidnapped. "Uh, yeah. Press 2-5-8-0-2-pound. That should get you in."

A brief pause, then, "Got it. See you in a little bit."

I rake a hand through my quiff, throw on a clean shirt, and watch with subdued glee when Piper pulls into my parking spot. Ten seconds later, we're locked in a warm hug.

"I've missed you," I say into her fiery mane of barely controlled hair.

"I've missed you too," comes the muffled reply.

Once inside, I point to the kitchen. "Want me to make you something? If you like Mexican food, I have pretty much anything you could want."

She stares at me.

"Grateful neighbors," I explain.

"Ah. Uh, no thanks, I can't stay long. My schedule has been

apeshit crazy, but I just had to see you. I have things to tell you that I didn't want to say in a text."

We sit on the couch, and I fake a relaxed pose. I noticed the heart-shaped locket once again around her neck. "How's your dad?"

"He's...okay. Still going to therapy, in and out of doctor's offices, the usual." She makes a guilty face. "Obviously, I had a lot of explaining to do that night."

I wince. "Does he hate me?"

"He doesn't know what really happened. As far as he's concerned, you were only along for the ride, just like the papers said." She sighs. "He was angry at first, but when I told him you gave us your half of the reward, he mellowed out fast."

I smile.

"You didn't have to do that, Bax."

"I know. But I wanted to. After all the crap you've had to deal with, with your dad and Jackson and Gavin and stuff, I wanted you to be able to go to sleep without worrying what was going to happen next. For a while, anyway. Besides, I'm good for money."

She nods. "Speaking of Gavin, he contacted me a few days ago. To apologize."

"For reals?" I ask, shocked. Did not think Pretty Boy had that in him.

"Yeah. Surprised me, too. Told me he regrets everything he did and said after Jackson died, and that he only blames himself for our falling out. Then he promised he'd never make trouble for me or my family again."

"How about that," I muse. "Are you two going to stay friends?"

She ponders this. "I doubt it. Our social circles are just too far apart, you know? Any relationship we have would feel like going through the motions. I'd prefer to remember the way he was when we first met, and not try to force it to be something else."

I remain silent. I know there's something important she wants to tell me, but I'll let her get there on her own.

She doesn't keep me waiting long. "Did Austin tell you I took a leave of absence?"

"He did. Is that really what it is?" I'm unable to keep the concern from my voice.

She takes my hand, squeezes it. "I promise, I will be coming back. I have a whole bunch of interviews scheduled for the next few weeks—newspapers, radio, even *The Today Show*, can you believe it?"

I whistle. "Holy shit, Piper."

"I know, right?"

"Can you handle all that attention? I mean, you're not exactly an extrovert."

"True, but I look at this as an opportunity. Rather than use my *fame*," she uses finger quotes around the last word, "to toot my own horn, I'm going to raise awareness about Guillain–Barré. Maybe someone with influence and connections will hear my dad's story and do something to help."

Just when I think I can't admire Piper more. This girl has a heart as big as all outdoors. "That's awesome, Piper. I hope you raise a billion dollars for the cause."

"That would be epic." She laughs, but it tapers off. "Like I said, my schedule is pretty filled up for the next few weeks. After that..." She stares at her lap. "I'm leaving town."

I try to hide my disappointment but probably fail. After a moment, resignation sets in. "That's a good idea," I mumble. "You need to get away from all this. Where are you headed?"

"My maternal grandparents have a nice ranch-style home in Wyoming. I've only seen them once since Mom died twelve years ago, and they miss me. They've agreed to have me over for Thanksgiving."

"Wyoming, huh? Won't it be freezing?"

She waves the comment away. "Eh, I don't mind the cold. A few weeks of clean air, Grandma's cooking, and Agatha Christie are all I need to clear my head."

"A few weeks? When will you be back?"

"Probably not until after my birthday."

I grimace. "So I'll miss it?"

"We can celebrate when I get back, okay?" She smiles, her eyes twinkling behind her cat-eye glasses.

"It's a deal." I move to my kitchen, digging another certificate out of the drawer. "But just in case I don't see you before you leave..."

I hand it to her, and watch her face light up when she recognizes it. "You actually went out and got me a spa day."

"I keep my promises," I say with just a tinge of smugness.

The look she gives me melts my heart, and the Piper I met that first day at Hill O' Beans reappears. "I keep my promises too, Bax, so here's one of my own." She sets the certificate down and faces me full-on. "If you ever, *EVER*, need me for *anything*, I'll be there. Whether it's for a case or if you just want to talk, you call me. Understand?"

I nod. Holy crap, I want to kiss her so bad. "Got it."

"Unless it's another serial killer," she amends. "Then you're on your own. One is enough for me." She winks.

"Totally get that." I laugh, and she stands. Guess her too-brief visit is over.

She pauses near the back door and faces me. "If all goes well, I'll be resuming classes in January. I'll probably be back at Hill O' Beans by then too."

Damn, I hope that's true. "Call or text me anytime. You can even Zoom me from Wyoming, once I get Trina to show me how Zoom works."

Piper beams. "That girl's a pistol. I'm not worried about you when she's around."

I move to open the door, but she stays my hand. Moisture suddenly clouds her eyes. "You're an amazing friend, Bax. And I don't mean the ESP. I'm truly thankful I have you in my life."

I find myself unable to speak. My body ignores my brain and edges close to her, and my face leans in. She doesn't flinch, or retreat, or stammer out an objection. Rather, she leans forward too.

Oh, my. It's going to happen. We're going to kiss. She wants it. I want it.

After this, we won't just be friends. We'll be something more. Maybe not in love, maybe not boyfriend and girlfriend, but the possibilities are there.

In that moment before our lips meet, I play out our relationship in my mind. I could be good for her, and she could be great for me. And I'm not just talking about the sex, which I know would be amazing. I'd be there for her. Support her. I'd never treat her the way Gavin did. I'd be more like...

Jackson.

The guy she should've ended up with. The guy she deserved.

The guy I'll never be.

I can't do it.

At the last second, I move my lips to her cheek. It's warm, soft. The heat of my breath glances off her skin, then I pull back. Behind her glasses, her eyes flash with disappointment, but it's quickly replaced by appreciation.

She steps back and lets me open the door. One final smile and a "See ya," and she leaves.

I watch as her car drives away, through the entry gate and out of sight.

The huarache's gone room temperature, so I nuke it back to an edible level. My eyes fall on the coffee maker.

When I started at Hill O' Beans, scoring a date with Sydney seemed like a worthy goal. And it still is. But this thing I have with Piper...it could be life-changing. No, it already is. Do I have room for both of them in my life? Can I really maintain relationships with both girls without screwing them up?

Guess I'll find out how good at adulting I am. If I can be that for Trina, I can for everyone else too.

For now, though? I have a bet to win.

Chapter Thirty-One

I pull my two-wheeler into the strip mall parking lot, getting my first view of Hill O' Beans in over a week. The dining area looks busy, as usual, but not so crowded that I'll have to walk sideways through the place. I check again to make sure the doctor's note clearing me for work duty is still in my jacket pocket, then lock my ten-speed in the bike rack.

I flash back to one month ago, the day I joined Austin's team. I remember how unprepared I was, how I'd spent my entire shift stumbling around like a donkey with four broken legs. The prospect of keeping up with the fast pace of a popular coffee shop seemed impossible for an ex-delinquent with no experience and not even a high school diploma. Thanks to Sheila, Austin decided to take a chance on me.

Because of this place, I've learned a skill at which I hope to become better still.

Because of this place, I made the best friend I've ever had.

Because of this place, an unrepentant killer will never take another life.

The ESP...well, that would've happened anyway, likely under less horrifying circumstances, but I can't hold that against Hill O' Beans.

"Velllllcome."

I'm so lost in my own thoughts as I pass through the front door that Hobula the Vampire's disembodied greeting makes my skeleton nearly jump out of my skin. I gasp, clutching my chest and trying to keep my heart from leaping out my throat.

I grab an empty chair for support, then look up to realize I'm being laughed at. Not only by customers, but by Austin, Imani, Sierra, and two people in aprons I don't recognize.

Anger flushes my face, but it morphs quickly into embarrassment, then acceptance. Yeah, if I were them, I'd laugh at me too. Nothing funnier than watching someone get the pants scared off them, especially a guy who should have seen it coming.

"All right, you got me." I grin. "Give the guy with the head injury a break, will ya?"

I make my way to the register, and my boss and coworkers flash approving smiles. They step aside to reveal a two-foot banner on the wall behind them, just below the TV. "Welcome back, Bax," it says. Dotted around the letters are my coworkers' signatures and well-wishes.

Aww, guys. Don't make me cry. I'm in a precarious emotional state this week.

I step behind the counter, fielding high-fives and fist-bumps from Imani and Sierra. I'm introduced to Hill O' Beans two newest employees, Amari and Kiara, both of whom started their training this morning. Amari is a tall guy in his early twenties, born in the U.S. to Nigerian parents who is putting himself through engineering school. Kiara, who I guess to be my age, is a petite girl with a head full of thick brown hair who speaks fluent Spanish. Both, Austin tells me, are learning the ropes quite well, but I'm to answer any questions and offer help if they need it.

After clocking in and donning an apron, Austin sticks me on the register for the duration of the lunch rush and lets Imani and Sierra school the noobs. Amari is polite and clearly eager to learn, which will serve him well here. Kiara gets a little flustered after messing up her first few attempts but brightens when she cranks out her first successful PSL.

Traffic finally slows, then stops, around one-thirty. Sierra hands me the plate of hotteoks she promised. This batch includes a dipping sauce made from apple butter and sprinkled with cinnamon. If possible, they're even better than the last time. There are too many for me to eat by myself, so I share. No one goes away disappointed.

By two, the trainees have been sent home for the day, as has Imani. I've wiped off the counter next to the register a dozen times, so I start shooting hopeful glances out the window, looking for Sydney. Sure enough, she strides in at ten past, smiling that gorgeous smile when we lock eyes.

"There you are!" She drops her satchel on an empty table and makes a beeline straight for me. "It's about time you showed up for work again."

"Aww, did you miss me?" I tease.

Her face flushes a deep red. It's adorable. "Maybe a little. Coming in and not being able to banter with you just isn't as fun, you know. Were you really in the hospital?"

I face the wall, showing off the hairless patch cut into the back of my head. The wound has healed enough to not have to wear a bandage anymore, but I imagine it's not pretty to look at.

"Ugh." She makes a disgusted face. "What happened? Did you trip over your overconfidence?"

Oh, you wanna play, huh? "Nope. I was practicing my victory dance, and I slipped and fell. Stupid, really."

She puts her hands on her hips, mock-frowning at me. "You haven't won yet, bub."

"I'm about to. One Bax Special coming right up."

I gather together the ingredients for Sydney's usual, except for the nondescript plastic baggie I threw two cups of Nesquik in this morning. I'm about halfway through my preparation when a jingle signals another customer.

"*Madre de dios,* Bax, what did you do to your hair?"

I turn to see a familiar face, looking considerably more haggard than the last time I saw it. "Nico! I don't think I've seen you in here before."

He sidles up next to Sydney, who moves to one side. "Never really been into coffee," he explains. "But Izzy's in one of her moods, and if I don't come back with something to calm her down, she's going to turn into the *chupacabra.*"

"Yowch," I sympathize.

"You're the guy who cut Bax's hair?" Sydney inquires.

He faces her, visibly affronted. "I didn't just *cut* his hair, sweetie, I sculpted it. Transformed it from the dumpster fire he came in with to the slammin' coif you see now."

"Well, I think you did a great job." Sydney smiles, doing the smart thing and appealing to Nico's vanity. Good move, girl.

"*Gracias,*" he says with a head-bow. "Till he had to go and ruin it, that is." He shoots me a hairy eyeball.

"Hit my head a few days ago," I say. "Had to make a choice—preserve your awesome work or bleed to death. No offense, I chose life."

Nico shakes his head in mild disapproval. "At least wear a hat or something until it grows back. It's embarrassing." He sighs, then turns back to Sydney. "So...what's good here?"

"I'm really not the right person to ask," she confesses. "I always get the same thing, mocha chai latte. *Buuuuuut,*" she gestures at me, "Bax is making me something brand new, something he created. He says it's even better than my usual."

"Oh, *really?*" He flashes his gleaming pearly whites. "Put me down for one too."

Thanks to muscle memory, crafting a second of my creation is no problem at all. I notice Austin, watching me from several yards away. Regardless of how the acid test goes with Nico and Sydney, it'll ultimately be up to Austin whether my version of an MCL is menu-worthy.

"Austin," Nico coos. I imagine the come-hither look on his face as he eyes boss-man's impressive biceps.

"Nico," Austin replies with feigned politeness.

"Still with the same guy?"

"Three years now."

"Heartbreaker."

I end the soap opera by adding the chocolate powder, stirring, and praying that the love for my drink continues to be universal. I set the cups down in front of Sydney and Nico, then step back to gauge their reactions. Nico wastes no time in snatching the cup up, blowing on it, and taking a sip. His eyes close, then go wide, and his eyebrows vanish into his pompadour.

Sydney, rather than taking her own sip, inhales the aroma like she's at a wine-tasting. She blows on the hot beverage several times, waiting for Nico's verdict.

My personal stylist puffs out a wanton breath, then sips again. "Bax...it's amazing. If this doesn't calm Izzy down, nothing will." After another sip, he says, "I'm going to the restroom. When I get back, I want two more, to go, and one of those yummy-looking cranberry muffins." He winks at Austin as he passes by. "Give that kid a raise." Then he disappears into the men's room.

I cross my arms, beaming at Sydney.

She chuckles, breathes on her cup again, then takes a wary sip. Not much, just a few drops. Her eyes close as the warm liquid slides down her throat.

I count the seconds, waiting for her opinion. It doesn't come. She takes a second sip, then a third.

Dammit, Sydney, quit torturing me!

She fixes those amazing baby blues on me, and a smile curls the corners of her mouth.

Should my heart be beating this fast?

"It's...really good, Bax," she says. "In fact, it's delicious."

"Sooooo..." I lean forward. "I win?"

Her smile fades away. "Not so fast. The bet was that you

would make me something *better* than my usual. This," she points to her cup, "is just as good, but it's not better."

If my anticipation were a balloon, it would be making farty noises as the air slowly leaked out. Is she *serious*? "Come on! You really going to play me like that? Do you know how hard I worked on this? Just for you?"

She puts the cup down, then leans across the counter. "Easy there, tiger. If you recall, this whole 'bet' thing was your idea. You could've just asked me out."

My righteous indignation dribbles away, and Bax the Fish-Faced Doofus returns. "I could've...really?"

She nods.

"That would've worked?"

Another nod. "But you were so determined to earn it." Her face softens, and I suddenly remember why I find this girl so captivating. "No one has ever tried so hard to get a date with me. Ever. It's really—"

"Pathetic?" *Shut up, moron!*

"Flattering. And sweet."

I gulp. "So...you'll go out with me?"

She takes my hand. "I'd love to."

Score.

I have a date with a freckle-faced angel.

"You, um, gonna stick around for a few minutes?" I ask.

"Yeah." She pays for the drink, takes her cup, then sits down at her table. "Join me when you get a break."

I'm so ecstatic at the thought of dating Sydney, I haven't noticed Austin has come up behind me. He points at the baggie, sitting innocently on the back counter. "Make me one. *Now.*"

I whip up three more in short order, including the two for Nico, who's back at the register. I hand one to Austin, slap to-go lids on the other two, and slide them over to Nico. We watch together as Austin takes one sip, then another. His brow furrows, and he smacks his lips in puzzlement. "The taste is familiar, but I can't quite place it. What is it?"

I stifle a laugh. "Nesquik."

The look on Austin's face is so priceless I want to frame it. His jaw drops, and for a few moments, he's reduced to stunned silence. "Nesquik?" he splutters. "I have taken coffee-making *classes*, read dozens of books on the subject, scoured a thousand recipes online. And you come up with chocolate milk mix." He places the cup down, then busts out laughing. "That is pure... effing...genius, Bax. I wouldn't have thought of this in a million years."

"Sounds like he likes it," Nico singsongs.

"I can sell the shit out of this." He thumps me on the back. "Come Monday, this is going on the menu."

Oh. My. God.

Nico holds up his palm, which I gleefully high-five. "Way to go, little man!"

"Thanks, dude," is all I can say. "And thanks, Boss. This means a lot to me."

"Just cultivating creativity in my employees." He takes another sip, and mmm mmms again. "But it needs a name. A good name that'll get people's attention. We can't just call it an MCL. Tell me you have something in mind?"

Crap. It's only now that I realize I still haven't figured out what to call my creation. I made a list of possible names a week ago but threw it out because they were lame as shit.

Then my eyes fall on Nico, and lightning strikes my brain.

I've got it. Oh, man, do I got it.

"It's called...the Sexy Bax."

Cue the choir music. Or Justin Timberlake.

A legend has just been born.

Suck it, Carl.

It's pretty close to the end of my scheduled shift, so Austin lets me clock out a few minutes early. After I assure him I'm healthy enough to work a full shift, he schedules me to open tomorrow and Saturday. I thank Sierra again for the hotteoks, then join Sydney at her table. She's worked her complimentary drink down to the bottom of the cup, which in itself is also complimentary.

"Sexy Bax, huh?" Her expression is playful, and a dimple I never noticed before appears on her cheek. Be still my heart. "You don't think that's a tad pretentious?"

"I think it's got a nice ring to it." I can't resist the urge to mess with her head a little. Call it payback. "In a few weeks, folks will be lined up for a taste of sweet, Sexy Bax. It'll be epic."

"Then I'm honored to have been present at the birth of a dynasty." She winks. "About our date—I've been invited to a Halloween party tomorrow night. You wanna come?"

"I...actually can't." I scrunch my face in contrition. "I have a thing at my townhome complex. I can't miss it."

"No prob. You working Saturday?"

"Until two, but I'm free after that."

Her face lights up. "I have a volleyball match at three. Want to be my cheering section?"

A chance to see my girl in action? Count me in. "Hell, yeah. Do you play as fiercely as you negotiate?"

"Harder."

"I pity the other team, then."

"We should be done before five, and then we can go wherever you like. What are you thinking for dinner?"

I plaster a knowing smirk on my face. "Do you like brisket?"

"Are you kidding?" she asks with a *duh* expression. "I'm from San Antonio. I was raised on brisket. Trouble is, I haven't found a place in Arizona that does it the way I like it."

"And how's that?"

"Pot roasted to perfection, swimming in jus. Heaven on earth."

Smugness factor increasing. "Then I have just the place."

"Really?"

"Really really."

"If you're right, and their brisket is as good as you say, I may kiss you on the mouth."

I grin evilly. "Do you kiss as well as you play volleyball?"

She leans forward, and the smile she gives me raises the hair on my neck. "Better."

Everything's coming up Bax.

CHAPTER THIRTY-TWO

"I'm gonna wreck it!"

I step through the open double doors of Arbor Vista's activity center, fake hands held high over my head. My lanky frame is about as far from Wreck-It Ralph's as it can be, but between the overalls and the wig, the rest is a pretty close match. Even closer to the real thing is Trina's Vanellope Von Schweetz costume, complete with the brown skirt and the green hoodie. She even has tiny candies stuck to her raven-black wig.

It's Gina's outfit, however, that grabs the most attention, decked out as she is in the plastic space armor of Sergeant Tammy Calhoun. She does look rather incongruous at the moment, carrying her ginormous blaster in one hand and a cake in the other.

The Arbor Vista gang rush up and high-five my oversized mitts, squeeing over how cool we all look. I expected the usual array of ghouls, goblins, and superheroes, and am not disappointed.

I survey the largish room, which has plenty of grown-ups— only half of whom got into the holiday spirit by dressing up— talking to each other and enjoying the atmosphere. A selection of light pop and rock hits pour from a pair of speakers standing in front of an entertainment system. Ted, dressed as an alien from the planet Mustache, works the thing like a pro. I may have totally misjudged him.

After the greetings are complete, I move over to the food tables, which contain a variety of sweet and savory dishes. I polished off the carnitas when I got home from work, so the first thing I help myself to is a slice of the pumpkin upside-down cake Gina and Trina baked together. There aren't enough adjectives in the thesaurus to describe how delicious it is.

Speaking of Gina, I told her about my imminent date with Sydney, some of which will be spent at Harrigan's. She oohed and aahed like a proud mom and told me she'd arrange to have the closest thing Harrigan's has to a VIP table reserved just for me. It's great to have connections.

I fill a plate up with finger snacks, remove my Ralph hands, and find a seat in a folding chair near the wall opposite the sound system. I'm about halfway through my second slice of cake when all motion in the room ceases. It's like someone has thrown a switch. Even the music has dimmed to a low thrum.

There, standing in the doorway, is a family of five. On the left, the mom is pushing a dual stroller containing two fussy toddlers. Next to her, the dad is gently nudging forward a girl in a witch's costume bearing a nervous expression.

Cheyanne.

I set my plate on the seat next to me and watch the scene play out. This is the first time I've seen Cheyanne since Harold's basement. She looks otherwise healthy, but the confidence I'm used to seeing in her face is gone.

She edges forward, searching the crowd for someone. Probably Trina and Crescent, who I last saw helping themselves to some snacks. Cheyanne locks eyes with me first. Her chest heaves, and she rushes forward, the black pointy hat flying off her head. I barely have time to edge off the chair before she slams into me, engulfing me in the hugest hug I've ever received. Her entire body vibrates as she clings to me, soft sniffles issuing from her nose.

"You came for me," she squeaks. "You risked your life for me."

I look up to see every grown-up and kid in the room watching us, but I tune them out. Relief at seeing Cheyanne back in familiar surroundings overwhelms all else. "Couldn't let anything happen to my friend, could I?"

She pulls back but doesn't release me. "You saved me."

"And you saved me," I point out, earning a wan smile. "You know what that means, right?"

She shakes her head.

"It means we'll be friends forever." Corny and unrealistic, yes, but it's what she needs to hear. If she's going to put this night-mare behind her, she has to know all her friends and neighbors are supporting her. Including me.

Cheyanne sniffles again and lowers her head. I worry she may break down crying, so I place a finger under her chin, lifting her head until our eyes meet again. "Hey...what do you call a witch who goes to the beach?" I ask.

She blinks a few times, then shrugs. "What?"

"A sand witch."

The chuckle, light at first, builds up steam and escapes through her nose. She smiles, a real one this time, and laughs. "That's pretty funny."

I wink at her. "You hungry?"

"Starving."

I gently turn Cheyanne around until she's facing the far wall. Trina and Crescent stand together, awaiting their turn with bated breath. "There's a table full of goodies somewhere in this room," I whisper. "Why don't you ask those two to show you where it is?"

Rather than join her friends, she faces me with a huge grin. Then she gives me a quick peck on the cheek before bounding across the room to join her besties. Their reunion is maybe the most adorable thing I've ever seen.

A moment later, the music and idle conversation resume. Mr. and Mrs. Macias make their way over and give me wholehearted thanks of their own. I hand Cheyanne's discarded hat to her dad who, as it turns out, is the head groundskeeper at one of the many Major League Baseball spring training parks in town. He tells me if I ever want to score free tickets to a game, he's my guy. I don't tell him I'm not a fan of the sport, but I keep his offer in mind in case Sydney is. Connections.

Once the eating and mingling taper off, the kids' portion of the party begins. A metric ton of wrapped candies is brought forth and poured into every child's bag, thus taking care of their trick-or-treating needs all at once. Games are played, and Trina defends her crown as Arbor Vista's apple-bobbing champion. Cheyanne doesn't take part, but she cheers on her best friend with tremendous gusto.

By eight o'clock, most of the younger kids and their families have called it a night. Cheyanne gives me another grateful hug before she and her family leave as well.

With the crowd continuing to thin, I call Crescent over. I compliment her incredible costume and face paint, which make her look like one of those creepy kids from a Japanese horror film I can't remember the title of. "Do you mind if I ask you something?"

She sits next to me. "Go ahead."

"You and Trina have been friends for a long time, right?"

"Over three years, ever since my parents and I moved here. Why?"

I drum my fingers on my knees. "Did she give you the Trina Test when you met?"

A smile that would probably look a lot sweeter if not for the scary makeup appears on her face. "Of course she did. She won't call anyone her friend until they take that silly test."

"Has it always been the same three questions?"

She thinks for a moment. "The third one has changed a few times, but the first two have stayed the same."

"Do you remember how you answered?"

Crescent nods. "Chocolate or vanilla? Vanilla. And cats or dogs? Definitely cats."

I furrow my brow. "Then I'm confused. You answered the exact opposite of me. My friend Piper also answered differently. How can we all have passed?"

Even through the makeup. I see Crescent roll her eyes and give me a "grown-ups are *soooo* dumb" head-shake. "You just don't get it, do you?"

Evidently not.

"The Trina Test isn't about answering the questions *right*," she explains. "It's about answering them."

I shrug, losing IQ points by the moment.

"What do you think most people do when a little kid comes up to them, wanting to ask them a bunch of random questions?"

This doesn't take me long to figure out. "Probably ignore her."

"Or tell her to go away. I mean, who has time to waste answering a little girl's silly questions?"

Crescent's right, of course. And that realization burns. I'm glad I wasn't that dickish when Trina and I met. "So anyone who actually does answer—"

"Passes. And maybe, just maybe, is cool enough for her to be friends with," she finishes.

My first thought is—that's a bit naive. It's a pretty big jump to assume that just because someone is friendly, it means they're also a good person.

Unless, of course, the test is being given by someone who can read auras.

Oh, *WOW*.

It's brilliant. Absolutely brilliant. So simple only a kid could think of it.

Only Trina.

"I'm guessing you've figured it out?" Crescent inquires.

"Yeah." I see Trina, standing near her mom. Gina's engaged in some bit of idle conversation with Ted, who does not resemble the cheerless guy I met the day I moved in. Trina turns her head, and our eyes meet. I slip one of Ralph's gigantic hands on and give her a friendly wave. She waves back.

"We are very lucky to have her as a friend," I muse.

"Yes. We are." Crescent pats my shoulder. "Happy Halloween...*Bernard*."

I facepalm. "Cheyanne told you."

"Yeah."

I shoot her a mock-scowl. "Crescent, please...I prefer Bax."

"I know. Just messin' with ya." She flashes an evil grin, waves her fingers like she's casting a hex on me, then walks with her mother out the door.

I scan the mostly empty room and become lost in thought.

To think where I was just over a month ago—I had no family, no direction, only Sheila and a vague promise to myself that I was going to make my life better. The roller-coaster that followed was something not even the wiliest psychic could have predicted.

Who knows where I'll be by New Year's?

The next thought that passes through my head is daunting. And thrilling.

I have no idea what's coming next.

Just how I like it.

TO BE CONTINUED...

Author's Note

First off, if you're reading this part of the, *thank you* so much for taking the time to enjoy my book!

If you enjoyed *The Bax Mysteries Book One: Killers*, you would be doing me a tremendous favor by leaving a review on whatever retail site you purchased this book on. A review need not be long, just a couple of paragraphs or even a few sentences.

I hope you will consider picking up a copy of *The Bax Mysteries Book Two: Ghosts* at some point in the near future. I assure you, Bax's story is only getting started...

About the Author

 Patrick Hodges currently lives in Arizona with his wife, Vaneza, and various furry animals. He enjoys reading (duh), and writing (again, duh) but hates 'rithmetic. He is an avid sports fan (Go Diamondbacks!) who will talk books or movies with anyone at any time.

To learn more about Patrick Hodges and discover more Next Chapter authors, visit our website at www.nextchapter.pub.

Check out Patrick's other books!

The James Madison Series (YA Contemporary):

Book One: Joshua's Island

Book Two: Ethan's Secret

Book Three: Sophie's Different

Promises: A Joshua's Island Christmas

The Wielders of Arantha Series (Sci-Fi/Fantasy):

Book One: Pawns

Book Two: Queens

Book Three: Endgame

Soraya: A Wielders of Arantha Prequel

The Bax Mysteries Series (Paranormal Mystery):

Book One: Killers

Book Two: Ghosts

Book Three: Elites

Book Four: Allies (coming soon)

Killers
ISBN: 978-4-82413-069-3

Published by
Next Chapter
1-60-20 Minami-Otsuka
170-0005 Toshima-Ku, Tokyo
+818035793528

22nd March 2022